Wicked

Andrea Arven

First published in Great Britain in 1991
by Nexus Books
338 Ladbroke Grove
London W10 5AH

Copyright © Andrea Arven 1991

Typeset by Phoenix Photosetting, Chatham, Kent
Printed and bound in Great Britain by
Cox & Wyman Ltd, Reading, Berkshire

ISBN 0 352 327995

Prologue

AD 2075

She was quite close when he saw her first. It had been a big fire and it was out now, but he had been sent around the back here with his hand-held heatfinder to check there were no hot spots that might re-ignite when the firemen were gone.

She picked her way across the rubble with the delicacy of a cat, coming towards him. No member of the public should have been here. He was tired and dirty and he wished she would go away. He turned back to the ruined building, resolutely continuing his scan, but not before he had seen that she was tall, elegant and lithe.

She was also masked. That meant almost certainly she was of the upper classes, the rich bitches who led fashion and did as they pleased.

Not with me, he thought sourly.

Suddenly her perfume assailed his nostrils. His air-mask was hung around his neck and he had been breathing the acrid aftermath of the fire since it had come under control. The clean beauty of the smell of her broke through his bad mood and he looked at her. It was night and the fire was out. There was little light close to them, but if it was dark, she was darker. She wore a one-piece garment that sheathed her body like a second skin and he saw her velvet black against the paler background, all richly rounded contours at breast and hip, with long shapely thighs above slender calves. She dropped to her knees in the filth at their feet and without saying a word she reached for his overtrousers. He went into shock as she hit the release button and felt for and found the trousers he wore underneath.

The heatfinder scanner was slack in his hand now. He braced himself as his heart pounded. He had heard of this kind of thing but barely believed it. It was always what happened to someone you only knew of at third hand, never to yourself or your immediate acquaintance.

Her hands went busily about their business with an assurance that could only have come from practice. By the time she had his cock out, it was strengthening and lengthening of its own accord. Her head tilted slightly back. He saw some white throat exposed, and the fall of black hair over her wide shoulders.

Her lips parted. They shimmered in the gloom. Her wet mouth was a dark invitation and he wasn't going to refuse.

As she drew his cock in between her lips, he felt dizzy. He had never been sucked. His wife wouldn't do it, nor had the few girlfriends he had had before marriage. The heat touched his gland and his cock leapt in her hands. She withdrew for a moment and laughed throatily, a soft husky sexy sound. Then she cradled his balls with one hand, ringed the base of his prick with her other, and began to suck him in earnest.

The world vanished and all that remained for him was his need to keep upright and the fabulous thing that was happening to his cock. He felt it stretched and drawn into the hot furnace of her mouth, compressed between her cheeks, tortured by her teeth and battered by her tongue. His cock squeezed and rhythmically pulsed as she drew on him.

She made the 'o' of her lips tight as she forced her head towards his groin, pushing his foreskin back and bathing his gland in wet warmth. Her teeth gently abraded its sensitive surface and he felt it swell and bloom in the hothouse of her mouth. Her tongue writhed around it and squeezed with the muscular power and agility of a boa constrictor. He gasped and shook as her fingers roved in the jungle of his groin and teased his balls and gripped the root of his cock.

Looking down he saw that her face was dark but that around his cock the ghostly glimmer of her lips made a shimmering ring that seemed to have a life of its own, ethereal, sensual, wicked.

Then she drew back, sucking fiercely on him almost to the point of pain. Again, he felt faint with the pleasure of it and his cock jerked and danced in her grasp.

She began to speed up and he groaned as his knees sagged.

2

She drove down on him and sucked back and he felt his juices accumulate. His balls ached. His gland was on fire. His prick seemed to swell and swell and suddenly it burst open and his spunk flooded out into her mouth. His hips jerked helplessly as he drove into her mouth in the extremity of his climax. She sucked and swallowed and sucked and swallowed and at last he was done.

She released his sagging prick and flicked round it with her tongue. Then she sat back on her heels. He groped for his trousers.

'Look,' he said in an urgent whisper. 'I've got to know who you are. How do I get in touch with you?'

'Why should you?' Her voice was barely audible, indifferent, yet sleek.

'It was wonderful,' he said hoarsely. 'I must meet you and repay . . .'

'You owe me nothing.' She got to her feet in a fluid graceful movement. She was like a purring cat. Content within herself, she had no need for him now. She began to move away.

'Your name?'

'No name.'

She turned and moved quite swiftly over the uneven surface. Soon she had blended with the night, and her darker blackness was absorbed and lost within its fragmented shadows.

The fireman fastened his clothing as if in a dream. He switched on his heatfinder and continued his steady scanning of the dereliction about him. His groin tingled and glowed. He could still remember in his muscles the pull of her mouth. But he wanted more than memories.

Once the city had been a patchwork quilt of vigorous, lusty, varied life, but that was long ago. Technology had shrivelled the workforce, and those that operated the machines now almost as clever and certainly as well-educated as those that invented and refined them. The few got richer and the many drifted. The city crumbled, slowly, almost luxuriously, showing its bones in a decay that was as obscene as a velvet-clad corpse. The rich retreated into their own world and fashioned it as they liked. Few bridged the two worlds. The fireman was one of them. The law enforcement agencies were another. And, quite naturally, so were the lawbreakers.

Particularly the pirates.

Those that do not have enough long for more. The human species entered its technocratic future burdened with the hopes and fears of cavemen, for evolution is fuelled by sex and sex hasn't changed worth a damn in half a billion years.

What those who don't have enough fail to realise is that those who have everything have nowhere to go. To the extent that this is true, the pirates who lived in squalor in the city and made their money thieving had the drop on the rich who lived in the jungle up in the hills, even if neither party realised it.

The pirates preyed upon the rich. The rich fantasised about the pirates. Made heroes of them. Lusted after them.

Sex is a great leveller.

Fee Cambridge ran her fingers the length of her pussy and back again. She sucked them thoughtfully before repeating the process. She took her time, letting the tips of each finger sense the warmth and wetness whilst between her legs she felt her own caress, rimming the entrance to her body and moving towards her little shaft, her tiny male member, aroused and quivering at the attention it was receiving. She was lying on one side on her bed, her legs sprawled open, watching herself frot her sex and play with her own private parts.

After a while, she noted almost absently that her pussy was fat and engorged, the flesh standing proud and flushed with readiness. She reached for something lying on the bed beside her and put it between her legs. She pressed its cool flat surface against her vulva, pushing up with increasing strength till her sexual flesh was crushed against it. She was flat on her back now, her legs drawn right up and folded at the knees so she had maximum spread. Her eyes were shut as she held the thing against herself and concentrated. She flexed internal muscles, squeezing her own pussy, and then very carefully she withdrew the artefact and relaxed her body.

4

She opened her eyes and looked at it. It had a glassy surface, crystalline and reflecting. The alkaline-acid balance of her exterior sex, a measure of her randiness, was accurately recorded on its surface where a chemical reaction between herself and it was etched.

She had kissed the mirror with her juicy cunt and the kiss was now recorded as a smoky etching to cloud the pure surface. Still naked, she rose up from the bed and carried it over to her dressing table. She opened a phial and using a dropper she put one or two drops of clear liquid on to the mirror's surface.

Gradually it stained blue. The deeper the etching, the more powerful the original reaction, the darker the blue. After a short while the process was complete. Fee fixed the mirror on the wall of her bedroom and looked at it.

Infinitely glowing as if lit by interior light, the shades of blue made a shape at once haunting and evocative. The double line, long, slightly asymmetric, with deep blue pressure points and a paler interior hung with speaking silence upon the wall. Near its base where the hole of her entrance had pressed, it was a deep royal blue, almost black in its centre. Where her clitoris had pressed was a small sharp point of rich colour, sapphire sex.

She would wrap it and send it to her husband. It was the latest thing in Valentines. Perhaps he would get the message and at last she would be satisfied. Her body ached for penetration and like the monkeys that swung in the jungle outside her home, she wished she could bend double and suck herself to satisation.

Fee Cambridge was a highly intelligent woman and she was aware that there was a variety of solutions to her problem. She had found herself increasingly favouring one of them. It was the craziest, the most dangerous solution but after months of conjugal neglect her sexual hunger was now so deep that she was beyond thinking rationally on the subject. She ran her tongue around her lips and remembered the taste of a man's spunk. Not her husband's. It was good but it was not good enough.

She didn't just want what she could do to a man. She

wanted what a man could do to her. And she was beginning to know what sort of man she wanted to do it. If she couldn't have her husband, presumably because he didn't want her that way any more, she wanted someone very special. Someone with power. She was very angry with life at the moment and a weak man would be crushed by her need and the force of her furious personality.

She wanted to lose herself and the violence of her need in the violence of a man. And she thought she knew where to go.

1

Once upon a time this had been a fantasy, but it had been repeated so often in her mind that now it was for real, she was confused. She was in the black shadows of a night-shrouded wall, all but invisible, herself as black as the night, save for her exposed white throat. Anyone close to her would have seen the pulse throb, and skin rising and falling rhythmically, too fast. It was the rhythm of fear.

She moved swiftly with a curious gliding movement, keeping so close to the wall that her leather jacket brushed it now and again, leaving a powdery trail where the chemocrete decomposed in the acidic air of the polluted city. Her pinsharp heels clicked a tattoo that matched her rapid breathing. Her breasts strained against the material of the silken tee shirt she wore.

Fee Cambridge was on the borderline of failing to distinguish reality from dream and she was afraid. Not only was she afraid, she was intensely excited. Her long slanting eyes glittered. The ancient sodium lighting drained them of their natural ice-green colouring. They were mysterious slits, made more so by the mask she wore that covered her upper face, concealing angled cheekbones and a fine, sharp-chiselled nose. Her lush full rounded voluptuous lips were revealed, very strong, luminescing slightly in keeping with the current fashion for 'ghost' lipstick that glowed in the dark.

The wall crumbled to an end. Before her buildings rose like an old man's mouth full of diseased stumps. Now the walls seemed friendly compared to the impenetrable shadows round the buildings' rotten roots.

She shot a glance over her shoulder, hearing her jacket creak as she did so. She could go back.

Her eyes narrowed. She thirsted, and the means to slake

her thirst were ahead, so she believed. She ran her pointed tongue over her lips and dreamed again of a man's spunk in her throat. She would go on. She set off past the tenement blocks.

A light flickered and there was movement. She became aware of several people close to her.

'You want something sister?' a low voice asked. 'Suck it, smoke it, snort it, fuck it – we supply it all.'

'The pirates,' she said. 'I want to find the pirates.'

A laugh answered her. 'Take the wide road, sister. You can't miss it. It goes straight to hell. That's where you'll find the pirates.'

'I'll see you there, brother,' she said, confidence making her suddenly reckless.

'I'm there already. Didn't you realise?'

She kept her back straight and walked hard and fast. Then she remembered – no one here had anywhere to go. She forced herself to slow down, to appear less urgent as she went on through the shadows and occasional lit patches. She would not show fear even if she felt it. They must think her one of themselves or they would pounce.

Other voices muttered from the dark, offering her the various services this part of the city had in abundance. Once or twice she was tempted. It might be raw, but entertainment here packed a punch that nights spent in front of a screen watching the exposed neuroses of the rich rather lacked. It had not previously occurred to her that rats have a zest for corruption. In the state she was in at the moment, any zest was better than none.

But she had set out to reach the pirates and there might not be a second chance. She might never get up enough nerve again. And a craven part of her knew that she might not survive this chance.

The highway was before her now, up on its pillars cutting across the sky in a multi-laned trackway that kept those from the other world, her world, from becoming contaminated with the human rats that swarmed down here in the dangerous shadows. Fee flicked her long black curls back over her leather-clad shoulders with sudden arrogance. She would make it. She could survive down here. She wasn't as effete as most of her kind. Then she saw the bonfires.

They flamed under the highway itself. Her heart leapt as huge gouts of flame flared up, reddening the figures gathered round about in the glare. Old furniture bulged and warped in bizarre simulation of a conventional room, but here it was in the open and grotesque. The effect was enhanced by cables running crazily through oily puddles and across rubble. The cables brought power to the music equipment that boomed frenetically, the sound bouncing between the highway supports. She was surprised to recognise the tune and acknowledged that for the first time she was hearing the music as it was intended, its discordance and shrieking vibrations in their proper context. It was a raw sexy scream in the night and it belonged here.

Overhead, supercharged autos screamed past, expensive microworlds of synthetic comfort for those who could afford them. Fee smiled and straddled her legs. The cars always made her feel excited and it was more true down here where they were wonderful and unreal and literally far above anyone around. She put her hands on her hips, exhibiting a confidence she did not quite feel. Still the pulse throbbed in her naked throat.

They were dancing she saw. Some danced with their bodies woven together by the beat, undulating in concert, their rippling bodies entwined like hermaphrodite molluscs coupling simultaneously at either end. Some danced apart, their curious jerks and postures body language of an ancient kind. Their message was clear to read. She watched them and read it, licking her lips again and feeling the heat rise in her own body. She began to sway.

Shockingly, a knife blade gleamed blood-red at her exposed throat. She was so intent on watching the scene before her that she had not heard him approach. She tensed, feeling his body at her back. She could not see him, only his hand on the knife, but she could feel him and smell him and with an older, less-defined sense she knew he was strong and confident.

'You got an invitation, lady?'

9

'I want to find the pirates.'

'And if you've found them?'

Carefully, so as not to disturb the knife, she rotated her bottom against his groin. Fear and exultation worked a chemistry in her body that made every nerve alive. 'What do you think?' she whispered, giving each word its full value.

He laughed. He kept the knife where it was and ran his other hand down her left side, feeling her contours. Then he slid a palm round the front of the leather skirt she wore until he cupped the mound of her sex. She thrust forward into his hand.

His lips were at her ear, in her hair. She felt the warmth of his breath as her heart raced and her breat heaved. 'You're very hungry, little girl. How come? Ain't you got no man?'

Fee raised her hand slowly and pushed the knife away from her throat. She turned in his arms and faced him. 'I didn't say so,' she said.

He was big, broad-shouldered over a barrel of a chest, and his wide face was framed with curls as black and wild as her own. He wore a single eyepatch and the ear on that side glittered with gold rings. Her breathing went ragged as she took in his bare chest matted with a wiry growth of hair, criss-crossed by two great studded leather straps from shoulder to hip. He smelt of leather, sweat and the acrid night. His shoulders were blue-tattooed so that it seemed the night itself made intricate patterns on his paler flesh. His broad forearms were veined in hard ridges and his smoother upper arms bulged with muscle. His leather trousers had an oily sheen that glowed dull red in the reflected light of the fires, and the metal studs of his chest straps threw back ruby pinpoints of flame.

Fee trembled and put her palms flat on his strange, rough, naked skin. She ran them slowly up him, over the straps and on to the satin at his neck. He held his arms open around her, allowing her this, watching her face as she absorbed his texture.

She closed her hands lightly about his neck and at last looked up and met his gaze. She slid her hands on up, linked them at the back of his neck and pulled down on him. He resisted just long enough for her to realise how feeble her strength was compared to his, then he lowered his head over her straining body and their mouths met.

His own sweet and fiery hot, demanding, commanding, and leaving her in no doubt as to his power and his will, he took hers.

Her response was total. She pressed into him and sucked eagerly at his mouth. He must have sheathed the knife because he caught her under her buttocks with his two hands and hoisted her expertly. Her legs came round his waist and still their mouths fed together as he supported her against his chest. Her hands ran up into the hot ragged silk of his hair and she gripped it and pulled his head back, kissing down on his mouth as she rode his hands, making no attempt to mask her need as she had masked her face.

Then she released him and looked into his face, trying to read his thoughts and see her effect on him. Her breasts heaved close to his face as though she had run a great race. She brought a hand round and moved down the neckline of her tee shirt so that one full rounded globe of flesh was revealed, white in the darkness between them. She fed the nipple into his mouth.

He bit her. She jerked with surprise and pain, arching her body back, but he held her and kept his balance, sucking hard on the offended flesh. She groaned deeply as the nipple elongated and stretched in his mouth, hardening with desire as it did so. Quite slowly, his thigh muscles bulging with the strain, he lowered himself until she was astride his bent knee, feeling its muscular strength hard between her soft thighs, pushing up against her sex.

Her vagina convulsed with desire.

He freed her second breast and sucked it strongly. She ground herself against his thigh and moaned slightly, deep in her throat.

He lifted her free of his leg and laid her roughly on the ground. He began to undo his trousers.

'Here?' she said, her voice cracking slightly.

'You wanted to find the pirates, you said.'

Her tongue flicked. Her eyes were wide open and the

11

pupils dilated so that they looked black. A pinpoint of flame was reflected in their depths. 'Yes,' she said.

'This is how the pirates do it.'

Her breathing quickened till she panted. The music entered her blood and thudded inside her. As he lowered his big body down over her she saw only flame and darkness as her senses reeled. Then she saw his shaft, pale and long and thick with its furred base in shadows. She lifted her knees and opened them but he pushed them aside and moved on over her till she saw the firelight flicker even along his shaft. It was like a club encased in a silken envelope of skin. Her nostrils flared and her eyes blazed as she smelt the musk of him. He laid the end on her lips and she opened her mouth in welcome.

Above her the faint stars reeled as she tasted his manhood. He was saltily luscious, fat and full in her mouth, the strange flesh of his erection elastic and firm. She closed her eyes and drank his goodness, sucking him, kissing him, nibbling his springy muscle.

He moved, penetrating her mouth deeper. She sucked the length of his shaft and felt the rough mat of hair it sprang from. Her body ached with lust for him and helplessly she arched her back as her own need made itself plain.

Slowly he withdrew from her mouth, bending over her to lick between her parted lips. Now at last he pulled back enough so he could reach under her short leather skirt. She felt his hands hot on her thighs and shivered. He pushed up, hard, and shoved her thighs apart.

Her cunt was quite naked. The pallid flesh bulged, hairfree, and she wore no garment to cover her nudity.

The pirate looked down for one long unwinking moment at her ripe mound with its dark slash below, and then he laid his rough palm over its arrogant upward thrust. The depilated skin was satin smooth and he rotated his hand over it, at first gently and then with increasing force. Fee moaned and pushed up and suddenly he gripped her plump sex-flesh and pulled.

She cried out and jerked. He felt her wetness as the interior of her slit brushed against his wrist as she writhed in his grip.

Her white thighs were cut by the two dark lines of her suspenders that supported her black net stockings and in her eagerness to have him violate her inner sex, she forced her knees down until they touched the ground.

He slid his second hand under her buttocks and lifted her hips clear of the ground so that her vulnerable parts were sandwiched between his palms. Her eyes were tight shut. She felt his thumbs begin to separate her petalled flesh. Their roughness abraded her and they were harsh in her secret places.

Again her vagina convulsed within her.

He rubbed her labia and she throbbed in response to the friction. Her flesh became pulpy and he felt its increasing softness and thickness and laughed. Now one thumb nuzzled further, uncloaking her own little shaft, and her breath hissed as he rotated it.

His other hand parted the lobes of her bottom and she felt his hand hard-edged against her rear.

She steadied herself on her elbows as he lifted her sex clear of the ground and brought his face down to meet it. She felt his head warm between her thighs and cried out as his lips found hers and his tongue probed where his thumbs had been.

His sucking was powerful and exquisite. Her flesh bulged into his mouth and she felt herself grow hot and wet. Her clitoris vibrated and sharp spasms of intense feeling flared through her stomach and spread up in a glow through her chest. She was up on her shoulders now, her legs over his shoulders as he ate down on her. His tongue was a hard prong inserted into her, delicious, a forerunner of the monster to come.

Fee sobbed. She couldn't stop herself. The walls of her cunt trembled and fluttered. A ripple grew in her, grew more intense as she shuddered violently, and she snarled in her frustration as her orgasm erupted. She hadn't wanted to come yet. She creamed into his mouth and felt his teeth as he realised what had happened. She jerked hard against him as she pulsated inside, out of control, driven by an engine of sex she could not master.

13

He sucked her climax and drank her wine. Then his mouth released her and he lowered her on to the ground again. She opened her eyes wide and looked up at him.

His mouth trapped hers and she tasted her own juice in him. Her breasts were crushed against his muscular chest and the studs embedded in his leather straps bit into her. She longed for the imprint of his maleness to be in some way permanent on her soft body. She wanted to be marked by him, to bear his brand, to be his beast.

He was far from done with her. He took one of her hands and laid his shaft in it. She savoured the breadth of it, its knotted veiny strength, its swollen ripe end. She began to frig him, feeling his cloak of skin withdraw over his engorged knob. She ringed him at its base and squeezed.

At last he was manoeuvring for position. She guided his weapon between her legs and lined up her throbbing tumescent core. He pushed forward and entered her moist interior in one mighty thrust.

Fee Cambridge adored the mystery of man and she adored the ultimate expression of manhood, when the male member was fed into her body and caused to explode within her, both seeding and satiating her lust. Now she gasped in both shock and triumph at having the pirate inside her, clasped by her special and very experienced muscles. She gripped him tightly and felt his response ripple the length of his cock.

He withdrew till he was almost out of her, so nearly that she mewed slightly in fear he would slip, and thrust in powerfully again.

Her mouth was wide open, her head thrown back in a soundless scream of pleasure. He drove into her and she heard from somewhere the whine of an auto powering over the highway behind and above her. It took megabucks to achieve that synthesis of power and beauty roaring through the night over the cesspool of a city, and between her legs something like it speared into her, an organic synthesis of violent beauty that she writhed up to meet and contain. He speeded up and she felt herself begin to throb hotly and pulsate against his sweet torture. She was stretched, racked by his mighty rod and she took it greedily.

Now the bones of his groin thudded into her flesh with each mighty stroke. She felt him swell, felt her own thick hot cunt grow pasty as she came again to climax. Her chest heaved. She gripped him with her cunt and at last he cried out, his shaft rippled and jerked and bucked within her and the hot liquid jetted from him to her. She milked him in her frenzy, her orgasm upon her as he thrust his final strokes. Her inside burned, the fire reaching up to glow through her whole body. Then the fit was past. She began to relax. The heat softened and eased and, like a healing tide, satiation flowed over her.

She saw the stars again, faint above the city lights. Twin shafts cut the night as cars hurtled by overhead.

He withdrew from her carefully and sat back. He fumbled in a pocket and brought out a torch. He held the light steady on her face so that her dilated pupils shrank to pinpricks and the pale colour of her eyes could be seen within her mask.

'Who are you?' he asked. There was a sheen of sweat over his face.

She felt glutted and wild, power running in her at her triumph. 'This,' she whispered.

He sat back and looked at her. Her long legs sprawled apart so that he could see her hot scarlet slit foaming with love juice under the pale mound at the base of her belly. It was strange to him that she had no crest of hair there and he reached out and felt again the smooth skin where there should have been a jungly growth to match his own. Her full breasts lolled shamelessly free from her tee shirt, and round her head black curls tumbled wantonly. Her mouth was bruised and hot from passion. Her upper face was still masked.

'Why did you seek us?'

'I want to join you. I want to be a pirate.'

His laugh was short and brutal. 'Where've you been, lady? Pirates are men. We have our women but they ain't pirates.'

'I will be a pirate,' Fee hissed. Her desire for self-abasement was temporarily relieved and she was accustomed to men who were malleable to her will after fucking. 'If you won't let me, I'll do it alone.'

Now his laugh was full-throated. 'Just like that?' He was genuinely amused.

15

She was getting angry. 'I'm as good as you.'

'In some ways, maybe. Not in others, little girl.'

'I'm as clever.'

'It takes more than that.'

'Give me a chance,' she wheedled in a silken voice.

He heard it and grinned inside himself. Only the rich whined quite in that way when their will was thwarted.

'No.'

'Frightened?'

In the silence that followed her lightly-flung challenge, Fee had time to feel the fear she accused him of. She reminded herself nervously that she did not understand these people. They were not predictable in her terms, obeying either a different set of rules or no rules at all.

Her heart started to pound.

He adjusted his trousers and then lay beside her in the dirt, raised on one elbow so that his face was close to hers, above it.

'You're toothsome,' he murmured. 'You have a wild set of muscles to wrap my prick in. And I like the touch of mystery, lady. I like the mask. Neat. But if you ever accuse me of being frightened again, I'll peg you out on the highway up there in starsville and when the autos have smashed your pretty bones, the crows will pick them clean. Right?'

Her flesh cringed with fear. Almost she agreed and prepared to beg his pardon. She believed him utterly. But something crept up her spine, some damnable reckless urge to go all out and not count the cost.

'Fuck you,' she said.

He hit her across the face and she laughed. His mouth met hers again and they kissed crazily, almost biting one another in their ferocity. He fell back away from her and she followed him round, coming on top of him and kissing him hungrily. Now she was astride him, tugging at his trousers to free his raising sex.

He was hard already. She lifted herself with a yell and dropped down on to him, taking his rigid muscle into her spongy-wet inner place.

She screamed.

2

Fee felt as though the top of her head was coming off. Her whole scalp rose up and she thought her hair was being torn out by the roots. She could still feel the pirate's cock in her, just, but she had reared up to ease the pressure on her head. The man between her legs began to shake and she opened streaming eyes to peer down and saw he was laughing.

Someone above her was pulling her off his sex by yanking her hair out. Now they kicked her hard in the back and the pirate laughed harder, his cock shrinking within her. He made no move to help.

'He's mine,' hissed a furious voice. 'Get the hell out of here and off his cock or I'll blind you, you thieving bitch.'

Fee gave way to the pressure and staggered to her feet. She turned and blindly swiped at her aggressor. The man on the ground grabbed her ankle and mercifully her hair was released. The woman who had attacked her danced backwards out of reach. She had bright white hair sticking out all around her head and a full-lipped petulant face suffused with rage.

'You cow,' roared Fee. 'How dare you!'

Lazily the pirate hauled himself to his feet, keeping a hold on Fee. He worked his trousers back up and fastened them thoughtfully with one hand. The two women glared at each other. The pirate now held Fee's hands by the wrists. Her skirt was still caught up, revealing her bald sex, and suddenly the other woman kicked at her.

Now the pirate did pull her back so that she was grazed by the flying shoe, but no worse.

'Is it a fight?' he asked. He didn't sound very concerned.

'Send the virus back where she came from,' hissed the newcomer. 'I'm enough for you.'

'Enough for any man,' agreed the pirate cordially. 'But I was enjoying myself and you put a stop to it.'

17

'If she wants you, she'll have to fight for you.'

'What?' said Fee. Yet she thought she understood.

'You don't know much about our ways, do you?' said the pirate. 'She has the rights of it. She fought for me once and won. Now she has the right to stop me playing elsewhere if she doesn't approve.' He shook Fee slightly. 'I don't think she likes you, lady in a mask.'

Fee found her voice. 'You mean, if I want your body, I have to fight this hellcat.'

'And win,' he said amiably.

'You get no say in it?'

'Well, it's no use fighting for me if I don't want you,' he said apologetically. 'A woman can't force me to shaft her. And if she attacks my woman anyway, I can see her off myself if I don't want my preferred goods damaged. So you see, I have some choice in the matter.' His amusement was evident.

'You aren't serious?' The newcomer radiated fury. 'You can only just have met her. I'll tear her pretty skin if you want, but I don't see that she can mean much to you. Run her along, Will. I'll amuse you tonight.'

'Well?' said Will.

It was a moment before Fee knew he spoke to her. 'You would let me fight for you?' she said. These people were animals.

'It was you who wanted to be a pirate,' explained Will gently.

'And if I win?'

'I am your territory.'

He let go of her at last and stood back. A crowd had drifted over during the altercation and people stood around, curious to see what would happen. Fiona could smell the tension aroused in them by the thought of a fight.

She was Fiona Cambridge. Was she out of her mind? The thought of tamely turning tail and walking out of the situation was intolerable to her.

Her eyes narrowed as she looked the pirate over. He was superb. He was the fulfilment of her wildest dreams. She looked at his chosen mate.

The girl was smaller and younger than herself, urban thin

18

but vivid in her way, smouldering as she was with anger. Fiona could imagine her smouldering with passion, and suddenly jealousy lanced her at the thought of Will being pleasured by that thin agile body.

'Your name?' she said, speaking directly for the first time. The roots of her hair still tingled.

'Mammet.'

'Is the fight now?'

The crowd hissed and stirred and Fee sensed a movement from Will. The blood sung in her. So he wanted her to win, did he? Maybe he was tired of his vicious little creature, maybe she had struck some cord in him herself. Whatever, she was sure that he did things to serve his own ends and not hers or Mammet's.

She remembered again his thick strong stalk of sex. There were a thousand things she wanted from his body. And only one way to get them, it seemed.

'Now,' said Will.

They moved nearer to the fires to get light from them. Some cleared the ground of rubble and stones. The crowd grew and swelled, murmuring with delight. Two women came to Fee and Will faded.

'Take off your clothes,' they told her.

'All of them? In front of the crowd?'

'Yes. You can keep drawers on but it isn't advisable. Mammet will tear them from you, anyway.'

Fee reflected that she wore no drawers anyway and began to strip.

The crowd was chanting now, clapping and whistling as the two women bared themselves for the fight.

'I lay a condition,' Fiona called suddenly in strong voice.

'No conditions,' shouted Mammet, 'save we fight with our bodies only, no other weapons.'

'My mask remains.'

'Let it be,' said Will and then Fee saw him, facing them, sitting at peace over what was to happen. She stripped proudly and walked over across the empty arena to stand before him.

She had reason to be arrogant. Her body was long and tall,

19

slim at the waist but flaring at hip and bosom, graceful, feminine and strong. She straddled her legs and put her hands on her hips, no longer concerned by the hot eyes on her nakedness. Her two women helpers tied back her hair for her.

'Are you worth this, pirate?' she asked for all to hear.

'That is your decision.' His eyes raked her body insolently. She wanted to kiss the hair on his chest and run her fingers over his tattoos. Her desire for him weakened her and she tossed it aside.

'I'll fight your little thing to teach her a lesson, so that she knows she must put no hand on me and I walk where I please with no need for her permission. I'll see if I want you afterwards.' She shrugged a shoulder.

The crowd roared with delight. It occurred to Fee suddenly that though there were men clustered around Will dressed much as he was, in black leather strapping, some with chains across their chests, and tight breeks that ended just below their knees, he dominated them in size and force of personality. Was he their leader? That would add a dimension to this crazy contest and sharpen the crowd's appreciation of what hung in the balance. Moreover, it would explain their ecstatic reception of her rudeness to him. She did not feel dislike for him in the crowd; only awe and an acknowledgement of supremacy.

Mammet came forward. Her white hair was licked back close against her narrow skull. She had small, pointed, black-tipped breasts, and a pale fuzz in her groin. Now she saw Fiona's naked mound and she stared.

'What happened to you, sister?' she jeered in insult. 'Ringworm?'

Fiona did not know what ringworm was, but she got the point of the jibe. She clubbed her hand and lashed out.

Mammet danced backwards, her eyes narrowed and her little body taut. Fiona moved straight in with her heavy breasts swinging, feinted with her hand and kicked Mammet on the knee.

Her foot hurt astonishingly but she had the satisfaction of seeing Mammet drop to ease the hurt joint. She tried to follow the blow with another but Mammet punched her on her bald mound. Fiona hit the girl in the face and Mammet launched herself up and fastened small yellow teeth into Fiona's right breast.

Fee never felt the pain. It was disease she feared, down here in the filthy city. She got Mammet by the hair and lifted the girl clear off the ground, still fastened to her breast like a ferret. Mammet started to punch her body but Fee hit her in the face until her teeth released her skin. Fee rattled her but the ferocity of the girl's attack on her brought them both down.

They rolled together on the hard dry ground with the crowd roaring all around, biting and scratching at each other. Fiona gasped as suddenly they were deluged by something warm and slimy and wet.

A bucket of something had been emptied over them. It was hard to keep a hold of each other as their hands slithered helplessly.

Mammet seemed fascinated by Fiona's sex. She kept going for it, allowing Fee to hit and punch her body. Once or twice the girl landed a blow on Fee's vulva, but her own man's spunk was ointment on what she sought to assault. Fiona's superior height and weight began to tell. She was better fed, stronger and fitter than the younger girl. Health and strength had always been a prerogative of the rich. Her will to win was as strong as her body and at last she got astride Mammet and pinned her to the ground.

The girl writhed between her legs and Fiona's eyes began to glitter. Her blood ran too strong for her to feel much pain in the lust of battle, but the thin body trapped below hers was arousing other instincts. She ignored the thrashing arms and pinned Mammet by the throat. Her big breasts swung and their tips brushed the girl's own little points. Her breath heaved and her heart pounded but she was filled with the exultation of victory. It was right she should win. She was the superior animal.

Both women were shiny with whatever had been flung over them. Firelight ran red up and down their gleaming bodies which were beginning to darken here and there with bruising.

21

A young man stood up. He was slender compared to the older men, and smoother skinned, but he was handsome and he had a patrician turn to his lip.

'I will take Mammet, if she concedes Captain Will to the new woman.'

A sigh of regret ran through the assembly. They knew their fun was over.

Fiona waited for Mammet's reply. Her sex was bruised by Will's fierce assault and by Mammet's bony fist. The girl's ribs pressing up into it were not unpleasant.

'I'd fight for you, any day,' called a husky voice from the crowd and they roared with laughter. Mammet veiled her eyes and bared her teeth.

'You have won,' she said bitterly.

'You haven't done so badly,' muttered Fiona and something close to a grin flitted across Mammet's face. Coming back to her normal senses, Fee was appalled to see the grazing she had inflicted on Mammet's cheekbone.

'You won't hold Will,' hissed Mammet. 'He is wild and he likes them young. You only win because he wants it. Now get off me.'

Fiona stood up and was surprised to find that she was shaky and felt sore in quite a few places. She ignored Will and went over to her clothes, pulling them on and shrouding her long full magnolia-pale body from the greedy eyes around her. She had her back to the arena and was startled when an arm came suddenly round her neck and jerked her back.

'Now you have won, my pretty,' said Will, 'you must claim your reward.'

'My reward?' Fiona felt dull and old and tired.

Will spun her round. 'I will explain, since you are so ignorant of our ways.' He kept his voice very low and intimate, but his tone was hard. 'A man cannot just make trouble between the women and cause them to fight. He must demonstrate he is worth fighting for.' His voice had become silken and he waited for Fiona to catch at his meaning.

'Worth it? How?' she said.

'What have you been fighting for?'

'Your body?' She felt stupid and out of her depth.

His hands came up and pulled the pins out of her hair so that it fell down about her shoulders.

'If I don't prove myself worthy, no other woman will ever challenge you for me. And when you prefer another man – '

She tried to pull away. 'No,' she mumbled.

'It is our way,' he insisted.

She looked up at him. 'You want this?'

'You and I,' he murmured so softly that no one else, however close, could have heard, 'know where you are from. But these about us do not. They would tear you to pieces if they knew. They do not tolerate games being played in their country, and here you will find there are no police to protect you, no patrols to keep you safe.'

'You know where I am from?'

'Aye, and why,' said Will as his head dropped over hers and his mouth found her lips.

She had forgotten already the fiery taste of him and to find that there was a mind within that powerful rugged scarred body aroused her on a different level than the crude scream for sex she had come here to satisfy.

'I am going to fuck you now,' he murmured.

Her blood started to pound. 'I don't want to,' she said. 'Not in front of these people.'

'Then you forfeit the fight. I will give you ten minutes to start running; then I will tell them where you are from. I can smell it in your hair, rich bitch,' he said. He shook slightly with sudden laughter. 'You'll fight, you vicious cow, because you can't bear to lose. But you are too squeamish to show that pretty box of yours fully to the eyes that have already feasted on your nakedness.'

'Damn you,' she said.

'I am damned already. You can do nothing to me.'

'Or for you. So why do you want me?'

'I didn't say that. I didn't say you could nothing for me. And, by God, you will, if I want you to.'

He split her tee shirt open and laid his tongue on the sore place where Mammet had bitten her. Then he led her back into the arena. He turned her round and pushed her down on her face. Before she could recover he had heaved her skirt up

23

over her hips and he pinned her with her rear stuck up before him. She felt his groin press up against the cheeks of her arse and at last the flame of lust shot through her.

These people lived by rules she had never heard of. They lived like men and women might have lived in the Stone Age. But she, Fiona Cambridge, had come amongst them and won out, beaten them at their own game, and now she had the best of it. With her face pressed in the dust she felt herself impaled on his clublike prick. He took her quickly, without sophistication, asserting his right to satiate his body on hers and her right to have a man who could satisfy her. She had fought for him and won and he had to prove in public that he was worth fighting for. The crowd roared cheerfully. They were having a good evening's entertainment.

Her outer sex beat sorely under Will's assault, but it was pleasurable pain. For a very long time this place between her legs had nagged her and destroyed her peace of mind. To be satisfied, even savagely satisfied, was more than enough, was a hundred times welcomed. A joy was unleashed in her and Fiona felt herself move incredibly to climax.

Will came in her. His spunk flowed hot and thick. There was no doubting his virility and manhood. He withdrew and Fiona heard the noise of the crowd beat against her ears. She jerked herself round, pushed the surprised Will back, and remounted his prick before it had time to shrink.

Now he was on his back as he had been when Mammet interrupted them. Fiona rode hard on his member, keeping it stiff even though he had climaxed. Her own orgasm came as splintered pain and pleasure and she opened mouth wide and yelled exultantly into the night.

Will caught her, kissed her mouth, pulled free of her and pulled her skirt down. He fastened his breeks and stood up, half-hauling Fiona up with him. Her legs went crazily askew, her knees touching, and he supported her. He led her over to the seat from which he had watched the fight and sat her down beside him.

'Now,' he said smoothly, 'it is the turn of Mammet and Jon.'

Fee hardly saw the two slender bodies weaving the age-old

pattern of lust and satiation in the dirt before her. Her eyes hurt and she was very tired. Will's arm was round her and it felt very good.

'Your name,' he said, watching the pair before him with a slight frown on his face.

'They call you Will.'

'They call me Captain Kid.'

'That's a hell of a mouthful.'

'Will.'

'Billy the Kid. Wasn't he a cowboy?' Her words were crazy, like her thoughts. Was all this really happening or would she wake up safely in bed? Safe. And bored.

'Captain William Kid was a pirate when they used ships, lady. Three hundred and fifty years ago. Your name, I asked.'

She hesitated a moment. 'Skelton.'

'Skelton?'

'Yes.'

'You aim to hang around?'

He was fast, she acknowledged. He was no slouch in the mental sphere.

'Not all the time.'

There was silence between them. He did not ask her where she might go when she was not here with him.

'I find you here?' she asked eventually.

'Sometimes.'

She tilted her head and looked to where the bonfires burned and the couples had danced or slunk about the shadows.

'Do you live here?' she asked curiously.

He took his time answering. 'That's a hell of a question,' he said eventually. 'Don't let anyone else hear you ask it. They might ask where you live, that you don't already know.'

He turned his head and looked at her coldly. His black eyepatch was a menacing reminder that he was of another world and as yet untamed.

'You are a prince among men,' she said suddenly, not having meant to reward or compliment him. The words came out of her hunger and his appeasement of it. 'Captain

25

William Kid, it is a pleasure to be fucked by you.' She meant it. She heard her own intensity, her own sincerity. It was real.

His hand slid up her skirt and he gripped her wet woman's place. 'You move good,' he breathed. 'I could do this again.'

The crowd dispersed, Mammet and Jon had done and were now away, arm in arm, to some place of their own. The fires burned low and she and Will were almost alone in the shadows.

'I have to go,' she said, struggling to keep the uncertainty out of her voice. He could stop her by force if he chose.

Yet he did no such thing. She stood up, towering suddenly above him, for he still was still sitting and her ankle boots had three-inch heels. She turned and walked rapidly away.

It was very late, deep in the night. The shadows muttered evilly as she passed and she caught the murmur of crazy talk, the whinny of sick laughter. Now she carried a small knife in her hand in case something threatened her. She needed to get home, to be safe. Her thighs trembled from her sexual gluttony and her mind reeled with what had taken place, and with her new knowledge of herself, of what she could do, and what she could be if the need arose.

Will was a man indeed, built to satiate the most demanding of women. Somehow, she had to find her way back down here, find him again and claim her rights.

Maybe they were all like him, down here in garbage-land.

She stumbled in her tiredness, wet-thighed and sticky, but for all her bruises and sore places, there was a smile on her face.

It had been quite a night.

3

Sunlight poured through curving glass domes and bathed the man at the kitchen table in a yellow radiance. He wore a midnight-blue overshirt belted at the waist over blue slacks that ended just below the knee. The open neck of the shirt showed the bronzed column of throat which supporting a handsome head with a firm, clean-shaven jaw. He had bright intelligent blue eyes.

Rollo Cambridge was good looking and he knew it.

'Fee,' he yelled. He heard his wife move through the apartment and wondered why she was late for breakfast. He was in conference in ten minutes and they hadn't aligned their schedules for the day yet. Bland music filled the room from all around. A light, electronic voice warbled about its pussy love, so sweet and soft and cuddlesome.

'Fee,' he called again, and looked up irritably as she came at last into the sundrenched room, moving sluggishly, evidently still half asleep.

His eyes widened in astonishment. He was accustomed to seeing her crisply and fashionably dressed at this hour. Now she was buck naked.

His eyes were drawn down the length of her body despite his annoyance with her. Her hair was tied up, for she had just come from the shower, and her exotic face was clean of make-up. Green eyes slanted above prominent cheekbones. Her full mouth quivered as she took in his gaze. Her long slender neck led his eyes to sloping creamy shoulders and full heavy breasts tipped dark ruby with large nipples. Her warm white body narrowed at a high waist and then flared with arrogant womanliness over rich and promising hips. Before he took in the long pale downslope of her thighs, he saw the blunt pouting nakedness of her hairless fanny, the fold within it inviting his eyes, and any other part of him that might care to follow, to enter and sample the dark delights within.

She was a tall woman with much of her height in her long legs, legs made, it seemed, to wrap round a man as he penetrated her mysteries.

She leant against the kitchen doorframe and lifted an arm to scratch lazily behind one ear. He saw the small tangle of damp hair in her armpit.

'Fiona,' he said uncertainly.

'Come back to bed, Rollo.' Her voice was husky. The rigours of the night filled her with sexual heat. Her body abrasions were skilfully masked and healing rapidly with spray-on antiseptic newskin. It had an anaesthetic effect but even so she felt sore and ached in various places. Yet the small unfamiliar pains served only to excite her. She looked at her handsome husband and remembered what was masked by his clothing and she longed for it up in her, where the pirate had raided her the previous night. She had enough for both men, and more.

'I've got a conference in seven minutes, Fee.'

'Cancel. Tell 'em you're sick. Let's bodysynch, Rollo.'

'What's the matter with you? Have you been taking pills?'

She crossed the room, her breasts swaying under their own weight as she did so. She stood by him and lifted an arm to release her black tumble of hair. There was a time when the sight of the tender flesh of her underarm had driven him wild, though it was hard to believe that now. She put a hand under one breast and lifted its weight till the nipple almost brushed his face.

'Suck me, baby,' she whispered.

He recoiled as if disgusted. Her eyes narrowed and became glittery. All of a sudden she looked dangerous, like a roused cat. As if in response a tiger walked past the glass walls of the kitchen through the luxuriant riot of vegetation beyond their apartment walls. Its orange stripy tail twitched as it saw the humans, so close yet beyond its feline reach. The machine-croon from the radio seeped round the room in saccharine whorls of sound.

'Put some clothes on, for Heaven's sake.' Rollo's eyes

28

flicked to the vidicom with its button in the screen-on position. It only needed to buzz with Fiona in this wild mood for her to be displayed to less indifferent predators.

He saw her against the jungle that surrounded their home and suddenly her pale body excited him after all. He checked his watch.

'Honey, my mind's on this conference. I can't switch tracks. We couldn't replay this scene in a few hours, huh?'

Fiona sat on a stool and lifted her heels to rest her feet on a rung between its legs. She let her knees fall apart and Rollo saw a moist gleam at the apex of her legs. He swallowed.

'I don't think so, darling,' she drawled. 'I can't tell if I'll want it then.'

He rose to his feet and flicked food crumbs from his clothes. 'I'll make you want it,' he promised. He swigged down the last of his coffee. 'Wish me luck, baby. This is the big one.'

'Hang in there even if it gets tough,' she said ambiguously.

Rollo didn't have the time to analyse this so he took it at face value. 'You're gorgeous, sweetheart. See you later.'

Then he was gone. Fee Cambridge grinned to herself and touched her fanny. It was sore as hell. The thumping it had taken during the royal rogering she had received the night before had bruised it so that she could feel it all the time. It gave her a pleasurable sexual tension and it felt so puffed that she had lain before her mirror with her legs splayed wide that morning to examine if it was swollen beyond its normal voluptuous convolutions. She had fingered it languorously, half-pinching its fatty plumpness, trying to remember how it normally felt. She loved the look of her rose-fleshed vulva, gloried in its bareness, and liked to stroke her own flesh in self-adoration.

She liked Rollo to watch her do it, only he didn't seem interested any more.

She stood up and went over to the laminated glass walls of the kitchen and leaned on their coolness for a moment, staring at the man-planted jungle outside. The tiger was gone, a sinuous patch of colour that blended with the barred sunlight spilling down through the canopy. Parakeets shrieked in the trees and made a flash of brilliant colour amongst the heavy green lushness. A tiny orange monkey swung chittering through the trees.

Her house was like an igloo, a deluxe pleasure dome of technologically-advanced comfort attached by tunnels to walkways and other house domes, none too close, all equally sophisticated, all surrounded by rioting vegetation where many had learnt at last to replace what he had destroyed down the wanton ages since he first wielded an axe. The cities decayed but the world zoo advanced, inhabited by sealed units of humans who could see nature but not touch it. It was forbidden to enter the jungle, of which more was planted every year.

As to who was in the cage looking out and who outside looking in, that was a moot point. The tiger had the answer, if anyone cared to ask.

Fee laughed and made her way over to the vidicom. Instead of turning the screen off, she positioned herself so that most of her nakedness was out of its viewer. She dialled Diana.

The big blonde answered quickly.

'Hi, there,' she said. 'What can I do for you? Oh, Fee. How's tricks, baby? Still as bored?'

'The short answer is no. Can I come over for breakfast, Diana?'

'Are you wearing anything, lady?'

'Not a damn thing.'

'Is that how you've been getting your kicks? Phoning strangers and giving them a eyeful? Fiona, that's low-class stuff.'

Diana chided her friend gently but with real curiosity. All of them fantasised about doing just that at some time or another, but no one ever admitted to giving way to temptation.

'I'll put something on before I come over,' Fee promised.

'Don't mind me. I'm all for the body beautiful. The patrols might be amazed though. Make their day, I should think.'

'I'll see you in twenty minutes,' said Fee. She wasn't

30

reduced to flashing the guards that patrolled the Zoo. Yet.

In her bedroom she buzzed her maid, Janine. Within a minute or two the young girl came to see what her mistress wanted.

'I need to get dressed, Janine. And my hair needs fixing.'

Janine's eyes flickered over Fiona's superb body. Fiona had never covered her nakedness before her. 'What would you like?' she asked.

'The mandarin, I think.'

Janine fetched the heavy stiffly-embroidered garment with the stand-up collar and held it for Fiona's final decision. It was black with ice-green dragons appliquéed on to its sumptuous glossy surface. The dragons were the precise colour of Fiona's eyes.

'Yes,' she said with pleasure. It was a beautiful dress.

'The apricot lingerie, ma'am?'

'No underwear.'

'None?' Janine was startled and she blushed slightly. She had a waist-length frizz of wheat-pale hair that swung in a heavy curtain as she moved. She did not have to wear a uniform, as some private maids did, and so was in a black one-piece, broadly belted at her waist, that clung to her adolescent contours. She was just sixteen, the legal minimum age for a maid. Her large round eyes were cornflower blue, and with her peachy complexion she had an innocent vulnerable air.

She held up the dress but Fiona said: 'Perfume first, Janine.'

The maid returned the dress carefully to its hanger and fetched the atomiser that her mistress indicated. Fiona raised her arms and held up her hair, closing her eyes.

Janine walked gently round her naked mistress lightly clothing the pearl skin with a fine spray. Fiona felt the momentary coolness at breast, buttock and thigh. Some of her grazes faintly stung. There was something insolent in her voluptuous enjoyment of the service and Janine lowered her eyes from the revealing curves. Always they turned to the hairless pudendum, to her secret shame. Fiona's bare bulge of sex fascinated her.

31

Fiona smiled.

Now Janine held the chosen garment and Fiona shrugged into it. Janine knelt before her to attach the little hooks one by one. The dress was created for luxury, not practicality. When Janine reached Fiona's breasts, where the material strained to take in their pliant fullness, Fiona reached in herself and settled them against the cold material making Janine abandon her fastening so that the deep plunge was revealed below her throat.

'My hair,' she said, going to sit at her dressing table.

Whilst the girl brushed her hair and then began skilfully to twist it into a fashionable knot, Fiona felt through her skin the dress.

Last night she had revelled in mud and slime. She was never filthy. Her house was aseptically clean, she did no dirty work and she bathed frequently, more than once a day, and had done so for as long as she could remember.

To feel dirt was a revelation. To see her skin smeared, to feel her hair grubby and dank with whatever had been thrown over herself and Mammet, to taste something stale and sour was almost beyond experience. Yet last night she had rolled in the gutter with a vulgar little hellion, scratching and biting for the sake of a man's cock.

She had rutted on the ground like a dog. She had allowed a stranger at her cunt and revelled in his caresses and his brutality. She had performed the sexual act publicly within a crowd like a paid whore at a sex party, in some crude celebration of bizarre customs native to the squalor of the city. There, there was no shame, no modesty, no privacy, no self-control.

Fiona filled her lungs and felt her breasts strain within the dress. Rollo had rejected her body. Not once, but over and over again, including this morning. Well, it was her body and she owed no fealty to him, husband though he was, if he did not make use of what was his. If Rollo would not answer her need, she would find ones who did.

Till now, she had been faithful to him in her fashion. She had made night-time excursions and found men's lively members, but she had kept her own body inviolate, pleasing herself only in so far as she pleased some stranger in the night with her eager, experienced mouth and hands. She had confined betrayal to tasting the climax of others and using the memory to masturbate herself to orgasm when alone.

Last night marked something new, a new departure. She had to have manflesh within her and the feeling of self-disgust engendered by Rollo's rejection had sent her to the sewers of society.

The thing was, she had enjoyed it. She laughed aloud and Janine jumped nervously.

'That's all,' said Fee crisply. 'I won't want you again before, say, four this afternoon. If you see the master, tell him I've gone over to Diana's for breakfast and we might take in a massage or something. I really don't know. He'll be in conference for hours, I expect.'

She leaned forward to put a flick of make-up on her face. The bare look was currently fashionable. Nevertheless, she put drops in each eye that caused her pupils to swell and she enhanced the shape of her lips. No ghost make-up. That was for night-time only.

'What shoes, ma'am?'

'The black sandals.'

Janine knelt to slip Fiona's silk-clad foot into each high-heeled shoe and do up the little gold buckle that held them in place. Fiona looked down on her wheaten head and wondered if Rollo ever synched with the girl. Before last night she would have sacked Janine and raged at Rollo if such a thing were true, but now she wondered if she wouldn't be relieved to know that Rollo still had that much libido in him. Janine was really very pretty in a rather wholesome way.

Fiona stood and Janine moved away and surveyed her mistress. 'You look lovely, ma'am,' she said with sincerity.

Fiona knew it was true. She couldn't help it. She was born beautiful and had the money and the time to make the most of it.

'Do you ever fuck my husband?' she asked casually.

Janine went white with shock at both the word used and its meaning. Then she coloured to a deep rich beetroot red.

'Oh, ma'am,' she said hoarsely.

33

'He's a good-looking guy.'

'But, I mean,' the girl struggled pitifully.

'Silly child,' said Fiona. 'If it is happening, I know who will have made the first move.'

'No, I wouldn't, please.'

'And if you are, the worst I might do is pay you a packet, give you a decent reference and send you on your way. It wouldn't be your fault, chick. I know that. Rollo can come on like a moonrocket if he wants to synch flesh and he doesn't like to be thwarted.' He used to come on like a moonrocket, she added sourly in her mind. He hasn't for some time to my knowledge.

'I mean I'm not, we don't, he doesn't . . .'

'He doesn't much with me, either,' said Fiona calmly. 'I just wondered whether it's because he's on-line elsewhere or because he just doesn't want to switch it on any more.'

Janine was getting over her shock. 'But he looks so sexy,' she blurted.

Fiona spared a moment to think of the impact of Rollo's looks and personality and wealth on an underling like little Janine.

'Yes, he does,' she answered the girl. 'It just goes to show how looks deceive.'

Janine began to go red again but curiosity was getting the upper hand. Fiona had never unbent in this way to her before.

'Can't you, er, give him something? Pep him up, I mean,' she ventured.

'Sure. But it's an admission of failure, don't you think? Dull, too. I feel I'm entitled to a little fun, if I'm to wake him up. It's my chemistry I want to do the business, not something bought through a screen-ad.'

Fiona was speaking almost idly, enjoying shocking Janine and enjoying using her as a reflector of Rollo's undoubted charisma. Yet as they left her lips, her words began to take a shape, take a life of their own. An idea like a cold ripple began to cast a vague shadow across the warm current of her mind.

'I see that,' said Janine.

'Have you got a boyfriend, honey? You don't have to

34

answer. I pay you to maid me, not so that I can pry into your personal life. But all of a sudden I want to know.'

Janine blushed furiously again. 'No, ma'am. I'm shy with men, really. A bit frightened, too.'

'What are you telling me, child? Surely you aren't still a virgin.'

'Yes, I am. And it's a terrible nuisance.' Janine was in deadly earnest so Fiona resisted the impulse to laugh.

'A nuisance! You make me feel old-fashioned. I thought it was supposed to be precious. I admit it's rather a long time ago for my own part, but I am sure that that was how the argument went. One tends to forget these things.'

'I bet you do remember. I bet you wanted to be rid of it as fast as you were able. Of course I want to enjoy men. But I know I'm going to be hopeless and I'm shy and I'm frightened I will be hurt and they'll laugh at me. It doesn't matter how much you are told, you just don't know what it will be like.'

Fiona laughed. 'OK, OK, I'll cut the flummery. I unloaded my virginity as soon as I was able. He was a lifeguard on a surf-beach and we did it between the combers. And I bet he did the trick with a dozen others like me that summer. There was nothing that guy didn't know about tight little twats and we just about stood in line to let him oil our locks. They called him Slim Dick and I didn't get the joke till about a year later. Now there was a man who knew how to resource himself,' Fiona added, suddenly caught up in her own memories. 'A less confident man might have had himself implanted so he could fill up with a fat one, but that guy stuck to small containers and got his thrills with what nature gave him.'

She remembered who she was speaking to and looked at Janine. The girl was wide-eyed with a maggot of curiosity in her general embarrassment.

'Look, honey, I've got to go. Diana's expecting me. Maybe I'll think about your problem, hey? You never know, I might come up with something.'

Janine flamed a deep scarlet. 'You wouldn't, you wouldn't tell Mr Cambridge, would you? I don't think I could bear that.'

'Of course not, said Fiona smoothly.

So that was how the land lay. It was hardly surprising, Rollo being what he was (or appeared to be) and this little inadequate child trembling on the threshold of sexuality. The shame of it was, she didn't even realise what she had revealed.

Fiona smiled within herself. Surely some good would come of all this new information. Some good to herself, that is. She was beyond thinking about what others needed. Her own needs gnawed too deep.

'I appreciate your honesty and I'll respect your confidence, never fear. I'll see you later, dear. Goodbye.

Fee was thoughtful as she rode the moving floors underground to Diana's. They lived in what was officially named the Jungle, but common usage had defeated officialdom and now everyone knew it as the Zoo. Iconoclasts liked the near-consonance between Zoodom and boredom. But part of living in it was that you could not walk around outside or go out for any reason whatever. It was no nature park outside, just nature pure and simple. People stayed in house bubbles or public domes and moved between them through tunnels filled with soft music and patrols. These guards served a double purpose. They protected Zoo-dwellers from the irritations of the common ruck who could not afford such luxurious living and had no place among the richest in the land. And they prevented the Zoo-dwellers from breaking out into the jungle. The natural jungle, that was. What Fiona had done down in the city was in no way forbidden. But if it were known, she would arouse disgust among her kind and lose caste. The whole point about the Zoo was that you might live alongside tigers, but you did not contaminate yourself with the squalor of human failure.

Rolling in the mud was no social asset. Perhaps that was why Fiona had enjoyed it so much.

Diana's apartment was ten minutes away, a near neighbour by Zoo standards. The big Scandinavian let Fiona in and then went through to make coffee.

'I've eaten, slugabed. What can I get you?'

'Crispbread will be fine.'

'Don't tell me Rollo did the business this morning. You look distinctly hung over.'

'No such luck. I took myself mother-naked into the kitchen and offered him a mammary but he recoiled in disgust.'

Diana looked sharply at her friend. 'You'll be meditating revenge.'

'You bet, sister.'

Diana wore tight pink shorts over harlequin tights. Her strong bosom was strapped firmly by a leather waistcoat buttoned tightly across it. What dazzled the eye, however, was not the leathery sheen of her formidable torso, nor the way the pink of her shorts strained across her shapely pelvis, but the holes cut in the leather of her waistcoat so that her big rosy nipples projected through and were on plain view. A gold chain attached to a little gold ring piercing each perfect female member, connected them, tip to tip.

'Love the gear,' said Fiona.

'Not too shocking?'

'Only the first time. I've seen others, though yours is very nice. I've been thinking about getting my own nipples pierced but I haven't got around to it. I love the jewellery.'

'You want to shop today?'

'I feel like a massage.'

Diana laughed. 'Ordinary or intimate?'

'Intimate, friend of mine. Willing to come along?'

'You bet. Hey, look at this.' Diana lifted her arms and linked her hands behind her head. She had thick tufts of flaxen hair in her armpits. These had been dressed with little pink bows that matched her shorts.'

'Cute. I really like it. I'm a bit sparse there myself.'

'The same coiffeur dresses your fanny thatch if you want it. You have plenty down below, Fee.'

Fee smiled a deep slow smile and slowly shook her head.

'You what?'

Fee said nothing, only continuing to smile at Diana.

'Fee Cambridge, is there something you haven't told me?' Diana's eyes flicked up and down her friend. 'Hey, show,' she suddenly demanded.

'You want to see?'

'I certainly do.'

Fiona reached down and got a hold of the hem of her dress. She crossed her arms over so that her bosom bulged between her arms. She wriggled and began to work up her tight skirt. The tops of her stockings came into view, then her thighs.

She wore no panties and moved very slowly as she revealed what lay at the base of her belly to the curious eyes of her friend. Nothing sullied the whiteness of her skin, for she wore magistocks which needed no suspender to keep them aloft.

Her mound told its own story. Its satin hairless surface gleamed slightly in the sunlight in Diana's kitchen. Fee parted her legs to get her balance and hoisted her skirt quite free of her sexual parts.

Diana gasped and bent her head to look closer.

'Honey, all that gorgeous black stuff you kept down there. All gone.'

'I thought it spoiled the view,' said Fiona huskily. She was enjoying showing herself to Diana. What had come over her, that all she craved was to exhibit herself?

'The view is bizarre, to say the least,' said Diana. 'But fabulous. This would knock Teddy sideways.' Her husband's name was Theodore. 'Can I look closer?'

'Sure.'

Diana knelt down and inspected Fiona's strangeness from close to. Fiona's mound of sex was like some strange fruit, at first a globe, then parting into two lobes. In that division lay a woman's mystery, her art, her enticement. It seemed to Diana that Fiona's skin pouted out towards her, bidding her touch and feel the rounded smoothness before sliding her fingers within the division to sample the moist edibility it cloaked.

'Can I touch?' she asked.

'Yes.'

Her hand came up hesitantly. She touched Fiona and felt the flesh at once satin-soft and smooth, yet firm and elastic, sheathing the bone within. She stroked it, forgetting it was a woman's sexual part, so fascinating was it to her. She slid her

38

hand over it to cup it and sense it with her palm, rotating her palm slightly at the deliciousness of the texture it held. Without her conscious volition, her fingers slid round and caught themselves within the division, the gash, the slit in the fruit, and she felt against the sensitive tips Fiona's wetness of sex and the lively little cone of flesh that was her clitoris. Her fingers curled up and penetrated deeper, dividing the labia that clung modestly to shield the entrance to Fiona's body. The warmth drew her. Her fingertips penetrated and the breath rattled in her throat. Her eyes rose slowly and she met Fiona's icy gaze as the glass-green of her eyes stared down.

She had two fingers in Fiona's pussy. 'I'm sorry,' she whispered.

The tension drained out of Fiona's face and the intensity of her blazing eyes faded. 'Don't be,' she said. 'I love you, darling.' She dropped on her knees to face her friend and caught Diana's shaking hand. She slipped the fingers into her mouth and sucked her own essence from them. Then she bent her head and kissed her friend on each of her chained nipples.

She sat back on her heels and smiled. 'If my shaven pussy has this effect on you, why the hell won't Rollo dig in?'

'He must be crazy. What a texture, Fee. I'm going to think seriously about doing this myself. God, it's so sensual, baby. It just sucks you in. I could cradle it all day.'

They got up and grinned at each other. 'The next craze, they say, is to have a hole down there in your clothes so folk can see what a pretty diddly thing we all keep hidden. Hey, how you would feel then, Fee? Drive the men wild.'

'Unless they are all like Rollo,' said Fiona savagely. 'He must have the libido of a plank of wood right now.'

'He's the best looking husband around,' said Diana. 'Far better looking then the ugly oaf I'm married to.'

'The sexy ugly oaf,' corrected Fiona.

'Yeah, he's sexy,' agreed Diana. 'And he rogers me like hell. But he doesn't work like your Rollo and we don't earn your sort of money.'

'Moderation in all things,' said Fiona gloomily. 'Except sex. Let's go get a massage, Diana, and the more intimate the better.'

4

They took the tunnelway back to Fiona's house to fetch her car. The massage parlour was at a considerable distance from the Zoo and it was necessary for them to use the great soaring highways that flew across the city sprawling on the plain below.

Diana did not have a car. Although her apartment was almost as lush Fiona's, and she dressed at the height of Zoo fashion which was at once expensive, rapidly-changing and extreme, there were ways in which her lower standard of living manifested itself. She did not have a personal maid. And she did not have a car.

Fiona's car was no ordinary beast. Many drones had cars, ordinary computer-assist models. Zoofolk called them drones but they were just the middle classes, suburb-dwelling and respectable. They despised the outrageous overtly sexual Zoofolk and the Zoofolk despised their bourgeois mentality.

No, Fiona's car was one of the new turbocharged monster machines. It was a thing of superb beauty, elegant design and state-of-the-art technology. Shaped like a rocket flattened at the bottom, it was made of corrosion-proof titanium overlaid with unbreakable glass. Fiona's was deep smoky-brown, a tobacco-coloured tube of power designed to wing its passengers, as the advertising said, at speeds in excess of three hundred and fifty miles per hour. It would do this in total safety and superb comfort, free from accident or breakdown and as free as possible from highway piracy. It was for these superautos that the great highways up on stilts had been built across the seething corruption of the no-hopers in the decaying cities. It was the only way the very rich could move through the very poor and be safe.

At an earlier time highway cops that patrolled with helicopters and more conventional cars had driven through the cities. But the poor shot the helicopters down for sport and if there were survivors, they ransomed them for large sums of money, a somewhat brutal equalisation of the national cashflow.

The monstermachines up on the special roadways were safer. Even so, they were not absolutely impregnable. The self-styled pirates were computer hackers who attacked the powertubes via their control systems as they blasted over what was, in effect, enemy territory.

Such attacks were rare, or rather, rarely successful. The point of them was to capture the effete hothouse flowers who owned and drove the cars, and ransom them. The penalty for this crime was endless imprisonment and the car designers worked constantly on the problem of making the cars hack-proof, but the problem was not yet overcome.

Once Fiona's car was out of its hangar and had trundled up the local ramp, it began to soar in speed as it matched itself to the highway. Fiona watched the screen – the computer screen for there was no windscreen – and keyed in her destination and desired time of arrival. The car would do the rest, dealing with other traffic, coping with any variable conditions there might be and taking them to their destination as specified. Theoretically, if your car contained the programme 'World Map', you could choose anywhere in the world, even Antarctica, and sit back and let the car do the rest.

It was a beautiful machine, a perfect slave, a thousand times more powerful and, within its limits, faster-thinking than its operators.

The surge of power gave Fiona the thrill it usually did and the car settled to a quiet zoom as they rushed through the polluted air over the cityswamp. They left behind them their own homes, nestling within the folded hills overgrown with jungle. Some kinky crooner recently had likened the jungle to a woman's vulva. The folds were soft and plump and many, thick with luxuriant pubic growth, the house domes nestling like microbes within the interstices of the sexual landscape.

The Zoo was rather proud of the comparison.

The car rushed through the air, planing above the roadway on a friction-free airpad. The only way one could see what passed by outside was to play a tape, slowed to watchable speed of the outside world. The cars cocooned their owners from the ugliness of reality.

'They say the city comes alive at night,' said Diana, comfortably sprawled on a couch.

'That's what they say,' agreed Fiona. She smiled to herself.

'Do you ever think about the pirates?' asked Diana.

'Sometimes. It wouldn't be so bad. People get home again in one piece if the ransom is paid.'

'You fancy, uh, what might happen between being captured and going home?' asked Diana, her mouth curving naughtily.

'They say the pirates are powerful men,' said Fee softly. 'It might not be so bad.'

'You're in a pretty bad way,' said Diana. 'If you fancy multiple rape you must be desperate indeed.'

'It's not rape if you like it,' said Fee sweetly. 'And if I get wet at the thought of muscular brigands ripping my knickers off and banging into me, then that is Rollo's fault. A year ago I would have primmed my lips like a drone and tut-tutted.'

'Never,' mocked Diana. 'But keep your fantasies to do with the city rather than the jungle.' She laughed. 'No one would blame you for letting a pirate between your thighs if you were captured, but don't ride the tigers. It's illegal.'

'There are tigers and tigers,' said Fiona. 'We'll be arriving shortly.'

The parlour was undoubtedly kinky, but it was classy, clean and discreet. Several Zoo women used it and if they didn't make haste to tell their husbands, that was their own affair. The guilty thrill aroused by a visit was spice to the occasion.

Fee and Diana signed in and paid and had their bodies scanned and passed as healthy. 'You require single cubicles or do you prefer to remain together and take a double?' asked the dark white-smocked woman at the desk.

'Double,' said Diana firmly. 'Seeing you get all het up is half the fun, Fee. Let's get to it.'

42

They were shown into a small room with two couches, each attended by a young male masseur. The men had bare chests tanned golden brown with flaring shoulder muscles and powerful biceps. Each wore a broad leather belt over skin-tight flexitrousers that ended just below the knee, revealing shapely muscular calves. The trousers outlined their buttocks, mound and cleft, and also their sexual equipment in every exquisite bulging detail.

The young men smiled as the women were shown in. 'Ladies,' said one. 'May we assist you to get undressed?'

'All the way, buster,' said Diana happily. 'I'm here to enjoy myself.'

Each of the men advanced on each of the women. Diana's man flicked her hair free and touched her chained nipples. 'Very nice,' he said. 'I can see you are a lady in synch.'

'Glad you approve,' said Diana saucily. Her attendant began to unbutton her waistcost lingeringly, allowing her large bosom slowly to reveal itself. Fee and her man waited and watched. The whole point of the excursion was to get turned on. Fee was quite happy to watch and openly admire as her friend was laid bare.

The chain unclipped and the waistcoat was slipped back. The attendant reconnected the chain and now Diana's big freckled breasts swung free, hanging down under their own weight with the chain brushing the skin of her stomach. The man worked close to Diana, touching her as if by accident, very lightly, brushing and arousing her skin and sensitising it to his touch. He slipped the waistcoat right back off her shoulders and saw her coiffeured armpits. He admired their intricate tiny styling with the absurdity of pink bow.

Now he knelt before her and unzipped her shorts. He eased them down over her stomach and firm buttocks and she stepped out of them. Her flattened bush could be seen through the material of her tights. Now he began to unroll her tights from the waist, slowly, allowing her stomach to ride free, and then her sexual mound.

When her tights were at her ankles he looked up, his face just opposite her pubes. He raised one hand and gently fluffed her hair. Diana grinned. She adored a man's hands on

43

her big powerful body. She lifted each foot in turn and her tights were slipped off with her shoes. She climbed on to the padded couch and rested, entirely at her ease with nothing on. Her attendant took her breast chain in his mouth and sucked at it so that it gently tugged her nipples. She laughed delightedly.

Now it was Fiona's turn.

Her young man took his time with her hooks, sliding a hand down inside the dress to facilitate their undoing, pressing into her bosom as he did so. When several were undone, he met Fiona's eyes and calmly lifted each heavy globe free of the confining material and laid them delicately on the material of her dress. They were magnolia, thick and lustrous, against its glossy black surface. His warm breath caressed them as he continued to undo the dress until he could split it in two.

They all saw that Fee wore no underwear. Her naked body was startlingly in view the instant the two front panels of her dress parted company.

They all saw the magical bare bulb at the base of her soft flat belly, Diana's luxuriant hirsute growth quite absent in her friend. The attendant hissed but did not touch.

It seemed to Diana that it was even more beautiful, more sexy, second time around. The memory of its feel, cradled in her hand, came back to her. She realised suddenly what it had reminded her of. Though the shape was quite different, it had the silken resilience of a man's erect member, springy, firm, warm and elastic. Sharply there came to her the lust to see a man's erect cock up against her friend's naked mound. She wanted to handle a cock and press the two satin-sheathed parts together and then press the male one into the enticing divide below the bulb, between Fiona's legs.

Fee's attendant unrolled her magistocks from where they clung unassisted to her legs and removed her sandals. Now Fee was as naked as her friend and as unconcerned. She too climbed upon her couch and the two women lay down on their fronts.

'My name is Derek,' said the man who attended Diana. He adjusted the sugary omni-music so that it washed sweetly

44

over them. Fee remembered the raw frenzy of the gut-rock down where the pirates lit their fires and knew that her life was too bland and that that was a dangerous thing.

She was captive in her lush anodyne society but she had the scent of freedom in her nostrils.

The lighting was adjusted so that the corners of the room became shadowy and mysterious but the women were highlighted. Then the men hesitated a moment.

'What is it?' asked Diana langorously. She was fully relaxed, ready for he man to start.

'For a small extra charge,' said one of the men, 'we will remove our clothing before attending to you, if this would please you.'

'Yes,' said Fiona greedily before Diana had a chance to answer. 'Get it all off. Let's see you, boys, huh?' She felt extraordinarily free with her body public and unclothed. Excitement ran in her.

The men grinned at each other and each carefully peeled off his skin-tight breeks. Then they were as naked as their clients, golden boys from head to toe with long slender penises hanging free from encumbrance. The clouding of hair at their crotches was very fine and downy, softly strokable with a visible shine. They had almost no other body hair, their long lissom limbs free and smooth and gleaming.

Now at last they began to massage the women, beginning with their scalps and working the roots of their hair before oiling their palms and moving on to bare silky skin. Fee sighed and felt herself begin to relax utterly, knots of tension releasing under the expert manipulation. Now and again her masseur's skin brushed hers and if she opened her eyes she could see his prick swinging softly to and fro as he worked. It was a nice sight. It was a very nice sight. Once, when it was close to her hand, she reached out and stroked it and she smiled.

Occasionally she heard Diana groan with sensual enjoyment. It was a good idea coming here, she thought. A certain amount of peace began to descend upon her.

At her buttocks her attendant ground steadily into her

flesh. He separated her two cheeks, savouring the plump roundness of their contours, and she felt a stab of sexual thrill as she remembered the karate-hard edge of the pirate's hand pressing in that place the previous night.

The man who felt her and worked her was called Paul. He rotated her buttocks and slapped them and dug his thumbs into them. His hands slid between them and soon his thumbs were pressing where she had to give, on the entrance to her back passage, where she could afford no resistance. The slick oily experienced fingers dug and probed and worked her hole so that the tight ring of muscle began to give more and she groaned deeply with pleasure, wanting to lift her rear into his invasive hands.

He kept going. He increased the pressure and now his thumbs slid within her a little. It was delicious. She clamped on his fingers and heard him laugh slightly.

Now her orifice was right open and he worked round the edge of the sundered crinkled flesh, constantly penetrating her slightly. Her vagina began to run juicily as her anus glowed with its abuse and his thumbs sank further in.

Her mind ran to the previous night and she thought of a big rough violent prick, thought of it where the masseur's oily thumbs now penetrated, thought of the big invader exploding up her arse as it was gripped by her lust. She thought of sitting down on the pirate's prick and letting it bulge in her tight bottom whilst she frigged her own clitoris and he pumped her rear with hammer blows.

She thought of her missile-shaped car thundering through her and herself laughing as she was split into two, at last satiated, satisfied, and able to find peace.

'Roll over, now, ma'am, said Paul. Dazedly, Fiona complied.

He massaged her face, neck, arms, and hands, working with particular attention on her shoulders to ease and relax them. Then he took one of her breasts and cradled it, felt it all over, stroked it, rotated it, slapped it and pummelled it, and beat it with quick short strokes that made it pulsate as if it had a life of its own. It heated under his hands, the blue veins that marbled the flesh rising slightly and darkening. He began to work on her nipple, drawing it between his fingers, teasing it into erection and giving it little flicks.

When both breasts had been treated alike, they felt buoyant and glowing and firm.

He massaged her stomach, hips, thighs, ankles and feet. To do her calves, he rested her foot on his groin so she could feel his warm fuzz of hair and the silk of his slack member against her foot as he worked.

He came back to her thighs and made them open and fall apart as he drew nearer to her central secret place.

She lay with eyes closed, feeling his body graze hers gently, feeling the flop of his penis as it lolled against her relaxed flesh and rolled over her curving mounds. He climbed astride her, up on the table with her with his knees pressing against the sides of her legs and his penis dropping between and over her thighs in a gentle intimate caress.

His thumbs went inside her, inside her sex, and he frigged her. This was what he was paid for. This was intimate massage.

His fingers found her labia and her clitoris and he worked them and stimulated them. He kept slipping his probing expert fingers deep into her fanny and applying pressure within her.

Fiona began to writhe under him and her lips parted as she cried out soundlessly in sexual ecstasy.

Diana stopped her own massage to watch. She herself only climaxed when a man penetrated her fully. She knew Fee could climax from masturbation and it fascinated her to see her friend given over to passion, prey to great shudderings and sexual tremors that were evidence of the tumult within.

Fee's head turned from side to side. She was oblivious to Diana's curious stare or the eyes of the two men. All she knew was the masturbation of her sexual place. Her knees were drawn up and held wide open. Paul had both hands at her, one frotting her clitoris and one with two fingers deep inside her entrance. Both his fists ground into her vulva. Fee knew nothing except her approaching orgasm. She was utterly given up to her body. Her lips shaped the words, *please, please*, but no clear sound emerged beyond an inarticulate cry for release.

Her fanny shook and throbbed and spurted wetly. She drove her hips up into Paul's hands, gasping and thrusting.

The inner vibrations eased. Her juices ran freely and Paul's hands were wet. Her face went slack as her limbs relaxed, the crisis past. Her fanny throbbed with a dull insistence, the masturbation reawakening bruised flesh battered by a pirate prick the night before.

Fee's body lay as if tossed by the wind, completely at rest. Her eyes were shut and she had a half-smile on her face, an inturned expression like that of a contented cat. Her skin glowed with sex and the golden youth still knelt between her legs.

'And was your last thing a big boy?' he enquired in a silky voice. Diana came suddenly to attention. 'He certainly left his mark,' added the masseur.

'He was big,' said Fee and a shudder suddenly ran through her glowing body.

'I thought you might be sore,' said Paul. 'I could see you were all pulpy and soft.'

'Can I look?' asked Derek. He came and stood looking between Fiona's legs still flopped slackly apart, seeing her dark bruised vulva like a ripe fruit half-bitten, the juices running down between her legs.

'Fiona?' asked Diana.

'Tell you later, kid,' answered Fiona dreamily.

Now Derek returned to Diana and he slipped his hands up into the big woman's strong proud sex, but though she wriggled and sighed with pleasure, she did not come and indeed, knew she would not. Fee watched her, leaning on one elbow and still half-caught in her own fantasy. Diana's hairy mound lifted and her long thighs shivered but that was all. The freckled breasts could not fall apart as Fiona's had done, for the chain pulling on the pierced nipples, held them together. Fee wondered what it would be like to feel the chain between her legs, to rub herself on its cold unyielding bumpy surface.

Diana was watching Fee watching her. That was OK. She knew Fee got a kick out of seeing a woman's body in arousal. She did herself, especially Fee's. She was hair-trigger over sex due to Rollo's neglect. Diana wondered if he realised he was playing with fire. Fiona would make a formidable enemy.

'That was great,' she said. 'I loved the boy's dongos swinging around.' She touched Derek's prick and gave a sexy growl in her throat. He grinned complacently. 'It's nice sight,' she said and sighed.

'Ladies,' said Paul diffidently. 'There is another service this establishment provides.'

'No, no,' said Diana lazily. 'I get it from my husband when it's all the way up and in. That suits me fine. I'm just here to play games, you beautiful boys.'

Paul was shocked. 'We never synch with the clients,' he said stiffly. 'This is not a brothel.'

'My mistake.' Diana was genial and untroubled.

'What service do you mean?' Fee's voice was cool and husky.

The two men went side by side with each other. They were remarkably similar in size, build and colouring: a matched pair. Now they laid their arms about each other's shoulders.

'Derek and I,' Paul continued, 'will provide a little entertainment, should you girls like it.'

That there should be no doubt of what was intended, each laid his free hand across their bodies and grasped his partner's genitals. It was a pretty sight.

'You mean you boys will, uh, perform, if we sub up?' asked Diana. Fee caught the threadlike ripple of excitement in her voice.

Derek smiled a catlike smile. 'We like it,' he said softly.

'You want this?' asked Fee.

'I've seen it on the Screen, of course,' mused Diana. 'It seems different, right here in front of us in the flesh.'

'We won't be acting,' said Paul. His hand slid up his friend's shaft and the slender thing became erect and stood out before the young man.

'That's pretty,' enthused Diana.

'Let's do it,' said Fiona. 'Heaven knows I'm sick of men who don't. I'd like to see some male enthusiasm about the place.'

'Talking of which, what's this about your sore fanny, Fiona? You've been holding out on me.'

'An oasis in the desert. I'll explain later. On you go boys. Give us sight of some action.'

They got the two men to push the couches together. Thus the two women were side by side, reclining in Roman fashion, still quite nude but ready to watch and be entertained. Fiona felt her pulse begin to speed up. This was a neat idea, homo tricks before the two women clients. It was the sort of thing that made the drones rail on about decadence and the sick society, but for herself, she couldn't see the harm in it. It certainly had an esoteric appeal, though. This would be one for the record books. Her fanny felt warm and juicy at the thought.

Now the men moved to the rear of the room and drew back floor-length drapery to reveal a little stage with a large square couch entirely covered in fur. The lighting was adjusted so that the girls were in the gloom but the men were brightly displayed. A mirror faced them from the head end of the couch. Nothing would be missed of the action to follow.

Paul and Derek got on to the couch and knelt facing each other, chest to hairless chest, almost touching. Their tongues poked out from their mouths and touched, tip to tip. Then they entwined and brought their faces close in so that openmouthed they kissed each other wetly and fully and deeply. Their hands began to play over each other's smooth bodies, savouring the touch of male skin with male skin. When they adjusted their bodies it could be seen that their pricks mimicked their tongues. Each was erect and touching tip to tip, swollen knob to swollen knob. There was a succulent delicacy about their touching. Their lavish enjoyment of each other's sexual parts was evident, yet they were sensuous and careful, not greedy. They were gloating over each other and content to take their time.

They began a complicated, slow, elaborate ballet of structured movement. Each struck a posture and held it, maybe with one limb raised and arms apart, and the other caressed and explored the exposed part. They broke pose to kiss and lip each other, and gradually they began to concentrate on

50

groin and buttock, using hand and tongue to arouse and fondle. Then, slowly, Derek stood up, letting his erect member rub up his friend from groin to face as he rose. He stood straddled before his kneeling friend. Paul lent forward and delicately he took the end of Derek's prick in his mouth.

Diana hissed slightly in excitement and squirmed next to Fiona. In response, hardly aware of what she was doing, Fiona reached a hand across and felt her friend's heavy breast. Diana did not stop her and Fiona's hand slid out over the full curve to find the nipple. She traced its length and pliant firmness and felt the cold resistance of the piercing gold.

Derek began to pump his hips as Paul sucked him. They saw the long slim shaft sink between the lips of his mouth and as Derek drew back from Paul's face, the wet column glistened between them.

Derek stopped and Paul sucked his knob, opening his mouth so that his tongue could flicker snakelike over the bulbous head. His hand came up and he began expertly to squeeze Derek's balls.

Derek's head went back and he began to pant. He pumped vigorously and the other's cheeks sucked hard as he powerfully worked his friend's prick. Then Derek was coming. They saw his shaft throb as he gasped. A moment later Paul opened his mouth and the women saw the creamy spunk on his tongue. With a sigh Derek dropped to his knees and placed his open mouth on Paul's. They kissed deeply, their throats working, swallowing the shared spunk.

'Wow,' said Diana softly. 'Is that a sight!'

'Glad we stayed?' whispered Fiona. Her hand dropped from Diana's breast and she curled her fingers round Diana's warm stomach. Diana trembled slightly. 'You bet.'

Now Derek turned and presented his backside to the girls.

'It's Paul's turn,' he said sweetly.

Before their startled eyes Paul began to massage Derek's rear much as he had done for Fiona earlier. He worked the tight valve open, inserting two, then three fingers and plunging them deeply into Derek. Then he raised himself and his erect shaft. He took his fingers out of Derek's rear and began

51

to push with his own member, pressing in between the lobes of his arse, driving to penetrate his male body.

Both women saw the effort it took to push the swollen end of penis at the tight aperture. Yet though there was strain evident on Paul's face, there was bliss also. Derek's face was reflected in the revealing mirror. He was transported with delight, his lips drawn back baring his teeth in a rictus of pleasure as his flesh split and gave way before the assault.

Paul's swollen gland slid into Derek's arse and he thrust forward, driving the length of his wand fully in until his hips and thighs rested against the cheeks of Derek's bottom.

Fiona felt Diana's tension and let her hand drop from her stomach into her hot humid place. Diana eased her position to allow her better access. Fiona ran her fingers gently inside and felt her pulse flutter rapidly as Diana's warmth and elasticity enveloped her groping fingers.

Paul began to fuck into Derek's arse with his glistening golden shaft, and the girls were mesmerised as it went in and out, in and out. It made the most delicious and lascivious sucking and plopping noise, a fat wet noise of sexual congress.

Now Paul was excited, thrusting deeper and harder and muttering in his lust. He grasped his friend's hips and slammed hard into him. Then he yelped and they saw him come. He held Derek's cheeks hard apart and his prick bulged as he ejaculated into Derek.

Then, for a moment, he hung limp over Derek's bent back before starting to withdraw. Both women strained to see. The narrow penis came out half-limp and foamy. Best of all, before the valve closed its secrets from view in tight fawn flesh as Paul removed his prick, they saw a dribble of spunk in Derek's cleft, oozing from his rear.

Now Paul dropped his head before his enthralled audience and put his tongue right out. He licked his friend's dribbling arse with long strong licks, then penetrated anew the riven flesh, this time with his tongue, and sucked hard.

Both men kissed each other with extreme affection and sweetness. Looking douce and wicked, they turned to the women, a pair of satyrs loose in the modern world, escaped from mythological times to worship Pan anew.

Diana began to clap. Fiona still had her fingers within her hole and she felt Diana's muscles work as she clapped. The spongy wetness invited her to linger but she knew she could not. Not now. Not here.

Diana congratulated the performers but Fiona turned over what she had learned about herself within her mind. It was being quite a day.

For some reason, little Janine came into her mind.

Fiona smiled, her green eyes glittering coldly. Life wasn't quite without interest after all.

5

On the way back to the Zoo, relaxed in the auto, Diana quizzed Fiona.

'Give, baby,' she said. 'Who synched with you if it wasn't Rollo? Who's made you sore?'

But Fiona had had second thoughts. Some ideas had come to her, big ideas that needed thinking over and investigating.

Illegal ideas.

However good the friendship, she couldn't involve Diana until she had things clearer in her head. Indeed, because she was fond of the big Scandinavian, she wouldn't do anything to harm her.

It was all nonsense. She was just flirting with the idea of danger. Nonetheless, it would give her a kick to sort it out in her mind and pretend she might go through with it. Meanwhile, it would be only sense to keep quiet about the root of her plan.

The pirate. Will and his lovely rogue cock that went where he willed and did not understand the boundaries of reticence and decent behaviour and good manners.

No, best to keep silence and hug her gutter sex to herself.

'I'm making too much of a mystery,' she said lazily. 'It was just a new vibrator and I used it too much. I am so damn fed up with Rollo choosing the desert instead of the wellhead. The man takes a pill every night and is dead to the world.' She giggled. 'I suppose I could wreak my vengeance on his sleeping body but it would be like necrophilia, you know? I kind of go for movement and response. Anyway, I took refuge in the nun's delight last night and went a little over the top.'

Diana was disappointed but did not press for salacious details. 'You want to stay for lunch?' she asked. 'We could shop after, if you felt like it.'

'I think I'll go home,' said Fiona. Her eyes were hard, like emerald chips. 'I'm tired and I suppose I ought to align with Rollo over lunch. We didn't match schedules this morning, as you can imagine.'

'This scheme he's working on,' said Diana. 'It'll be really big if it comes off.' There was a note of envy in her voice.

'I guess,' said Fiona. 'If it does, I'll have to help with the organisation. I'll have less time free.'

'You'd enjoy that, wouldn't you?'

'Yeah. I like work, actually. I just don't like it to get in the way of my sex life. At the moment Rollo is totally sublimated and I don't got for that, no way.'

'Would you screw around?'

'Would I tell you if I did? Be real. We know the same people. I'd have to be discreet.'

There was a great deal of overt sexual display and open sex talk in the Zoo, but though few of them admitted it, they weren't so different from the drones in the way they behaved. They made more noise about it, that was all.

Human sexual behaviour has always been much the same. It is the fashion for its presentation that varies, that's all.

'Lay off Teddy,' said Diana. Her tone was light but she meant it. She might let Fiona dabble in her fanny but she wasn't going to share her man's equipment. Oh no.

Fiona's cold green gaze enveloped the blonde. 'I value your friendship maybe more than you know, huh?'

Diana licked her lips. She remembered how nice it was, Fiona's fingers within her during the live sex show. She remembered her own fingers within Fiona. That was almost nicer, if possible.

'I know,' she said.

Fee was there when Rollo came out of his work station. One room of the luxury apartment was entirely given over to telecommunications and it was from there that Rollo conducted his business affairs, rarely meeting his associates in the flesh. He could have an on-screen conference with up to twelve personnel with the equipment he hired, and if it happened that he needed more, he could hire a bigger slice of satellite and put them on line. They had no need to waste time and resources jetting around the world. Business was conducted through the small screen now and that was the world as far as Rollo was concerned.

He was engaged in floating a company to pipe water from the wet northwest to the arid southeast. This was a project that had been on the books for over fifty years, ever since drought became a regular feature of the southern summer, but still no one had yet got around to the engineering and financial logistics necessary. Rollo was filling the gap. He was developing a consortium and financing it through the marketplace with himself as head and Fiona as one of the directors. If it fell into place she would become involved on a day-to-day basis. She had a genius for organisation and was a natural partner for him, hard-headed and clear-sighted, and if he hadn't forgotten she was a sexually active and needy woman, their relationship would have been perfect.

As it was, Fiona was hellbent on revenge.

Rollo had forgotten their exchange of the morning and was still vibrating from his business activities. He ate a salad without noticing it, discussing the personalities of the men and women he was dealing with and the various timings suggested for the launch date of the new company.

'Give us a name, Fee,' he said. 'Something strong and sexy. It's got to make people think of power and success and confidence.'

She stared at him in amazement. The man had no idea what went on in her head these days.

'ThroughFlow,' she suggested. 'FluidFlow, SuckSouth, StreamLine, OnStream, SouthFlow, DeepWet, Soak-Down . . .'

'OK, OK, print them out baby. Nothing too raunchy. No Zoo-smell. We want to appeal to all levels. So no going over the top.'

Not for you, maybe, thought Fiona with sweet savagery. But I might.

'What are you going to do this afternoon?' Belatedly Rollo remembered his manners. In most marriages where one partner earned enough for both, the other usually watched a lot of Screen and video between dates at the gym and neighbourly socialising. Upright members of society did good works and pontificated in local government.

Fiona wasn't very upright. 'I'm horny. My lover's coming round,' she said.

'Don't joke about it, woman. Now I have to go.'

Fiona had had a big night. She went back to bed and fell asleep.

After she woke, she showered and, still in her houserobe, she settled to her computer. She was determined to be a pirate. She hadn't been mouthing off the previous night and she was mad that they would not let her join them for a raid or two.

So she would go it alone. The pirates hacked cars. They only occasionally achieved success – it was not an easy thing to do. But Fiona had several advantages that they lacked.

Firstly and chiefly, she had a car of her own. The pirates never had a car, never could take one apart and learn how it was made as far as its computer Control-net, its Connet, was concerned. Connet cars carried protection against hacking, or piracy as everyone called it. When the internal guidance computer, the Connet itself, was overridden by external instruction, as in hacking, it melted down, totally self-destructing.

The Connet defined the car. It was the most expensive component, worth more than the rest of the car put together. So meltdown had to be a disastrously expensive procedure.

The manufacturers reckoned it was worth it. Even when they succeeded in hacking a car and bringing it to a halt, the pirates could not use what they had stolen. The Connet was lost, melted, defunct and unanalysable. Until it was replaced, the car could not be driven. So all the pirates could do was break the door locks and take the passengers hostage, the passengers being by definition rich, since only the very very rich could afford a Connet car in the first place. They were then ransomed back to their ever-loving families and the car was towed away, to have its computer replaced if the owner could afford to carry the insurance. The pirates never got a look in.

The SkyPolice could hack into a car to stop it if they believed it contained a criminal, and that also induced melt down. Of course, Connet owners were rarely criminals and if they were, they didn't attempt to flee in their cars. There was too much to lose.

The cars were fitted with a manual override which shut down the Connet without destroying it, but you could only do this after hitting an emergency switch that sent an automatic Mayday signal that would bring down the SkyPolice, AirAmbulance and FireCopters within five minutes. And it took ten minutes from pressing the emergency switch before you could engage manual. The cars were joyrider-proof. The destination programme could be entered by anyone, but only those whose genetic fingerprint was recorded as a permitted user could operate the Connet and actually engage the programme.

Rollo and Fiona, and absolutely nobody else in the world, could drive their Connet unless they themselves enlarged the permitted user record, something they had no intention of doing.

So Connet cars kept their internal secrets. But Fiona had a second advantage. She was a computer whizzkid herself and had actually worked for the automanufacturers at one stage in her life.

She planned to hack a car. She would learn what she could from her own but she had no intentions of inducing meltdown. She didn't care what she did to the car she hacked – meltdown would be inevitable but she would run no risk of damaging her own property.

The police would never know. It would just be one more act of piracy on the highway.

Rollo had bought the car but he rarely used it. Indeed, he hardly ever left the apartment except on sporting or social occasions. It was Fiona who used it for transport.

She did a couple of hours' work and then emerged and called for Janine. The young girl came and helped her mistress choose a tight black skirt with over-the-shoulder straps that revealed almost the entire breast apart from the nipple.

'It's a lovely dress, ma'am,' said Janine, 'but a little dated. They expose the nipple now, you know.'

'Mmm. I was with Diana today. She had this great

58

waistcoat that covered all of her except the sticky-out bits. And those were pierced.'

Janine stood back and looked at the dress. Then she came forward and felt the material, rubbing it between her fingers. Fiona's nipples brushed the back of her hands.

'If you gave me twenty minutes I could adjust this for you,' said Janine. 'The straps are wide enough and strong enough, I think.'

'Go ahead. I'll make up.'

Fee stepped out of the dress and Janine fetched her sewing box and settled in the corner to bring the dress into fashion. Dressed only in suspenders, flesh-pink stockings and four-inch heeled shoes, Fiona sat at her dressing table and got to work on her face.

Rollo came in. He saw his wife's all-but-nakedness and his eyes flicked, slightly shocked, from the blind stare of Fiona's hairless crotch to Janine, bent submissively over her mundane task in the corner. He came and stood behind Fiona and began to massage her shoulders. She leaned back against him, the action pulling up her magnificent taut breasts so that each nipple pointed into the mirror and was there reflected, pointing back.

Her eyes went up from her own body so that she could watch him in the mirror. His lean face was beautiful, his eyes as brilliant in colour as the wing of a hummingbird. His hair was a long silken sheet, brushed carelessly back to reveal the planes of his face, and she longed to sink her hands in its warmth and revel in his animal fur. He was dressed all in black for the evening, his overshirt spangled with dull silver medallions, and Fiona could see his muscled body move within the embrace of the cloth. He was a black panther of a man and for all the use he was to her, he might as well have been gelded.

He bent to kiss her shoulder. 'You given up on underwear?' he asked.

'Sometimes. Janine's altering my dress.'

His hand came over her shoulder and cupped her breast. She saw he was watching it in the mirror.

'Rollo,' she said, soft and low.

He let go of her. 'I'm tired, baby. I thought a gentle evening. It's late already. I've got some stuff to look over.'

The green eyes went diamond hard. 'It still could be gentle,' she said deliberately.

'Let's eat, Fee.'

The tension went out of her and she stood up, moving with lazy grace, somehow insulting, going across the room to her maid. Her high heels made the muscles in the backs of her calves taut and her buttocks moved seductively up and down in relation to each other. Standing up, her nakedness was more apparent, her bare-breastedness, her naked dome and naked arse emphasised by her suspenders, stockings and her two clothed companions.

'Are you done yet?' she asked. One leg relaxed with the knee bent, she stood close to Janine seated over her task. Rollo watched them from the dressing table.

'Just finished,' said Janine, heatsealing the final seam. Her eyes, on a level with Fiona's belly, slid up her mistress. Fiona moved back slightly and Janine stood up. She held the dress up for inspection.

Carefully Fiona stepped into it and Janine fastened the short tight skirt and smoothed it over Fiona's hips. Then she eased each strap into position and carefully teased the nipples through each of the holes she had just made.

'Just rub them a little,' said Fiona huskily. 'They'll get stiffer and it'll make it easier for you.'

Across the room Rollo licked his lips and light gleamed on the tight skin over his cheekbone. Janine frotted her mistress's plummy nipples and they stood proud, dark and firm, through the dress.

'That's great,' said Fiona. 'Fix my hair now, baby. And I need plum-coloured earrings to match.'

Janine's eyes flicked up to meet Rollo's and down again. 'They need ghost cream,' she said. 'Then they'll glow in the dark.'

Fiona came over by Rollo and sat down in front of the mirror.

'You do it,' she said to Janine.

Rollo had propped himself half-sitting on the dressing

table to one side of the mirror. Janine now went to the other side and picked up the tube of luminescing cream that Fiona used for her lips at night. She leant round in front of Fiona so that her hair swung in a heavy curtain across Fiona's knees.

Fiona noticed two things. The first one was how far gone in her adoration of Rollo Janine was, and how much the girl was enjoying this by-play even if she didn't quite realise what was going on. The second thing she noticed was that the wheat-fair hair took on Titian lights under the artificial lighting of the dressing table.

Janine's tongue came very slightly out from between her lips and she gripped it with her teeth as she concentrated. Carefully and slowly she ran the tube of cream round the dark aureoles of Fiona's breasts. She applied it thickly. Then she put the tube down and with one finger she began to massage the transparent cream into the flesh and the projecting nipple.

'You do one, Rollo,' said Fiona.

His blue eyes were very bright as he leant close to his wife, his arm brushing Janine's hair. He rubbed Fiona's nipple till it was covered with a film of cream. Fiona saw a pulse flutter in his temple.

As she sat there, her husband at one breast and her maid at the other, with nothing but a stifled silence between them, the plan Fee had been struggling to formulate fell into place with smooth precision. She almost laughed out loud.

Janine stopped and drew back. She was flushed a pale delicate rose, a faint wash of colour that Fiona thought had nothing to do with the intimate contact with her body. It was the nearness of Rollo, the lion man, her master. Fiona reached up a hand and took Janine by the shoulder, pulling her gently down.

She touched the young girl's lips with her own. 'Thank you,' she murmured. 'You are very precious. I wouldn't be without you.'

Rollo's eyes flickered. Fiona began to purr with contentment.

She gave Rollo one last chance. Late that night she stopped him before he took his sleeping pill.

'I want to go down on you,' she whispered. He lay on the satin sheet quite naked and breathtakingly beautiful. His body was mature and arrogantly firm, his muscle tone excellent. He was a shapely man, wide at the shoulders and narrow at the hips. His manhood lolled back across one thigh.

'I'm almost asleep, Fee.'

She ignored this, turning round in the bed and taking his member in her mouth. For a moment she tasted heaven as it thickened between her lips and she began gently to tantalise it to full erection with little sucks and kisses.

'Fee,' said Rollo. She felt him go soft within her mouth. 'Give me a few days, huh? When the pressure eases, maybe.' He put a pill in his mouth. In a few minutes he was deeply asleep.

Fiona sat there considering him for a while. Then she got off the bed and went along the corridor to the maid's suite. She tapped on the door.

A sleepy voice called out and Fiona went into the room and on and through to the bedroom.

Janine was reading in bed.

Fiona went over to her and took the girl's hand in her own.

'It's me, Janine. I'm sorry to interrupt you. I want to show you something.'

'Now?' Janine sounded puzzled and alarmed.

'Come along to my bedroom. I've something to show you.'

She stood and obediently Janine climbed out of bed. She was wearing something in artificial silk with a cluster of pink frills that came to midthigh. It was liberally adorned with little teddy bears wearing pink bows. Her heavy hair was plaited into a single thick rope.

Fiona took her hand again and led her back along the corridor to the master bedroom. She took Janine in and led her to the bed.

The girl gasped as she looked down on the sleeping man.

'You told me you were a virgin today.'

'That's right. That's the truth.' Janine's voice was squeaky and her eyes were round as saucers.

'Have you ever felt a man?'

She didn't pretend not to understand. 'No,' she whispered.

'Touch Rollo. Go on. He won't wake.'

Still holding Janine's hand she guided it down onto her husband's sex. She lifted the soft silky shaft from where it nestled in its warm bed of fur and pushed it into Janine's hand, closing her fingers over it so that it was cradled in their nervous grasp.

'I know you've got the hots for him,' she said gently. 'That's OK. I do myself. But Sleeping Beauty here needs waking up. I don't mean that literally. I mean sexually. The prince needs a princess. You help me to arouse this guy and bring him back to sexual life and I'll double your salary and let you bite on his apple, too. You get me?'

'I, I don't know.' Janine held Rollo's prick as if it was a venomous snake. Yet she could not let it go.

'Put it this way. You are a virgin.'

'Yes.'

'You don't want to be.'

'No.' Janine was vehement.

'You fancy Rollo.'

'I can't help it, Mrs Cambridge. He's so gorgeous.'

'Yes, isn't he?' said Fiona dryly. 'Now, tell me. If you want to become fully a woman you need an experienced man, yes?'

'Oh, yes,' said Janine fervently.

'Well, despite his present supine state, Rollo is an experienced man. And he is attracted to you.'

'He is?' Janine startled eyes flew to Fiona's. 'Oh no. He couldn't be.' She was as pink as her nightwear.

'I knew tonight. So did you.'

Janine hung her head. She kept her hold of Rollo's cock, though.

'What turned him on was you fiddling with my body. You didn't mind that, did you? Touching me, I mean.'

Janine fixed her eyes on Rollo's balls relaxed at the base of his shaft. 'Actually, I liked it,' she mumbled. 'I think your body is fantastic. I wish mine was like it. It makes me feel really funny to do things to you.'

'I thought so.' Fiona's voice remained calm and she

masked the flare of triumph within her. 'Would you mind if I touched you?'

'I don't know. I've never thought . . .'

'Take your nightshirt thing off.'

Stiffly, Janine released Rollo and removed her nightshirt. She did not meet Fiona's eyes. She stood, miserable with embarrassment, her arms hanging at her sides.

Her body was warmly peach and slightly chubby, her breasts endearing and her stomach a rounded perfection. Crisp fair curls hid her sex. She was indescribably sweet.

'Run your hands down Rollo,' said Fiona after a moment. 'He won't wake. Sit on the bed.'

As if in a daze Janine obeyed. Tremulously she began to caress the sleeping man, growing bolder as he did not wake. She felt his chest and shoulders, she ran her hands lightly down his arms, and then she returned to his sex. She was fascinated by his heavy soft limpness. She bent over him, trying to see him better in the dim light, and her rope of hair hung heavily to one side, the end brushing his thigh.

Fiona took the weight of the hair in her hands and then began methodically to unplait it, shaking it loose and then drawing it over one shoulder so it spilled down Janine's back and tumbled about her lower shoulder and caressed her breast on that side. Now she could see the girl fingering her husband's sex. She began to stroke her naked back.

'Kiss him, if you like,' she said softly.

Janine bent her head and touched dry lips to Rollo's chest.

'Kiss his manhood,' whispered Fiona. Her breath stirred the hair by Janine's ear.

She felt Janine shudder. Her head drooped, as if heavy, and with her pale gold hair spilling all around she brushed her lips against the silken sheath of Rollo's golden shaft.

He sighed and stirred very slightly.

Janine held herself stiff, bent over him, her bottom slightly lifted, trembling. Fiona ran her hands under the firm sweetness of her youthful buttocks.

'Kiss him,' she murmured.

Janine whimpered in her throat, opened her mouth and kissed Rollo, tasting him with her tongue. As she did so,

64

Fiona inserted her fingers in the opened cleft between her bottom cheeks and ran her fingers lightly along it till she felt the dampness of sexual opening and the soft brush of intimate hair.

'Kiss him,' she said, her own hand trembling as one finger sought for and found Janine's tiny member. She caressed it with a mothlike touch.

Janine lifted Rollo's prick and put it into her mouth. She sucked lightly, her eyes shut, as Fiona probed delicately below her.

'There's a fire burning in you, sweetheart,' said Fiona. 'Let me help you with it.'

Janine released Rollo and laid her burning forehead gently on his cool chest. She gave a small stifled sob.

'Lie down beside him on the bed.'

Her head came up. 'May I?' she pleaded.

'Come on. On your back.'

Janine's face glowed as she moved carefully around the bed and lay beside Rollo, allowing her body to touch his in as many places as possible. Her expression was beautific.

'Relax now and open your legs.'

'Oh, please. I mean . . .'

'Don't be scared. I just have to check you really are a virgin and you aren't having me on before we get too deep into this thing.'

With a nervous eagerness Janine let her legs come up and fall apart. Very carefully Fiona inserted a finger into the extreme end of Janine's little pussy. The girl stiffened and became rigid, her eyes squeezed shut. Fiona went a short way into the tight small orifice, and then smiled and withdrew her finger. She had felt the obstruction. She bent over Janine and kissed her on the lips.

'You angel. Nothing but the truth. Your little fanny is divine. I envy Rollo his forthcoming pleasure.'

Janine blushed. 'What do you mean?'

'Why, what do you think I mean? Rollo is going to have your sweet body, if you want him to.'

'If I want him to? Oh, Mrs Cambridge, it's my dream. But he doesn't want anyone like me. He has you.'

'You undervalue yourself and what you have to offer,

sweetie. You have something rare and precious. The first time you give yourself to a man matters. It needs to be good and it needs to be important to him. I think you will be, for Rollo. You are young, beautiful and untried, and you adore him. What man could ask for more?'

As she spoke, Fiona absently ran a hand over Janine's breast. She continued to stroke her whilst the tension went out of her young body.

'You want to touch him some more?'

'Please.'

'Go ahead. May I play with you a little while you do?'

'If you'd like to,' whispered Janine.

She turned to the sleeping man and for a long moment she worshipped him with her eyes. Then she ran her hands over him, coming back to his sex, lifting it and feeling it and finally cupping his balls and weighing them in her small palm.

Whilst she did so, Fiona aroused her own nipples and then brushed them against Janine's smooth skin, stroking Janine on her breast and back.

Then she thought she had maybe pushed things far enough for one evening. She kissed Janine on the shoulder.

'That's enough for tonight now. You run along and think things over. And take tomorrow off, so you can catch up on your sleep.'

Janine turned round, her young breasts swinging and brushing against Fiona's.

'Thank you,' she whispered, with shining eyes. 'It's been fantastic. I hope you don't change your mind.'

'You might change yours,' said Fiona, veiling her eyes.

'No.' Janine was suddenly fierce. She reached up her face and kissed Fiona hard on the lips. Fee was astonished and for a moment didn't react. Then her mouth opened and she felt Janine's tongue enter. Her hands came up and she clasped the girl's shoulders and for a moment the two women clung together, kissing with sensual abandon.

Janine picked up her nightshirt and fled.

For a long moment after Janine was gone Fiona stared down at her sleeping husband. She remembered the sight of those young eager hands and lips about his loins. She thought of Janine's freshness and simplicity and air of worship. Her mouth twisted wryly and she was visited by a powerful desire to slap Rollo hard and beat him with her fists.

The Valentine had arrived that day. Rollo had laughed, put it to one side and forgotten about it.

6

Fiona let three days and nights go by and then she asked Janine if she might come to her room that night. Janine was agreeable. Indeed, she was eager.

During those three days Fiona had seen her eyes following Rollo about the apartment upon the occasions that they were in the same room, which was not very often. During the three nights, Rollo had continued to sleep the sleep of death.

When Fiona came along the corridor that night she hardly knew herself what she was doing. She was accustomed to being honest with herself and she knew that this played no part in the revitalisation of her husband. She was sure that had Rollo continued to satisfy her as he once had done, she would never have felt driven to explore the peculiar byways of sexual practice that now enticed her. She had begun by trying to find some sort of satisfaction for herself, some acknowledgement that she could arouse and satisfy men. That had led her out into the night where she had knelt before strange men and taken their essence into herself, herself anonymous and of the night. She had told herself that this was not adultery. Her body remained inviolate whilst she indulged her strange fierce passion to taste a man in his orgasm.

Yet it had not been enough.

She yearned for danger. A madness had come over her and her safe comfortable life had become a prison that she broke out of. The pirates were figures of great romance in her world, the subject of countless romantic adventures on the Screen, but the reality was quite different.

It was darker, dirtier, fiercer, more dangerous than she could ever have imagined. It pleased her that she knew the truth. It pleased her as she moved, beautiful, aloof and fashionable, through her elegant world that she knew the truth and they did not. As her fingers felt fine fabrics, as she ate luxurious food, as she enjoyed each and every refinement of her privileged life, part of her was on the ground rutting with Will, her cheek pressed in the dirt and his cock hard and arrogant shafting her from the rear in the hot public gaze.

She could remember the texture of his wiry chest, muscled under its leather straps. She could remember the sheen of firelight on his greasy breeks, how the bulges of his manhood were revealed. She could remember the fiery sweetness of his mouth and the rich musk of his groin. His skin was scarred and pitted. One eye was blind. Tattered elf-locks hung like Medusa's snakes from his head.

She longed to rake him with her nails and feel his calloused hands mastering her body. She felt none of the soft fawnlike devotion that made Janine melt and blush every time she saw Rollo. Instead she felt the fierce longing to abase herself, debase herself, and be purified by lust in the savage domination of her violent lover.

Even as these feelings washed through her, some kernel of good sense, a latent desire for self-protection, knew that she could play with fire and risk a little burning, but really she had too much to lose. Even as the danger attracted her, so she must plan to replace it with something new, something spicy, something not quite so frightening.

Diana, big, warm and womanly. Janine, sweet, girlish and infinitely appealing.

These were new fields to explore, new sensations to experience. Rollo's lack of interest had launched her on a strange journey and she would not shrink from what she discovered along the way.

She tapped on the door to Janine's suite and entered it.

Her welcome dispelled any qualms of conscience she might have regarding her interference in the girl's sexual development. Janine was a ripe fruit waiting to be plucked, crushed, split and sucked. Let Rollo sample her ruptured sweet moistness, if he would. Far better it was him than some other man not appreciating the prize he had, or too cold-hearted to reward Janine's warmth and eagerness with a like

69

enthusiasm. As Janine's arms went round her in welcome, Fiona reflected that there was plenty for them all.

Janine kissed her mistress with saucy confidence. Their tongues met and mixed and for a while they did nothing except taste one another and explore mouth to mouth.

Fiona drew back at last and slipped off her robe. In her turn Janine took off her pastel slip with red love hearts all over it, and the two women were nude together.

There was something lovely in their bodies being essentially the same shape, yet such a variation on a theme. Janine took one of Fiona's breasts in her hands and began to examine it in frank detail, feeling its weight and shape, its undercurve and long, elastic nipple. In her turn Fiona took one of Janine's breasts in her hands. It was smaller and firmer than her own, the muscles more springy with youth. She touched her nipple with Janine's and the girl laughed and they were content to play like this for a while.

Then Fiona dropped her dark head and began to suck Janine's nipple.

'That's so good,' whispered Janine.

Fiona treated both breasts alike and submitted to the same caress from Janine.

'Suck harder,' she ordered gently.

'Doesn't it hurt when I do it that hard?'

'I like my baths stinging, my food spicy and my sucking firm. It's all a matter of taste. As you get older, you like your experience to be more intense. I'm twice your age, Janine.'

Then Fiona suggested they varied what they did a little. 'I want to play between your legs,' she said. Her eyes were slitted as she watched Janine, waiting for her response. Each time she was bolder, coarser with the girl, she watched to see if Janine recoiled.

Not yet.

'Won't it hurt me?' Janine was wide-eyed and curious but she certainly was not disgusted.

'I'll leave your fanny alone. The inside of it, I mean. That's for Rollo and I don't intend to spoil what you are going to offer to him.'

Janine blushed and her eyes dropped. Fiona could see that

she loved to hear of her impending violation. Her breasts rose and fell in her delicious agitation.

'You have a lot more sensory equipment down there than what's inside you, sweetie.' Fiona's voice was low and husky. 'Why don't we find out about it?'

Janine lay back, her pupils dilated and her eyebrows somewhere up at the top of her forehead. There was no way Fee was going to admit that she herself was on new territory. Moreover, her longing to feel Janine's private and personal body was now so powerful that if she had been resisted, she might have boxed the girl's ears and told her not to be so stupid and bourgeois. Janine's malleability was useful, but not in itself a turn-on for her. Fiona wanted a female body to satiate her lust. She had no requirement for devotion.

She found she was trembling as Janine obligingly opened her legs. She tried not to let her mounting excitement show. She must remember to exercise restraint and not get carried away and frighten the girl.

Fleetingly, as the stunning moist sweetness of Janine's sex was revealed to her greedy eyes, she remembered Will, dark and powerful and lacking in all restraint. Ah – that was what it should be like between two lovers. It should be fierce and abandoned, an animal coupling with the added savour of human intelligence.

But for now, there was the sweet hors d'oeuvre of this little untried female organ laid out for her delectation, her secret pleasure. The girl was clay in her hands.

Fiona ran her hands up inside Janine's thighs and felt them quiver. They were faintly dusted with soft hairs, thickening to make the ripe curly mat that framed her pussy. Fiona felt and tickled the soft hair.

'Do you like that?' she murmured.

'I feel strange inside.'

Fiona caught her lower lip between her teeth. As gently as she might separate two leaves of gold foil, she picked apart the slightly sticky labia and for the first time caught the faint, sweet new mown hay smell of Janine's open sex. It quivered before her eyes and she did not know whether Janine moved or her own vision was blurring in her intense excitement. She felt a pulse between her own legs and she knew sharply how she would love to do what she was doing whilst a man shafted her and fucked her own urgent cunt. Her lips curled into a smile at the thought. She ran her fingers round the entrance to Janine's body and imagined how, if she had a penis, she would thrust the big hard thing in, riving the reluctant flesh and making it fit to be used, to be enjoyed and in its turn to enjoy.

She ran her fingers up and down the lovely place, wetting them with her mouth to make them slide more easily, and gently pressing them against the little entrance.

She licked them again, her pointed tongue dark against the bright rosy colour of Janine's sexual parts, and then she uncloaked Janine's clitoris and began to frot the tiny soldier.

'What's that?' gasped Janine.

'Like it?'

'It's incredible.'

'Have you never played with yourself down here?'

'No, never. Oh,' shrieked Janine. 'That's so good.'

Fiona suddenly bent her dark head and put her tongue where her fingers had been. Janine gasped and went rigid. Then her breath hissed as her back arched, Fiona's hair warm between her thighs.

Fee had never in her life tasted anything so wild and sweet and ambrosial as the virgin musk of Janine's untried fanny. She was a woman who adored the powerful thick taste of a man in climax, it feeding her imagination and her sexual drive in equal parts. But Janine was like the wild rose hip, tangy-sweet and good. Indeed, the girl was a briar-rose, simple and naive and natural, not yet bent to a man's hand.

She sucked the tiny clitoris and vibrated her tongue against it and then closed her mouth over Janine's entrance and began to suck hard. It was a moment before she realised she might break the fragile membrane in her greediness, and she tore her mouth away from the virgin wine lest she should spoil things for Rollo, coming after her to sample this place.

It was hard not to laugh out loud.

She released the girl and sat up. Janine was panting, her pretty little-girl breasts heaving.

'Did you like that?' asked Fiona. Her voice was low and mellow, her tones honied.

'It embarrasses me,' said Janine. 'Your mouth, down there.'

'Do you want to do it to me?'

'Yes.'

The slight note of reluctance in Janine's voice pleased Fiona. She worked her way on to the bed and lay back, her legs drifting apart.

She closed her eyes. 'Now, Janine, you must do just what you want to do. Don't be afraid of anything. Explore all you want. Know no boundary. Go inside me, if you want. You have the freedom to do anything. You can't hurt me or offend me or embarrass me. I long for you to know what you want to know, child. It is a privilege for me to help you overcome your ignorance and your fears.' Fiona's voice was like thick cream, richly inviting, caressing, warm and permissive.

First Janine laid a hesitant and slightly moist palm over Fiona's depilated mound, as Fee had known she would. Janine fingered it and palmed it and laid her cheek on its satin smoothness. She ran her tongue over it and dried it with her hair. Then she slid her fingers on down into the dark exciting wet crevice below the gleaming magnolia dome.

Fee kept her eyes shut. The shaking fingers were naive as they explored through her long weaving walls of erotic flesh, but they were fresh and delicious and she felt transported with pleasure. This business with women was wonderful, yet she was assured of her own heterosexuality at the same time, for even as Janine pried into her most intimate orifice, even as the girl's fingers slid within her hot, succulent, experienced cunt, she dreamed of having a man's cock at this very moment deep in her throat that she might suck it as her pussy was invaded.

Her fantasy was rudely broken by Janine withdrawing and beginning to cry.

'What is it?' asked Fiona, injecting concern into her voice to overlay the impatience at the interruption.

'I knew there was something wrong with me. You are so large. I haven't played with myself, honestly Mrs Cambridge, but of course I have felt myself when I'm dealing with, you know . . .'

'Yes. But what's wrong?'

'I'm too small. I'm not normal. No wonder I am so afraid of men. Mr Cambridge will laugh at me if he ever tries to get inside me and he'll think I am just stupid and not properly made.'

She was really crying now. Fiona cast about in her mind for some way of convincing Janine of her normality.

'Listen to me,' she commanded sharply. Janine sniffed and her shoulders shook. Her eyes were already reddened and she looked pathetic as a lost puppy-dog.

'I'll prove you are perfect,' said Fee. 'Just give me a moment.'

Janine stared at her doggily, hope in her damp eyes as she cast round the room. Then she found what she was looking for and she came back to the bed. She held in one hand a slim penlight torch, maybe three-quarters of an inch in diameter.

She held it up before the puzzled girl. The tearstreaks down her face gave her a woeful appearance. Fee smiled reassuringly.

'You know what homosexual men get up to,' she said in a pleasant brisk voice.

Janine writhed. 'Yes. Sort of.'

'What orifices they use, not having a woman's fanny.'

'Well, as far as I know, their mouths and, er, their bottoms,' said Janine. She giggled uncomfortably.

'Right. Now trust me. I won't hurt you but you will be surprised and you might not like it. Turn round and go on your hands and knees.'

Obedient to the last, Janine did so. Fiona found some cream and greased the penlight.

'Relax, now,' she said.

She nuzzled the thin greasy tube at Janine's trembling bottom. With the fingers of one hand she tried to hold open the tight pucker of flesh as she attempted to slip the penlight inside. She pushed and Janine squeaked with horror. The very end, the narrowest part, had penetrated Janine and now the penlight projected from between her quivering buttocks.

74

Fiona resisted a surprising urge to thrust the thing brutally in.

'Do you want me to push it any further in?' she asked.

'No,' said a muffled voice. 'I don't like it.'

Fiona took one last regretful look at the instrument held in place by Janine's locked bottom, shaking slightly as the girl herself shook, and removed it.

Janine turned round, her face crimson.

'Look,' said Fee. 'That's how far it went in.' She showed Janine where the thickish cream was pushed back and wiped off by the restriction of the girl's tight valve.

Fee smiled. 'You see, when a man is homosexual, he likes to be penetrated that way. His rear gets softer and looser and he learns to admit even the gross inflamed penis of his male lover. An erect penis can be a very thick long thing, yet he takes it greedily up into himself because that's what turns him on. Even heterosexual men like a finger invading their backside. Well, many of them do. They find it sexy and stimulating if a woman puts a finger up their backside and moves it about a little. Women like it, too. I do. Feel me. Remember, I like it.'

She turned over and presented her rear to Janine. She knew her own puckered skin was dark like her nipples and that a wisp of hair still remained in the crevice between her cheeks.

She felt the hard penlight begin its violation of her rear. Janine pushed and Fiona relaxed her muscles and felt the lovely intrusion, the stretch of wall as it expanded to admit the invader.

She clamped her muscles tightly. Janine gasped and let go. Now it was Janine's turn to see the torch trembling, held by muscle power, projecting absurdly outwards.

Fee rolled on to her side with the penlight still sticking out of her arse. She rubbed it slightly on the bed so that it thrust a little further in. She tingled delightfully within.

'I'm tight,' she said. 'I'm not as tight as you, though. I like to be entered like this. I like a finger inside me. Rollo's finger,' she added slyly. 'He likes it, too. He likes doing it to me and me doing it to him. And because I occasionally do this, have this done to me, I am looser. I can accommodate the invasion. My backside has expanded and grown used to being entered. And that is exactly what will happen with that sweet little unused fanny of yours. It is made to receive an erect penis, full of lovely expanding flesh that will fit all sizes and lengths and give a man pleasure whether he is big or small. That little cunt of yours,' Fiona chose the word deliberately, 'will cling to his cock and he will love it. You begin small and tight but you get bigger and more elastic. Once your membrane is broken by Rollo, you will hunger for big sex. There is nothing abnormal about you, Janine. I promise.'

Janine sat for a while, considering. Fee felt she had been rather clever and was conscious of smugness. She slipped the penlight out of her rear.

Janine peeped up shyly from under her hair. 'I've been silly, haven't I?' she said.

'Go down on me, sweetheart, said Fiona huskily. She couldn't wait any longer.

That first time a woman laid her mouth against her intimate flesh and kissed her and sucked her juices. Fiona would never forget. Janine knew little of what pleased, but she was aroused herself and going quite well on instinct. She had none of the knowledgeable skills of Rollo and nor had she the ferocious expertise of the pirate, but she had a quality that all Fiona's male lovers had lacked, something indefinable, something that could only have existed between two women.

It was strange, because Fiona was not adulterous by nature. She would have remained satisfied with Rollo had he continued their early vigorous and innovative sexual life. There had been men in her life before Rollo but they were pale and insignificant besides the fires of her passion for and with him.

The pirate had been her first infidelity. Janine was her second. She lay dazed with pleasure as Janine's tongue ran up and down the length of her fanny, thrusting carefully between the fleshy lobes and occasionally penetrating the outer reaches of her pussy.

Then the two of them came together and held each other

sleepily in their arms. They kissed fondly. Fiona was surprised at the real affection she was beginning to feel.

'Have you been happy tonight?' she asked.

'Yes, I have, Mrs Cambridge.'

'Do you want to do this again?'

'Yes, I do.'

'I'll make sure you get Rollo, I promise.'

'Won't you be jealous?'

'That's not your problem. I don't mind if he synchs with you. You deserve it. I'm very fond of you.'

Janine sighed, blurry with sleep. Fiona kissed her one last time and slid from the bed.

The plan was going well.

7

She needed a gun. She would have preferred to make a simulacrum but she did not have the resources nor the engineering skill. In the end she joined a gun club and acquired the real thing.

It was old-fashioned because handguns weren't made any more and their only legitimate use was in gun clubs where devotees practised ancient skills, firing at targets.

The gun was heavy, a Smith and Wesson revolver with an action so stiff that Fiona was hopeless unless she cocked it first. With the hammer back it had a hair trigger. She learned to fire it rapidly by knocking the hammer back with her left hand and firing it almost instanteously with her right. It was not much different from what had been used two hundred years previously when the West was wild.

There were handguns, both revolvers and automatics, in dwindling numbers in the criminal world, but they were all museum pieces, really. The police used cryogen sprays, as fine as lasers, that literally caused their victims to 'freeze', albeit temporarily.

But if Fiona was to be a pirate, she needed a gun.

Captain Will Kid had laughed in her face and dismissed her desire to be a pirate as absurd. It rankled. What had originated as a half-sexual desire to join in on a raid had become a dedicated ambition. She would hack a car. She would be a pirate herself.

The decision to go ahead alone cleansed her somehow of the toxins in her blood, toxins that had built up from years of easy living, shopping, watching the Screen, years of smothering boredom. In some strange way it validated her new sexual liberation, her exploration of deviant carnality.

They were bound up together, this manipulation of husband and virgin, this manipulation of self and danger. She was risking everything she cared for and it was glorious.

She knew she would go back to find Will. She wanted a trophy. She wanted a hacking.

She bought a bigger knife and a pair of close-fitting untearable gloves. She acquired some very specialist hardware. And she got the gun.

One night she was ready. She let Rollo knock himself out with his pill and then she slipped into a pair of man's trousers and a black over-sweater. She wore soft black shoes and a black sack jacket that masked her curves. She put her little interceptor computer into a knapsack and fastened it on to her back. She wore a mask that shrouded her hair and upper face and she pulled a cap low over it.

She looked like a slim man, not very tall.

She let herself out of her house and into her hangar. She kissed her smoky-brown gleaming machine as she went by and then let herself out onto its darkened ramp. She could not used the lit moving walkways. They were not only patrolled, they had scanner cameras trained on them. But she had devised a route by which she could get out and away unseen.

She climbed the sides of the ramp and went over the edge until she could drop on to the netting over the Zoo. Full-size trees were growing beneath it and so she was very high in the dark night. She felt the rising warmth from the sleeping jungle and some night thing shrieked in the canopy as she passed.

She travelled for some two miles across the rigid steel wire, moving as quietly as she was able. Since the apartments that she and her friends lived in were totally burglarproof, calibrated to their owners' DNA, this area was not guarded. She kept clear of the occasional house domes, some still lit, that she saw below her amongst the vegetation. Their yellow light spilled upwards turning the black trees brilliant emerald. The glass was polarised so that she could not see in, but they would be able to see out. She was careful to keep in the dark.

At the edge of the Zoo she dropped down to the ground. Away to her left were the dim rows of hydroponics houses where the food that fed them all was grown under controlled conditions. It was forbidden to take food in animal or vegetable form, from the wild.

She was in nowhere land. Before her the ground dropped away and the city lay in urban liquefaction, a desolate tired open sore belonging to a former age but not yet quite withered away. It stretched like an ill-lit smear to the far horizon. All that was bright and clean was concentrated into the brilliant bands of light that were the great highways cutting the sky like lasers above the city. Each carried its cargo of shrieking superautos, a million credits of the most sophisticated technology known to man. Even the space stations hanging up there in the magnetosphere were not more complex in their engineering.

She would hack one. If she failed tonight, she would be back. And then back again until she succeeded. Only then would she stop.

Fee began to trot downhill towards the city.

She did not go to where she had found the pirates on the previous occasion she had entered the city. She stopped short at another great glittering chemoconcrete wall with soaring graceful lines, rising to support the mighty highway above. She was dwarfed into insignificance here in its shadows.

Her opinion of the pirates, already high, rose higher. She had to climb this support wall. From her knapsack she took gravgrabs. Deep in the heart of the chemically-bonded silica walls were iron girders. Her gravgrabs were electromagnets. She would walk up the wall.

She put the first one against the wall, its rubber skirting sealing it. It was heavy. In the handle was a button and when she pressed the button the electromagnet hummed into life and locked solid against the wall. Unless the current was interrupted it would tear the fabric of the wall before it failed to grip.

She put the second gravgrab against the wall above the first and switched it on. She tried to keep her feet against the wall so she did not hang, but it was with difficulty that she released the first gravgrab and swung it up and reclamped it.

Press, release, move up, press, release, move up – she was in agony after a few minutes and the wall towered above her. Captain Kid had said you needed to be strong and she had laughed at him.

A third of the way up. She trembled at the drop below her and her muscles were in agony. Hanging from one arm she reached carefully into her coat pocket and took out the harness. She was sobbing as she connected it to the grav-grabs. Then she slid her exhausted body into its uncomfortable embrace and hung there, supported against the cold quartz wall by slings, her arms no longer taking the strain but resting.

She stayed there a very long time, deciding whether to go up or down. Finally she went on up, more from a stupid and exhausted obstinacy than for any rational reason. There was no rationality to what she was doing and she knew it.

She rested again. Then she went up again. It took her two hours to reach the top and she hadn't even started what she meant to do. She was merely getting into position. She was awash with sweat and trembling with fatigue. Above her, the fence leaned out into the night.

She sat in her slings and threw her grappling iron at the top of the fence. She counted her throws. It took her twenty-five shots before the metal prongs engaged and she could pull down on the rope and feel it hold. She found she didn't want to leave the gravgrabs and slings. Suddenly they were safe and familiar. But finally she did, abandoning them there in the meantime, and allowing herself to swing sickeningly out into emptiness before she could climb the rope. She had professional climbing equipment for this but it was still terrible.

She reached the top of the fence and climbed over it. Suddenly she was safe, on the now-favourable slope, and she was able to scramble down till she stood on the highway itself.

An auto screamed by, scaring the wits out of her. She might as well try to stop a rocket. Nonetheless she huddled tightly against the fence, having first checked that she was not so unlucky as to land by a security camera. That was why she could not walk along the highway. Not only was it dangerous, but the frequent monitoring would have exposed her long before she was in place.

She set up her little computer and switched it on. The

infrared cells would give her only two or three tries and she had no means of recharging them from a heat source up here.

It was cold as the sweat dried on her. The wind was an enemy this high up, pulling her and disorienting her with its unfamiliar malevolent strength.

Another car screamed by, scything the night with its power and invulnerability.

Only they weren't invulnerable. You could hack into them if you knew how.

Fiona forgot about the wind and the danger. She huddled protectively over her little computer and began to feed in the programme. Her hands flickered sensitively over the keys, adjusting as she went. It was blueprint-dedicated, something she had invented herself. That would place her chances of success infinitely higher than the pirates, who, no doubt, had to use general-ability, non-specific machines. Moreover, her programme was roughed to match the Connet already, using her remembered knowledge from when she herself had worked for the automanufacturers.

It was not so very different from an old-time burglar turning the tumblers of a safe by ear and experience.

A car was coming. Fiona could see it miles away if she cared to look. Instead, she concentrated on intercepting its developing signal with her computer.

The car came closer and closer. She did not look up. Data flashed across her screen and she read it at the best speed she could manage. As she decoded, she adjusted the programme, fine-turning it. For a split second she caught the diagrammatic representation of a circuit board in flow-mode and her screen blanked as it overloaded with data.

The car passed its signal fading, and her screen came alive again with her programme rough on it.

She needed more power, more time. It was impossible.

She shook herself mentally. Connets weren't shielded. They wouldn't work if they were shielded. Therefore they radiated their precise electromagnetic signal. Fee had already roughed in the frequency-variation pattern within which all Connet cars came. Each car was individual but it had to lie within certain parameters and those she knew about. She had to decode the signal as a car passed, retune her own computer so that it was a precise match and then instruct the car to come to a halt. The Connet couldn't even recognise that the signal was coming from the outside. All it knew was that suddenly it had two sets of instructions and they didn't match. So it melted down.

Like a ray of light Fiona understood how a car should be hacked. She had known all along, only she had not worked it through and seen the consequences.

She didn't need to issue stopping instructions. She could preset any instruction without even knowing what it was. Two sets of instructions regardless of their content, would induce meltdown. The car would stop automatically.

She let the next car go by whilst she reprogrammed. Now, as soon as she matched signal, her machine would fire a random instruction, the one nearest the frequency pattern to use least time. She had only half the work she had thought she had.

The screen began to flicker and break up. Another car was coming, its signal overriding her programme and distorting it. Once more her fingers danced over the keys as she tried to find and match patterns. Gradually it began to fall into place. As she decoded each part it stabilised on her screen, losing its eye-bending jigger.

She was sweating under her mask when her ears tuned to a new noise. She concentrated on the computer but the noise was intrusive. Suddenly she woke up to what it was. A helicopter. The SkyPolice. She slammed the off-button, losing all the ground she had gained, and bent her body over as close to the fence as she could get, resisting the impulse to look up. The SkyPolice used normal vision as well as infrared and ultraviolet. They might actually see her.

The car she had been attempting to hack whistled by harmlessly. The sound of the copter increased to a roar and then passed on.

It was some time before Fiona unfurled herself. Her heart was pounding. It occurred to her to get out whilst she still could. Capture would mean mandatory prison. The rest of her life.

Several cars went by at spaced intervals whilst she crouched recovering her nerve. Then she decided. She would try once more. After the horrors of this night she would never again get up nerve and strength enough. Once more and she would feel she could honourably give up and go home.

Again she played the keys, immediately absorbed and forgetful of all else. The pattern fell into place section by section. She became faster, she knew almost in advance. Part of her was laughing, exulting at how close she was coming with this one. Soon she would be safe and could go.

Unbelievably a car was stopping. She stared at the screen, stable at last, the unique pattern displayed. She looked up as the beautiful sleek blue tube halted and settled on its airpads.

Fiona stood up, putting the little computer off. Before she did so, she saw the pattern waver and fragment and drip, viruslike, off the screen. The Connet was no more, physically melted into a meaningless dead jumble of electronic fragments.

Fiona slid the computer into her knapsack and took out a laser pencil. She walked across to the car and broke the lock. She couldn't take the passenger captive but she could retrieve some trophy from the car, something to take to Will, something to prove what she had done.

Another car whistled harmlessly by, automatically putting itself into a different lane since this one was obstructed. Its passenger would not even know an act of piracy was being committed.

Her passenger would, though. She was trying not to laugh as she reached to open the door, fumbling with her other hand for her gun. She had no ammunition, of course. It was a shock, then, when she saw across the curving roof another gun, its wicked black eye pointing at her.

All she could see were the arms that held it, its shining smug menace and the top of the one that threatened her, a dark featureless head. She swallowed, her throat suddenly dry.

'This one's mine,' she said, trying to make her voice guttural and deep. It was peculiar with fear.

'Back, ' said a male voice.

She backed until she was against the fence. Immediately two figures appeared from either side and held her. They removed her gun and knapsack. The man who had threatened her now had the passenger out of the car.

There were more pirates. Swiftly they forced the terrified passenger into a large bodybag and manhandled it to the fence. They could all hear the whirr of the returning helicopter. The bag was run up the fence and then the captured passenger was lowered with terrifying speed. He vanished down into the night, plummeting earthwards. Two of the pirates followed him, abseiling down the rope.

Now Fiona was hustled up the fence. She was on the rope with a gun in her face. She grasped the metal clip and shot downwards after the others. Her bladder felt close to collapse with fear. If the police had taken her she would have spent a long time in prison, unless she could plead some temporary mental aberration and get off. But these men might kill her. And they would certainly assault her. Jokes with Diana were one thing but real gang rape was quite another.

How far did Will's jurisdiction extend? Could she get to him?

She could scarcely remember the drop to the ground, she was so out of her mind with fear. What craziness had brought her here? Was she so bored she would throw it all away, all her life, Rollo, everything? Skelton. She had called herself Skelton after the wicked Barbara Skelton.

Wicked Barbara Skelton had turned highwaywoman and died of a bullet fired by the man she loved.

At the bottom she was struck from the rope and her hands dragged behind her and manacled. They still didn't know she was a woman, though they would find out soon enough.

Someone lifted a slab out of the ground and they all went down into the hole. The bodybag with the unfortunate victim was lowered and the slab replaced and with two of the pirates carrying the victim, they set off along an ill-lit stinking wet tunnel.

A gun prodded Fiona in the back and she stumbled along as best she could. There were six men in the pack, all powerful in build, dressed in leathers with the cross-strapping over their powerful naked chests that was stylistically the pirates' own uniform. Some were tattooed, their muscular arms embellished with dragons and the skull and crossbones. They all had shaggy hair and wild dark faces.

Despite herself, Fiona's spirits began to rise. In a rough way they were attractive men. They looked fierce but not mad and there was discipline in their behaviour. Maybe she would be ransomed like the poor mutt in the bodybag. Now they knew her to be unarmed, surely they would not execute her out of hand?

How would she explain being captured, if she was ransomed?

Side passages led off. The band stopped and two different men took the bodybag. For a moment they were all busy. Suddenly Fiona ran to one side and jumped down several steps. She staggered, regaining her balance, and then doubled low and ran fast, weaving as she went. She was an expert runner. She swerved to her right and went on down the new tunnel fast. She heard a bullet whang beside her. Not for them automatic sighting. They had to rely on skill and in the poor light that wasn't enough.

Cursing her manacles she ran on, settling to a steady speed that she knew she could maintain. If only she dared to stop she could step through her manacles and get her hands in front of her.

Brickwork chipped close to her as another bullet missed. There were more side passages and she went along them, turning as often as she could in an effort to shake off pursuit.

She was tiring. Her muscles had already undergone strenuous activity that night. It was not good underfoot as broken bricks from the crumbling hundred-year-old walls formed a loose rubble over a slimy undersurface. She blundered round a corner and saw rats.

Their eyes were tiny gleams of light, their sleek bodies adapted to the dark wet conditions as her own was not. She stifled rising panic. They were mammals like herself, intelligent and adaptable. It was just that they had adapted to living in filth and it was natural to the human mammal to fear the rare creature that failed to fear it.

They scattered slowly as she went on through them. In the bad old days people used to die from rat bites. Was that still true? She didn't know. She could hear no one behind her now and then she saw metal rungs set into the wall leading upwards. So what if they were rusted and untrustworthy. There must be another manhole up there and after the risks she had already undergone that night, a broken rung was trivial.

She needed her arms. Fee sat down bringing her linked hands under her backside to behind her knees. She was intent on doubling a leg to get it through the chain when she heard something and pain exploded in her face.

She fell back against the wall in shock. All she could think about was her face. She blinked her eyes and was aware that she had both of them still. She worked her mouth. It was painful but her tongue moved and she could not taste blood. It was her cheek. She had had a bullet graze her face. Now she could feel it stinging and the hot flow of blood beneath her mask.

The men came up towards her. She got her hands in front of her and staggered to her feet. The first one reached her and hit her so that she struck the wall. Her shoulder was grabbed and she was heaved up and punched in the stomach.

She doubled over, gasping and wheezing for breath, unable to claim the immunity of her sex. But then they tore off her headgear and the black mass of her hair tumbled free about her bloody face.

'Christ,' said one of the men. 'It's a woman.'

They backed off slightly and watched her curiously as she stood, trying not to snivel, gradually straightening herself as the pain eased in her guts. The tension came out of them. She was no longer a threat but an object of curiosity, something to turn over in their minds.

The three of them remained quietly together in the dim yellow gloom of the festering tunnelway as if they were the best of friends. Fiona felt their curiosity turn to consideration. Each metal stud across their chests had a pinpoint gleam of light, like the rats' eyes. They were superlative men, raw, wild and making no concessions to fear. Fiona's tongue came out and she licked her lips, tasting the blood that trickled down one side of her face. Unnoticed by her, the pain from the blow to her stomach had been replaced by a manic fear, a sense of impending crisis.

Each muscle in her body began to cramp, she stood so still. Her heart pounded unevenly, painfully, in her chest. The pain in her cheek was a like a knifeblade twisted in clean flesh.

Her breath rattled. The bigger of the two men smiled and took a step towards her. She flinched back and he laughed, grabbing the stuff of her clothes and tearing her loose sack coat apart and off.

He tore the good material as if it had been paper.

He pulled up her over-sweater. It forced her manacled arms up and her chin went up also as she nerved herself.

Both men looked at her naked breasts speculatively. They hung full and heavy, a rich curve below each one, the dark nipples pointing in arrogant welcome towards the watchers. The thieves. The pirates. Fiona's breath suddenly sobbed into her lungs and her breasts moved, alive, a touch of exotic body-perfume underlying the smell of fresh sweat and the rank odour of fear.

The big man used her rucked over-sweater to trap her arms and then he caught her trousers at her hips and pulled them roughly down. She screamed and he cuffed her, quite amiably, across the good side of her face. Then he pushed her head down to his crotch and held it pressed against him. The other man went round to her rear.

Fiona began to shake. She felt the rough insertion of an exploratory finger. I don't believe this, she thought to herself. This isn't happening. Then her whole body jerked and she would have fallen save that the big man held her and steadied her.

Thief's cock, stealing her inner space, stealing her cunt and its warm welcoming juices ready to flow for the right man. Her cunt knew no difference and Fiona found herself impaled whilst a man rutted against her. Her eyes were shut and she smelt man-smell from the groin of the one who held her. Each jerk of the thieving body at her rear made her cheek sting. Each fill of cunt sliced pain at her cheek bone. She felt the blood flow, salt tears adding to the agony, and she felt her treacherous body warm and lubricate until the pain was like the shout of orgasm racking her body.

The man holding her dropped to his knees and forced her face up until he could trap her mouth with his, his hands running under her to hold her swinging breasts, taking her body as it shook to the assault from his partner. Fiona felt the heat and the power of the two men, one at each end of her body, and suddenly she submitted, not through fear, not through common sense, but to the demands her own sexual engine made on her to enjoy herself, to take what was offered, to turn the rape of her body into her own rape of experience.

Her mouth worked and she felt the shock of the man kissing her.

The one at her back finished and slid his satisfied member out of her body. He stood up and stretched with pleasure, fastening his clothes. The big one stood her up and let go of her.

Her hair was as wild as the pirates' own, her face crimson-black on one side with spilt blood. Her jumper was caught at her armpits and her hands were fastened in front of her body, bunching her full breasts and deepening the valley between them. Her legs were slightly straddled for balance, her trousers caught down about her knees, and for the first time both men saw the pale base of her belly where she should have been black and hairy.

The big man ran a calloused hand up her thigh, their eyes meeting.

'Let me go,' said Fiona huskily. She made no move to escape his slow intimate investigation of her body.

Wordlessly he shook his head, the corners of his mouth curling up slightly at her foolishness. The side of his hand entered her vulva and pressed up into it. His thumb stroked across her depilated mound.

Fiona widened her stance very slightly. 'Afterwards,' she said.

'I can't do it, sister,' he said without regret. 'I can't let you go.'

He spun her round and her head was once more pushed down. Now the smaller man held and steadied her in her bent-over position. She felt the big man's cock enter her, easily as she was so wet, and he began in a leisurely way to take his pleasure.

It had never happened to her before. She had never received two men, one after the other, like this. She felt the enormous strangeness, the newness, of a full cock in her spunk-soaked body, a different cock. When it bloomed and she was filled over again with male wetness, she felt a melting weakness, a disabling desire to curl up and worship at their two dissimilar temples of phallic pleasure. Her personality fled, she was all body, all opening, ready to receive and receive again a man's demand and turn it to her own deep satisfaction.

They pulled her clothes roughly together and took her rubbery compliant body between their own and ran her back along the tunnels, through the watching rats, till they arrived at their pirate nest, down here in the black bowels of the earth.

8

The room was warm, well lit, and dingily furnished with a large table in the centre. Food and drink, among other things, were on the table. People sat around or stood propped in corners, all pirates and some women.

At the head of the table, dominating the room, sat Will, Captain Kid.

'Hey Will,' said one of Fiona's captors. 'We got us a poacher.'

'So I heard.' Will's voice was a lazy rumble.

'Take a look at this.' He stepped aside and the other man pushed Fiona into the room, in amongst them. She heard the concerted hiss of their indrawn breath and tossed her hair back defiantly. She met Will's gaze. She saw his eyes darken as his pupils dilated in shock.

She took two steps forward. No one stopped her. She held her body as proudly as she could, shoulders well back. She smiled.

Will absorbed her man's clothing, her wild hair and her bloody cheek. His eyes went slowly up and down the length of her.

'Well, well,' he said softly.

'I said I could do it.'

'You stopped the car with this?' He gestured at her computer on the table beside him.

She nodded, still smiling. There was wet warmth between her legs under her clothes. She wondered what Will would have to say about that, when he knew.

Will sighed and tapped the table. 'You were on my territory,' he said.

'I'm a thief. I don't have to ask permission where I thieve.'

'You are quite wrong about that. You've made a very big mistake.'

'I don't hear you.' Fiona injected contempt into her voice. 'A bullet did that to you?'

'Yes.'

'Another can put paid to your damned insolence.'

The indifference in his voice made her angry. 'Do it,' she challenged.

The tension in the room was electric. Will stood up with the easy grace of a big cat, supremely confident. He came up to her, towering over her, and looked down into her slitted eyes, laughing at her defiance as if it was no more than the bite of a fly. 'It would be a waste,' he acknowledged.

She smiled in triumph.

'But I like to lay waste,' he added. 'I'm a pirate, remember.' His smile lacked warmth and Fee felt a trickle of fear.

'So am I, now,' she said, feeling her voice in danger of cracking. She was exhausted. She couldn't take much more of this.

Will looked round the room. 'We've met this lady before. She and I have unfinished business.'

Someone said: 'We are all hungry men, Will.'

Their captain laughed. 'She's a meal that can satisfy more than one, if I choose.' He felt some movement in Fee and his eyes flicked first to her, then to her two captors.

There was a moment's silence. 'We didn't know you knew her,' said one of them. There was no discernible emotion in his voice.

'She's the foreign bitch,' came a shrill shout suddenly. Mammet had recognised her. She jerked forward and was restrained by the man beside her, her new lover from the night of the bonfire.

'She's put herself outside the rules,' said Will in a flat voice. 'I'll deal with her.'

He hustled her through to another room and then through that to a bedroom. They were alone and Fiona felt overcome with weakness. She went ahead of Will and sat on the bed. She tried to make her brain work but she was too tired.

Will came over and sat beside her. He put one finger under her chin and lifted her face so that their eyes met. She controlled herself so that hers did not slide away. The eye-patch remained anonymous, cold.

'Where are you from?'

'Take these chains off me.'

'I ask the questions, you answer them. Where are you from?'

She remained silent.

'Do I have to hurt you?'

'No.'

'How did you know how to stop a car?'

'I'm a good hacker.'

'That's obvious,' he acknowledged patiently. She was only just becoming aware of the mental and psychic strength of the man, a match for his great muscular body. 'But it takes resources as well as luck. The equipment you carried was the best. Brand new. You've got money. You've got class. Where are you from?'

Still she didn't answer. She could not cudgel her brain to move, but something moved within her, knowledge and cunning at work on some more atavistic level than she had known she possessed.

He came astride her so that she fell back on the bed with him leaning over her. He put a hand in her hair. The glitter in her hard eyes softened and she knew within herself how much she wanted him. It pleased her that she lay beneath him in her sweat and dirt, on a stale bed in a converted sewer. The man over her had threatened to kill her. She was manacled and helpless against him. No friend of hers knew where she was.

Yet she was subduing him. Her own luscious body, damaged and abused beneath his, meant more to him than all his threats, more than anything. In her way she was winning this exchange, exhausted though she was. Power surged through her.

Deliberately he stripped her of everything, jumper, trousers, shoes, pants, using his knife to cut her clothes away from her body till it lay long and white beneath his. He saw its narrow-waisted, full-breasted promise. He saw her heavy large plum-coloured nipples, erect at the nearness of his dominant body. She felt the air strike cool at the wetness between her naked legs and hoped he would not be put off because his men had used her before bringing her to him, her rightful mate. She hoped he would punish them for taking what was his, even if it was done in ignorance.

She was all his. An unsteady flame burned in her. She was crazy to have him in her. Her lips parted in expectancy.

He put his two hands under her armpits and hefted her to her feet. He gripped the chain that fastened her hands and raised it. Before she had taken in what he was doing, he lifted her slightly and dropped the chain over a large hook driven into the ceiling. Then he let go of her and stood back.

Her arms were raised high above her head and trapped there, at the wrist, by the chain between her manacles now caught on the hook. She could stand on the ground in her bare feet, just. Her nakedness was all vulnerable, all exposed.

Will walked round her and laughed. 'Very attractive,' he said. He slid a rough warm hand down her back, into its curve and out again over her bottom.

She wanted to sweat it out but her arms had taken too much abuse that night, what with the climb up the wall to the highway. 'You don't have to do this,' she said, her voice honey-thick and low. 'You know I'll come to you willingly.'

He was at her back. He reached round her and ran his hand possessively up over her ribs and onto her breast. She felt his lips on her shoulder and shut her eyes, dizzy with relief. It was all right. Her body had won. Only tiredness could have made her doubt such a thing.

'I know,' he said. 'Why?'

'I have to explain?' She caught the raggedness in her tone. 'Synch with me. Match us. Do it.'

She couldn't believe it when he moved away. A cold draught spilled into the room and she knew he had opened the door. She couldn't bring herself to turn round where she hung, in case he saw the defeat in her eyes.

When he came back he wasn't alone.

Will brought the girl in, a tiny thing with a mass of tangled red hair and a waif-white face hidden within. A rat's face, thought Fiona savagely, pointy and sly. If she was free, she would have killed them both. She did not believe she was capable of such anger. Her body shook with it and the chain above her rattled, mocking her.

Will ignored her. He lay on the bed whilst the girl eagerly stripped herself. Her body was red-fair and freckled with bone-thin limbs and a flat arse more suited to a boy than to a female. She peeped round through her mat of hair to look at Fiona and she smiled. She had mud-coloured eyes, light brown and stupid.

She began to undress Will where he lay slack in the bedclothes. When he was bare she lowered her face over his groin and Fee heard her mouth at him, heard the noises she made exciting him. She sat back giggling and played with her achievement, letting Fiona see what would be hers to enjoy. Will's face was bland and blank. He did nothing except submit to the girl's caresses. Then she raised herself on her knees, astride his colossus, and lowered herself with much shrieking and moaning over his erect shaft. Again she peeped spitefully at Fiona and then she laughed as she rode up and down on the quiescent man.

His body was unbelievably beautiful in the naked glory of its masculinity and power. Fiona hung weakly, crushed by what he did to her, unable to tear her eyes away from the thin squirming girl stealing his manhood and debasing what she believed they had between them.

The red-haired girl screamed and lowered herself and stroked Will's chest, rubbing her face in his chest hair. It was only as she kissed his body that Fee realised he had never laid his lips upon her.

'Thank you,' he said coolly. It was a dismissal. The girl climbed sulkily off him and ostentatiously opened her legs so that for a moment Fee saw Will's spunk on her little white thighs amidst the freckles and the red pubic hair.

She dressed, hooding her eyes and covertly watching Fiona. Will lay supine, his eye all but closed, his used member lolling against the dark, strong, curling hair on his thigh.

Then the girl was gone. The silence stretched, longer and longer.

Presently Will said: 'You are a rich bitch, aren't you? Out slumming. Looking for a quick thrill down here in the dirt. Getting your kicks in the raw.'

Fee didn't answer. She felt afraid. The contempt in his voice stung worse than her open cheek.

'Did you go back last time and tell your girlfriends all about your pirate lover?'

Fee licked her lips. 'No,' she said hoarsely.

The word hung between them. She understood now what she meant to him but she felt no triumph. He could master himself, master what he felt for her and subdue his flesh as she could not. He was stronger than her.

He got off the bed at last and came over. He crouched down beside her and with his two hands he encircled one of her thighs. She felt his warmth close to the core of her and was unable to control the surge of lust. He ran the collar of his hands up and down her thigh quite slowly. 'Such a smooth body,' he murmured and he kissed her thigh.

He released her and stood up. He faced her and Fee knew he saw the tears that rolled silently down her face. He lowered his head and took one of her nipples in his mouth. He rolled it round with his tongue and she could not tell the salt tear in her bloody cheek apart from his hot mouth at her breast.

'Will,' she sobbed.

He looked into her face and smiled at her. 'You can do better than this, Skelton,' he said with gentle mockery. 'Does it take so little to subdue you?'

She ignored the pain in her arms. She swung her legs up and gripped him around his waist, arching her back so he staggered as her groin thrust into him. He laughed and caught her up, flicking the chain off the hook. He carried her over to the bed and threw her down on it. He unlocked the handcuffs and kissed the inside of each wrist where the metal had abraded her.

His body was fantastic, a powerhouse of raw muscle alive with sexual mastery. His mouth closed on hers and his stubble stung her broken cheek and made it bleed again. He transferred his mouth and began to lick and suck her blood.

Her body arched up under his as her need convulsed through her and she laughed, feeling his hairy muscularity all the long smooth length of her. He was erect already and her rage and exhaustion were forgotten as her blood sang with lust and excitement.

She pushed him away and swung her face down on his glorious manhood. She laid her bloody cheek on his prick and licked the red smear off.

'You're crazy,' he said. His thumb slid into her and she groaned and bore down on his hand, her muscles gripping him as she tried to masturbate on it. He pushed hard fingers round between her buttocks and then drove one into her rear entrance.

She gasped and jerked up from him, driving his thumb deeper into her pussy. He kept his finger where it was in her rear, pushing it further in though she tried to escape him. He pinched his finger and thumb together so that he could squeeze the wall of lightly-muscled inner flesh between them, the wall of flesh that separated within her body her vagina from her rear passage. His other hand held her breast and he kissed and sucked the nipple, sucking it so hard it was drawn deep into his mouth.

She was beside herself, riven by his crude invasion of both her places in one go. Her hands were meshed in his hair and she knew his mastery of her was beyond wit and cunning, beyond everything.

He released her so suddenly she fell forward on the bed. He put his hands under her stomach and heaved her backside in the air so that she was on her knees, her face crushed into the bedclothes. He held her buttocks apart with his two hands and drove into her.

For a moment she did not know what way he had penetrated her. She was split, filled, heat boiling from his source in her. Then she felt distinctly his knotted hardness in her fanny and without being able to control it she came, instantly, a hot wet eruption of lust that bathed his swollen shaft as it thundered into her.

He felt her tighten and slacken, felt the increase in temperature and the slidiness of her orgasming hole.

'You hot bitch,' he said, and he drove into her sex, still in spasm from her climax. She gritted her teeth and tried to regain control, tried to milk him, pushing back against him and feeling his balls swing warm and full against her.

She couldn't stop yelling. He was holding the cheeks of her backside apart and it made her moan with joy that his eyes feasted on the dark inner line in the cleft of her buttocks, the soft crumpled flesh of her rear revealed even as he worked himself deep in her fanny. She could feel him build to climax, knew he knew she could feel him, knew her own texture was changing as she became soft and pulpy and thick, ready for his discharge. Then he ejected into her and her muscles clamped tight on his cock as it pulsed free of his sperm, his body jerking till it was empty. She throbbed in response and at last he was still.

The room was redolent of their coupling. She could hear their ragged breathing. He withdrew slowly, stretching out the pleasure, and she felt a warm trickle slide from her long dark purple slit down onto one white rounded thigh.

She fell sideways on the bed and turned to him a face dazed with passion. She moved her heavy thigh across and lifted herself and bent over his crotch. Her tongue licked through his wet pubic hair. She ran it down the length of his love-shiny prick and laid her head on his thigh. Her ice-green eyes were lust-darkened to emerald deepness.

He ruffled her black curls.

'What am I going to do with you?' he said.

'I have to spell it out?'

He drew her beside him where he lay and kissed her mouth and eyes.

'You've broken the rules. I can't ignore it.'

'Do you usually do this with rule-breakers?'

He laughed. 'They are usually men.'

'Rules are made to be broken.'

'Not my rules.'

She stirred against him. She licked his lips and opened his mouth with hers and ran her tongue around his strong white teeth. She couldn't take seriously the threats implied in what he said, she couldn't take her own future seriously. All she knew was that she was free, freer than she had ever been, all her previous existence fallen away so that she was new made over to be the essence of her carnal nature, here on a bed with the pirate. All her bodily needs were gone save for this one, to join with him sexually and focus his strength and violence into an assault of her willing body. The contrast between her own smooth, perfect beauty and his scarred magnificence aroused her. The world was four walls. Her place in it was the bed. Her future, past and purpose were in the imminent union. She wanted to enter his body like a virus, enter even his cells and cause his DNA to grow and change him so that on the most profound level they were one.

'I want you again,' she said huskily. 'I want you in me again.'

She began to use tongue, lips, fingers and pressure of flesh to arouse and stimulate him. She roved over his body, exploring each part, parting his hair, feeling and licking into each crevice, each fissure, till she knew the most intimate taste and feel of him. She censored herself over nothing. Whether she was between his toes or between his buttocks, she held back over nothing, allowing no shame, no restraint in her unhurried, luxurious, slow investigation of his body.

Then she began to concentrate on his masculinity, on his sex, enveloping his used member with warmth and life and regenerating it to serve her will. She sucked the end first, gently, and had the satisfaction of feeling it come alive and swell under her tender ministrations. She took his balls and separated them in their sac of flesh amd moved them until his roots began to tingle with desire.

As his flesh expanded she nibbled the length of his shaft, savouring the veins, drawing back the foreskin and tenderly kissing the red bulging end.

When he was big she lowered her sodden pussy on to him, allowing him to slip easily within her but then crushing him with her inner muscles, not moving her body at all save for the inner masturbation of his prick with her cunt. Then she lifted her body so that the head of his prick rested just within her, and balancing herself she began to frig him very rapidly using the bony ring at the entrance to her body to excite his cockhead as it slipped in and out.

His breathing changed and his good eye shut as the tension of love-making rose in him. She stopped her light rapid movement and instead she lowered herself so that he sank deeply into her, then she ground together their groins before withdrawing almost to the point where he fell out of her. She sank hard down, rose right up, again and again.

'Christ,' he murmured. She purred and sat high on him again, just using her internal muscular power lightly to play with his hot hard end.

His hands gripped her hips. He pushed up. One hand slid up her front and felt for a breast drooping melon-heavy above him. She curved her supple body down over him and kissed his mouth passionately, then his ear, running her tongue within it and nibbling the edges of it. She smelt the sweat in his hair and saw his roots were dark with it. She licked it like a cat, savouring the saltiness.

Despite herself, her fanny convulsed. He felt it and laughed and drove up again into her. As he held her and thrust, she felt she was being penetrated to her very core and beyond it, to some new realm. She threw back her head, steadying herself with her hands, feeling his sex support her and lift her to a height of pleasure she had not known existed. He lunged up and up and up and she started to come, beside herself, gasping and shouting as her insides rippled with flames of lust till each wave was submerged into the torrent of orgasm.

He came himself, piercing her with joy, his cock blazing as it creamed until she was full, full up, and at last, satisfied.

She lay dazed beside him, her eyes unfocused, inhaling the smell of sweat and sex. Her own hair was as wet as his. Where their heads lay together on the pillows it was not possible to tell whose black curls were whose.

She slept, his mouth open and on her unhurt cheek so that she felt his breath warm and possessive on her and it was very good.

She woke to hear talking.

So deep had been her sleep that she was disoriented, her internal body clock not working, and she did not know where she was or what time of day or night it was. She lifted her face, puzzled, and felt Will's rough warm body inside her.

He was propped up, smoking, facing someone in the room and talking. He was still entirely naked. She was sprawled in bare-arsed abandon beside him.

Will slapped her rump. 'Go back to sleep. This is man's talk.'

She rolled on her side and looked to see who else was in the room. She blinked in surprise. It was the bigger of the two men who had captured her in the tunnel, the one most like Will. Perhaps he was the man who had shot her.

He stood tall in his leathers, his eyes raking her nakedness and sex-soaked body. Fiona felt a thrill of danger. Will was unpredictable. If he was satisfied, as he might well be after the red-headed bitch and then her own powerful loving, would he hand her over to another? She knew already he did not care about her own opinion of what went on, riding roughshod over her and watching her bend to his will.

Part of her liked it.

But she didn't want to synch with any other man. True, he was a pirate and all pirates held a sexual fascination for her. Further, he was far from ill-looking. He was like Will, though not so broad and tall, and his tousled hair was a lighter colour, and having two good eyes made him almost a handsome man in a rugged way. But he lacked some spice that Will had. Perhaps it was the aura of command. Fee didn't care and was too lazy to analyse it, though one reason for the pirates' apparent similarity was explained to her. They all had well-developed chests and arm-muscles. She knew why. Shinning up those walls for a living was bound to build muscle tone.

Despite the man's undoubted attractions, Fiona felt slavishly lustful only for Will. He was the boss and he was a superb and ferocious lover, and altogether a dangerous man. Her tiger.

'Meet Chain,' said Will.

'Hello, Chain,' she said. Her mouth curved into a sly smile. Her hand moved and she touched Will's limp penis. He gave a shout of laughter.

101

'She's a very horny bitch,' he said to Chain.

'What are we going to do with her?'

'What do we always do with poachers?'

'Not that,' said Chain with a wide grin, nodding down at Fee caressing Will's groin.

'They've not been women before,' said Will.

Chain came over to the bed and sat down by Fiona. He ran a hand down her side, considering her upcurving hip and smooth long flank. Fee rolled on to her back between the two men, deliberately playing with fire. She let Chain's hot eyes see the hairless pallid dome at her belly-base, above the wet fissure of her used sex. Its twin lobes were puffy and swollen and from between them her dark long labia protruded invitingly.

'What do you do with poachers?' she asked. Her voice was languid and thick with past sex.

'We hang them upside down under the highway and slit their gizzards for the crows,' said Chain. His hand came over her belly, her mound grazing his inner wrist. 'It seems a pity this time.' His eyes were like Will's but with more warmth in them.

'There are other women,' said Will, sounding bored.

She twisted like a snake and was up before he could react. She struck him ferociously hard across the face, her eyes blazing chips of fury. Will caught her wrist and Chain bellowed with laughter.

Will took her second wrist and with iron strength he easily overrode her resistance, forcing them both back behind her where he held them with one hand. His face was inscrutable. Fee saw the muscle bunch as he drew back his free hand.

She laughed. 'Which cheek will you hit?' she mocked.

Chain murmured in shock. Will hesitated, a shadow of doubt crossing his face. Fiona lifted her face and held it at an inviting angle, waiting to see if he would strike her.

'This one,' he said. He pulled her flat on her face across him and smacked her bottom. He smacked hard and it stung. Fiona heard Chain yell with delight and then Will smacked her with abandon.

She writhed, humiliated by what he did and who watched. She could not break his vicelike grip of her.

Both men were yelling and shouting now and Fiona felt her bottom jerk up after each blow as if welcoming the next. Her eyes stung with angry tears but she could not stop the compulsive lifting, almost as if she was rising to a man shafting her.

Her fanny burned.

She tried to wriggle free but Will held her easily with his one hand as he smacked her. Too late she realised her hot red arse was glowing like a beacon, like a red rag to a bull. Her efforts to escape only tantalised. She felt her legs dragged apart and she tried to kick out but she was held, helpless.

She was panting and groaning as she felt herself invaded. Will held her down across his own naked body. Chain it was who thrust into her, between her scarlet tormented cheeks.

Her monkey-red rear throbbed with the invader fat within it. Her backside was all one hot peppery tingle that combined with the soreness from her earlier congress, and she found that her juices began to run, the love-battering sweet and fierce where she should have been able to resist.

Then he was done. He had filled her over again and removed himself from her. Will rolled her over, her whole body suffused with a sexual flush that was partly rage, partly pleasure. Chain was doing up his trousers.

'Every time you strike me,' said Will mildly, 'I'll give you to one of my men.'

She wanted to speak bravely but the ferment of emotion within her would not let her trust her voice. She tried to make some gesture of defiance but she could not. She could not even wipe her nose, and Will held her hands so tightly that they hurt.

Chain said: 'She's crying.'

Will shrugged. 'She's a woman. She doesn't want to admit it. She needs to be taught a lesson.'

Chain grinned. 'I like the syllabus. But I think I had better go now.'

'Make sure I'm not interrupted for a while,' said Will.

At the first gentle kiss from Will, Fiona collapsed against him.

'You shouldn't have done that,' she sobbed. 'You shouldn't have had him do that to me.' She felt an undercurrent of ecstasy at her own excess of emotion, at the totality of her subjection.

'There are three reasons why I should,' said Will. 'Chain is my good friend. That's the first. Secondly, I enjoyed watching him shaft you. And thirdly, you were far out of line.' He kissed her and held her to his chest. She heard the hard steady beat of his heart.

'You are going to kill me,' she whispered. 'You are going to synch with me and kill me.'

He held her face between his two hands so that it was close to his. He kissed it very delicately. 'Isn't it worth it?' he asked softly.

'Dying?' She didn't understand.

'You've got what you came for. What does tomorrow matter?'

She whimpered slightly.

He laughed and kissed her again. 'See, Skelton? You can't be a pirate. We all know that in the end the cops will get us. They have too much going for them and they get better and better and the cars get harder and harder. Or we will fall from the highway, or get shot, or have a car hit us. We live with death so we make today good. Tomorrow doesn't matter. But sweetheart, you don't think like that. Zoo baby. My beauty in a cage.'

Fiona heard his words and knew that they were true. She didn't want to die. She had wanted to live with some danger to salt her life but she did not want to live with death as her grinning companion. Tomorrow mattered.

'Where you come from,' said Will quietly, 'people sit in offices and speak all day long into machines. They move money around and call it work. And you sit in your bubble houses, your plastidomes in the Zoo, bored to death, watching the big Screen, shopping, drinking with your friends and the most dangerous thing you ever do is to sleep with one another's partners. You are intelligent enough to know that that is not real life. That is why you have come down here amongst us. You want to know what it feels like to

104

be alive, to taste excitement and fear and danger. You don't understand that what gives spice to life is the nearness of death. Life is a game in your world, Skelton. In my world, life is a triumph. A temporary triumph over death.'

He let go of her face and held her in his arms and began to make love to her very tenderly and gently. He kissed her all over till her body first eased and then aroused. He came round on top of her and entered her quietly, without force. Gently he fucked into her, a steady soft rhythmic arousal of lust.

She had not found him tender before, not seeking that in him, and she was disarmed and confused as he intended her to be. This was his mastery complete, the other side of the coin he bought her with.

Her body took a long time to come to climax but he waited for her with infinite patience and control. She almost slept, hypnotised by the sliding velvet shaft filling and softly releasing her sanctum, a delicious possession of what her husband had rejected. Having destroyed her, Will remade her, and he knew what he did.

He whispered to her as he slid tirelessly in and out. 'My sweet lady come into the rough to taste a real man and she's out of her depth but she's so sensational with her poor under-used body that no one has known how to fulfil before. Now you are mine, lady, mine to possess and keep for my pleasure because you need me, need me to complete you and make you full.'

She murmured and rose to him, knowing she would climax again, feeling her tired muscles tremble in the sweet agony of orgasm. He felt her too, knew she was close and kept her there, in ecstasy, at but not over the peak.

Then he let her cry out and tumble over into climax, releasing himself within her so that she bloomed hot inside, a roiling voluptuous slow orgasm that throbbed through her tortured flesh, causing her to shudder and vibrate in his arms whilst her vision dazzled and blackened.

They lay close together in a kind of peace. Then Will asked if she wanted to use a bathroom, and Fiona thought with faint surprise that they weren't quite so animal after all.

She was heavy as she left the bed, her limbs dragging and slow, but the thought of being clean at long last appealed to her again. The bathroom was crude but the plumbing worked and the water was hot. She found soap and spent a long time lathering herself, washing away the spunk and the sweat and the fear on her body. She cleansed her cheek and for the first time thought it should be dressed. When Will joined her she asked for a can of Newskin.

'Newskin?'

'You have some surely?' Her brow knitted.

'Oh. I know what you mean. That stuff you spray on that heals wounds. We don't have it.'

'Why not? It's fantastic.'

'Sister.' Will was patiently amused. 'It's a bio-engineered catalyst, an enzyme that promotes the growth hormone so that the skin cells grow in a localised area at a furious rate for a limited time. Enough to heal. Enough to anaesthetise. Enough to prevent scarring, I guess.'

'Sure.' Fiona was impatient.

'It costs a damn fortune.'

'I hacked a car tonight. I know the ransom you boys ask.'

'We don't often succeed in hacking cars. There are quite a few of us to support. And we don't give a toss about scarring.'

Fee turned back to the mirror and looked at her split cheek, raw and red. It had never occurred to her that she might scar. She wondered how soon you had to spray a wound. There had never been a delay before on the rare occasion she had hurt herself or been with someone who was hurt.

She switched her mind from the problem and instead she washed Will, serving his body by cleansing it all over and at the same time enjoying the length and the strength and the breadth of him, learning it and implanting it deep into her memory so she would be able to recall it at will. She enjoyed also the contrast between Will and Rollo, at last satisfied enough to forget sex for a little while and think of other things. Rollo was smooth and bronzed and sleek, almost feminine with his satin skin. Will was rough and rugged, with knotty muscles and scars and callouses and a hard hairy body. He was very tall, well over six foot, and broad with it. She felt her own lissom womanliness, her slightness and frailty beside him.

She dried him carefully and powdered him, rubbing his wet washed hair for him, willing to perform any service he required. She knelt on the bed after she had towelled his hair, finger-combing his wet tangles. Then she all but touched his eye-patch.

'This,' she said. 'Have you lost the eye completely?'

'It's still there,' he said. 'It's blind. I took a chip of metal in it one day when the helipolice got too close.'

'Couldn't you get it fixed?' She knew it was a stupid question even as the words slipped out of her mouth.

He was laughing at her. 'There are no fancy hospitals for the likes of us,' he said. 'We have some bush doctors and I wouldn't let one of them near my eyes. We kinda learn to do without.'

She sat back on her heels, her mind running easily as suddenly it was faced with a comprehensible problem, one of organisation, rather than culture-clash. 'Perhaps I could get you into hospital,' she said. 'It's the documentation, though.'

'The documentation is available for money,' said Will. 'It's the money, lady. We don't stop a car that often. That reminds me. How come you struck lucky with your first shot? If this was your first shot.'

'It was my first attempt,' said Fiona. 'I don't think I could ever get up that damned wall again.'

'So how did you do it?'

His voice was lazy but Fiona felt the chill as his will met hers. She licked her lips. 'I'm talented on computers. We talk the same language.'

'And?'

'I spent a lot of time preprogramming.'

'You think we don't? What else, Skelton?'

'I used,' she hesitated. 'I used to work for the manufacturers. It's where I met my husband.'

She could have kicked herself. She should never have said

107

those last words. It was getting too dangerous here with the captain. He was a subtle and a devious man and he was using her own body against her. He was brutal and tender by turns but it was all planned all a deliberate manipulation of herself. He did not have a spontaneous, uncontrolled bone in his body.

He held her eyes for a slow moment. Then he lifted her left hand and looked at her ring. It was made from two bands of gold held together by twining platinum vine-leaves, minute swags of grapes represented by tiny ruby chips. It was a beautiful exotic toy, the gift of a rich man. As Will looked at this symbol of her other life, Fiona knew fear.

'Do you,' he asked softly, 'have a car?'

'Yes.'

'Jesus.'

In a moment of piercing clarity Fiona knew what she had done, what danger she had exposed herself to. Will's life was predicated upon the monster machines, the superb rocket-beasts of the forbidden highway, the ultimate symbol of success and self-aggrandisement. He was seeing her in a new light. She was not just a rich bored woman looking for rough trade. She was not even just a skinful of juicy sexual tricks, with a face and a body to drive men wild with lust.

She was the owner of a Connet. She had a one-million-credit machine, the ultimate in travelling luxury, the ultimate ego-machine, the ultimate expression of human personal power in an apolitical age, just to get her from A to B.

The ultimate penis. A three-and-a-half-hundred-mile an hour hotrod, a gleaming titanium shaft loaded with power, a synthesis of technology and greed.

This man had just fucked a woman who had a million-credit vibrator at her command.

Which way would he jump? Fiona felt a lurch of excitement. She was living on the edge. It could get to be a habit.

'Stay here with me,' he said softly. Pleasure rose hotly in her. He had gone for the woman, not the car.

'No.'

'I can make you.'

'Your loss.'

'I can make you want me any time I feel like it.'

'I want you all the time, anyway.'

'Then stay.'

'If I stayed,' she said, 'I will become just another woman to you.'

'You think so little of yourself?'

'I have an edge with you.'

'You do?'

'I have a smooth rich husband to synch with me. I wear the latest fashions. I have so much money I can't be bothered to add up what I spend. I have a Connet car.'

'Is that how you see yourself?'

She heard the contempt in his voice. 'I can't hold a man like you with looks and sexy tricks,' she said, her voice low and rich. 'And I want to hold you. If I go away and come back, you will know I dance to your tune. I will come back smelling of that other life, the one you can't have. You might be rough trade, my tiger-man, but I am luxury trade, carriage class, Zoo bred. If you are a tiger, I am a leopard, sleek, a thing of infinite riches. Yet I choose you. I come down to the sewer and I choose you. You know that I cannot keep away from you, even after all that you have done to humiliate me and hurt me.'

Will lay back on one elbow, his good eye narrowed, watching her, thinking over what she said. Now he smiled. 'That did you good. I did you a favour.'

She let it go. 'You have your life,' she whispered. 'I have mine. Don't we get our hype from the contrast between us?' She leant over him and brushed a finger over his lips. 'You and me. Yes? Honesty between us.'

'If you say so.'

She knew he would never be honest with her. He would never be safe. But she did not wish him changed.

'One thing.'

'Conditions, Skelton? I don't think I accept conditions.'

'No more of that business with Chain.'

'You didn't like him?' Will grinned broadly.

'That's got nothing to do with it.'

His powerful hands enclosed her wrists and he ran his hands up her arms and down again. 'I'm not your husband No one hits me. No bitch, however pretty, however sexy hits me in a little temper and gets nothing back.'

'Chain shot me tonight. He and his pal knocked me about before they knew I was a female, and then when they did they took me, one after another, as if I was nothing, just a hole on legs. Then Chain fucked me again whilst you held me down the two of you laughing at me and degrading me for your sport. You owe me, Captain Will Kid.'

'You poached. I've given you your life.'

'You got the passenger from the car I stopped.'

'I owe nobody.'

They stared at each other with hostility. Fiona thought of the long walk home. She was desperately tired.

'What's your real name?' he said in a flat voice.

'You know all you need to know about me. And some.'

'All I know about you is that your body is magic and you weave a spell I can't resist, try as I might. I would rather kill you than lose you, Skelton.'

She couldn't help it. She rose to his bait, a willing victim. She kissed his nipple and sucked the tiny hard disc. Her hands went down and she found his rear, rubbing the flesh when she had found it and seeking entrance. He fell back and she came on top of him. She turned herself round and put her mouth to his slack shaft. Her fingers quested on round, into him, and he groaned suddenly and his prick hardened. She invaded his backside still more and felt his breath hot between her legs. He ran his tongue her fissured length and then sought out her clitoris and began to suck it.

With her finger she masturbated his rear whilst she sucked his cock to life. She exulted when he rose up and hardened properly. What a man! Her own fanny burned from the treatment it had taken that night and she only aroused him now because her departure was imminent and she longed for him.

It would demean her for him to know how starved she was, how near she was to dearth though she glutted herself with him. She could not bear for him to know of Rollo's continued

110

rejection. How could she admit she feared to have his bloated weapon enter her again that night, because she was sore and it would hurt?

She had an idea. It made fear and excitement shoot through her in equal amounts.

She slid her finger deeper into his rear and felt him jerk and wriggle. Her mouth released his cock and she willed herself to forget its thickness and length.

'Mount me,' she said hoarsely. 'Here.' She pushed at his anus and he shuddered, his back arching.

His tongue slid hot and wet from her pussy up between her divided buttocks until he was sucking at her rear entrance. She quivered, loving it and terrified in equal parts. She had never admitted a man in this way. She didn't know if she could.

He moved out from under her and came on to his knees. 'Do you have any cream?' she asked, panic washing through her. She didn't think he would back down if she asked. There was a cruel streak in him.

He moved and for a moment fumbled out of her sight. Her wet wrinkled flesh fluttered of its own accord, nervously. Then she felt a cold jelly shock against her arse. He penetrated her with his finger, working her, softening her and greasing the passageway. She moaned, sweat starting on her upper lip and beading her hairline. His finger left her and she felt the club of his sex press against where it had been.

He had to push hard. She had a vivid picture of the two boys at the massage parlour. Then, with a succulent plop, Will got the end of his massy cock inside her and she yelped with pain.

She was being seared with red-hot needles, lanced by the gross muscle within her. Her bottom spasmed and she groaned deeply. Her buttocks stung from the beating they had received and her clitoris set up a sharp clamour of tingling pain. The heat of her fanny burned and all her rump glowed, within and without.

'More,' she whispered.

He drove further into her. She felt split in two. She clenched her rear muscles and he laughed.

'Too much, greedy sister?'

'More,' she hissed through gritted teeth.

He clove her and lust erupted through her body. 'Fuck me,' she shouted and he was doing it, riding into her, the pressure in her everywhere, guts, groin, vulva and womb.

This man could do anything to her and she would love it.

She bucked down on to him and he took her hips to steady her.

He took her fast. He must be tired himself. She felt him swell and she felt the soft thuck of his balls on the backs of her thighs. He thrust hard and she felt him flower within her, his hot liquid a welcome gush. As her arse filled, his cock relaxed and he began to slide out.

He watched his handiwork for a moment, seeing his own juice smear her lovely cleft. He lay down beside her and Fiona looked at him, trembling still but triumphant and adoring.

'You bitch,' he said. 'You clever bitch.'

'Not all one way, eh?' she croaked. Something had happened to her throat.

'That look of worship in your eyes,' he said.

'Yes?'

'I kinda like it, Zoo baby.'

'Will,' she groaned.

'Don't say it. Go now. Or I won't let you.'

'You have to give me some clothes.' She gave a crooked laugh. She was close to falling at his feet. Her eyes couldn't focus, she was so full of him and what he did to her, for her.

'I reckon you've earned new clothes,' he said. 'We get the computer and all the little toys you brought in tonight. And the passenger.'

'And my soul, pirate.'

He laughed. 'Yeah. And that.'

9

Fiona took to her bed for two days pretending she was unwell but refusing to allow a doctor access. She was exhausted and sore and needed time to recover mentally as well as physically.

Over and over again during that two days she visualised the powerful naked body of her pirate lover. Just thinking of him was enough to arouse her. Her mind dwelt on the details of what she had gone through and she found that she was angry and softened by turns. She knew she had a fundamental weakness where Will was concerned. Though she gloried in her toughness of character in general, it pleased her to be so abased a creature with the pirate.

She revelled in the luxury of her life, feeling it as she had never felt it before. She, who had wallowed in sexual frenzy in the night with the dregs of society, was now lapped all about with pretty toys and soft living, waited on and pampered and having her will served by her paid employee.

The knowledge that the bullet might have shattered bone instead of grazing her, the knowledge that she had come close to being killed, further excited her.

By the time she was able to treat her torn face, it was too late to prevent scarring. She explained it by saying she had turned too quickly and caught her face on a sharp point. As an excuse it was thin but no one had any reason to disbelieve her and think she lied. She kept a close eye on the news and saw reported that another car driver had been ransomed. So her victim was home again, a poorer man, unless he was insured against piracy as many of them were.

The episode with Chain stayed in her mind and her principal emotion was a kind of fascination that it had really taken place. She remembered the frenzied moment, her bottom burning, Will forcing her down, Chain dragging her legs apart to plant his thick thieving member within her. She tried to imagine what she must have looked like from the rear with her reddened cheeks and writhing legs opening to give glimpses of her wet sexual crevasse. She could visualise Chain, his leathers opened at his groin, holding himself with one hand and kneeling forward on the bed between her struggling limbs, forcing her rear up till he could sink his shaft within her furious body and trap her with his sex, master her resistance and turn it to a kind of fierce accepting angry joy.

She had hated watching the red-haired girl suck and fuck Will as she hung helpless and rejected. Will had enjoyed having his mate impale her after he had taken his own satisfaction from her.

She tried to imagine Diana, whom she cared for, in the cellar with herself and Will. What if she had witnessed Diana caressing Will's body and using it to pleasure herself? She had no trouble recalling Diana's generous sex with its riot of fair curling hair. She set herself to picture Will's dark powerful cock sliding up and within Diana's intimate tresses, going on and into Diana till the blonde writhed with joy at the invader. She imagined it withdrawn, glistening, then sliding back up and into her friend.

What would she do? She would stroke Diana's breasts. She would run her hands underneath Diana's rear and feel on round until she could lightly clasp Will's swinging balls and caress them as he shafted her friend. She could let her fingertips gently flutter up without impeding his action so she could feel Diana's split labia and moist vulva, feel the softness of hair, feel the strength of Will's wet shaft going in and out.

In unwitting mimicry of her wallowing in sex, Rollo wallowed in work. He needed her now. Things were coming together for him and he wanted her computer mastery to get the details under control, to create organisational programmes that would keep the growing consortium under his control, a structure that he could command and keep on top of.

She could do this. She would do this for him, and for herself, as soon as she was able.

Diana came to see her.

'What's wrong? You don't usually keep in your bed.'

'I'm shattered. A momentary imbalance. Too little of this, too much of that. Don't nag me, Diana. I'm enjoying myself.'

Diana sat down. 'You look different, Fee. Is it this lover of yours?'

'I didn't say I had a lover.'

'Your body language does. You look so sexy I could give it to you myself if Teddy hadn't done the business twice already this morning.'

Teddy was her husband. Fiona knew she wasn't bragging. The pair of them went at it like stags in the rut.

'What is this man,' said Diana, 'that after a session with him you have to take to your bed?'

'He's . . . he's . . .' She couldn't say it.

'Will you leave Rollo?'

'No.'

'Is the guy married?'

Fiona laughed aloud. 'I've no idea. I shouldn't think so.'

'Where d'you meet him? Do I know him?'

'You don't know him.'

'You sound very sure. Why don't I know him? And if I don't, why are you so foxy with me? Who is he, this fantastic lover of yours?'

'He doesn't belong to our life,' said Fiona with difficulty. 'I found him a long way away.'

'Out of the Zoo?' Diana looked at her friend doubtfully. Suddenly Fiona understood.

'You stupid ape,' she said. 'I know what's in your mind.'

A guarded look came down over Diana's face. 'You do?'

'Friend of mine, I couldn't take your husband if I wanted to. And I would do nothing to harm our friendship. I don't believe he would let me, either. My lover is not Teddy, Diana. Forgive me, but your husband is not the only man in the world who can dazzle a woman with the quality of his synching. I've found another.'

'I know he's not good looking. But you've been so desperate. I just wondered.'

'I still aim to get Rollo's pole up.'

'You do?'

'I have this sneaky little plan.'

'Are you going to tell me?'

'I think you'll be shocked.'

'So shock me. Don't patronise.'

'I'm going to use Janine.'

'Who?'

'My maid.'

'Your maid, for Christ's sake!'

'I said you would be shocked.'

Diana thought about this for a while. 'How?' she asked.

'Have you ever fancied it with a woman, Diana?'

Diana put her head on one side and looked down at her friend. 'I never thought about it till that day at the massage joint. I got really hot. It was good when you touched me. Mind you, I was already hot as hell from the massage and then seeing those two guys perform. God.' Diana threw her head back and laughed. 'That was really something. I've never seen anything like it.'

'It's sexy watching other people at it, isn't it?'

'It's on the Screen all the time. I don't bother with it.'

'In the flesh, Diana. Real people. People you can smell and hear. And touch.'

'I guess so. I'm not sure. I don't think I'd like to perform in public.'

'Janine has the hots for Rollo. I'm fixing it so Rollo sees her screwing. Then she will make a play for him.'

'That's bloody dangerous, Fee. Handing the delectable Rollo over to another woman. And Janine is just a kid.'

'She's sixteen and she wants the guy badly. I can't arouse him. If she can, maybe we can both get the benefit.'

'You'd share him?'

'I don't get him at all at the moment. Half a loaf, Diana.'

'You amaze me. I can't take this in. Who's the guy who is going to perform with Janine so Rollo can get excited about it?'

'That's my little secret.'

'Your lover?'

'No chance. I told you, he's not in our world at all. I met him somewhere completely different. And he would no more play games at my ordering than he would . . .'

'Would what?'

'I don't know. He's not tame. That's what I like about him.'

'You can get a long way in that auto of yours,' said Diana jealously.

So that was fine. Diana thought she meant that Will was somewhere geographically distant when she said he was in another world. It wasn't miles that made the distance, though. She could walk, given sufficient time, to Will's world, but it was still a different world altogether.

After she was up and about again Fiona worked hard with Rollo for a while, doing her bit for TransFlow, as the new company was called.

There were meetings via computer link-up with engineers. They were fixing the specifications that would form the basis of the tenders from construction companies.

The whole property and land side was a horrific tangle. Where they could, it made logistical sense to use the old ruined waterways already owned by the water companies who would be buying what TransFlow carried. These would not need to be deregistered as farming, recreational or wild land, and the old canals made a natural line for the pipeline to follow.

Rollo was no fool, either. As a side project and quite unknown to the other members of the consortium, he was investing in a little company that had produced a successful process for turning sea water into fresh. Desalination had been viable for over half a century but it had remained expensive and clumsy. The new filtration plant not only removed the salt dissolved in sea water, but also the trace magnesium, silver, iodine, uranium, gold, nickel, copper, cobalt and so on, collecting them in a commercially viable manner that would underpin financially the production of fresh water which was the filtration plant's main purpose.

Rollo had always backed more than one horse in the race and his personal finances reflected his acumen.

He came to Fiona. 'I need to buy the patent on the water filtration plant,' he said. 'If the pipeline gets out of hand and we can't continue to raise finance, or if our costs soar and make the water companies look for a cheaper solution, we'll control it. You and I won't lose personally. I have first option on the patent but I have to come through with the money pretty soon or they can offer it on the open market.'

'How much for the patent?'

Rollo told her. Fiona's eyes narrowed. 'We don't have that much money spare, do we?'

'No. My credit is fully extended with TransFlow. I have to have it there because it gives investor-confidence, if I'm seen to be out on a limb myself.'

They looked at each other. 'The car,' said Fiona eventually.

'It could be a year. I mean, we could be without it for a long time, baby. We'll get it back in the end, of course, when TransFlow regenerates my personal holding. Do you mind very much?'

'Give me a couple of days, Rollo.'

'No longer, Fee. I mustn't miss this. We need the insurance.'

'I understand.'

The plan came to her fully formed, the product of Rollo's own words. Her request for a delay had been merely to accustom herself to the shock of being carless. But now she thought she could see a way round it. If she could work an insurance fiddle on her car, she might be able to raise the finance and keep the car at the same time.

She got busy. She put stage one into operation that same evening. There was no time to lose.

She had to get hold of a car computer control system, a Connet, that had been subjected to hacking. She needed one in meltdown. She toyed with the idea of asking Captain Kid

to help her but rejected it. He was too uncertain, too dangerous. Moreover, he was not a wheeler-dealer like Rollo and to
a certain extent like herself. Will was a taker. He wouldn't
make deals.

She vidicommed an old acquaintance from her days of
working at the autofactory where she had learned and used
her computing skills. She picked a guy in middle management, a career failure who knew he would go no further, a
man who would never afford to buy one of the beautiful
machines he worked to help produce.

This man had tried to make the grade with her but Rollo had
taken her from under his nose. If he felt he could get one over
the successful high-flying Rollo Cambridge, he might break
his company oath and supply her with what she wanted.

Fiona prepared for the call by making herself as seductive
as she knew how. Then she dialled him. His name was Jamie
Andersen.

'Hey, Jamie,' she said when she got through. He was a
nice-looking second-rater which made what she wanted to do
that much easier. She would have done it anyway.

His lips parted in astonishment. 'Fee,' he said. 'Fee
Bronson.'

'Fee Cambridge,' she corrected prettily.

His face downturned. 'Yeah. So how is Rollo these days?'

'Abstracted.'

'What?'

'Bound up in business. I don't want to talk about him. I
wondered how you were.'

'Me? I'm fine. Just the same. You know.'

'You're a nice guy, Jamie. We used to be friends. I'm
awfully bored. Rollo is always busy. Let's meet up and talk
old days at the factory. We used to have fun.'

'We did? We did,' he repeated more firmly. 'Yeah. Let's
meet.' He gulped.

'Tonight.'

'Tonight?' he yelped in amazement.

'If you can't make it, I understand. Everyone's always
busy.'

'I can make it, Fee.'

119

'I'll bring my car. Maybe we can go for a ride.' She gave this the full throaty treatment. Jamie turned a dull red.

'You have a car. An auto. One of ours. Of course you do.'

'Let's ride, Jamie, and catch up on old times. I'll come over, then?'

'Yes. Sure. I'll be ready. And Fee?'

'Mmm?'

'I'm glad you called.'

'So am I, Jamie. So am I.'

She dressed to kill. She put on the tight black number with the peep-hole nipples, full ghost make-up, and she had Janine fix her hair into a scented profusion.

Having been neglected lately, Janine was inclined to be sulky, Fiona kissed her tenderly on the lips.

'Darling,' she said huskily. 'Business is at a critical stage and when Rollo turns on to you, I want you to have all his attention. I think things will move next week.'

'I thought that maybe you didn't like me any more,' mumbled Janine.

'Me? Oh baby, I didn't realise you liked me so much. I mean, I thought I was just a means to an end with you, Rollo being what you really wanted.'

'I do want him. I still don't understand why you don't mind. But I like what we do together, Mrs Cambridge. I mean, I get really excited.'

'I like it too, honey. I was worried in case I got greedy and frightened you off. But if you want to play with me just because you like it, we'll certainly play some more. Lots more.'

The sun came out in Janine's face. 'That's wonderful,' she said earnestly.

'Now I have to dash. I'm meeting an old workmate and I want to impress him. You know, show I haven't gone matronly or developed lines or sag or anything.'

'You,' gasped Janine with incredulity. 'But you are fabulous. So beautiful. So sexy.'

'Bless you, child. Just what I want to hear.'

Fiona kissed Janine thoughtfully, savouring the female mouth mixed with her own. The girl's adoration of herself pleased her and was counterweight to her own adoration for Will. She liked the idea of Janine serving her as maid and yet lusting privately to touch and be touched in intimate deviant caress. The girl's mouth was honey, and her submissive attitude aroused Fiona sexually. For a moment she fantasised playing Chain to Janine, wearing leather and high heels and invading the helpless girl caught squirming across some man's lap. It would be fun. She would love to see Janine writhing, with spunk oozing from her body's most private entrance, her breasts crushed and her bottom reddened with abuse.

Already in the mood for the evening's games, she went to the hangar to fetch her auto. She would seduce Jamie, hardly a difficult feat. She needed him compliant to her will. He was going to steal for her, after all.

Jamie admitted her and with a kind of eager unease led her into his sitting room. The lights were dimmed but Fee could see it was a classic middle-income bachelor pad. Jamie did not live in the Zoo, of course, but his home was no slum though the windows were opaqued so that he could not overlook nor be overlooked by his neighbours. Dronesville. Respectable, dull, and boring.

One wall of his sitting room was given over to the mandatory big Screen, off in deference to her arrival, and Fiona supposed he had been watching one of the sex channels before she arrived. There was a feel in the air, half-hopeful, half-shameful. She would have liked him more if he had had the boldness to leave it on so that couples writhed as they talked. There would have been an honest vulgarity in that which would be more attractive than his furtive demeanour now.

He was dressed in tight tan slacks that were not quite the fashionable length below the knee, and a stiff heavily-embroidered overshirt. They had been all the rage a couple of years back. Rollo still had one or two at the back of his wardrobe somewhere.

He fetched her a drink, a good malt whisky, which was one up to him, thought Fiona, for the damned stuff cost a fortune. Synthetic alcohol was cheaper but it was nothing like as good as the real thing.

Jamie could not keep his eyes off her clothes. Exposed nipples were a new fashion for the Zoo. Down here in Dulltown no one would be wearing them for a year, and then they would be toned down somehow. No doubt Jamie had seen them on actresses in the broadcasts, but Fiona could bet hers were the first Jamie had seen in the flesh, as it were. He probably had a succession of girlfriends who had shed their clothes at the appropriate moment, but that was not the same as seeing beautiful, rich, desirable women walking around with the tips of their tits on show.

The dim lighting enabled her to sit so that her nipples projected and glowed in ghostly fashion. Let him get an eyeful. He was going to pay for it.

Parking her car outside was doing his credit good in the neighbourhood, she had no doubt. No one down here would ever have ridden in one of the rocketcars. There would be old-fashioned computer-assist models but they were excluded from the highways, the sexy skylanes that roofed the city and were for the turbomasters alone.

'This is nice, Jamie,' she said chattily. 'How are things with you?'

'Much the same, Fee. You look great, really great.'

'You like the gear?'

'Love it,' he said huskily.

'You don't think it's too extreme?'

'Some women,' said Jamie and coughed to clear his throat, 'couldn't carry it off. You can, Fee. Believe me.'

'I've missed the old days, you know,' she said mistily.

'You don't look as if you have.'

No fool, then. 'I gave you a hard time. You want to know why?'

'I doubt it. It can hardly be flattering.'

'I'm a flyer, Jamie. I knew the sort of life I wanted and Rollo has given it to me. Rollo has given me everything, except . . .'

'Except what?'

'What you would have given me.'

'What's that, Fee?'

'Fidelity.'

She couldn't do it. She couldn't betray Rollo and her own sexless relationship to this man. She couldn't admit Rollo didn't screw her any more. It suited her own ego and her perception of loyalty to Rollo to pretend he synched around.

'Those goodlooking guys, they always play the field,' muttered Jamie. 'You know that.'

'Come out in the car, Jamie. I'm being boring. Let's have some fun together, for old time's sake.'

'Of course. Whatever you say.'

He recognised the car. There weren't that many Connets made in any one factory and anyone who really loved them could keep an individual count. He stroked the smoky glass-brown exterior. The titanium body was vitriplated in shatterproof obsidian giving the car a deep opaque lustre.

Fiona touched the lock and it admitted them. She saw the neighbours watching and gave them a good eyeful of her clothes and legs. Inside she fixed them both a drink and asked Jamie if he had any idea about where he wanted to go.

'The coast,' he suggested.

She programmed the computer and they started up. The gas turbine motor hummed and the car rose on its airpads. It was set on local, to detect bodies and other heat sources, and would go at slow speed until it reached the highway ramp, some distance here from the houses. The ramps ran close to the rich dwellers in the Zoo because they were the only stratum in society that could afford Connets. There was no point in building service roads here that would never be needed.

They bumbled quietly along, Fiona concentrating on building Jamie's ego. She knew she would have to make the come-on. Some men liked it, some didn't. She had to hope that Jamie was so besotted that whatever his normal preference, he didn't care in this instance.

The screen indicated they had reached the ramp.

'Help me put her up,' invited Fee.

The car was keyed to her DNA. Jamie took her hands within his and lightly held them, playing the keys lovingly, his body pressed gently against her back and his head at her shoulder. The motor rose in pitch until they could not hear it.

123

They were pushed back as the car shot up the ramp and joined the highway. They were up in the stars, below the velvet arc of sky, enclosed within the Connet web and carried madly within it.

There wasn't a lot of time.

10

'Jamie,' said Fee. She twisted her hand within his and pressed his to her breast. His palm felt the naked nipple surrounded by material.

'Fee,' he croaked. His lips came onto hers as she fell back into his arms.

'I've always wanted you,' she murmured. 'I was afraid that if I got entangled I would miss out on the high life. I wanted that so much as well. Was that very wicked of me, Jamie?'

'I expect so,' he said breathlessly. 'You were always a little wicked, Fee. I think that's why I wanted you so much. Then that smooth bastard got you.'

'You've got me now,' said Fee. Her arms wound around his neck.

He wasn't bad. He wasn't bad at all. In fact, he was quite agreeably good. She was a snob, Fiona realised. Just because a guy didn't make it to the top at work, it didn't mean he wasn't a clever operator between the thighs.

She came on hard, sensing he liked it. He kissed her and then pulled down her strap exposing the entire breast. He held it and kissed the plummy nipple, teasing it expertly till it was proud and long. He caught it between his fingers and went hard at work on the other one with his mouth.

The car hissed along at two hundred and ninety miles an hour. Jamie got his hand up her skirt and found she wore no panties.

'Oh, dear God, Fee. You could drive a man insane.'

'Take me, Jamie. Make it worth while.'

He had her skirt up and was pulling her legs apart. Then he stopped, gazing on her revealed parts.

'OK?' she asked.

His face was transfixed. He never heard her. He began to

pant. He fell on to his knees before her and a curious expression, compounded of fear and wonder and bewilderment, crossed his face. Very, very slowly he brought a hand up. Fiona could see it was trembling. He touched her with the force of a moth's wing, the slightest of touches, on her uprearing bald sexual mound. He lifted his face and met her gaze with something like pain in his eyes.

'Fee,' he said.

'What is it, Jamie?'

'I never thought I'd see this. I never thought it could be so good, so strange. So blunt. Then that sweetest, sexiest slit below, leading back. Fee Bronson, you are the stuff of dreams.'

It didn't seem the appropriate moment to correct him over her name. He used his fingers with delicate strength to open her wide and gaze deep into her steamy interior.

His lips moved but no sound came out. He simply knelt there, looking, holding her open so that her heat was caressed by cool air.

The intense visual scrutiny and appreciation was very flattering.

He bent down so that he could look closer. Fee flexed her fanny muscles.

'You are like fruit,' he murmured. 'Soft, split, fermented fruit, dark and juicy and intoxicating, inviting teeth to bite deeply into you.'

'So bite me,' said Fiona softly.

'You'll make me drunk.'

'Suck my juices, sweetheart. We've waited long enough.'

But he didn't. Not then. Instead he released her skirt and removed it, laying it carefully to one side. Now she wore nothing but long sheeny stockings and suspenders. Round her throat was black velvet and more of the same was twisted deep and cunningly into her hair.

Jamie began to shed his own clothes. He stripped quite well. He must use the gymnasium, thought Fiona idly. She didn't remember whether he had when she worked at the factory. She hadn't been interested enough in him.

He had fair hair and his prick stood out of a curly golden

126

cloud. She was surprised to see he wasn't getting down to the business. She knew she wasn't going to mind this time with Jamie. It was quite fun.

'Fee,' he said.

'What is it?'

'I want you to suck my cock.'

'Is that what you like, lover?'

He brought his groin level with her face.

'Go down on me, Fee Cambridge. Suck me off.'

His getting her name right gave her the clue. He wanted her abased. He wanted her humiliated. He wanted to feel on top after all these years, in command.

Fee changed her tone from flirty to humble. Anything to oblige. He wasn't just going to get his cock sucked by Fee Bronson. Rollo Cambridge was going to be right down there, humbly sucking alongside.

He was slightly scented. This was a common male habit, she knew, but not one that pleased her overmuch. The smell that turned her on was clean aroused male. She didn't want a perfumed prick.

She sucked gently at first, finding his threshold where pleasure turned to pain. The art was to keep a man there, just the right side of pleasure but at its most intense. She worked his shaft, nibbling and licking and eating at the hair from which it sprung. Her hand came up and caressed his balls, cupping them and squeezing them. Then she back-tracked the length of his shaft until she was at his tumescent head.

He was overexcited. The car, herself, the forbidden (forbidden for her, that is) and illicit nature of what they were doing, were all too much for him. When he climaxed he would be out of control.

Fee sucked the eye of his gland and tasted salt. She took the whole end into her mouth and squeezed and sucked hard. He was panting now. She opened her mouth and played her tongue, pointed and hot and sharp over his quivering flesh. She ringed the base of his prick with finger and thumb and plunged her mouth right over him, drawing back slowly, pressing hard.

He was groaning, shaking with mounting passion. She drew back onto the head, sucking hard, rhythmically hard, and at the same time frigging him with finger and thumb. Her other hand tickled at his testicles.

She felt him come with her hands first and opened her mouth to take what he had to give. He spurted into her, shouting and shaking, and when she knew he was unloaded she pulled back and lay back, her lips slightly parted, a trickle of spunk coming from one corner of her mouth.

He stared at her, aghast. Now he had had what he wanted, he was ashamed.

'Kiss me, you bastard,' she said thickly.

His mouth was hesitant. Maybe he had never done this before. Fee had little idea of what other women liked or encouraged men to do. She herself had always wanted more. More intense experience, more variety, more tricks and flavours in her sex.

She pushed up so that his mouth was hard on hers and knotted her fingers in his hair, driving their mouths together whilst she sucked his tongue and licked his inner mouth. He recovered himself and began to kiss her back, his tongue darting round her mouth and exploring the taste of himself in her.

Her eyes were chips of ice as he lifted his face from hers.

'Turn round,' she commanded. Her expectation of obedience was insulting. He hesitated a moment and then obeyed her.

The giant car quivered as it hurtled along the highway.

Now she had his rear before her. She considered. Between his legs his prick hung down, limp and soft. Fiona smacked his bottom.

'Hey,' he protested.

'Shuddup,' she said and ran her nails over one buttock. A set of three shallow red weals stood out. She smacked them hard. He jerked out but remained silent, his head down, his bottom up.

Fee looked round the car and saw Jamie's trousers. She slid the slim leather belt out of the tabs and coiled it round her hand so that she held the buckle. She backed away from

Jamie a little and then brought the temporary whip down with a whistling crack across his buttocks.

He jerked violently and cried out but he did not stop her.

'You filthy bastard,' she said and whipped him again.

'Fiona,' he whimpered.

'Mrs Cambridge to you,' she said. She whipped him again, hearing the crack of leather as it struck living flesh. 'Me, sucking the likes of you, eh?' His backside was glowing red, the plum-coloured lines across it the same colour as her nipples.

She checked down between his legs. His prick had stiffened a little already. She gave him one more vicious flick. She hadn't broken any skin but his rear was signal red and must sting like hell. She was astonished to find she was wet between her own legs. She was enjoying this.

She pulled his buttocks back towards herself a little which had the effect of making his male equipment dangle down instead of being safely tucked between his thighs. His scrotal sac hung with a sparse collection of crinkly blonde hair around it. The stronger shaft of his purplish dong, half-erect, hung lower.

She must be careful, she thought. Her clitoris tingled. Judging the blow nicely, she lashed him gently across his balls. He screamed and put his arms over his head. She lashed him again, fighting the impulse to use her strength. His prick was hard erect now, swinging nicely.

Fee put her mouth to his anus and sucked hard. She could feel his flesh vibrate with shock at the unexpected assault. He writhed. She invaded him with her tongue and felt his valve spasm. She spat on him to make him wet and then invaded him with her finger.

'Oh, Christ, no,' he moaned, bubbling with fear. But he didn't stop her.

She drove her finger further in. 'Turn over,' she ordered.

Carefully he pivoted on her finger, so brazenly up his arse, bringing his leg up and over till he lay on his back before her. He was red-faced and distressed but his prick stuck straight up in the air, ramrod hard.

'This is bad, huh?' she asked silkily.

'I can't, I can't . . .'

'So how are you going to punish me for being such a naughty girl?' As she said this, she pushed her finger even harder in.

His back arched as he lifted his buttocks from the couch, absorbing her probing finger, his mouth open and his eyes shut. His vertical rigid cock was beautiful. For a moment she thought he had failed to catch what she said. But he had heard her and was gradually becoming aware that the game was changing. He sagged down and his eyes opened. He peered blearily at her. When he spoke, his voice was hoarse.

'I'm going to whip you,' he said.

Fee removed her finger and cowered back. 'Please don't,' she whimpered.

Jamie sat up, shaking a little. 'You bitch,' he said. 'I'm going to make you suffer.'

She squirmed back, then turned her back on him, presenting her rear, her pale pointed buttocks an open invitation to abuse. 'I can't look,' she squeaked.

There was a delay. She had no doubt he was considering the strap. She poked her bottom right out as provocatively as she knew how, and thought about Will smacking her. Her fanny vibrated slightly, moist and excited.

She screamed. It stung incredibly, a burning hot line across her buttocks.

'Take that,' he yelled and the whip whistled audibly, cutting through the air to land stingingly on her proffered flesh. It burned.

'And that,' he cried again. In a sexual frenzy he struck her several times more and Fiona felt the blows merge and bloom into a fiery all-over heat that expanded and flooded through her in a hot sexual tide. As he struck her again, the thin piercing sweetness of the blow was desirable and arousing.

Then he was in her, taking her from behind, shoving his stiff prick into the open wet invitation of her upraised orifice.

He plunged deeply and aggressively, taking her hard and fast in his need. Then Fiona became aware of something most peculiar.

She was hot, wet and thoroughly aroused. Jamie was doing

130

the business just fine. But she couldn't come. There was no climax. She felt Jamie coming, heard him gasp, felt his heat and flow in her, but beyond a couple of perfunctory muscular spasms, she did nothing herself.

She had only ever made love for pleasure. This was the first time she had gone with a man out of calculation, for an end other than sexual satisfaction. Maybe that was it.

Now he had rolled her over and was stroking her wet hair back from her brow and kissing her face gently with little soft kisses.

'Fee, oh my darling, you beautiful creature,' he was murmuring. She felt a rush of maternal protective emotion. Poor Jamie. A sweet guy, really and not untalented. He looked all in.

She fetched them both a fresh drink and tidied up a little, adjusting the air conditioning to reduce the smell of sexual congress.

'That's quite a muscle you keep down there,' she said.

'A man could die for you,' he said romantically.

I only want you to steal for me, she thought sweetly. 'Jamie, I'm one bored woman. You took me out of myself today.'

'You want a repeat and I'm on, Fee.'

'I've been playing with computers lately.'

'Oh yeah. You weren't bad, were you?'

You patronising bastard, she thought coldly. I was the best.

'Does Rollo use you in his business endeavours?'

'Don't let's talk about Rollo. Can you do me a favour?'

'Name it, sweetheart.'

'Get me an old Connet. A bust one. One in meltdown.'

'Hey, that's not so easy.'

'I guess not.' Fiona ran a tantalising finger up his chest, through his little mat of wiry hair. 'Nor is it easy for me to get away like this. I want to play around with a melted Connet, maybe see if I can fix it.'

'You can't fix a computer after it's melted.' Jamie was positive. He was an electronics expert himself, though not up to Fee's standard.

131

'Wanna bet?'

'It's crazy, Fee. You could buy one. God knows, you must have the credits.'

'I could buy a good one,' she corrected. 'I want one in meltdown.'

'The factory erases them. You know that. They are all accounted for.'

'Mmm-hm.'

'I mean, I would have to fix the records. And for what?'

'For me.'

'But it would be no use to you.'

'So you think. And you might even be right. I don't want to blow the one in this car. Even Rollo has limits and he doesn't expect me to waste hundreds of thousands of credits on a whim.'

'Forgive me, Fee, but it is just that, a whim. I thought you had more sense. You can't do anything with a melted computer.'

'I think I can. The melted computer does no good at the factory. I'm not depriving anyone of anything. I'm recycling waste, if you like. It would be a challenging toy for me. I like that.'

She gave Jamie a challenging look as she said this and licked her lips. 'I'm sorry,' she said slyly. 'I like to live a little crazy and I expect my men to do the same.'

'You bitch,' he said helplessly. 'You know I'll do it.'

She laughed gloriously. 'Fuck me again, Jamie. Then steal me a computer. That turns me on, yeah.'

'Yeah,' said Jamie. He would play it her way now.

They didn't get out of the car at the coast. With considerable ingenuity Fiona managed to keep Jamie well entertained all the way back to Dullsville. She was shattered when they got back to his apartment, but not as shattered as he was. Jamie could hardly walk.

She arranged to pick up the computer the following day. Her schedule was tight. She couldn't afford to wait.

One of the good things about Rollo was that if he agreed to something, he didn't keep raising the issue again and rehashing it. So he said nothing that night about selling the car, nor the next day.

Early afternoon Fiona drove to Jamie's and picked up the ruined computer which he had brought out of the factory in a box at lunchtime. Fortunately he had to get back to work so she gave him a quick uncomplicated rut on his couch and was able to get away. Her mind was detaching from sex now. She was thinking electronics.

However, she had her plan to keep to. After re-entering the car outside Jamie's, she slid a prepared siphon between her legs. She sucked Jamie's semen from her fanny into the sterile tube. She had also relieved him of three pubic hairs. She put these into a plastic envelope and tucked all her spoils into the glove box.

She drove home and without washing changed into the dress she had bought that morning. It was the most dazzling and daring she could find at such short notice. If she held still, it looked silver-black. If she moved, it coruscated into a hologrammatic rainbow of pure colour. Moreover, though it did not have nipple peepholes, it did have clear panels over her breasts and the upper half clung to her body, showing the powerful swing of her firm full breasts and their delicious convex lines underneath leading up to the tilting outwards-pointing nipples. In addition there was another translucent panel at the top of her rear cleavage, so that the beginning of that lovely cleft, dark with mystery and illicit promise, was clearly visible.

Fiona wore a harness as underwear. A broad elastic band led between the cheeks of her buttocks, spreading them apart, firming them, making them pout so that each globe of flesh appealed to the touch of a masculine hand bold enough to adventure.

At the top of her cleft it divided to come down over her belly crosswise. Each strap then went under, between her legs, round the inner thigh to join again at her rear.

When Fiona was naked but for this strange device, it caused her depilated gleaming mound to project even more bulbously than usual. Between her legs, the twin straps pressing against her inner thighs also pressed against her labia so that when she parted her legs and lay back, her sexual parts bulged outwards greedily, as if to take for themselves what they longed for to give them purpose and fruition.

Fiona stood for a moment, assessing herself in her mirrors before leaving once more in pursuance of her plan. The dress clung and shone with living three-dimensional colour when she moved, and with subfusc richness when she did not. Her excited breathing caused her proud, partly-revealed bosom to lift and fall rhythmically. She wore four-inch heels and they made her leg muscles taut and bold. At their top her cradled, divided arse was at the same time covered yet enticingly prominent.

She could feel the sweat from her lunchtime session with Jamie still on her body. She could feel a faint stickiness between her legs where she had not cleansed him from herself. Her heart pounded, her nerves were playing up, but she felt that none of this was amiss. It all fitted the part she was about to play.

11

As Fee drove slowly up the local ramp, she checked her equipment. Her face shimmered in the gloom of the darkened interior. Beside her was a box with gay wrapping paper over it, such as one might use to giftwrap a toy for a child. Also beside her was a tray of delicate instruments, tiny screwdrivers, a soldering iron, some gold nodules and some of platinum.

The melted computer was also there.

She programmed the car with her destination and as it was made to do, it queried her peculiar order. She reprogrammed the same set of commands and this time they were accepted.

Soon after it had entered the highway, the car came to a stop as she had ordered it to. As it stopped, she sprang into action. Wearing gloves, she opened the door nearest the fence and shut herself on the outside. She then broke the lock with a laser pencil.

Back inside she removed the loosened fascia in ten seconds flat. Now, delicately, flat on her stomach, she began to disconnect the Connet, working at her fastest speed. After five minutes of concentrated work she was able to slip the tray with all its multiple ceramic chips and simple neuron web out from its aperture. She delicately disconnected the hacking alarm and placed the Connet carefully in the prepared box, packing it around and dropping in the laser pencil on top.

Now she took the melted-down version of the same thing, a toffee-ish tangle of components like burnt sugar, and slotted it into the empty aperture. She began to connect what was left of its structure to her car's controls.

The minutes ticked by.

She triggered the hacking alarm. Its signal could do nothing to the good Connet now. She tightened the fascia back in place and dropped the alarm and her tools in on top of the Connet, with her gloves. She sealed the box and shoved it into the luggage compartment.

Her eyes flicked round the car's interior. It looked right. Through the open door she could hear the whirr of the SkyPolice copter coming closer and closer. She reached into the glove compartment, took out the syringe and with a moue of distaste she opened her legs and squirted cold semen up into her body. She arranged the three pubic hairs around the mouth of her fanny. There was no time for artistry, she thought with a bubble of hysterical laughter. She thrust the syringe into her bag, hauled up her skirt, forced the bodice of her lovely new dress apart and slapped her own face a couple of times. She hit herself violently on her vulva to bruise it and then flung herself back. As a last gesture she touched salt to the corners of her eyes.

When the police found her she was crying, sprawled back in her car, her sex exposed.

She heard the first man as he reached the open door.

'Hey,' he called out. 'The victim's still here.' He audibly gulped as he took his first clear view of Fiona. He remembered he was a policemen. 'Lady,' he said hoarsely. 'You OK?'

'The bastard, the bastard,' sobbed Fiona. She writhed a little to give the trooper the full benefit of her oozing fanny.

'What's going on?' The second man was there. He saw Fiona and made a sort of strangulated gasp.

'They raped me,' sobbed Fiona, trying ineffectually to pluck her skirt down over herself.

'Here? They didn't take you?'

She struggled upright and now the first man was in the car with her. She flung her arms round him and pressed her wet face close.

'I'm so glad you are here. Why weren't you here earlier? You could have saved me.'

'OK, lady. We'll get you to a doctor. We don't understand why you weren't taken.'

Fiona pulled herself free and hitched her skirt most of the way down, wiping her face. Tumbled black curls spilled around her white face, framing it and highlighting her long angled green eyes. Her perfume assailed the troopers' nostrils and as she moved, her dress flickered into brilliance. One perfect white pear-shaped breast spilled free of the torn bodice of her dress.

'I don't know,' she said tragically. 'They were animals.'

Both troopers felt simultaneously their cocks jump with jealousy for the pirates who had been uninhibited by considerations of decency and uniform when confronted with this luscious classy piece of female flesh.

'I had a gun,' Fiona continued. 'The pirate laughed and took it off me and then suddenly he fell on me like a mad beast. He did terrible things,' she added in a husky whisper. She shut her eyes and let her long wet lashes trembling with unshed tears lie on her cheeks. She needed to keep their minds on sex, not crime. The last thing she wanted was intelligent doubt.

She started to sob again. 'I heard the helicopter and they ran away.'

The troopers had no difficulty in following the sequence of events. Indeed, their problem was to tear their minds away from visualising certain salacious details.

'A gun,' one of them was sufficiently in command of himself to say. 'How come?'

'Loaded?' asked the other.

'Of course not. I tried to bluff him. I belong to the Glades Gun Club. I was carrying the revolver in the car but I wouldn't have ammunition of course. You know that. You only get what you use.'

'Where's the gun now?'

'The pirate took it. Oh, oh, they've melted my car down. What am I going to do?'

'You haven't been taken for ransom. I'm sorry, lady, but you got off lightly. Your insurance will settle the car damage.'

'What happened to me was far worse than ransom,' whispered Fiona. 'Get me out of this.'

The troopers radioed for a tow to take this undrivable car away to the repair shop. The computers were always replaced as soon as the insurance gave the go-ahead, new Connets

137

coming direct from the factory by special delivery.

Fiona herself was taken to the police station by helicopter, the troopers all solicitous help for the ravaged woman.

'Do you want to vidicom your husband?' they asked.

'No. Not yet. Not till I can see him and reassure him that I am OK.'

She managed a tremulous knock-kneed walk that had every man she came into contact with green with envy for the pirate's experience.

At the station a doctor examined Fiona. She lay comfortably whilst he slipped things up her fanny and found evidence of male invasion. She could only hope that Jamie had remained as honest as he appeared. If he had a criminal record his DNA would be on file and his spunk identified. She was relying on the dullness of his past behaviour.

Wearing a clean police shirt to cover the nakedness of her exposed bosom, Fiona was led to be interviewed by the captain of police.

Like the troopers he was a big man, handsome in a rugged way, with narrow blue eyes and pock-marked skin. He approached the interview carefully, not sure if she was hysterical after her recent experience.

'This interview is being recorded,' he stated at the outset. 'Would you like some other person present of your choice?'

'No, thank you,' she said huskily. 'I feel quite safe with you.'

'Your name?'

'Fiona Jasmine Bronson Cambridge.'

There was a silence. The fraternity who owned the beautiful monster machines was not large. They were also the top most echelon of society, the richest and the most powerful. The captain had a professional memory and political wisdom.

'Are you Mrs Rollo Cambridge?' he asked eventually, after his mental circuits had made the connection.

'Yes.' She moved slightly. Her dress exploded with light. The captain's eyes flickered.

'You care to tell me what happened, Mrs Cambridge? We can have your husband here, you know. Or a lady friend, if you prefer.'

138

'I'd rather get this done with,' she said, raising tragic eyes to meet his. 'I was driving along, not thinking, you know.'

When the captain drove it was an old computer-assist model, pre-Connet technology, and he had to use local roads and handle his car and concentrate. Not for him the powerways under the sky.

'I know,' he said.

'The car started to stop. I knew it was the pirates. We, we joke about it, we women, you know. We don't believe it will ever happen to us.'

She managed some tears at this point for the foolishness of women.

'I was damned if they'd get me. I had the gun and when they broke the doorlock I held it up.'

This was a detail she was proud of. She had lost her gun to Will the night she had played pirate and been taken. Now she could account for the loss convincingly. Guns were tightly controlled and even if she had never gone to the gun club again, she would have been checked up on. Since people had been forbidden to carry arms, violent deaths had dramatically decreased. The pirates hadn't killed a victim in years.

'Then what happened?'

Fiona hung her head. 'This really big man pushed into the car. He just laughed when he saw the gun. He reached over and took it straight out of my hand. He said something dirty to me, something very crude. I can't repeat it. I felt so humiliated. I slapped his face.'

'You did what?'

'I slapped his face. He went berserk.'

'What did he look like?'

Fiona took her time. She mustn't be too good. 'He was big, like you,' she faltered. 'Broad-shouldered. He looked enormous in the car and I guess I was terrified.' She began to pant, reliving the experience. 'He wore this black leather gear all sweaty and shiny. His chest was almost bare and he had tattoos. He was huge. And hairy.' She let her voice rise and burst into tears. Now she had the image of a big menacing gorilla in the car with her frail little self.

The captain moved protectively and Fiona came closer to him on the couch.

'He was dark,' she said and as the words came out of her mouth she saw the gaping wound in her story. It was no good describing the black-haired Will when she had blond pubic hairs in her crotch. And she mustn't be too specific. The police might hold DNA records of several of the pirates. 'He seemed to loom over me and block out the light. Maybe he wasn't dark, it was just the light at his back, but that was how he seemed to me.'

'Did he have an eyepatch?'

'An eyepatch,' she echoed stupidly. 'No. I don't think so. He had a bandanna around his forehead and it was down on his eyebrows, but I am sure he had two eyes. You mean you know these people?'

'We know their leader. He wears an eyepatch. They call him Will Kid.'

'Who?'

'Will Kid. He's a very dangerous man and a very powerful one in his way. Bad all through. He leads the biggest gang of pirates in the city in these parts. Others only operate on his say-so. He's a hard man and we would love to get our hands on him and take him out of the scene. You were lucky you didn't meet him.'

'Will Kid,' said Fiona, as if fascinated.

'That's not his real name. He uses it. It's some pirate's name from back in the seventeenth century.'

'What is his real name?'

'Henson Carne. A rogue and bloodthirsty villain. Yet I've been told he's attractive in a way, to women, I mean. I don't mean to insult you,' added the captain hastily.

'Captain, I want to tell you what really happened.' Fiona spoke in a low voice, her lip trembling. 'It's why I don't want Rollo here. I don't want him to realise how bad I am.'

She laid a hand on the captain's chest, leaning forward earnestly, allowing the shirt to come open so that her breast was visible. She saw his eyes dip and come back to her face. He didn't say anything.

'When the pirate was in the car,' she said shakily, 'he had

this terrific aura. I don't know whether he knew my gun was loaded or not. I think he enjoyed the risk. I hit him and he grabbed my arm and twisted it back behind me and tore my dress. No man has ever treated me like that. It made me feel really peculiar. He was so powerful and I was so, so weak. Then he kissed me. Please, you have to understand. Someone has to understand. These people are mythic figures. They star in big Screen drama all the time, impossibly romantic and sexy. And there I was, being kissed by this incredible man. I didn't know if he was an actor or the real thing. I was so confused. I began to respond. I admit it. I began to respond to his hot lips.'

The captain reached over and wiped a tear from her cheek. 'You're scarred,' he said. 'How did you get hurt?'

'A silly accident at home.' Fiona liked the thin white line left by the bullet. She could have had her skin treated but she thought it gave her a wicked, sexy look.

'To what extent did you respond?' asked the captain. His voice was low and gravelly, almost caressing.

'I gave him my breast.' Fiona took her hanging breast and held it up to the captain, as close to his face as she could. It was blue-veined and porcelain in texture.

'He went to haul up my skirt,' she continued, keeping her breast where it was and speaking in a low intimate whisper. 'I lifted my bottom so he could do it more easily. His mate was yelling at him to hurry up and he was laughing. I felt mad. I was filled with lust. I thought I could delay him and it pleased me. I took his hand right into me, like this.'

She held the captain's eyes with her own. She took his unresisting hand and led it between her parted legs, on and into her fanny. He felt her jutting smoothness and the warm wetness below and within. Nothing impeded his hand in her groin. It slid to feel her arched taut buttocks held by the webbing of her harness. A thumb slipped into her whilst his fingers tried and failed to find her intimate fleece. His face dropped so he could touch her breast with his lips and Fiona put her arms round his neck and drew him closer, into her body.

'You are very like the pirate,' she whispered. 'Big and

strong and very male. It was only when he got out his sex and began to thrust towards me that I realised what I had done. I had practically invited him into my body. I didn't mean it. I was acting out a fantasy and suddenly it turned to nightmare.' She moved on the captain's thumb so that it went deeper within her.

'I understand,' he said. 'We all have our fantasies and you lead a protected life, there in the Zoo. It's no wonder you lost control.'

'I did. I admit it. I'm so ashamed. I wanted to be rogered by this wild man who lived outside the law. It's so wicked. I'm so wicked. And he fucked me really hard, you know.'

The captain swallowed.

'And I came. I had an orgasm. I said I was raped but when the pirate took me, I had a sexual orgasm.' She rotated her fanny on the captain's thumb and tasted the sweat that broke out on his forehead. Rainbow light flickered from her dress, dazzling his overloaded senses.

'He turned to his mate. "You want her," he yelled. I started to scream. The other one got into the car. I was shouting "no, no, no", and then the helicopter was there and the pirates were gone. I guess I passed out. I don't even know if the second man took me.'

'I think you saved yourself by allowing that man to take you. He probably would have raped you, anyway. Because you inadvertently gave him some encouragement he took longer and spoiled the kidnap. You have been a very clever and a very brave woman.'

Fiona was holding the captain by the neck, riding up and down on his thumb.

'You think so?' she whispered. 'I was living in a fantasy and it turned horrid.'

'Sometimes,' said the captain, 'you can't resist acting out a fantasy.' He removed his hand from under Fiona and stood up, releasing his clothes. She fell back on the couch, watching him.

'I'll edit the frigging tape,' he said. 'No man can resist you. You are the most beautiful, the most bewitching thing I have ever seen. I should think even Kid himself would wave away half a million credits of lost ransom money to have you. You're worth anything.'

He came over her, a big man with a paunch. His prick was short and thick and full of juice. As he rose and fell, taking her firmly but without frills, her dress shimmered surreally.

Fiona loved it. She didn't need to do this. It was no part of her plan. She did it because she liked it, because she was elated at what she had learned about Will, and because the captain reminded her of Will in some subtle way. There is not that much difference between the hunter and the hunted.

She had herself played pirate and if he had proof of that, this man could put her inside a prison for tens of years. He could break Rollo and ruin his life. He was her adversary, her dupe, and she adored having him risk his job to lay her.

She fucked with abandon, clinging to his tough work-hardened body. He was grizzled, an older man than she was used to, but it did him no disservice in her eyes. Moreover, as a policeman, this man risked his life to protect her and her sort. The pirates and the police were both armed and occasionally one or the other was killed. They played life for real.

Fiona was caught in her own fantasy. Almost she believed the tale she had told.

She could only hope Jamie's spunk was not on record. If that was so, she would have been a little too clever. But the congress with the captain was insurance, in its way.

She lost herself and her doubts and thoughts in climax. There was no problem with orgasm here. This bull of a man was not Jamie, and though she fooled him, he was a genuine threat to her, a real power. Fiona loved power.

They took her home much later. She begged to be left alone with Rollo though they offered to come in and explain and help. She said she could manage.

She went first to shower and to douche and to change into a loose robe. With wet hair and looking surprisingly childlike, free of make-up and sophisticated clothing, she joined Rollo in their sitting room. She knew already that bad behaviour seemed to cleanse her temporarily. She looked her most innocent, her most saintly, after her wickedest behaviour.

He was bathed in music, a glass in his hand, half asleep. A sheaf of specifications lay disregarded at his side.

Fiona went over to him and knelt before him and laid her head on his knee.

'I missed you,' he said. It was not a condemnation. He touched her wet hair.

'I'm very tired, Rollo.'

'Are you all right?'

'Yes.'

She saw his blue eyes crinkle as he grew puzzled. Then they went cold. She could tell what he was thinking.

'I'm going to take a pill and go to sleep. I'll tell you in the morning.'

'Should I know now?'

'It's all right, Rollo. I promise.'

'I'm on satellite tomorrow from eight o'clock our time.'

'Can you take the evening off? I'll do a special meal. I have news and I think you'll be pleased but I am so tired I can hardly keep my head up right now.'

He was thinking she had a lover. 'You know I trust you, Fee.' he said.

'I know.'

'I couldn't share you.'

Her senses thrilled. He might not be getting it up her, but his feelings were still strong enough to make him consider her his territory and not to be violated by others. The problem was that his sexual motor needed overhauling and getting back to work and Fiona had confidence in herself as chief mechanic.

'Look forward to tomorrow night,' she said lightly. 'Keep it free, darling. We'll enjoy ourselves.'

She got her feet and blew him a kiss.

She slept late the next day and woke feeling very good. Successful impudence gave a much brighter glow to the day than tedious virtue ever did for her. She rang for Janine and invited the girl into her bed. They cuddled for a while and Janine played dreamily between Fiona's legs, sweetly fingering the erotic flesh. Whilst she frotted Fiona's clitoris

144

into delicious arousal, Fiona kissed her mouth and breasts. Her mind ran on the comparison between the captain of police and the maid, the soft youth of the one and the hard sexual wisdom of the other. Janine's fingers were dear little intruders. The captain's thumb had been as thick as a slender penis, and as knowing.

At last, and with reluctance, she drew back. 'Listen,' she said. 'I'm going to get dressed now. I have a couple of calls to make and then I want to go shopping. I need a dress and I need some fancy food. I am wining and dining Rollo tonight because I have things to tell him that will please him. I know I've been neglecting you lately because our affairs have been a little complicated but you mustn't take it to heart. I love you, baby.'

'I'll help you to look wonderful tonight,' said Janine. 'What about the dress you bought yesterday? Has Mr Cambridge seen it? It's so beautiful.'

Fee smiled. It was a good idea to wear the same dress she had committed her various crimes in. It added a piquancy to the coming occasion. It was a pity that she alone would be able to appreciate that.

'It's in the linen basket,' she said. 'It's been torn. Can you see if it can be mended? It needs laundering too. If you can fix it, I'll wear it.'

She spent a pleasant day. She informed the insurance company about her car and they checked immediately with the police who informed them that the car had indeed been hacked and taken off the highway in an undrivable condition, and that there was independent confirmation that Mrs Cambridge had been assaulted though not kidnapped. Jamie's spunk was earning its living. The insurance company agreed to forward funds to Fiona's account for the new Connet. Then Fiona had the repair shop holding her car send over her luggage from it by special delivery. She explained it was a children's computer and was fragile and so could they handle it with especial care.

The bank informed her when the money was credited to her account. She moved the money straight into one of Rollo's business accounts. She took delivery of her own

145

Connet and unwrapped it. She rewrapped it expertly using the box she had got from Jamie containing the hacked Connet that he had stolen for her. Now her own perfect Connet was in an official autofactory box. She sent it by special delivery, using a different company, to the repair shop. The repair shop installed it and the car was fully functioning and back in her personal hangar by the evening.

So far so good.

She concocted a meal based around shrimps embedded in part frozen fresh pineapple pieces, splinters of sharp fruit and ice containing the salty morsels, with a walnut and mayonnaise salad, asparagus tips in lemon butter and honey ants. Then she bathed, allowing Janine to sponge her gently all over, lingering in the nooks and crannies of her body to remind her pleasantly of their presence. As she lazed there in the scented foam, eyes half-closed, Janine titillating her private places, it occurred somewhat naughtily to Fiona that one day in the distant future, when she was tired of Janine or Janine of her, it might be nice to have a male maid. Someone young, it should be, maybe eighteen, a tender bud of new-fledged manhood. It would please her to have some golden boy to service her body and care for it, before getting Rollo to satisfy her lust.

Janine washed and dried and dressed her hair in artful confusion, a silky tangle that invited the hand to enter. Then Janine oiled her body all over so that her skin had a dull pearlised lustre and she gleamed and faintly caught the light.

The rainbow dress was perfect. Fee slid into it quite naked, it being her sole garment.

Rollo was late but he came. That was the main thing.

She sat very still in the room when he came in. For a moment he didn't see her, for when she was still, the dress was a dull silvery-black. The table was laid with beautiful food and there was greenish-white Portuguese wine and a heavy ruby burgundy.

Rollo was tired. He stood a moment, dressed in his usual midnight blue, his eyes a bright gleam as he rubbed at his shoulder muscles. Fiona knew she could do him better than that.

146

'Hello,' she said, her voice pitched low with the slight husky catch in it that made it so potent a weapon in her sexual armoury.

'I didn't see you there. This looks very nice.'

He came down two steps and she rose to meet him, a cascade of brilliant colour and light. His breath hissed.

'Do you want to bathe before we eat?' she asked. 'Nothing will spoil.'

He nodded gratefully. She followed him to his bathroom and took his discarded clothes. She ran water for him and put herbs and minerals and oils in it. He stepped in and lay back, permitting her to perform for him what Janine had performed for her.

She sponged his body very gently all over whilst he half slept in the buoyant watery caress. She lifted his manhood and washed under and around his balls, between his legs and within the cleft of his buttocks. Gradually his lassitude changed from one of exhaustion to a pleasing erotic daze as the sponge stroked in and around his groin. He was lapped in sensuality, no demands being made upon him except that he enjoy himself and relax.

Eventually he climbed out and Fee dried him and made him lie down. She oiled him, entering every crevice, and massaged him, releasing the tension knotted into his muscles. It was whilst he was lying on his back that she became aware he was watching her. Those very blue eyes were unwavering.

She was a shimmer of three-dimensional colour as she moved down on to his sexual equipment. She massaged his penis until it hardened and she stroked the lengthening, thickening shaft.

She let him feel her hands on his balls, cupping and cradling, lifting and separating and gently rolling. She pushed his knees apart and went behind his balls, stroking and knuckling at his rear entrance.

His penis curved gracefully, half erect. Fiona ignored its lissom invitation and finished the massage.

He put on a short black robe, roughly belted, with a dragon climbing up its back. They went through to eat.

'I love the dress,' he said. 'It's worthy of you.'

She smiled and handed him the notification from the bank of the money in the company account.

He looked at it, puzzled. Money was his working resource and he had a good idea all the time of what was where and this was a colossal sum he knew nothing about.

'I don't understand,' he said.

'It's the money for the patent. Is it enough?

'Have you sold the car? It's worth more than this, Fee.'

'The car is in the hangar. It's perfect. Is this enough?'

'Yes. More than enough if I use it as a credit base. Where did it come from, Fee?'

She smiled, a Mona Lisa smile.

'Your jewellery? I don't want that.'

'No. I don't think I own that much.'

'What, then?'

'I'll tell you after we've eaten.'

His eyes flicked up to the wall. Where Jamie had a giant Screen, the Cambridges kept their collection of original art, Picasso, Poussin, Jackson Pollock.

'Fiona,' he said. 'You go out a lot and you dress fabulously and you are dog tired when you get home. What have you been doing?'

'I haven't whored for it, Rollo.' She was amused. She was almost telling the truth.

His hand trembled on his glass. His prick retained the memory of her hands, so recently stroking and arousing him. 'I told you I couldn't share you, Fee. I know you are wild. That scar. You are so beautiful it drives me crazy. Sometimes I wonder why some other man doesn't try to take you away from me.'

'What would you do?'

'I'd kill him. Or you.'

'Then it's a good thing I'm not going away, Rollo. Eat your food.'

By the time they were eating fruit and drinking a luscious grapey wine, they had moved to the couch. Fiona told him what she had done.

'I've pulled an insurance scam.'

'What?'

'I acquired a computer in meltdown. I took the car out on the highway and disconnected our Connet from it and installed the hacked one. I triggered the hacking alarm and when the police came I said the pirates had attacked me.'

'Don't tease me, Fee. I'm not in the mood.'

'I was at the police station last night. Today they confirmed that I had been hacked to the insurance company who released the money, which I transferred into this account. The repair shop re-installed the original computer, though they don't know that. We have the car back. And the money.'

'It's illegal.'

'It sure as hell is.'

He started to laugh. 'You crazy witch. I almost believe you. What if you had been caught out?'

'You'd get visiting rights to my cell.'

'You planned all this for me?'

'For us.'

Her eyes were hooded as she watched him. He wasn't stupid and his mind was working over what she had told him.

'How did you explain why you weren't kidnapped?'

'I told the police I had been raped on the spot and the HeliPolice arriving scared the pirates off.'

'Were you raped?' His voice was cool.

'There were no pirates.'

'Weren't you checked at the police station? Why wasn't I called?'

'I begged them not to. Sure I was checked.'

'Then they know you weren't raped.'

'I had semen in me.'

Rollo's face went dark. He reached a hand into her hair and gripped it tightly. 'Whose?'

She didn't answer. She felt a rising excitement. So he really cared.

His hand slid round and held her throat. Her pulse worked madly, fluttering under his palm like a trapped wild thing.

'Whose?' he said again, his voice bitter and cold as a glacier.

'I milked you, you bastard, whilst you were asleep.'

He stared at her, working it over, seeing if he believed her. His hand started to relax.

'You clever, beautiful, magical bitch,' he whispered. 'You succubus.'

He kissed her hungrily and she gave herself to him wildly. He lifted her up, sliding her dress up over her naked hips. His robe feel open over his erect golden sex. He lowered her onto it, slowly, allowing her sex to flower open around the head of his prick and engulf it and swallow it inside so that he sank deep upwards into her hot clinging wet flesh. He sat her down in his lap and pushed upwards till he was fully sheathed within her and could feel her tight pressure all around his swollen muscle.

He kissed her greedily. 'You vampire,' he said. 'Thief. Criminal.'

Fiona clenched her interior muscles and he laughed, his eyes brilliant and as blazing with colour as her laser dress. She tipped wine from her glass into his mouth and then lapped up what spilled. He fell with her on him and felt her rip his robe apart and kiss his chest, sucking his nipples. She dripped wine into the cup at the base of his throat and she drank from the skin.

His cock swelled with pleasure and he arched up with her riding him like a horse. He reached for and found the fastening of her dress and released the bodice so that it fell away from her. Her beautiful pendant breasts swung free, the flesh pearlised and dully glowing, the nipples dark with lustrous promise, sweetmeats of desire.

Rollo caught a breast with his mouth and felt its soft weight on his face as he nuzzled up into it. He found the nipple and sucked it into his mouth, feeling it firm and lengthen and tasting it with his tongue. He sucked hard so that the aureole came within him and the breast distended. Fiona moaned and he felt her tighten round his prick. Her cunt gloved him closely, clinging, sucking, gripping him. He sobbed for breath and then pulled out of her, knocking her sideways on to the deep furry pile of the floor covering. She went on her back and he was over her immediately. He put his slick-wet prick between her lovely breasts and rolled it there, feeling in their yielding pillowy fullness a cool clasp after the heat of her volcanic interior.

He moulded her breasts, one in each hand, and masturbated between them. Then he moved back and rolled Fiona on to her front. He stood up at her head, facing her back, and he lifted her legs right up off the ground so that her body arched in a hard curve, her head at his feet. He supported her thighs and held them apart with his hands. Standing between her legs, holding her helpless, he laid his stiff prick in her slit forced moistly openly before him. Her bare bulging mound strained and he frotted himself the length of her vulva, allowing the weight of his erect member to hold itself down on her dark quivering flesh. Then he removed it and crouched down, sinking his face into her slit. He sucked her whole mound as it thrust bluntly into the air. Then, remaining straddled over her, he sucked her to climax.

Her musk-fruit was divine, dark and delicious and heady on his tongue. Her convolutions of flesh stretched in his mouth and he licked harshly her full length before lapping deep within her tumid hole. He felt it fluttering and the muscles in it contracting around his thrusting forceful tongue. He ran his tongue round inside her and set his lips to suck as though he would draw her into his mouth entire. He bit her vulva and felt it vibrate between his teeth.

Then his mouth was flooded with her wine and he heard her sob as she came. He bit and sucked down and then finally he allowed her to roll down and over on to her back, lying on the floor. Her eyes were wicked green slits and in her suffused face the livid white line of her scar stood out clearly.

Rollo pulled off her dress, his balls aching for penetration. He opened her slack heavy legs and knelt between them, finding her wet little clitoris quiveringly erect. He thumbed it and tongued it and then he tipped wine from his own glass into her body. Bending his head he drank from the chalice of her sex. Then he reached over to where the remaining food was. He found a meringue stuffed with cream and with one firm blow he crushed it between her buttocks so that the cream oozed and spread and smeared all around her rear.

He assaulted the mess with his face, his tongue darting and probing till he found and penetrated her greasy creamy rear orifice.

Fiona's whole body was jerking with desire as she attempted to masturbate herself with his tongue up her backside. He felt the rapid muscular contractions of her valve and he knew her whole vagina was flexing powerfully.

He tormented her no longer. His cock was crazed to be inside her. He had always adored her greediness and lack of restraint. He wiped his face and looked down at his frantic pleading wife, desperate to be filled.

He remembered her talk of rape and his skin flushed darkly. 'I'd kill the man who took you against your will,' he said harshly.

'Fuck me,' she croaked.

His hand groped for and found a second cake. With Fiona watching him he impaled his rigid cock through its sticky structure. Leaving it speared on his sex he began very slowly to insert himself, at long last, within Fiona's cunt.

The bulbous red head ruptured the tight ring of her entrance and slid on fatly within the wet slimy dark of her. As he pushed, the meringue cracked and broke away so that cream spilled out over his shaft, into his pubic hair and on to his swollen balls.

He felt the cool cream and the slightly rough meringue, the whole sticky ooze of it, in contrast to her slick wet sliding satin heat. His prick was silky hot and sticky cool. He pushed slowly his full length savouring the clench of her on him, knowing she was gripping him as tightly as she was able. Her cunt was as clever and tricksy as a laundered bank account, as a creative tax return, infinitely rich and endlessly satisfying. He remembered after one of his earliest big deals stuffing banknotes up inside her, seeing how much money he could fit within her, then all the fun of getting it out again. He had masturbated himself into handfuls of money that was already wet with her juices. She had eaten a hundred-credit note smeared with his sperm before his eyes, laughing as she did so.

His cock rippled and he had to take care not to come.

Her cunt, its craving for his full swollen muscle at last answered, tried to milk him, gripping and sucking at him, reluctant to allow his withdrawal before his renewed thrust.

His own eyes were slitted as he concentrated ferociously on drawing out the pleasure of fucking to gluttonous lengths.

He drove in again and again, seeing her eyes were unfocused now and knowing that in his mastery of her body he could take her to heights of sexual experience she was unable to find anywhere else. She was high on him, drugged with sex, her pupils black pinpricks in the ice-green of her eyes.

He felt her lose control. She vibrated on his shaft and then she orgasmed, seething round his cock so hard he thought it would split and burst open before his spunk was released. He gave a great cry as his balls exploded and violently he thrust and thrust and thrust again.

Fiona came back to herself as her cunt fluttered in the aftermath of climax. Little aftershudders shook her.

She was soft and loose and trembling as she cradled his spent cock within her, her post-orgasmic ripples soothing Rollo's throbbing cock, stroking it into peace. Spunk trickled from her entrance around the base of his shaft to mix with the violated cake where their thighs rubbed together.

'You superb bitch,' he said hoarsely. He withdrew himself slowly from her, watching his slimy shrinking prick leave her wallow bit by bit. A golden glow spread from his peaceful balls up through his stomach. His prick struck his thigh softly with a wet thud and he grinned. Fee was watching him from under heavy lids, her mouth slightly curved and her whole body soft and tension-free.

Rollo looked down at what he had just vacated. The luscious flesh had bruised and darkened to a plummy glow. The labia were puffy and sticky and the slit itself dribbled cream-flecked spunk in a pearly trail across the marble tones of her pale thighs. The upreared dome of her naked mound was warm satin, pale gold above white and purple.

She was a sluttish queen of lust, sumptuously equipped to strip a man raw. She was his. Rollo bent his golden head and gorged on their come.

Fiona was dizzy and spaced-out with satisfied desire. She was aware of Rollo's cool gentle mouth about her parts, cleaning her and bringing her back to life. She opened her eyes wider and slowly began to focus on the beautiful man at her cunt. She smiled a wide catlike smile of pure satisfaction. At that moment she would have died happy.

Rollo lifted his head and looked at her. She saw his blond mane was almost black with sweat. He smiled back at her, then swept her up into his arms and carried her through into their bedroom.

He laid her out on the bed and placed himself so that he was face down in her groin, feet to the pillow, his head resting comfortably on her thigh. He reached out with his tongue and vibrated her clitoris sharply so that pinpricks of desire radiated up through her love-sodden body. He spread his legs so that he straddled her and she could look down into his sex.

'Fuck my arse, baby, the way I like it,' he said.

She reached for the oil and began to massage his rear. She took her time, savouring his small muscular contractions. Then she held his buttocks apart with her hands and licked the oily place, pushing with her tongue and feeling his tightness reject her.

Now she put in a finger and rolled it about. He moved pleasurably and bit her clitoris gently so that she was speared again with little lustful prickles.

Fiona opened his backside and slid in a second finger. He groaned and writhed on her as she worked them slowly into him as deep as they would go.

After a while she got a third finger in. Now he was shuddering on her hand and sweating, his valve held right open as she tortured him gently with her three fingers, trying to hold them wide apart to make the violation more severe.

'That's enough,' he said from between clenched teeth.

'The hell it is,' she snarled and she reached for the vibrator she now kept her side of the bed. She slotted the terrible thing in, driving it slowly home, and she heard him howl and jump. Joyously she switched it on and watched greedily as it shook in his riven orifice. He squirmed and writhed before

154

her fascinated eyes, the plastic column clenched between his buttocks and feverishly jerking.

She began to smack his buttocks, seeing the imprint of her hand on his smooth skin. She smacked with as much sting as she was able and his cheeks began to glow hotly, still with the automatic device leaping inside his arse.

'I'm going to come,' he cried out, half-strangled. Immediately she released his arse by switching the thing off and pulling it until it was almost out, with only its head inside him. She wormed down the bed and took his gland into her mouth. She stroked his stomach gently to allow him to recover a little.

'Come inside me, Rollo,' she asked. 'Unless you think you are good for one more time.'

'I don't know, honey. I'm out of practice.'

Fee slipped him safely within her fanny and with delight felt him expanding to fill her. She sighed with pleasure and ran her hands through his sweat-soaked hair. At that moment she could not have cared less if she never saw another pirate. This man was enough, more than enough, if only he could be brought to do this more often.

Without him even moving he was bringing her up to climax again, so beautiful was his growing cock within her. She felt her own texture change and began to pump herself on him.

He came quickly but she was with him and they clung fiercely until at last they fell apart, dizzy with each other.

'You sensational thief,' said Rollo. 'You should have been a pirate yourself.'

He fell asleep.

12

TransFlow threw a launch party.

This was an in-the-flesh social occasion to wine and dine and entertain everyone who might be of use in the venture. Thus there were politicians, financiers, top construction people, lawyers, accountants and government men – anyone, in short, who might help with getting the new company successfully floated. The gathering was leavened with media people and celebs, all to add decorative gloss. TransFlow needed to look important, successful and confident at this stage. It only needed enough backers to believe in it for the dream to become reality.

They hired a hotel up in the snow zone where the air was thin. The guests came by microlight, helibuzz, helicopter or private plane.

Fee had already been interviewed by the media in her home concerning TransFlow, in which she was playing an increasing role. Her combination of intellectual mastery and sexual heat cast a spell over her audience that her exotic beauty did nothing to lessen. Fee Cambridge was the stuff of men's dreams.

The evening began with the directors, including Fee and Rollo, welcoming their guests, all two hundred of them. Then they all sat down to eat. Conscious that every woman present would attempt to outshine her neighbour, Fee avoided peacocking. All the men were in sober formal black and white, Rollo looking indecently handsome in the severe clothing. To emulate them Fee wore a dress of stark simplicity, bone-white, dead-white, just a pale shaped sheath from cleavage to thigh without any decoration or relief save that provided by her voluptuous curves within it. Round her neck she wore a fine strip of black velvet. She mimicked the men in her clothes, and the contrast highlighted how very different her body was from theirs. The dress clung so that her shape was intimately revealed, her pendant breasts, her slim thighs, her smooth belly, and the dress was almost the same colour as her skin.

Her black hair was strained hard back shaping her skull, its thickness hidden in confinement. She wore no jewellery whatsoever, the only woman in the building not to do so. She was all white and black with only her green eyes lending her colour. They were the precise colour of the Rhône where it spates from the heart of the glacier.

She should have looked dowdy. Instead it was she who looked magnificent, whilst the richly dressed women around her looked cheap and their diamonds but gaudy glitter.

She drew every man's eye including that of her husband.

After the meal and Rollo's brief speech, there was an entertainment whilst the guests digested their food and cracked nuts and bad jokes and drank liqueurs.

The hall dimmed and a murmur of talk stilled as the players came on. There was a ripple of delighted shock as they entered and a burst of spontaneous applause. The man and two women wore nothing but a tiny black satin *cache-sexe* each, yet their bodies gleamed with oil and rioted in a fantasy of colours. All three of them were painted all over, every scrap of skin, so that colour and pattern and story blazed over their shining skins.

The man was an animal, a black animal with golden spots rippling over his hide. His legs and arms were striped gold and tan and buff and chestnut, and he wore a tail, a long firm black and orange stripy tail. Fiona was irresistibly reminded of the tigers around the Zoo.

The newly-formed Publicity Department of TransFlow was earning its keep. They needed to be stylish right now. There would be a time for mud and machines later on.

The two women were clothed in the jungle. Rich dark green exploded on fronds painted across their shoulders and upper bodies. Butterflies flamed across their breasts. A dragonfly shimmered, his long body aquiver over their stomachs, tail down, disappearing behind that scrap of black material.

157

Each woman had a gorilla on her back and snakes writhing up her legs. Green grew upwards from their feet.

Somewhere, drums beat.

The three began to dance together, their bodies an ecstatic union of fecund life. They ducked and curved and twined sinuously round each other, a dazzle of dark colour and life.

As the drum beat became an insistent urge to copulation, their dance became more suggestive, more arousing, and the tail of the man-tiger slid between the thighs of the girls and appeared to have a life of its own.

The company got a little hot. Fee found that her vagina pulsed gently in the rhythm of the drumbeat.

Finally the three performers were leaping up and down in a frenzy, throwing their upper bodies about in an apparent abandonment to sexual craving and satisfaction. Yet they barely touched one another and never lost the insistent beat nor their poise and balance.

They danced to a frenetic and indecent climax, the music stopped and the lights came up. The three linked hands, bowed and ran off.

The audience howled its delight.

Now was the time to mingle and dance and socialise. The hotel staff cleared all the debris of the meal away and served drinks. Fiona and Rollo touched lips and went to do their separate duty.

Ten minutes later, talking to a government official with more real power in the land than many a politician, Fee remembered that not long ago she had lain naked over the body of an outlaw whilst another man forced his muscle into her unwilling body. Unwilling to begin with. She had even begun to enjoy the degradation of having two men take her, one after the other, without consulting her will.

That sordid violation contrasted oddly with the luxurious wealth that now lapped about her. She could see that the official she was talking to was turned on by her. Would he want her still if he knew she had chosen to rut in the mire with a pirate?

Even the catfight with Mammet had more reality than the

company she was now in. She would bet that she could get better sex down there in the city than from any man present in this gathering of the great and the good and the powerful.

Except for Rollo.

After a time she made her way over to Jamie. He looked a little bewildered but he was holding his own, more so than the girl he had brought with him, a pretty bourgeoise.

Fee behaved beautifully.

'Jamie,' she cried huskily. 'I'm so glad you came.'

'I was surprised to get the invitation,' he said. His eyes took her in hungrily.

'Jacomo is in charge tonight. He's our head of PR. But Rollo and I fixed the guest list with him. I wanted you to come, Jamie. Now, introduce me to your friend.'

'Sonya, this is Fee Cambridge. Sonya Marston.'

'Hello, Mrs Cambridge This is very splendid tonight.'

'Isn't it? All meant to impress those with deep pockets. We need them right now. But call me Fee, Sonya. Jamie and I go way back. I used to work at the autofactory, you know.'

'Jamie said,' It was clear Sonya hadn't believed him till now.

'May I borrow him, Sonya? I would like to dance with him if I may.'

'Go ahead,' said the girl with a little laugh. She had little option.

As they swirled away into the crowd, Fee became intimate.

'It's good to see you, really good,' she murmured throatily into Jamie's ear.

'You've not been back to the house.'

'No. I've been fantastically busy with the company launch. And Rollo is a little suspicious. Like all guys who roam, he is very possessive. I can't afford to lose him, Jamie. Please understand that.'

'It's your brutal frankness and self-interest that turn me on so much, you witch.'

'Yes. I can be myself with you. I don't have to pose as a good girl.' She laughed and shimmied closer to him. Jamie groaned in his throat.

'Now, to get to business. The reason why I invited you tonight is because I have developed new software for TransFlow. I'm patenting it and setting up the computer department. I need a reliable top manager. One who can work with people and get the best from them, one who knows how to hire and fire, and one I can trust to have absolute loyalty to the company. To me.'

'Are you offering me a job?'

'Yes I am. At about twice your current salary. But there's a catch.'

'Which is?'

'If TransFlow fails, your job vanishes. No security.'

'And if TransFlow succeeds?'

'You might be able to buy a car in a couple of years.'

'It's quite an offer.'

'You have a week. Call me and let me know. I need someone and it's growing exponentially at the moment. I'll have the legal department mail you a sample contract of employment. High risk, high rewards. Shape up or get out. No room for mistakes. You understand?'

'I understand.'

'The risk will be reduced, however, by the patent.'

'I'm not with you.'

'Even if TransFlow gets rocky, I will be able to sell the software. I could set up a marketing company quite independent of TransFlow. If you were not personally part of the failure, I would guarantee you the transition to that company. So unless it was your own fault, there would have to be two company failures before you were out of work. And you would have enhanced skills and be re-employable, in that event.'

'It sounds good, Fee. You make it sound good.'

'If you decided to leave us and took more than your experience elsewhere, we would grind your balls to dust, Jamie. We don't allow our systems to be pillaged. We expect loyalty and if we don't get it, we use all the power at our command to crush.'

'I believe you, you cold-hearted bitch. The effect it has on me is make me want to rip that indecent dress off your body

160

and synch with you here in the middle of all these people. I'd like to make those icy-clear eyes of yours cloud over.'

Fiona grinned. There was no doubt that Jamie had come on terrifically these last few years. The guy had backbone. However, it was best to get things crystal clear. 'Sex is not part of the contract, Jamie.'

'I know. You made one contract and that's with Rollo. The rest of us get what's left over. I don't know why we bother. You bewitch, Fee. There's black magic in you.'

She laughed, delighted.

'How did you get on with the computer I got you?'

'The what?'

'The melted Connet I stole for you and risked my job for, dammit.'

'Oh, that. I got too busy. I threw it away.'

Then things got bad again. Work was fine but Rollo seemed to have forgotten his re-arousal. Fiona felt that her appetite was whetted for him and things were worse than ever now that he had turned monkish again. Of course, there was her half-started plan involving Janine.

Janine now routinely bathed her and massaged her intimately and sucked Fee's sex till she rolled with pleasure at the girl's knowing lips. In return she kissed and played with Janine till the girl was all one red sexual flush. But always she remained careful not to rupture that precious membrane.

Janine's sexual awakening changed her, so that she even walked differently. She carried her body with a proud assurance that made her more succulent than ever. Her youthfulness highlighted the voluptuous resonances that had developed in her flesh. She was a fig ripe for bursting.

'Darling,' said Fiona one day. 'Come to my bedroom tonight.'

'Tonight?'

'Yes.' Fiona named the time. 'Come then. Don't be afraid.'

'I'm not afraid,' said Janine and she smiled.

Fiona had bought sleeping pills at half the strength Rollo usually had and substituted them. He was very tired and slept heavily, but he was only drugged to half the extent he thought he was.

At the appointed time Janine came. Usually they played in her bedroom. This was something new.

'Now,' whispered Fiona. 'Take off your robe, sweetie.'

Janine obliged, a triumphant peachy bloom on her skin.

'Climb on the bed.'

'Won't he wake?'

'I don't think so. Not properly. Here, come between us.'

Janine stretched herself between Fee and Rollo. Fiona leant over the girl and began to touch Rollo. Skilfully she aroused him a little.

Apart from Rollo himself on that one other occasion, Janine had still not touched a man. She watched breathless.

'Now stroke him.' Fiona guided Janine's hand and tremblingly the girl touched Rollo's sleeping flesh.

He quivered.

Fiona encouraged Janine to cup his balls, to hold them and get to know them. She taught Janine how to play with a man but not hurt him in such a tender place.

Janine was an avid learner.

Rollo stirred in his sleep and murmured.

'Let your breast press against him,' whispered Fee.

Janine obeyed. Rollo moved and his lips formed against the breast. 'Fee,' he muttered.

'Touch his prick again,' ordered Fiona. Her eyes glittered. It excited her to see Janine at his sleeping vulnerable places. It excited her because Janine obeyed her and Rollo knew nothing of what they did with him.

'Use your lips,' she said. She wanted to see Janine go down on him.

The girl took Rollo's flaccid member into her mouth and rolled it on her tongue like a fine wine. Fiona smiled, catlike, and allowed her hand to slide under Janine's buttocks. She stroked the warm soft outer pussy whilst Janine gently sucked her husband. The girl sighed and squirmed.

'You realise Rollo is a little out of the ordinary,' said Fee.

'He's fabulous,' said Janine thickly.

'I mean he's circumcised, darling. Did you realise?'

Janine released Rollo's cock and looked at it lovingly. 'I thought he was a little different from the men on the Screen but you can't ask anyone about something like that. You look so stupid.'

Fee reached over Janine and lifted Rollo's member. He murmured again and the two women grinned wickedly at each other.

'See here,' said Fiona. 'This is his glans, permanently exposed because his foreskin has been removed. You already know the little eye where his juice comes out.'

'I long for the day.'

'*Moi aussi, chérie*. Being circumcised is supposed to be cleaner. And it desensitises the tip so that he can protract intercourse.'

Janine blushed and looked into Rollo's groin. Then, before the eyes of the two women, Rollo came erect. He muttered in his sleep and his hand jerked. His eyeballs rolled from side to side under his closed lids and his hand came round and grasped his own cock. He began roughly to masturbate himself, stopping every so often. His lips moved.

Fiona could feel Janine trembling. She pressed her own naked length against the warm softness of the girl and felt excitement course through her. She let a hand come round and she clasped a breast, holding the nipple.

Rollo suddenly ejaculated. Janine jerked convulsively as the pearly white stream gushed erratically from the end of Rollo's prick. He sighed and smiled and rolled on to his side, falling into a deeper level of sleep.

Fee pulled Janine round and stuffed the girl's fingers into her own cunt. She began to ride up and down on them, wishing they were longer and harder, desperate to complete her climax.

When she came, she kissed Janine passionately, rubbing breast to breast, stretching herself out and massaging Janine's fingers with her wet pussy. She had all but lost control, seeing Rollo like that, and she hoped she had not frightened the girl off.

She pulled back and looked at her. 'School's over for tonight,' she said softly.

163

'I look forward to the next lesson,' whispered Janine.

After the maid had gone back to her own quarters, Fee looked at her husband savagely. Her thoughts had been turning back to Will Kid recently and now her eyes hardened and became brilliant as she thought of being back down there in the city with him, risking everything. His big rough body, his harsh unpredictable ways, his conferral of sexual bliss – she wanted to go back. She wanted more. She was hungry for him. She wasn't yet ready to settle for the respectable life.

She had an idea. She had called herself Skelton to Will Kid because she had in mind the story of Barbara Skelton, lovely, bored and wicked, who had gone out into the night to play at being a highwayman. Barbara had begun by enjoying the dangers of a life of crime, holding up coaches at gunpoint and robbing her friends and neighbours. She had gone on to find sexual excitement in the arms of a gentleman of the road, so that each robbery had been consummated by rolling in the ditch in her lover's arms, or by going with him to some sleazy tavern, there to get a bed for an hour. Barbara was married to a good and wealthy man, but it had not been enough for her.

She died of a bullet. Fiona had already come closer than she had intended to paralleling Barbara. She knew she had been lucky and should now play safe. Will knew she came from the Zoo and might yet decide to ransom her, or even track her down and blackmail her. That would be very bad news indeed.

He too used a false name but she had discovered his real one. The police captain had told her. Henson Carne. So why had he called himself Will Kid? Had he picked a famous pirate at random or was there more to it? Had he, like herself, picked a name for a purpose?

Any clue to the enigma of the man would please her, and confer a certain power over him that she stood much in need of if she was to have further dealings with him. Fiona linked with her local library/info bank to put up on screen all they had on the notorious pirate.

She was astonished. The story she read was far more complex than she had expected. Here was no savage and greedy man leading a rollicking life dedicated to piracy, plunder and rape. Instead she read of an energetic, able and intelligent sea captain holding the commission of King William III of England to hunt down pirates and apprehend them with his private man-of-war, the galley *Adventure*.

Fiona even read a copy of the commission, giving its exact wording and dated January 1695.

Moreover, since England was at war with France at the time, he was further commissioned to attack French merchant shipping. This was known as a commission of reprisals. His government authorised Kid to commit acts against the French which were not piracy only because the two countries were at war.

Kid set sail from Plymouth in the *Adventure* in May 1696. His galley carried eighty men under his command and thirty guns.

He sailed for New York and took on seventy-five more crew. Then he sailed for Madagascar to find pirates.

Captain William Kid was a hunter, not the hunted. He was a policeman, not a pirate.

Fiona read on, perplexed.

Due to some dirty Caribbean politics at the time, those who were nominally on the side of law and order warned the pirates of Kid's coming. He therefore found no pirates for over a year and had no prizes to share with his crew and no funds to feed them and to maintain the boat. In the end, facing mutiny, he turned pirate to save himself and his boat.

In 1699 the King's pardon was offered to pirates who gave themselves up. Kid, not knowing he was specifically excluded, surrendered. He was anxious to return to a decent way of life.

It did him no good. He was hanged in Execution Dock, Wapping, London, in 1701.

It seemed an odd choice for Henson Carne to select Kid's name. Kid had been an honourable man forced by circumstance and betrayal to turn predator. He had died for it.

Fiona thought about this a good deal. She reflected that the captain of police had been both bitter and knowledgeable about Will Kid. Had he once been a policeman? Was he a lawman gone bad?

Fiona knew she was indulging in what probably was no more than an elaborate flight of fancy, yet it teased at her and made her long more than ever to meet Will again and penetrate the mystery of the man.

Meanwhile there was Janine. The *frisson* of danger that being down in the city gave her must one day be lost. She could not go on forever risking everything for the dark sensuous nights down in the mire and dirt of corruption. She must resolve things with Rollo so that her need for the city ceased to exist. She might not yet be prepared to give up her pirate lover but she could see the day coming when she must.

She went to Janine's room and had a long talk with the girl. Then she went up into the loft space above the bedrooms, where there was no plastic bubble-roof but a utility and storage area, and she made a hole in the floor with a drill. She drilled it big enough so that by applying her eye she had a good view of her bed below. She used a plug of white malleable material, children's modelling clay, to fill the gap. It would be easily removable.

Back in her bedroom she tidied up and inspected the ceiling. The textured white plastering gave no hint of the imperfection. Fiona smiled to herself. It was funny how everything worked in your favour when what you were doing was bad.

The master bedroom in their apartment had two bathrooms off it, one she used for herself, the other being for Rollo. It was Rollo's habit to shower last thing at night before he came to bed, and to shave. It was a courtesy to Fiona that he shaved then, and a tribute to their rich enjoyment of mouthwork on each other's bodies. He did not use the more normal depilatory creams because Fiona liked the faint tang of stubble, just enough to excite but not enough to abrade. He had not changed his ways since their sex life atrophied.

Fiona could predict from long experience his time in his bathroom. Moreover, he usually left the door ajar. She based her plan on this.

On the appointed night Janine came to the bedroom door and peeped in. Fiona nodded and the girl came on in. Rollo was in his bathroom drying himself after his shower and Fiona was lying half in bed dressed in a sumptuous négligée.

'Oh, Mrs Cambridge,' piped Janine. 'May I talk to you, please?'

'Why, what is it, Janine? Come in, dear. You look upset.'

'I know I shouldn't intrude. Is Mr Cambridge here?'

'Don't worry about him. He's busy just now. What is it?' So far, so good. Janine came over to the bed.

'It's just that I'm so upset.' The girl's voice trembled and she sounded close to tears. A good little actress, Fiona noted.

'Don't cry, Janine. Is it boyfriend trouble?'

'I wish it was. I think I'm going mad.'

'It can't be as bad as that.'

'It's . . . it's . . . Can I tell you something really personal, Mrs Cambridge? You won't laugh at me?' Janine's voice wobbled artistically. 'You won't tell Mr Cambridge? I couldn't bear for him to know. I'm so ashamed.'

This was the critical point. Either Rollo would resign himself and stay in his bathroom till Janine was gone, recognising that Fiona had to deal with 'servant problems,' or he would emerge and make his getaway.

Fiona thought he would probably take the easier option and stay where he was. Also, she thought he might be piqued to hear what Janine had to say. She was sure he was aware of Janine's heightened sexual tension. Rollo was older than herself, in his late thirties, at an age when a man might begin to doubt his sexual attractiveness and be reassured by the attentions of a young girl. This was silly. Up to a generous age, most men get sexier as they get older. Rollo was a prime target for an adoring teenager.

'I wouldn't tell Rollo anything private about you that you told me in confidence,' Fiona assured Janine. 'I take it this is in confidence.'

'Oh yes,' said Janine fervently. 'I can tell you because you are so kind to me. But I would be deeply humiliated if a man knew this, especially Mr Cambridge.'

'What is it, Janine? Can it really be so bad? Fiona's voice was caressing, almost purring. Rollo was staying put. She could be certain he was listening. Janine had purposely pitched her voice well up so that he could not miss what she was saying.

'You see,' faltered Janine. 'I've never had a boyfriend.'

'Never? How old are you?'

'Sixteen.'

'Of course. But you are young yet. Most girls start too young.'

'I don't think I am normal.'

'That is a very common fear. I don't mean to patronise. We are all insecure about ourselves underneath.'

'I mean, I want a boyfriend. I'd love a boyfriend, but . . .' Her voice trailed away.

'I don't see the problem. You are very attractive. You must have enough money to go out on your evenings off. Why don't you go on the hunt with a girlfriend? That's what I did.'

'All my friends have been humping for ages. I'm ashamed to admit I am a virgin.'

'You're a virgin, are you?' repeated Fiona, making sure Rollo got the message.

'Yes.'

'It's something to be proud of, I suppose.' Fiona was doubled over with mirth inside. She sounded so priggish, so know-all.

'I'm not proud of it,' hissed Janine. 'I think there is something wrong with me. I mean, I get feelings, you know.'

'I know,' agreed Fiona kindly, stifling laughter.

'Really strong feelings. But when I see a boy, I mean a boy of my own age, I go cold inside.'

'I admit the average seventeen or eighteen-year-old is not the most poised sexual adventurer,' began Fiona. She couldn't meet Janine's eyes. The girl was splendid.

'That's what I want,' cried Janine. 'A sexual adventurer. Some mature man, preferably gorgeous, who will take me and teach me the arts of love.'

'You've got good taste. I like to see ambition in a girl.'

'But how can I meet such a man,' wailed Janine. 'Even if I did, he would despise me for being young and inexperienced.

Just the sort of man I want is the sort of man who just wouldn't want me. A virgin's no fun for a man, is she?' Janine cried this last passionately.

'Well,' said Fiona judicially. 'That isn't quite true. I think it turns some men on. Older men, I mean, whose natural partners are all very experienced women. A virgin is a bit like a unicorn, rare and hard to believe in, but lovely if you happen to fancy . . . No. That's a bad analogy. But you see what I mean.'

'I can hardly go up to some lovely sexy mature man old enough to be my father, and say, hey, I'm a virgin, does that turn you on? Can I?'

'No,' said Fiona doubtfully.

'You know lots of lovely men, older men I mean. I don't suppose you could find out for me, could you?' asked Janine wistfully.

'Act as procuress, you mean?'

'That sounds awful. I'm asking for help. You would be doing me a kindness, not exploiting me.'

'I couldn't just turn you over to some elderly satyr. That would be clean against my conscience,' said Fiona self-righteously.

'No, but some man who was experienced and sexy and attractive, perhaps if you gave him a hint you knew a young girl who wanted such a man . . .'

'Janine, we all want such a man. You are describing the ideal man.'

'I'm sorry,' said Janine humbly. 'You must think I am disgusting.'

'Not at all. I'm glad you feel you can talk to me. But rest assured, your feelings are absolutely normal. You don't have anything to fear in that way.'

'I meant physically,' mumbled Janine.

'Pardon?'

'I mean, I don't think I am physically normal.'

'Physically?' cooed Fiona nice and clear. 'I'm sure you are physically normal, Janine.'

'How can I find out? I mean, if I knew I was, I might be more confident with men. But I can hardly check out another

169

woman. I feel too embarrassed to go to the doctor. He would just think me mad. Perhaps I am,' she added mournfully.

'Well,' said Fiona. 'I suppose I could check you. Or you could check me, if you'd prefer. Would that make you feel better?'

'Would you mind?' Janine was breathless with pleasure and gratitude. 'It would make me feel so much better.'

'Lie on the bed, dear, and open your legs.'

'But Mrs Cambridge,' fluted Janine in her little-girl voice. 'Did you say I could check you out?'

'Indeed I did, dear.'

'You mean you'd really let me look at you? Intimately?'

'In the interests of your happiness and wellbeing,' said Fiona, being plucky and noble. 'I am not a shy woman.'

'I've often wondered what you are like,' said Janine. 'As a mature woman, I mean.'

'Why don't you take a look?' Fiona let honey drip from her tongue.

'Now?'

Fiona made great play with her négligée, sliding it silkily up her body in a tantalising rustle. She opened her legs.

'Now, I'll just open my legs a little and you can see what a perfectly normal woman is like. I've had enough men to know, believe me, sweetie.'

They shuffled on the bed to give Rollo the full aural arousal, and mindful that he might take a look, they arranged themselves with Janine on her knees on the floor with her back to the bathroom, whilst Fiona sprawled with legs wide open on the bed, her knees bent over the end of it and her feet on the floor.

'You are so beautiful and strange without hair,' said Janine.

'Make sure you can see properly,' said Fiona outrageously. 'It isn't as if we will be doing this again.'

'Is this all right, Mrs Cambridge?'

'You can be firmer. You won't hurt me.'

'Oh,' gasped Janine. 'You are so beautiful and complicated.'

'Separate the flesh a little. That's right.'

The shaft of light from the open bathroom door momentarily widened. So Rollo wanted to see his wife with a girl fingering her private parts, did he?

'You are all dark and luscious and musky,' said Janine in a reverential voice.

'You say the nicest things. I don't know that a man has been quite so lyrical about my pussy. They tend to want to get down to the business or rather, up into it. You'll be as attractive yourself, sweetie, I promise.'

'No, I'm pale and tight and dry. I know.'

'Let me look. I am sure you are talking rubbish.'

The bathroom door moved slightly again as Rollo withdrew. Fiona sat up and the two women swapped places. Fiona made sure Rollo knew just what was going on.

'There now, Janine. Just lie back and relax. Slip up your nightshirt, that's right, up over your hips. Don't be shy, now. That's a good girl. Now I can see everything.'

'I'm so embarrassed, Mrs Cambridge.'

'Nonsense. Try shutting your eyes very tightly and then you won't feel as if this is real. Concentrate on what you are feeling down below.'

'Yes, Mrs Cambridge.' Janine was deliciously docile.

'No looking now. I don't want you to get all self-conscious and tighten up on me.'

'I promise.'

'You have the most adorable little silky bush, dear, that I am touching now. It has red highlights in it. Now I am touching your thigh. No need to jump. You have lovely thighs, young and rounded and firm. They are the most delicate peachy colour.' That ought to make the bastard sweat, she thought with savage glee.

'Now open your legs a little more. A little more. There now. The most beautiful little rosy pussy a girl could desire. Or a man for that matter.'

'You are just saying that. You haven't touched me. You haven't looked properly yet.'

'Honey, stay like this with your eyes shut and your legs open wide. I'm going to fetch a little cool jelly before I open you up. You will like the sensation. And it will help

171

prevent me from being too rough with a virgin rosebud.'

Fiona rose to her feet and went into Rollo's bathroom. He mouthed a bewildered expletive at her and she put a finger to her lips. She found the lubricant and crooked a finger. Rollo laid his head close to hers.

'Come in the room,' Fee breathed. 'Get a close-up.'

He raised his eyebrows and she grinned wickedly and caught him by the hand, dragging him with her back into the bedroom.

'Keep your eyes firmly shut,' she cooed.

'I am,' said Janine. 'It makes this feel remote, not real. It's like a strange dream.'

'Wearing a mask or going somewhere in disguise does that to you as well,' said Fiona. 'If you ever want to have a really great time, no holds barred, just go to a costume do or go with a mask on. That's when people really let rip.'

'I'll remember.'

'Now I'll just dab a little of this jelly on you. It's made as a sexual lubricant so don't fear it. It's very cool. Ready?'

'Ready.'

Fiona's face was enigmatic, closed and catlike. She turned to Rollo who was gazing at Janine's open-legged posture as she lay back on his bed. Her mound rose in sweet arrogance under its fluffy silken thatch of red-gold curls. Beneath it, between her thighs, peeped a pale gleam of flesh. Fiona pushed Rollo on to his knees at the end of the bed so that he was close to the tiny shuttered pussy.

She knelt beside him and touched his prick. It was hard. 'I'm just putting the jelly on,' she said. She motioned Rollo who daubed a finger thickly from the tube and then laid the finger with great gentleness on the trembling fissure before him.

'Ah,' sighed Janine.

'A little more,' said Fiona.

Rollo fingered Janine, touching her rosebud.

'These are what we call the labia,' said Fiona. Rollo delicately moved the petalled flesh. 'Is that nice, dear?'

'Yes. I mean, it's so strange. But I love it. It's wonderful. Would a man like doing this to me?'

'Oh yes. Far better than I might.' Fee grinned at Rollo. 'Now for your clitoris, your tiny man-member, your female penis.'

Rollo found and unsheathed the little cone of flesh. His face was intent. He frotted it gently and it trembled under his light touch.

'You flutter like a humming bird,' said Fiona. 'You are obviously in full working order, very sensitive and responsive. A man would like that very much, if he knew anything at all about the arts of love and wasn't just a greedy taker.'

'How can you tell the difference?' asked Janine dreamily. Her legs were wide apart and Rollo continued to tease her erect flesh and titillate her sexual parts. Fiona brought her own hand between her husband's thighs and grasped his swollen pole. She began to masturbate him expertly. He felt very good in her hand, strong, elastic and vibrant with lust.

'A little more jelly,' said Fiona. Rollo obliged, putting the cool transparent stuff in the heated gash of the aroused girl.

'The difference,' said Fiona, 'is in the method of attack. When they take you, you know. If a man is grabby and insensitive, don't go with him again. Go for a man who is artistic with your sexual organs and who works at how you feel. Usually the men who really love a woman's fanny are the best. They like to linger, to touch and arouse and look and feel at what you have between your legs. It is a little shrine to sex down there. They need to worship before they plunder.'

She could feel Rollo coming closer to climax. His shaft was hot and full and hard. With her other hand she began to stroke and fondle his balls.

'Now,' she said, finding it increasingly hard to concentrate, 'I will separate your lips and seek what is inside you. You are a virgin, you say?'

'Yes, Mrs Cambridge. Isn't it a good thing Mr Cambridge can't see us now? I don't know what he would think of me.'

'I do. He would be envious, child. No man could resist your sweetness. In go my fingers. I can feel your tightness. You are deliciously small, which is a very sexy idea for a man, honey. It means your pussy will grip his cock really tightly and

173

squeeze down on it.' Fiona squeezed Rollo's prick and felt him start to shake. His fingers were obedient to her words, within Janine, stroking and feeling inside her channel where no cock had ever been.

'You have a little obstruction in your secret haven. When this is broken by the first man who penetrates you, it will hurt a little, darling, and you will bleed a little. Afterwards you loosen up and you become naturally self-lubricating so that the delicious slithery satiny texture I can feel right now will be all you, and none of it from a tube. A man's cock will slide right up into you, making you feel full and powerful as you ride on his weapon and master it and give it great joy as you take it for yourself.'

Rollo had hooded his eyes and his face was sly and closed. He held Janine's pussy open with his two hands and very delicately intruded a finger which he stirred about.

'You are truly a virgin,' said Fiona. 'Tell me, dear, does it hurt when I touch you inside or does it arouse sexual feelings in you?'

Rollo was shaking, beads of sweat rolling down his forehead. His prick was so hard Fiona thought it might hurt him.

'This is absolutely gorgeous,' said Janine. 'If it was a man between my legs right this minute, I'd beg him to enter me.'

Rollo came, shooting onto the floor between Fiona's skilful fingers, struggling to keep his spasmodic jerks from alarming Janine.

'I'd adore to have a man come in me,' whispered Janine.

'You are absolutely normal, sweetie. I can assure you of that. If Rollo was here he would say the same thing himself. Your pussy is delectable. Almost I could eat it. But we must stop now or he might come in.'

Rollo clambered stiffly to his feet and moved back into his bathroom.

'Mr Cambridge is just my ideal sort of man,' said Janine. 'He is so attractive, so assured. I think he is beautiful, Mrs Cambridge. It is an honour to work for you both. The only trouble is, he makes other men look pretty second rate.'

'Rollo would be very flattered to hear you say such a thing. It isn't every man of his age who has a young and lovely virgin just aching to be deflowered by him.' Fiona was taking no chances that Rollo wouldn't get the message.

Janine sat up. Rollo was nowhere to be seen.

'I can dream,' she said. 'Gosh, that was wonderful, Mrs Cambridge. I really love being touched all round my intimate places. It makes me feel terrific. If only it didn't have to end.'

'Run along now and don't worry. A man will be lucky who gets you, darling.'

'Thank you so much.' Janine bent and kissed Fiona on the lips. Then she gave an exquisite little wriggle and dropped her shirt back over her hips. With a sly wink she left the room.

Fiona sat on the floor and waited. Slowly Rollo emerged from the bathroom.

'Maybe we shouldn't have done that,' he said.

'She didn't know. She liked it. Anyway, she's crazy about you.'

Rollo looked down at his limp prick. 'It was quite an experience.'

'You have a fabulous cock. I love playing with it.'

'What was it like for you when she touched you, Fee?'

'You want the truth or bromide?'

'The truth.'

'I kind of liked it. All that trembling girlish naive bit. I think she is a very hot little number, only she doesn't realise it yet. And what was it like for you, up to your knuckles in her little virgin twat?'

'Peculiar. She is quite unlike you.'

'How so?'

'With her it was strange. It was kinky. It certainly turned me on. But you are a full-blooded woman, Fee. Janine was a little shrimp patty. You are a lobster.'

'That's a compliment?'

'You are rich and dark and a feast in yourself. You are like forbidden fruit, dangerous and enticing. Sex with you always has the flavour of the illicit. You bloom, Fee, and make me ache to bruise you. You invite a man to split you open to extract your honey. There's not a dull safe bone in your body. You enchant me. You own me.'

175

Fiona kissed the inside of Rollo's thigh where the friction from his clothes rubbed the skin to silken smoothness.

'I want to bite on your muscle, sometimes, when it is fat and full.' She rubbed the end of his prick with her nose. It smelt sexy and was wet from his orgasm.

He put his hands into her black tumbled mass of silken curls. His voice was muffled.

'I want to come in your hair,' he said. 'I want to be dirty. I want to foul you. I want to spunk all over you.'

Fee took a handful of her own hair and put her face into his groin. She took his balls into her mouth and held them there. She wrapped her hair about his prick and began to abrade him back into life. The rough friction wakened him and he began to harden. He pushed her hand away and took her hair himself and began to frig his own prick hard. Fiona put her hands between his legs and gripped his muscled buttocks, squeezing them and sinking her nails into his flesh. She kept his balls in her mouth and sucked gently at them.

He pumped hard and with a gasp he unloaded, foaming into her black mane. He bent down and kissed her hard on the lips. She sat up and raised her arms, drawing up her breasts, feeling her hair. She rubbed it as if it was shampoo and laughed. Rollo kissed her armpits, sucking the tiny tousle of hair in each.

'I'll have to shower,' she said languorously.

'I'll wash you. And then I'll suck you to sleep.'

'Good,' she said, content.

13

After this Fee was happy, too happy to risk everything by
returning to the city. Rollo was wakening up from his long
sexual slumber and the very thought of Janine gave her a
frisson of pleasure. Even work was satisfying. The
TransFlow shares were selling well. Water was an increasingly valuable commodity in the overpopulated world.

She met Diana at the pool where they swam together for
pleasure and for health. They went shopping together and
Fee bought Janine some exquisite underwear. It was the least
the girl deserved.

Diana invited Fiona and Rollo to a party she and Teddy were
attending. Those who lived in the Zoo threw occasional parties,
elaborate affairs but successful in giving their community a sense
of adhesion other than the one supplied by great wealth.

Monroe and Diva Jackson were throwing this one and they
were too idle to make a formal list of guests. Instead they
invited those of their friends whom they met and asked them
to pass the word along. Monroe was into antiques and the art
world. It was to be a theme party, that of the ancient
Egyptians.

'Incest and Cleopatra's wigs,' explained Diana.

'Triremes and pyramids, more like,' said Fiona tartly. 'I
shall come as a warehouse.'

'A what?'

'A warehouse. Wasn't Egypt the granary of Rome?'

'Crazy woman. Honestly, do come if you can. I hardly see
you and even the virtuous have to relax sometimes.'

'I promise,' said Fee affectionately. 'But I can't promise
for Rollo. The international time zones give him screwy
working hours. I'll try and get him to come, though. He
lives, breathes and dreams TransFlow. It'll do him good to
be away from it for a while.'

'We bought some shares, Fee.'

'I bought some myself,' said Fee sweetly. 'I believe in the hard-working son of a bitch. If anyone can make this crazy enterprise work and show a profit, he can.'

'It's some relationship you two have.' Diana was laughing. 'Love-hate, yeah?'

Fiona became dreamy. 'Perhaps that's what I need from a man,' she murmured. 'Both sides of the coin.'

'You could have made a great courtesan in another age.'

'Part of me wants to be good. The trouble is, it is such a small part.'

Back at home in the apartment Fiona gave Janine the lovely underwear she had purchased.

Janine occupied a complete suite in the apartment. She had a bedroom, a sitting room and her private bathroom. Now Fiona gave that bedroom some thought.

It was a typical teenager's room. Over the bed was a huge menacing poster of a naked-chested young man wearing tight leather trousers with a suggestive bulge in the crotch. Behind him in weird perspective was a Connet car. Clearly he was meant to be a pirate.

Pop stars adorned other walls with surreal backgrounds from video stills. Between and amongst this immature elemental sexuality were the trinkets of girlhood, a teddy bear, fluffy toys, pierrot puppets and the like. The mixture of ignorant sex and sentimentality was overlaid with the smell of a cheap sweet scent.

Fiona thought it horrible. Utterly feminine herself, she had never felt the need for feminine props. She had abandoned the toys of childhood long ago without regret, unattracted by saccharine colours and nostalgia. She was a man's woman, not a grown-up little girl yearning for pink frills and pastel-shaded cuddly toys. She faced the world as an equal, ready to give and to take, and she didn't go in for fluttering eyelashes and weakness to arouse the protective instinct in a man. She didn't want protecting and she thought men had more interesting instincts to arouse.

The thing was, would Rollo reject this ghastly room for

reasons of taste, seducing Janine in his own bed, or would he go for the room as an extension of Janine and the perversion of her youthfulness and untouched sex? Rollo's big experienced sophisticated cock did not belong in Janine's sweet little pussy. Yet that was what he lusted for. The room was an aspect of the girl. He wanted to be an intruder. He was going to enjoy being out of place. He wanted to violate.

Fiona went back up into the attic and drilled another hole, this time over Janine's bed, plugging it invisibly as before. Now she was really ready. She grinned. She was being so damned naughty. She could hardly criticise Rollo if he got naughty urges too. Weren't they two of a kind, her and him, under the skin? She took her risks sexually, he took them financially and they both orgasmed on success.

Rollo was not free the night of the party so Fiona went over to Teddy and Diana's without him. She liked Teddy, an amiable gorilla of a man with a rumpled face, grizzled hair and a permanently sloppy grin. He had the quality of making all his clothes look slept in, though Fiona knew it was appearance only and Diana fought a useless war over smartening him up. He treated Fiona as a pal and she liked it.

The two women had decided to wear identical costumes. Both had hired Cleopatra wigs which hung heavily, being much woven about with beads. Janine came over with Fiona to make the women up in the Egyptian mode and to help them with their clothes. These were naughty. This was hardly surprising, the current fashion being for revealing rather than obscuring, and they had chosen to go as serving maids to royalty, attendants of the queen who at this stage in Egyptian history was always the Pharoah's sister.

Royal attendants wore, it seemed, long linen dresses that were pleated and hung to floor-length. The dresses came up under the bust, thrusting the breasts up but leaving them bare. Nipples were as much in fashion back then as now. Janine made up their faces from pictures copying tomb frescoes and then, as a finishing touch, both women put on a tiny square-cut goatee beard.

'Now wait a minute,' said Teddy. 'I am all for historical

179

accuracy when it comes to bared bosoms but beards! No way. I don't believe women were them.'

'They certainly did,' said Diana, who claimed to have done the homework on this one. Teddy was a statistician and could be forgiven his ignorance. 'Don't you think they are cute?'

'I'd feel naked without mine,' said Fiona and giggled. They set off for the party.

There were plenty of people Fee knew and could enjoy talking to. There were some new people it might be interesting to meet. There was good food and dancing and plenty to drink. Monroe showed her round his private gallery where he stored his treasures between buying and selling and made a pass at her. Fiona evaded his elderly fumbling and tried not to yawn.

She mixed. She chatted. She circulated and was polite and well behaved. She refused two offers of finding a more private room, one offer to leave the party and go to someone's apartment and resisted one drunken grope on the stairs.

She became more and more bored. She missed Rollo and envied him, shut in his work station making his computer draw stylised representations of the water route the pipes would be taking, breaking the project into manageable lumps for tender.

She was bored. Her wig was heavy and hot. The music was anodyne and dull, with none of the cunt-tingling power of the gut-rock she had heard in the city. The people were pleasant and shallow and she was bored.

She heard the latest gossip and scandal. Some of it she could see for herself. Diva always liked to shock. Fiona could hardly blame her for that but there was a touch of malice in Diva. Fee wondered if her husband's insatiable collecting of beautiful *objets d'art* had soured their relationship at some long ago time. Diva was like a jewelled turtle, a beautiful hard carapace on a withered and wrinkled skin. Monroe probably spent a great deal more time stroking ancient and valuable artefacts than he spent stroking his wife.

Now Diva scandalised the party by bringing her tame young man, obviously her lover, a sultry beast of perhaps eighteen years to her sixty, all brawn and swollen muscle.

He wore tight shiny shorts that showed the cleft in his bottom and the size and shape of his genitals in stark relief. He wore nothing else except for some aromatic oil that made him glisten, and a chain.

His wrist was manacled and a chain of gold led from the manacle to Diva. Thus she led him about and he had to follow. Fee did not quite see the Egyptian theme but Diva was quick to explain.

'He's my slave boy, dear Fee. Isn't he gorgeous?'

Fee looked at the boy. He smouldered back at her.

'Divine,' she said. 'Tell me, did he come with the chain on?'

'Sweetie, I let go this end and he'll be away, rutting with every woman in the place. What balls, Fee. I can't describe. They steam. Really steam. This man is an engine.'

'Steam, huh?' said Fiona. She kept her face straight.

'I'll tell you a secret,' said Diva. Dutifully Fiona leant closer. 'He likes doing it with boys, too.'

Diva hissed this last morsel from between magenta lips. No ghost make-up tonight.

'Does he do it with Monroe?' asked Fiona in velvet tones.

'I said boys,' snapped her hostess. 'I watch, you know. I just love to see their dinky things in each other. Aren't I awful?' She gave an arch snigger.

'Dinky things and steaming balls.' Fiona looked at the youth who was fully occupied in being magnificently sullen about a yard away from them. 'Honey, you are so experienced.'

'My slave has a big thing.' Diva was snapping again. Fiona grinned at the boy. He thrust his pelvis forward and flexed, under the straining material, his muscle. Fiona gurgled with laughter and fled.

After a while she sought out Diana and Teddy who had long since abandoned socialising and were dancing together, gazing moonstruck into each other's eyes.

Fee tapped a shoulder lightly.

'I'm on my way,' she said.

'Oh honey. Do you want us to come?'

'You stay. I'll go topsides, I think. I feel like being under the stars.'

'Good party?' asked Diana.

'Sure. The best. Steer clear of Diva and the slave, though.'

Diana giggled. 'Isn't she awful? All that teenage moodiness and not a brain cell in sight. She must have picked him out of a brothel.'

They kissed goodnight and Fiona drifted away. There was another piece of gossip that she had heard and she wanted to mull it over.

Out of the apartment she avoided the moving walkways and went up an escalator to the glass tunnels that wandered over the Zoo, above the man-made jungle that guaranteed their privacy and exclusiveness.

It was colder up here in the dark. The tunnels were not artificially heated and had grilles at intervals in their sides to allow the real weather to penetrate. Fiona strolled slowly, gazing absentmindedly at the foliage below, carrying her wig and beard.

The pirates had hit the news. This was the latest that she had heard. The police were making a determined effort to clear up the pirate nest and stop their predation in the rich. The number of successful hackings had risen lately and someone particularly self-important had been taken and ransomed. He was bitter about his thirty-six-hour captivity and making waves about it.

The SkyPolice had made sorties to ground level and used automatic weapons when they got there. It was rumoured that recently the pirates had raped a woman, leaving her sexually and physically crippled, unconscious in her car for the SkyPolice to find. The woman was in a psychiatric home unable to lead a normal life.

Fiona heard this media distortion of her own case with anger. She had made clear to the captain of police that she had urged the pirate on to assault her and that technically it was doubtful if it was rape. The fact that the entire incident was imaginary, the product of her fertile imagination and designed to help her insurance scam, added salt to the wound. She had been responsible for the biggest dent in the pirates' romantic image that they had received in years. It was her little computer, no doubt, that had increased their hacking success. Now they were attacked in force and their bizarre equilibrium upset.

The temptation to confess and effect some sort of redress was momentary. Her sense of fair play was not strong and she had the predator's instinct to take advantage of weakness. Yet she was ill at ease.

She could not return to the city, that was certain. Captain Will, Chain and the rest of the gang knew the risks they ran and would have to put up with the consequences of their own actions. It was their lookout, she told herself firmly.

But it would be a hell of a waste to put a male beast like Will behind bars, where he was useless.

Meanwhile, what would she do for fun, for danger? How would she keep her life on the edge, where she liked it to be? She had no idea.

Fee buried herself in work. She set up her marketing company so that the infrastructure was there should she ever want to activate it. She debugged the software she had developed for TransFlow. She installed Jamie and settled him in. He was working well, making independent decisions already and looking confident.

Rollo worked and did nothing else. Fiona calculated that in the previous six or seven months he had had precisely two sexual sessions with her. One of those was triggered by her indulging in criminal activity. The other was after she had aroused him by making him touch their maid's private parts.

The first giant diggers began to roll. Up and down the country the pipeline that was to link the northern wetlands with the drought-gripped south began to come into being. Fiona watched herself on the Screen, at the opening ceremony cutting the tape, and was bored.

In a fit of pique she decided to go to a brothel. Sex was for sale, wasn't it? In traditional societies men had gone to brothels for variety or perversion or simply for quantity, but for a long time they had catered for both sexes and all tastes.

Fiona checked the market to find a classy one and prepared to go.

She wanted discretion above all things but then she reckoned so would most of the clientele. She would go masked. Being masked removed inhibition for her and she acknowledged wryly that she was not over-endowed with inhibition anyway.

On the night she chose she had Janine scrape back her hair hard from her face and pin it tight. A few curls were freed off to cluster about the pins, but otherwise it was severe. She dressed against the prevailing fashion for tight trousers in long baggy ones, in black, which she wore with a full white cavalier shirt borrowed from Rollo's wardrobe. Overshirts were all the thing for men, but Fee tucked in its looseness at her waist. It was deeply frilled at wrist and throat, and she wore a small tight black jacket over. Only her eyes gave colour to her austere appearance. In her pocket was her mask.

She rode the moving walkways and then took a taxi to the locality of the brothel. She was amused when she arrived to find it was a traditional classical building with a vast dour façade, columned and porticoed in mimicry of ancient Rome. It must be a hundred and fifty years old, she thought, and for some reason this tickled her sense of humour. Brothels were as old as culture itself, she supposed, so it was right that they should be housed in historic buildings.

She ran lightly up the steps and into the subdued interior, more like an up-market nursing home than a palace of sin and sex. There was hidden lighting and soft music. But this respectable frontage concealed something entirely different, if Fiona's researches were correct. She approached the desk.

'Can I help you?' The woman was mature and charming, her clothes a symphony of controlled elegance and classic good taste.

Fiona had her mask on now. 'I should like to use your services,' she said.

'Have you a particular service in mind? I can give you a fully illustrated catalogue if you like. The catalogue is returnable.'

'Nothing fancy. One man and myself. Aged between

twenty-five and forty-five. A private room. I do not wish to be observed.'

'Would you like to walk through our public rooms and perhaps have a drink and relax a little? You will find many of our people there and perhaps you might make a selection.'

'That sounds fine.'

Fiona walked through the body-scanner in the compulsory health check and then authorised the deduction from her account using the DNA recorder. Then she took breath and prepared to indulge herself in the amenities of the house.

She moved from the vestibule as directed, her high heels sinking into the luxurious depth of the floor covering. She passed through great gilt doors and found herself in a long room, massive in proportion but graceful. The atmosphere was warm and slightly scented and there was the hum of male and female chatter. It was a civilised soothing scene and Fiona's spirits began to rise. Far from being overtly raunchy like Diva's party, this could almost be a social gathering for diplomats.

Except that many there were almost naked.

There were other clients like herself, and like herself some of these were masked. The girls wore diaphanous robes made of a material that became transparent as they moved. At one moment you could see the girls' entire charms laid bare, long lovely legs, beige bodies or beautiful black limbs and all the smoky shades between. But in repose, the material became opaque and was a discreet wisp that suggested but did not reveal.

For the men it was something different.

They wore nothing except chastity belts. Fiona had heard of these but never seen them. The belt took the form of a hollow cone of thick clear plastic, padded and softened on the inside. The man's penis was inserted into the cone, still on clear view, and its very end projected slightly from a hole in the apex of the cone. Fiona thought it was dazzling. The cone enclosed the penis so that it was far too wide to insert into an orifice. The balls hung freely at the back of the cone. The cone was kept in place by a tight-fitting belt that went around the hips and was locked at the back with a digital lock.

Although their genitalia were on full show, and their bodies were magnificently naked front and back, the men could do nothing until they were released from the locked device. The whole concept pleased Fiona enormously. She looked pleasurably around her, drinking in the details avidly, aroused by the sight of so much cock and titillated by its imprisonment.

She began to walk the length of the room. She took her time, unashamedly enjoying the goods on offer. As she passed, the men brazenly flaunted their naked privates, tempting her to unlock them and sample their prowess in the ancient art of fornication. Her severe clothes awakened the interest of the girls also and they swished their clothes suggestively as she went by in case her taste should be for them.

Fiona accepted a glass of champagne from a passing waiter. She sipped it, sauntering through the groups of people, and was approached by a man in evening dress.

'Does madame require any assistance?' he enquired suavely.

'I like them male and big.'

'Big in every sense or big in the particular?'

'Every sense.'

'Charles and Jonathan over there do a little body-building in their spare time,' the man murmured, 'and Chevro on the Louis Quinze sofa doesn't need to, since he is so large already. Clive, that's the man leaning against the fireplace, is under six foot but, my goodness, he is well endowed. Phenomenal. And he knows what to do with it.'

'I'll take a look at Clive.' Fiona moved over to the man who stood with an elbow on the mantelpiece apparently inspecting the Rembrandt over it. Fiona wondered whether Monroe sold antiques to these people. She had the feeling that the Rembrandt was the original.

As she reached him, Clive turned and noticed her. She saw he had the true sensual curve to his lip, the genuine mark of the sexually indulgent. She met his eyes calmly. He raised his brows and smiled enquiringly. Fiona's eyes dropped to his cone.

The enclosed quiescent prick reminded her of a fly in amber. Its stillness was surreal. Almost one expected it to

186

move and have life as though it was on film rather than trapped three-dimensionally within the plastic medium. It was perfect. Perfectly visible and perfectly detailed. Fiona stared at the penis attached to the living man with the visual greed of the voyeur.

She knew from experience that different pricks had different rates of expansion and the limp prick was not necessarily the best guide to what the fully erect member might offer in the way of size and thickness. But sometimes a big limp prick meant a huge erect missile able to plunge explosively into the woman's hot and needy place and if this was true of Clive, he was the best-endowed man she had ever seen.

Rollo was comfortably large with a good expansion. He had thickness and length and a particularly lovely knob, really flavoursome and shapely.

Will Kid was all rigid muscle and tensile strength. This was no contradiction. He was big and thick and hard, very veiny and textured, but elastic too.

Clive was simply satiny hugeness, a beautiful great smooth thing that made you itch to stroke it.

'I'd love to stroke your dick,' said Fiona bluntly. She was paying and she wanted to test the goods.

'My pleasure,' murmured Clive. His voice was low-pitched and throaty. 'Just a stroke or more than that?'

'Can I see it erect before I commit myself?' Fiona felt arrogant and a touch cruel. This was the one situation where she did not have to consider her lover's ego. A male whore was simple self-indulgence, almost masturbation at third hand. You paid for it, and an expert put it there.

'It has to come out of the cone,' said Clive. He lifted one leg and rested his bare foot on the fender. Fiona saw the muscle ripple inside his thigh. His feet were beautiful, broad with a high arch and delicate bones to the ankle.

She touched the tendon within the skin where it ran into the groin. 'You are nicely built,' she said. 'Can you move to match it?'

'Feel my balls,' said Clive. 'If you want to give me pain, that is.'

'Pain?'

'When a woman of your class and beauty and elegance feels me up and caresses my balls, my prick grows. It is in close confinement as you can see. The result is pain. Of course, that might turn you on. There is no commitment if you have me unlocked for a closer look. The management wants you pleased, not bullied.'

'Unlock, then,' said Fiona.

'Tell the management. I cannot be free unless you request it. I am helpless,' said Clive. He smiled.

Fiona found the man who had recommended Clive and said that she would like him unlocked. He gave her the code number and said that if she was not satisfied, to keep looking. The house was dedicated to pleasure. Upon her return, Clive turned round and Fiona eyed his tight muscled rump. Her hand just above his cleft, Fiona entered the code number and the lock opened. The strap came apart but the cone did not fall off. He turned and she saw the sheer size of the man kept it in place despite the hanging straps.

'You want to take it off? he invited. She reached down and eased the thing away from his groin, releasing the clinging flesh. He tossed the belt to one side.

'Now I can breathe,' he said.

She saw the silken column hang against his balls. She reached down and again ran a hand up his thigh. She let the back of her hand brush his scrotum and then she turned it and briefly caressed the warm soft hairy skin.

His shaft started to fill.

She watched, fascinated. His member firmed and grew visibly in length. Then it hung, half erect, half projecting forward.

She laid her hand curiously upon it, its warmth and texture demanding the fuller caress. Slowly she closed her hand about it and lightly stroked up, drawing back the foreskin a little. It firmed and she realised that inadvertently she was holding him too tightly. She relaxed her hold. The shaft continued to swell. She relaxed her hold some more and found she could barely make her fingertips meet around it.

She let go and looked at the man's equipment.

'I guess you know how to use that thing,' she said. 'It's not just a pretty cock.'

'There's only one way to find out,' he responded politely. I would warn you, though, I am not for the faint-hearted. I know now you can handle me. But can you cunt me?'

'There's only one way to find out,' said Fiona. 'Let's go.'

She linked arms and he smiled down at her. As they walked away a waiter collected the discarded cone. After sanitation another male whore would wear it until he took some client's fancy.

They walked the length of the room together, an experience in itself because, although Fiona herself was fully clad, Clive was rampantly naked and his erect cock cleared the way. Even in those decadent surroundings they managed to create a mild sensation as they passed. They went up wide curving stairs to the upper rooms. Clive led her through a thick panelled door into a room with an antique decor, a high-ceiling apartment with a bathroom en suite. The bed was designed as an ancient four-poster which Fiona found a nice conceit. It dominated the room.

'Before we settle,' said Clive in a meaningful way, 'I should tell you that we have a variety of specialities on offer. Some of them require certain apparatus and we would be better to move elsewhere.'

'Such as?'

'Would you enjoy being mastered and humiliated by me? The fact that you were paying for it would only heighten my enjoyment of pissing on you and rubbing you with excrement.'

'No,' said Fiona.

'Then again, it might please you to revenge yourself upon a man using me as proxy. I have a low threshold for pain and could be cowed by a strong dominant woman such as yourself, forced to submit to whatever degradations you wished to impose on me whilst I beg for mercy, a snivelling heap . . .'

'No,' said Fiona.

'Whips?'

'No.'

'Torture? The rack. The wheel. Manacles. You liked m
prick imprisoned, I could tell. And for a truly fabulous fee
would permit you to pierce my foreskin and place jewelle
studs about my cock. It is expensive since it renders me *hor
de combat* for a while.'

'I don't want you *hors de combat*. I want action.'

'Company? Male or female. Both. Watching or partici
pating. We have some very elaborate scenarios in which yo
are free to enact any role that takes your fancy. If I migh
prompt your imagination and indicate at the same time tha
there are no limits here, you could have your hand
embedded in two lovely juicy cunts whilst a great ebony coc
was stuffed in your mouth, and two more cocks fucked an
buggered you simultaneously. It's quite an experience,
added Clive mildly.

Fiona laughed. 'I'll bet it is. But I'm not sufficiently jade
yet.'

'Then I might offer you a long lingering session betwee
two adult people with an immense amount of talent betwee
them, a couple who are not only very able, but very resilient
There is much that expertise and experience can achieve.'

'That's what I want,' said Fiona.

'May I order refreshments for you? It would be as well i
we kept our strength up.'

'Oysters and champagne for me and whatever you wish fo
yourself.'

He ordered the food through the house-com system. Fiona
watched the muscles in his buttocks move as he walked and
began to feel excited.

'Whilst we eat,' he said, after putting down the com unit,
'would you like to watch some entertainment?'

'On the Screen?'

'In the flesh.'

'Others copulating?'

'No, though we can provide that if you wish. I mean
sophisticated, talented and original entertainment.'

'Yes,' said Fiona.

'Might I suggest that we have our food in a private loge
whilst we watch? We will see no others in the audience and no

190

others will see us. I would like you to eat naked, you see. I long to expose your body.'

'That sounds good.'

He leant towards her, his brown eyes shining. 'You are plainly a woman of surpassing beauty,' he said. 'You can't think how privileged I feel to be able to reveal your hidden curves and secret places.'

Something caught in Fiona's throat. She knew he was acting as he had acted when tempting her to sado-masochistic games, but he was so damned good at it.

'I will just arrange for our supper in the theatre,' he said. When he had done this he came back to Fiona and touched her shoulders, standing at her back. She shivered slightly. She was longing to touch him. He eased her jacket from her shoulders and took it off her. Then he loosened her shirt at her waistband. She felt his lips at her neck and laid her head back, offering him her white throat. Her shirt came free and his warm hands roved inside and clasped her body. His tongue flickered and touched her throat.

'There is no hurry,' he said. 'The night has a thousand hours for lovers and I will make every minute of every hour memorable for you.'

He unbuttoned the deep old-fashioned cuffs of her shirt and eased her arms out and took the shirt off her. He turned her round and looked at her.

'Your breasts are twin pleasure domes from Xanadu itself,' he said. 'But the scar on your cheek is fornication incarnate. Will you take off your mask?'

'No.'

'Your eyes. Green fire. I've never seen a woman like you.'

Now he knelt and undid the fastening of her black velvet breeks. Loosened, they hung open. Her utter nakedness and hairlessness within were revealed.

He caught his breath. He reached behind her and undid the fastenings of her boots. He slid one long boot off and then the other. Now he was free to draw down her trousers. As he did so, he put his tongue into her navel.

Her stomach fluttered.

He removed her trousers and she was left standing there,

as naked as he was. He walked round her as she stood viewing the long pale planes of her body, the full deep bus with its porcelain texture and between her hips the smooth rounded belly that flattened when she lifted her arms.

He ran a finger up the curve of her back and clasped her neck with his hand. He kissed her shoulder blades and behind her ears.

'Do you ever wear diamonds?' he asked.

'I don't like them.'

'On some women they are superb. They would be wrong for you. What jewellery do you like?'

'Gold. Pearl. Opal. Tiger's eye. Nothing fancy.'

'You have good taste. Brave, beautiful and, let me see. Do you like danger? I think you do.'

Fiona faced him. 'Don't get too clever,' she advised.

He acknowledged the rebuke. 'I will provide a robe,' he said. 'Let us go to the theatre.'

Their darkened balcony, its intimacy beguiling, overlooked the stage. The food was laid out on old lace in keeping with the antique fashion of the house. There was oysters, champagne, old brandy, as well as skewers of grilled meat, dripping in some heavy sauce.

They sat down. Fiona was astonished at her hunger. All her appetites craved satisfaction, it seemed.

Clive opened an oyster and ground a little fresh black pepper on to the muscle. He squeezed lemon and handed it over. Fiona threw back her head and tilted the shell. The animal slid into her open mouth and she swallowed its salty strength. She licked her lips with her pointed tongue.

Clive took one for himself and she saw his throat work. She ate two or three more and he did the same, laughing and wiping the juice that spilled from the side of his mouth. He poured her champagne but declined its bubbling coldness for himself.

'I do not have a good head for alcohol,' he said and Fiona warmed to this bizarre admission of vulnerability. 'And I would not detract from our coming enjoyment. But I do take brandy, though very little. For me it is bottled sensuality, fermented and distilled liquid sex. I can taste the sun in it and it warms my blood.'

192

They finished the oysters.

'I ordered these,' said Clive, picking up a skewer and rolling it in the thick rust-red sauce. 'They are a specially of the house. The sauce is very piquant and appeals to strong tastes. I think you might like them.'

Fiona lifted a skewer herself from its bed of peeled grapes.

'Allow me,' said Clive. He held up his skewer and bit a piece of the meat off. She saw the flash of white teeth. He offered his mouth to her.

She took the meat mouth to mouth, throwing back her head to get the morsel right in. The heavily spiced meat was delicious. He fed her again and she fed him, sauce spilling down their chins. A drop fell, fox-red, on her white breast. His tongue licked the sauce from her throat and breast and she murmured with pleasure.

He kissed each vertebra of her spine. 'It is going to be a privilege making love to you,' he said huskily.

'You have not entered me yet,' said Fiona.

'You will know it when I do.'

His greasy hands circled her breasts and massaged their fullness. 'It is time to watch the show,' he said.

A woman came on stage. She was very slender, very slight. She danced an ancient Balinese dance of extraordinary beauty and grace, plainly a celebration and potent with meaning.

Then a troupe of men came on stage and danced a Japanese dance of violence and death. It was magnificent but it was the magnificence of killing and Fiona did not like it.

Now another woman came on. She wore little save for an elaborate headdress and she crouched before a wicker basket and played a pipe.

The music reached into Fiona's blood so that she shivered. It was insistent, a mesmeric drone, monotonous.

A head appeared from the basket. The woman was a snake charmer but it was no cobra she wooed. The head was a flattened arrowhead, marked in bands of brilliant colour. Fiona knew that colour in reptiles and insects usually meant danger.

She saw the forked tongue flicker. She was fascinated and repelled.

The woman fluted at the snake and drew it away from it basket. It followed her, a sinuous curve of elegant death.

Now the woman lay back on the stage like a limbo dancer bending her upper torso right back until her shoulders rested on the stage, still playing all the while. The snake writhed between her open legs. Fiona stiffened. The head was lifted in the air and it was turned from side to side, almost blindly as if it was questing.

Something about the monotonous playing tugged at Fiona's memory. She felt she recognised the dirge and yet she knew that to be impossible. It teased her awareness.

Now the snake was right between its mistress's legs and its tongue flickered against her vulnerable flesh, the flesh at the apex of her open legs. Fiona saw that not only was she shaven about her sex, but her labia was pierced and she wore gold rings at the entrance to her sexual opening.

She felt Clive's hands down about her own sex, questing like the snake. She shivered and let her legs fall apart. On stage the snake moved its head up close to the proffered vagina. Then, to an audible gasp from the unseen audience, it tongued the woman's cunt and penetrated its head.

She played on and Fiona was visited by a revelation. She watched with a certain grim amusement as the snake's muscles quivered as it penetrated deeper into the woman's body. She stopped playing and carefully rose to her feet. Obscenely the snake hung between her legs, its body writhing slightly, its head invisible deep within her cunt. She displayed herself to a flutter of applause and then suddenly she grasped the tail and pulled the snake from her. She dropped it to the floor and began playing again. The snake returned to its basket as the woman straddled her legs and played on. Moisture dripped from her cunt in clear droplets.

Fiona was supreme with computers. She could hear the digital patterns in the playing of the pipe. The damned disgusting exhibition was no more than some very fancy work with a programmed robot. She laughed aloud. It was very clever. Her own cunt itched in shock at the performance.

Clive poured champagne on his hands and massaged Fiona's breasts with the fizzing liquid.

'You liked the snake,' he said.

'I'm into computers myself,' she answered slyly.

He hesitated, dumbfounded at her perception. 'Beautiful and highly intelligent with it,' he said. Fiona grinned mockingly. 'Jesus, I'm hot for you,' he said. 'Let's go to our room.'

They returned to their room and Clive ran a bath for Fiona and washed her and himself. She had been right. It was nice to have a man perform this intimate office whilst she lay in idleness feeling his hands on her body. Definitely, when Janine left, she would investigate the possibility of having a male maid.

After she was out of the bath and dried, Clive knelt and inserted a finger within her moist cavity and touched the velvet within.

'I'm going to make love to your breasts first of all,' he said. 'But I will come back to this place and make you scream with pleasure.'

Fiona was all compliance. She allowed herself to be laid on the bed and Clive massaged her breasts with aromatic oil. When they were flushed and aroused he took his own hanging prick and laid it within her hands.

Fee helped herself to a little oil and looked with interest at what she had been given. She began to work him gently, allowing him to rise within her hands slowly until his shaft was huge in her grasp. It only made her feel greedier, knowing it was hers to command. His skin was particularly soft and slidy, the foreskin retracting easily over the swollen end. The gland engorged and darkened as she handled him and she saw the eye gleam.

His balls were big and firm in their bag of skin. She cradled them and felt their oval shape and strength.

Clive began to kiss her skin. He sucked her and gently bit the sucked flesh. He went all over her like this till her whole body tingled in arousal though he had not yet touched her pussy or its sensitive surroundings. He stroked her breasts with his great cock, beating them slightly and rolling them with it. He held his gland and opened its eye and brushed her nipples with the slightly oozing tiny orifice. It made Fiona's nipples tremble.

Now his mouth was at her breasts. He rolled and sucked with brutal strength and when both were dark and swollen into prominence, he nibbled them delicately so that she almost came at the pleasure of it. He flagellated her nipples with his great cock.

'I want you to do something for me,' he whispered.

Fiona had trouble understanding his words. She was in a sexual daze, her whole body quivering with the need to be penetrated. 'Yes?' she said blindly.

'This little bladder. Will you insert it for me and then pump it up with this little pump till I tell you to stop?'

She took the rubbery thing with a certain disgust. It was pink and had a nipple on one end where the pump could attach.

'Insert it where?'

'Here.' He half turned and touched his anus. His eyes were gleaming with the depravity of the satyr.

'You want it in and pumped up?'

'Pumped tight. To hold me open as I attend to you.'

'OK.' Fiona felt quite interested in the procedure. He crouched with his backside in the air, his two hands hauling his buttocks apart. Fiona felt her fanny convulse as she looked at his neat crimped rear. There was a wisp of sweat-soaked hair in his crevice. On an impulse she leant forward and licked it.

'That's good,' he whispered.

Using her index finger she began to poke the rubbery thing within him. She rather enjoyed it. He stiffened and sighed as she went into him. He would be bisexual, of course. Evidently he liked this aperture to be invaded. With the bladder mostly in, she attached the pump and began to work it. As she pumped, air filled the little bladder. The whole thing began to expand in a figure-of-eight shape, fat within him and fat without but nipped at its waist by his anal muscle. Slowly it forced his rear open.

He was silent, welcoming the intrusion.

196

'Enough?' asked Fiona.

'More.' His voice was husky with strain as he adjusted.

Fiona pumped. Obscenely the bladder protruded from between his cheeks, holding them apart with its bulbous width.

'Enough,' he croaked.

Fiona stopped and carefully detached the pump. Then a cruel grin curved her lips. 'Just a moment,' she said with false sweetness. 'Don't move. I want to keep looking.'

She re-attached the pump and recommenced the action.

'What are you doing?' he gasped.

'Raping your arse, lover.'

'Stop,' he pleaded.

Fiona laughed and stopped. He eased himself up and sat back on his heels. Sweat filmed his brow. 'You wicked bitch,' he said.

Now that she could see him from the front again, Fiona saw that his weapon was a mighty thing indeed. Bloated with desire, it projected at a hard angle. When she touched its massy proportions, it leapt and quivered under her hand.

'Turn round,' she ordered.

He obeyed and she gasped with cruel pleasure at the pink bladder squeezing his cheeks asunder and holding his rear passage open to the point of pain.

'Walk about,' she said. She was very excited and breathing hard, her breasts rising and falling quickly.

He walked up and down the room, stiff-legged because of his split arse. His cock shook before him like a mighty club, swollen at its head.

He stopped and faced her. 'Lie back,' he ordered hoarsely.

She smiled her catlike smile and lay back at her ease on the silken pile of pillows mounded at her back.

He came on the bed and opened her legs. He looked at her for a moment. Then he turned himself round and opening her legs wide he put his mouth to her vulva.

In front of her the bladder wobbled and danced. She saw his scrotal sack full of juice, this balls distended. They joggled before her. She reached out a lazy hand and fondled

197

their fullness. Then, with her eyes half closed, she gave herself up to pleasure.

He bit her folded flesh, licked it apart and sucked it and flapped at her with his tongue so that she grew dark and rich. He worked each tiny part of her sexual flesh so that every nerve was set alight with lust. He worked from the very end of her slit to its apex. Then he went back to her rear. He had the sophisticated ability to suck her open and then blow into her as she shut. His tongue was very strong and he could penetrate her easily.

He thumbed her orifice open and blew into her. Then he ejected saliva into it and manipulated her so that the saliva dribbled out.

The trickling liquid aroused her, warm and wet, still more. She kept involuntarily gripping with her muscles. Her whole vulva seemed to ooze liquid lust. She seethed and it seemed to her that she must almost be steaming, such was the heat glowing up from every part of her wet places.

Yet only now did Clive move on to her clitoris. He tongued it and nipped it and licked it and sucked it till she was in an agony of desire. And then he moved within her. He held her open and he blew. He closed his lips over her and sucked so violently that her body jerked and she almost came into his mouth. Yet he controlled her even in this, puppetmaster of her lust. His tongue went in and licked round her juicy walls. Her whole passageway flowed thickly as she was stimulated to eruption.

All the time the pink bladder wobbled before her eyes.

He lifted his head. 'I am going to enter you now for the first time,' he announced.

Fiona was beyond speech. Her body arched helplessly. He turned round and drew his mighty shaft all down her body, stroking her with it. Then he began to butt at her entrance.

He pushed at her. She knew she was slimy with sexual heat but still he pushed, not sliding in.

'I'm going to hurt you now,' he said maliciously. By way of response she strained harder to draw him into her. Her muscles fluttered and shook. He pushed hard and his knob went in through the narrow entrance. Her cunt gave before the onslaught, welcoming him, drawing him on, squeezing, straining, bulging, grasping him and then, as he hesitated she dug her heels into the bed and reared up, driving herself up on him. His cock slid deep into her and she felt her eyes bulge.

Her back arched. Her blunt bald mound was up and straining. The pressure within her grew and grew. One at a time he lifted each of her legs from the bed and hooked them over his shoulders.

Fiona closed her eyes and entered paradise.

He moved gently at first, letting her get used to him and letting her own juices flow sufficiently to lubricate them both. She kept herself rigid, struggling to contain and retard her orgasm.

He began to work her. Each stroke was deep and incredibly long. It got harder to hold the barrier.

He expanded as he came free of the constrictions of her passage and then tightened deliciously as he went back in, held by her firm vaginal embrace. His actions created a ripple effect between the two of them as the pressure eased and tightened alternately.

The great gland at the end of his member nuzzled blindly within her as though it would possess her very womb in the profundity of his fucking. Fiona rose to meet him, thrusting at him greedily, her teeth bared into a snarl. Her fanny changed as it began to climax. Little shudders shook her, gaining in speed and intensity. Her cunt vibrated, hotter than ever about his cock, and fiery wet. Now pelvic spasms shook them both and Clive roared into her like a train thundering into a tunnel.

She felt his sexual blows dizzily and then the full force of her orgasm took over conscious thought. He held her at her peak and then released his own climax so that she knew the joy of his thunderous finale as she arrived at her own.

He held himself in her whilst she shook with aftertremors, enjoying the sensation of her powerful wet cunt about his diminishing organ. At last he withdrew. He sat back and looked at her long soaking body. It sparkled with sweat, giving it a gauzy texture under the soft lighting by the bed.

Gently he held her knees open, gazing into her deep ruby slit.

'I'll get the mirror,' he said. 'You should see this.'

He came back and held the glass so that she could see clearly what was between her legs. Her flesh was still pulpy and swollen, bruised crimson and purple. All over it was between each fleshy petal and tumbling from the slit itself was a cascade of foam.

'Work your muscles,' he said. She did and ejected a further stream of love juice.

'Isn't that beautiful?' he said. 'You are one spunky lady.'

He carried her into the bathroom and laid her on a frame on the floor which he then raised by hydraulic action till she floated clear of the ground in a comfortable harness-like arrangement. Clive sprayed her with a shower head, the jets of water making her body tingle with returning life, and then he dried her with a hot air blower.

He bent over her suspended there and put his mouth over her so that his upper teeth came down over her mound of Venus and his lower teeth sank into the fruity softness of her vulva. He closed his teeth slightly and shook his head, worrying at her pudenda like a dog with a bone. His tongue snaked out and before it was all washed away he drank some of their juices from the cup of her sex.

He carried her back to the bed where she lay passively, wondering what was coming next. He poured them each a glass of fine old brandy and gave her hers. The smooth liquid fire ignited a trail along her veins.

'Take out the bladder for me?' he asked.

She nodded a reluctant assent for she liked his straddle-legged awkward walk and the obscene pout of the thing. Now he reversed up to her and she released the valve in the bladder and let the air whoosh out. The whole thing now slid easily from his rear orifice. She took a little oil and massaged the offended flesh. He groaned a little and it slowly settled back into place. She slid a finger in to test its elasticity after such a stretching and to compare it with Rollo's arse, which she knew well.

Clive was considerably looser than Rollo had ever been, even in their most hectic days. She moved her finger thoughtfully inside Clive and realised she was enjoying being there very much. After a while she got Clive to roll over so that she could still penetrate his rear but she could also inspect his lovely cock. She handled it whilst she poked his arse, and found it swelled in her grasp.

He stroked her breast. 'I have many more games we can play,' he said invitingly. 'Is there something you fancy yourself?'

'I'm going to get astride this baby,' said Fiona, waggling his cock. 'I'm going to sit on it and take the whole damn thing right up me as far as it can go.'

He laughed. 'If you are going to ride me, I think you should have some suitable accoutrements.'

'Such as?'

'A cowboy hat. A nice suede jacket with lots of fringing. High-heeled boots with great rowely spurs. And a whip. A cowgirl needs to keep her horse under control, don't you think?'

'You have all this equipment here?'

'Certainly.'

Fiona enjoyed the dressing up. She slid the jacket on over her bare body and found the fringes tickled and excited her nipples where her breasts bulged free through the open front. Her hips and pelvis remained nude, her mound thrusting forward over her secret gash, and her buttocks pouting back under the rear hem of the jacket. The leather boots held her calves firmly and the high heels raised her so that when they stood chest to chest, Clive's mighty cock was on a level with her lower belly and she could nestle it at the apex of her legs.

The spurs were ferociously sharp and she found his nakedness vulnerable now she was partly dressed. She flicked the whip a couple of times and caused it to crack.

Clive dropped on his hands and knees with his back to her.

'Why don't you whip me round the room so I can show you my paces?' he suggested. Fiona flicked the whip at him but he did not perform until it struck his skin and by the time he had gone twice round the room, his arse was blazing red. She beat him until he mounted the bed where he rolled over. His cockstand was rigid, a vertical pole, just what she wanted.

She delayed enough to wrap the thong of the whip round his lovely great silken shaft and pull it tight. The flesh purpled and squeezed. She laughed and released him and dropped the whip.

'Take this now,' he said, passing her a riding crop. 'If you find me faint-hearted or not energetic enough when you are riding me, you can ginger me up with this and make me mend my ways. You have a right to expect a thoroughbred performance.'

Taking him inside her was a joy. Fiona lowered herself slowly till she was sitting fully astride him. She thought that if she was not already loosened by their previous fucking, she would not have been able to do this. She took the springy leather crop and tapped him smartly on his thighs, either side of which her rowels gleamed wickedly.

To her joy, he bounced violently and when he eased up she hit him again, urging him on till he was throwing himself up into her forcefully and frequently. He inserted a finger between their flesh and found her crushed clitoris which he teased as she went up and down like a piston. He used all his professional skill to time his climax to hers and when she felt the warm gush she had the added pleasure, as he swivelled expertly inside her, of feeling the lovely slithery liquid cascade about their joined sexual organs.

Fiona could hardly keep awake on the journey home. She stumbled through her own front door and found her way to her bedroom. She giggled at her crooked walk. Her thighs felt most peculiar.

Rollo lay asleep, a golden wasted king of a man.

She shed her clothes and fell on the bed. As she slid almost instantly into the deep sleep of exhaustion she held in her mind the clear mental image of the giant cock that she had had up her that night, in her cunt and in her mouth. Nor had Clive been content with that. He had knelt over her and masturbated himself until he came all over her breasts which he then massaged afterwards with his own spunk. Her skin still trembled at the memory. Her hand had its memories too, the velvet feel of the vibrant strength of him.

She fell asleep smiling.

14

The next day it said on the news that a notorious gang of the self-styled pirates had been successfully attacked and arrested. Two were dead, one policeman wounded and the rest of the gang in custody having been formally charged with highway piracy and kidnap.

Fiona heard the news with her fanny feeling twice its usual size and her brain feeling about half. She found she needed to know if Will Kid was in custody. She remembered her fantasy that he was a renegade cop. If he was, so much the worse for him. He would get even harsher treatment.

Down in the city they would know. Will had been king of his patch and if he was gone there would be a power vacuum to fight over. There would not be one who was not aware of it.

An idea began to form in Fiona's mind.

Then Rollo interrupted her plans. The directors of TransFlow had decided to meet in the flesh. They had things to say to each other that they had not the time to say at the launch party. The trouble with on-screen conferences was that there was no need for the subtleties of secretarial help. No one took notes. There was no minute of the meeting to agree to afterwards. The meeting was completely and entirely held on tape, copies of which were automatically sent to each participant afterwards.

Thus a whole range of subtle politically-motivated behaviour was lost. There was no 'feeling of the meeting'. There was only the bald record. The coldness and unarguability of the record inevitably controlled tongues. People only said what they did not mind being reminded of verbatim at a later date.

Minute-taking had always been a skilled and specious art and in the higher echelons of power this had meant that minutes were more a creative record of the power structure of a meeting than they were a plain recording of what was agreed. Now, like fire-making, it was a lost art, overtaken by the onward march of technology.

Each director brought with him something of an entourage and in the case of Fiona and Rollo, both being directors, theirs was a shared one. They were not the only marital couple on the board and there was an atmosphere of holiday as well as work about them all. Fiona knew they would be there at least a week and in other circumstances she might have enjoyed it. Rollo was supreme at these power games and she usually got a kick out of watching him at it, but she admitted to herself that her involvement with Will Kid was occupying the forefront of her mind and it was making everything else seem dim and unimportant.

They flew to Rio which was in permanent Carnival these days and Fiona endured hours of carambas and maraccas and Mexican hats and fancy costumes till she was sick of fiesta by any name.

She spent a great deal of time talking computers and she made crystal clear what was her personal baby and what belonged to TransFlow. She had used personally generated finance to set up her software company and it was now independent of the giant consortium.

She had time to review her recent sexual career. She examined the men she was now meeting in the light of Will and Chain and Clive and even Jamie, and decided that, regrettably, she had down-market taste in male flesh.

One of the directors made a sexual approach to her. It was a woman and Fee pretended she was hetero. For the moment Janine's maidenly charms were enough. She had no desire to move further along the lesbian path yet. Surprisingly, the gluttonous session with Clive's mighty dong aroused in her the desire for Janine's cool, sweet, fresh young body, so endearingly naive and endearingly urgent.

Rollo ate with her, danced with her, slept with her and talked with her. He did everything a woman in love wants her husband to do except fuck with her.

They flew home all pretty clear about what was going on in each other's minds. Construction was underway now and they faced the problem of controlling inevitably escalating costs. These must not eat into profitability. It was the biggest scheme that Rollo had ever got off the ground and he was determined that it should not fail for lack of his personal dynamism.

The night came that Fiona could no longer resist the lure of the city, and finding out what had happened to Will.

She dressed carefully. She must appear to be one of them. She wore a strange rubber garment that looked like skin-hugging trousers down the outside of her legs but was scalloped down the inside and held in place by a series of straps and buckles that revealed ovals of white flesh from top to bottom. In fond memory of Clive, she wore heeled ankle boots with spiky spurs.

On her top half she wore a tight bolero in the same black rubbery stuff as her lower garment, attached by five buckles and straps across her front. It made no concessions to her generous curving chest, rather it trapped the voluptuous flesh and held it tightly within its rubbery grasp.

She wore a gigantic silver zip about her throat and her hair was tightly bound with a hat pulled low over her face. She went cat-footed across the wire over the Zoo till she came to the wasteland between the edge of the jungle and the city-sprawl below. She had the feeling this would be her last visit.

She travelled quickly. It was different. The shadows were gloomier, the voices in the dark harsher and more on edge. There were no fires under the highway though still the twin headlights shafted the night as the turbomasters fired by overhead.

The headlights were unnecessary. The computers used infrared to steer the cars. Most Connet cars were never driven manually and only human eyes needed visible light to see by. The headlights were a concession to human quirkiness.

Fiona cast about her to see where any action was. She went on deeper into the city. She had checked out the manholes down to the old sewers and with shocked eyes she had seen the rubble-filled holes in the ground. They had been blasted out of existence.

She came across a wide street full of shops and eating houses. Music spilled from closed doors and dim light with it, so that the wares on offer, poor enough stuff by any standards, were rendered even less attractive by grubby shadows round the sleazy heaps.

She went on. On one street corner was a fight. A small crowd had gathered round it but Fiona crossed the street and went on by.

She went deeper and deeper into shadowland, panic growing slowly within her. This was madness. It was clear the city was neurotic with fear after the police swoop.

She saw two girls and approached them. They stopped and moved closer to one another, hostile to her. Their faces were pale and they both had long, improbably red, hair.

'Where is everyone?' asked Fiona.

'At the games.'

'The games?'

'Yeah.'

Fee heard bewilderment creep into their voices. Of course she must know where the games were, if she was of the city. 'Will the pirates be there?' she asked. 'If any are left.'

One of the girls suddenly guffawed with ugly laughter. 'If there are any left,' she shrilled. 'Oh yeah, that's where they'll be.'

Fiona went on. She cursed herself for not asking directly about Will Kid.

She became aware that certain shadows moved with her, intent about their own business. She felt one of a silent hurrying crowd. She must be going the right way. Everyone, it seemed, was going to the games.

The darkness ahead grew even more impenetrable. Fiona had long lost sight of the highway and she missed it. It was something familiar in this alien place.

She realised she was approaching a large circular building that reared up and blotted out the light before her. Others went that way also. Near to the ground were dim lights, oddly flickering. As Fiona came closer she saw they were torches, naked flame, burning in the sullen air with smoky defiance.

People were passing through a creaking turnstile. For the first time Fiona wondered about money. She never handled money. All her dealings were automated. She came closer and watched. This was really funny, she thought in a hollow way. She was the richest person there, richer than all these people put together and multiplied by ten. By ten times ten. More. But she had no cash and could not pay.

She leant against the wall and watched with narrowed eyes.

It was a moment before she realised she was being spoken to.

'You alone, sister?' a voice asked close to her shoulder.

She controlled her nervous start. 'What if I am?'

'I'm alone,' said the voice.

He was tall. It was hard to make out his features in the uncertain light but Fiona had the impression of a ferret, a narrow evil face set on a long thin body.

'What's that to do with me?' she challenged. She tried for the city-tone, a kind of aggressive boredom.

'You going in?'

'I don't have the fare, brother.'

'If I paid you in, maybe we could play some games together, huh?'

'Maybe. Are you good?'

'Good enough. Let's go.'

Inside was bedlam, more than a thousand people milling in hot dirty confusion as they climbed the stairways to reach the tiered rows above an arena brillliantly lit with floodlights and at the moment quite empty. The smell of food caught in Fiona's nostrils and made her gag. Hot greasy food crudely overspiced surrounded her. People wolfed at packets held in their hands and then threw away underfoot what they did not want. That and the sweet sickly overlay of synthetic alcohol was a nauseous combination.

They moved into the crowd, the man keeping close to her. Fiona could sense he was ready to grab her, to stake his claim on her body and exact first payment from her mouth for his generosity in bringing her in. She saw a particularly thick knot of people and vanished the far side of them, dropping swiftly through the rows and doubling back the way they had come. She attached herself to a group of three and walked close behind them, as if she belonged, till she was sure she had unloaded her sucker.

Now she began to search in earnest.

She went systematically through the great crowd trying to see if there was anyone she might recognise, either directly or by their gear, as belonging to the pirates.

Time passed and some activity was getting underway in the arena. The crowd was beginning to settle. Fiona knew she would have to start asking people. She was getting nowhere.

Two motorbikes roared into the arena, sand and gravel spitting from their tyres, to a roar of approval from the crowd. The riders gunned their bikes at ferocious speeds in the confined space round and round until one turned and went in the reverse direction. Now they passed each other twice a circuit, coming closer and closer to a collision whilst the crowd shrieked its delight.

Now they started weaving figures of eight. Each near-collision drew renewed whoops from the bloodthirsty crowd. Then the bikes almost did hit and one went over on its side, slewing across the floor of the arena with its driver trapped on it. The crowd yelled disapproval which intensified when they discovered the fallen rider had hurt his leg and could not remount. He could not walk. He was helped from the ring to roars of anger, his bike was dragged away and the other rider rode tamely off.

Fiona moved through the crowd. A man was standing with his arm round a girl.

'Hey,' said Fiona softly.

'Shove it,' said the girl briefly.

'You know where I can find Will Kid? Captain Will Kid? I heard he got unlucky but I didn't hear how much.'

The man shrugged. 'It ain't my business,' he said.

'Get lost,' snapped the girl.

Fiona moved on, resisting the urge to slap the girl. She didn't need trouble on top of everything else tonight.

She approached another man and repeated her request.

'Who's asking?' he said.

'A friend.'

'A friend would know.'

'I've been busy. I lost touch.'

'Lose touch again, you hear me?'

She began to get angry. This time she approached two women with their arms round each other. She repeated her question.

'Poor Will,' said one softly.

Fiona felt a cold hand clutch round her heart. 'Why do you say that?'

'Poor Will, poor Bill, poor us, poor fuss . . .' The girl's voice trailed away and she giggled. Fiona looked more closely and saw the mad eyes. She mumbled and moved on.

She was sickened now. She wanted to get away and she began to make her way to an exit. She was doing no good here, not to herself nor to Will.

Down below her the second act was getting underway. Flames shot upwards as lit rings of fire smoked into the night. There was no roof to the amphitheatre.

She looked down. Someone dived through a ring of fire and came out aflame. The figure stood there, arms outflung, cruciform and engulfed in fire.

This time Fiona was not too impressed. She knew the body could be coated in a synthetic resin and the flame would not actually be touching the skin. The figure below would be coated in silicone or something similar. But it looked good and she doubted that many in the crowd had much of a grasp of chemistry.

Under cover of the enthusiastic noise, she struggled to find an exit. Then, to her horror, she was grabbed. The man who had paid her entrance had miraculously found her again and he was very angry.

Twisting her shoulder from under his mean tight grip, Fiona ducked away from him, only the slipperiness of her rubber clothes saving her. She ran through the crowd, snaking into any gap she could find between the compressed bodies. She was followed by a storm of vituperation and abuse.

Then flame shot up before her and the crowd screamed

with one awful terror-struck voice. Something in the ranked tiers had caught fire. An errant spark from the show had found matter to burn in the crowd. There was instant panic as people pulled back from the menace, and like a great sluggish animal the whole mass of people moved up, seeking to get out the way they had got in. Individual screams drilled her nerves and spread panic faster than flames.

She assessed the situation in a split second. She remembered the stairs up from ground level leading to the entrance at the tops of the tiers. The thought of those stairs full of escaping people was more terrifying than the fire. Against the grain of the crowd Fiona began to go down, down to the sanded arena away from the exits.

The next half hour would be forever in her mind, the stuff of nightmare. She had made the right decision, of course, and as she worked lower she found others had done the same thing. The performers had an exit down here, far closer and safer than the ones up top, above descending stairwells and narrow passages.

The air was bad, over-heated and depleted in oxygen. The heat was intense, though Fiona's suit protected her. It might be rubber, but all high-quality clothing had flame-resistance built in. Her lungs were burning as she fought her way with the crowd towards what they all took to be freedom.

They passed through several big rooms and then flowed into a chemocrete corridor with offices off it. There was a door at the end and as she was spewed out through it, trying desperately to keep her balance, Fiona realised she was outside.

She began to run. She heard sirens in the night and became aware of firecopters whirring overhead. There was a great deal of screaming coming from the amphitheatre.

She took to her heels and fled. She ran on and on, easing her pace only so that she could maintain it, putting all the distance she could between herself and the horror behind. She ran through the city, through the wasteland and on to safety. She knew as she ran that she was cured of ever coming here again.

No one stopped her. No one interfered with her. She met

people running the other way, greedy to see the disaster firsthand.

At the fence she rested, sobbing against its familiar wire. Then she climbed up it, up and up till she was over the jungle and heading for the Zoo. Now she was safe she slowed up, used up and exhausted. She checked her wrist compass and headed across the dark plain above the canopy. An hour later she was on known territory, occasionally seeing the warm gleam of light spilling up through a bubble dome.

She found her ramp and ran home.

15

Fee Cambridge knew her place now. It might be boring at times but, if she was to survive, it would be within the safe confines of the Zoo. She didn't have the stomach for the city.

She had to incinerate all her clothes which stank of the fire and had scorch marks on them. For the first time she saw her activities as Rollo might see them. She was appalled by what might have been.

The experience faded like a bad dream. There was mention on the news of a serious fire down in the city but it was rare for much prominence to be given to anything outside the cocooned world of the Zoo. The media weren't keen to report what they feared to investigate.

Then Fiona had a new idea concerning the whereabouts of Will Kid.

She dressed herself in sombre respectable clothes and vidied the captain of police who had penetratingly interviewed her after the escapade with her Connet.

After some delay she was put through.

'Captain,' she said, looking pale and nunlike.

'Mrs Cambridge. How are you?'

'As fine as I can be, in the circumstances. I want to ask you something indiscreet.'

'Not too indiscreet, Mrs Cambridge,' he said with forced joviality. 'This is an open line.'

'It's about your wonderful roundup of those terrible brigands. My psychiatrist recommended I bring this into the open.'

'What's that?'

'Will you be preferring charges in that little matter we both know about, that traumatic experience I described to you that you were so sympathetic over?' She let her voice waver a little.

'Actually, Mrs Cambridge, we don't have the perpetrator of that particular misdeed, I am afraid. We tried to match DNA but it was no go. I'm very sorry. We don't have that man.'

'I have to tell you I am relieved. I could hardly bear the thought of the episode becoming public and what he might say.'

'Well, it doesn't arise. Possibly he is dead. We didn't get all the bodies. Your privacy will be assured in the matter.'

'Captain, I want you to know how much I appreciate your handling of this delicate issue. I feel in your debt and if ever the opportunity arises that I can do something for you, you may rest assured your discretion will be rewarded.'

'That's fine to hear, Mrs Cambridge. I'm just doing my job.'

'Did you get that one you told me about? Will Kid. The one named after the old-time pirate.'

'We certainly did. He is behind bars forever, I guess. I still feel good about it every time I think of it.'

'Good for you. And thank you so much.'

Poor Will. Fiona meditated upon his incarceration. There was nothing she could do to help him. The best legal defence in the world would not get him off the hook, for it was a hook of his own devising. It seemed an awful waste of a highly talented and well-hung man. She would simply have to forget all about him.

The best way to do this, she decided, was to further her plans concerning Janine and Rollo.

By way of preparation she took to playing with Rollo in his sleep, just to get him on the right track, as it were. It was not a process she enjoyed. It brought home to her her humiliating status of a wife who had ceased to turn on her husband. There was no fun to be had at all from tickling a man's balls if he in return resembled nothing so much as a sack of potatoes. Rollo might be stunning visually but sexually he was in the tuber class. It made Fiona want to spit.

She had a long conversation with Janine but felt the girl needed little schooling. She was a born actress.

Fiona felt no sympathy for Rollo as she wove her devious

213

net around him. He was only getting what he deserved. Indeed, he was getting far better than he deserved. Two women, herself and Janine, were working flat out to arouse his laggard sexual desire. Few men would find themselves the object of so much concern. She ought to abandon the libido-lacking son of a bitch.

Somehow she couldn't bring herself to do that.

As the night drew nearer, she drew in the loose ends and tightened the knot.

'Honey,' she said over dinner one night.

'Yes?'

Poor innocent lamb, thought Fiona cynically. She strove to keep her voice light and pleasant. 'Have you thought any more about Janine since that occasion in our bedroom?'

Rollo did not turn dark red nor did he drop his food. He was far too sophisticated for that. But Fiona, watching him narrowly for the slightest of signs, detected a certain rigidity in his posture.

'She's crossed my mind,' he drawled. 'I've been busy, of course.' He added this last hastily in case Fiona should get the right idea. 'I hope she's all right now.'

'I don't know,' sighed Fiona. 'She's the best maid I ever had and I am genuinely fond of her. I wish we could help her with her problems.'

'Her problems with men, you mean.'

'Her problem is that she doesn't have one. And because she doesn't have one, she doesn't have the confidence to go out and get one. She is really bugged by this virginity business.'

'Yes,' said Rollo in a dull voice.

'She is afraid to get herself a boyfriend because of the impediment of her virginity. She has the wit to realise a man likes a woman to know what she is doing.'

'Yes, of course,' agreed Rollo unenthusiastically.

'She hates to present herself in such a dumb light. I have assured her a man won't necessarily think like that. He should honour her for her abstinence. She says that might be what it says in the books but in real life men like women who like men. And women who like men have done it.'

'A vicious circle,' said Rollo.

'Absolutely. If only she could break the circle.'

'And the membrane.'

Fiona trilled with laughter. 'Neatly put. But you are right. Once she was started this whole problem would roll up and go away.'

'Yes,' said Rollo in that same curious flat voice.

'Isn't it funny,' pursued Fiona, 'to think of that lovely young girl like a ripe fruit waiting to be plucked. There is a unique experience for some man with the guts to take it. All her sweet young innocent rounded flesh awaiting a man's prick. Like Sleeping Beauty, only she needs a prick to wake her up, not to put her to sleep. He's going to be a lucky bastard who first gets his cock inside her, don't you think, Rollo?'

'Yes,' said Rollo and left the table in a hurry.

The next day when they were aligning their schedules, Fiona told Rollo she would be spending the evening with Diana and would not be back till late.

When Rollo finished work that night and had come through to eat, alone as Fee had told him he would be, he found she had left him a note telling him not to wait up. She knew how he needed his sleep these days. She and Diana were going to a benefit performance of the ballet and on to a newly opened restaurant that specialised in insect-based cuisine. She would be back late.

He spread some flow charts across the table and settled to eat.

He had finished his food and was working at the table in amongst the mess when Janine came into the room. She hesitated when she saw him there.

'Yes?' he said pleasantly to the girl, looking up.

'Please, Mr Cambridge,' she whispered.

'What is it, Janine?'

She burst into tears. 'I want to give my notice in.'

Damn, he thought, wishing Fee was there. He knew Fee was keen to keep the girl.

'Surely not,' he said in hearty voice. 'We like having you here very much, you know.'

'I'm just a nuisance. And I'm so unhappy.'

'You certainly are not a nuisance. I'm sorry you are unhappy. Is there anything I can do to help?'

'You, er, Mrs Cambridge, uh, oh . . .' She burst into renewed tears and howled dolefully.

Rollo gave a wistful look at his flow charts and stood up to do his duty. He went over to the distressed girl and put a fatherly arm about her. They sank together on to the step that led down into the eating area.

'There, there,' he said. 'I'm sure all this is not necessary.'

'Mrs Cambridge has been so kind,' said Janine. She gulped a couple of times like a frog and appeared to master her tears.

'She's very fond of you.'

'She's tried to help me but I am beyond help.'

'I think that is a little overdramatic, Janine. Things can't be that bad. Is it money? Perhaps we can help.'

'No. I'm fine for money. Mrs Cambridge pays me a very generous wage.'

Rollo cursed mentally. Money was the easy option.

'It's men,' said Janine melodramatically.

'Men? More than one?'

'None.'

'I beg your pardon.'

'None. Oh, Mr Cambridge,' cried Janine, drawing back from him slightly and facing him. 'Am I really so awful?'

She had slightly chubby cheeks, a remnant from her recent adolescence. Her pale face was woebegone and tearstreaked. Her pale hair swung slightly and glowed with life. Her large blue cornflower eyes swam mistily, tears caught like diamonds on her thick lashes. She was infinitely appealing.

Rollo leant towards her and carefully wiped the tears from under her eyes. He smiled, softening the brilliance of his own eyes. They frightened Janine but at the same time she adored them. 'No, Janine,' he said softly. 'You aren't awful at all.'

Innocence wreathed her. Rollo felt the full weight of his years and sexual knowledge. She moved closer to him. He felt the glow of her body-warmth and caught the faint fresh smell of cologne.

'Do you mean that?' she begged.

'The man that has you,' said Rollo, 'is a very lucky man.'

'That's lovely,' she whispered, an adorable faint blush lending colour to her wistful face. 'I wish it was true.'

Rollo took her face between his two hands. He drew her closer and tilted his own face sideways. His eyes dropped from hers to her lips.

He touched her mouth with his. She did not respond but neither did she pulled away. Again he laid his lips against hers, almost holding his breath, and this time he felt her lips flutter slightly beneath his. Her lack of knowledge, lack of gloss, caught at his heart and his loins. He pressed harder and opened her mouth with his.

She responded very gently, hesitantly, like a frightened bird. Rollo kissed her as sweetly as he knew, tasting the young freshness of her mouth, savouring her extreme and rare innocence. As her tongue moved slightly against his, he felt his cock rise sharply with desire. He pulled Janine into him and holding her tight against his hard body he kissed her deeply and thoroughly.

She pressed against him with a shy grace. He slid his hand round her neck under her weight of hair and felt her tremble as he caressed her sensitive nape.

At last he drew back. He held her face between his hands again and searched for her expression. She looked breathless with wonder, mute in adoration of him.

He smiled into her face. 'You see,' he chided. 'You are a lovely child.'

'But I don't want to be a child,' she breathed. 'Not any longer.'

Rollo's hands trembled slightly. His groin ached. 'What do you mean?' he asked carefully.

'I went . . . I want to grow up. To be a real woman.' She blushed again.

Rollo released her face and drew her against him. With his chin on her head he said in a flat voice: 'What do you mean, exactly?'

'You know,' she mumbled into his shirt. 'Sex.'

Rollo held still for some time. Janine held her breath.

217

Then Rollo moved again so that he could look at her. Janine saw the change in him and marvelled. He had lost the soft protective look and gained a sort of glittery hardness. The skin on his lean face had tightened. She felt the first sweet stirrings of sexual power.

'You want a man to make love to you?'

'Yes.'

'Has this ever happened to you before?'

Janine bent her head as if with shame. 'No,' she said in a stifled voice.

'Why don't you get a boyfriend? I'm sure the youths at the local disco will be willing to oblige.'

'I don't want a boy,' whispered Janine. 'I want a man.'

'Any man?'

'No.'

Rollo sighed. 'Who, then?'

'The best.'

'The best?'

'You.'

The silence grew and stretched between them. 'You see why I have to go,' mumbled Janine.

'What makes you think I am the best?'

The face she showed him was incredulous. 'For the likes of me? You are like Prince Charming. You're, you're perfect. So far above me. I'm a servant. Just a dumpy little virgin eating my heart out for you. I don't expect you to want me.'

His chin was on her head again. She felt his chest shudder with each strong beat of his heart. She closed her eyes and savoured the exquisite moment.

'You should never say such things to a man. You shouldn't belittle yourself.' He shook slightly.

'Why shouldn't I say them? I embarrass you, you mean?'

He clenched his hands into fists suddenly, deep in her hair so that it hurt. His eyes blazed blue fire. 'You silly bitch,' he said between his teeth. 'Because of course I want to fuck you.'

If he had intended his coarseness to make her recoil, he was mistaken. Janine took a hold of her shirt and ripped it open. Her young breasts spilled out. 'I beg you to take me,' she said. 'I beg you.'

Rollo came forward over her and began to kiss her ferociously, trapping her between himself and the floor. Janine found the change in him and his physical strength terrifying and exulting. 'I'll do anything you want,' she said hysterically. His mouth was on her breast. 'Tell me what to do.'

Rollo stopped and tore himself from her. 'Your bedroom,' he said. His breathing was ragged.

In the attic Fiona moved carefully until she was over Janine's bedroom. She had already removed the plugs of material from her two spyholes. Now she settled herself in absolute silence as her husband and her maidservant came into the room below her.

Her plan was working, it seemed.

Rollo moved the torn shirt back from Janine's shoulders and kissed them, taking his time and lingering over her strange flesh, so new to him. The shirt trapped her arms against her body and she closed her eyes and moaned faintly, pushing herself forward, offering herself to him.

He looked down at her breast. It was firm and shapely, the size to fit into a man's palm and his spread fingers, not large but beautifully shaped. He worked her shirt off so that her upper torso was bare. She hung her head as if in shame and her hair spilled all around in a long wheat-fair curtain. He separated it at the back of her head and kissed her neck there.

She did nothing to him, leaving his body alone and keeping her hands to herself. He took this as evidence of her shyness and ignorance.

He ran his hands down her back and she straightened and arched it so that her hair fell back and her breasts thrust through. Rollo put a hand under her chin and began to kiss her jawline and her ear.

Fiona watched silently from above.

Rollo had her mouth with his again. Hers was wide open now like some chick in the nest appealing for sustenance. He broke slightly from her and with their breaths mingling he said: 'I can't turn back. You are sure this is what you want?'

'I worship you,' whispered Janine. 'Do anything to my body that pleases you.'

'And tomorrow, when you help dress my wife. What then?'

'Mrs Cambridge is good to me,' said Janine artlessly. 'Look what she bought me.'

She broke from Rollo and reached for something over a chair. It was a satin chemise, a delicate piece of nonsense, creamy smooth with heavy ivory lace at its hem. Two slender ribbons supported it across her shoulders.

'Fiona has excellent taste,' said Rollo. His eyes narrowed as he watched Janine slip the garment on. He reached out one hand, palm forward, and laid the centre on her nipple outside the material. Gently he rotated his palm against the tip of her breast so that the material frotted her slightly. He felt her harden. He watched her face and saw it change.

'Take off your trousers,' he said.

She wriggled and slipped out of the clinging things. Under them she wore a pair of French drawers made from the same satin and ivory lace as the chemise. Rollo laid his hand on her upper thigh and slipped his fingertips under the lace. Her skin was firm and resilient. It was dusted with fine gold hair. He stroked her thigh.

'I want you to remove my clothes for me,' he said.

He stretched himself on the bed. Her face was serious and intent as she bent to her task. She undid the fastenings of his shirt and opened it shyly and looked at his chest, richly tanned and smooth. With trembling fingers she undid the top of his trousers. She fumbled over this task, not quite clear what attached to what. Rollo made no move to help her.

Then his trousers were undone also.

'Should I unzip them?' she asked.

'Yes.'

Her fingers reached awkwardly into his fly. She had been aware for some time of the bulge within his clothing. Now she felt the heat and pressure of his body. He was still confined by his undergarment.

'Take off my shirt,' he said. He sat up and faced her so that she had to come very close to raise it and take it off over his head. Only the material of her chemise separated their naked breasts.

He brought his hands round and found her waist, holding it under the chemise, feeling the top of her drawers and the

220

are skin above them. She did not have Fiona's slenderness but her skin was elastic with youth.

She sat with her hair cascading all about her, trembling lightly in his grasp so that he was almost unbearably excited. He slid from the bed and stood up. 'Finish undressing me,' he said.

She knelt at his feet and removed his house sandals. Then she slid her hands nervously under the waistband and took a deep breath. She pulled down, baring his groin. His cock sprang free close to her face. Her hair brushed against it as she bent to lift each leg and free him of his clothes. It quivered stiffly.

She bent right over before his naked body and kissed his feet, her hair a pool on the floor. Then she raised herself and sat back, looking at him, arrogantly naked and hard erect, a beautiful sexual man.

'This is what you wanted,' he said harshly.

'Yes. It's so big,' she said naively.

'You've seen erect men before.'

'On Screen. This is different.'

Above them Fiona sat back and rubbed her eye. Then she applied it once more to the scene below her.

Rollo bent one leg under him and sat on the bed. He took Janine in his arms and kissed her again, sliding a hand up under her chemise and finding her breast. He played with her nipple till it was long and erect. She linked her hands round his neck and shook slightly with what he did to her. She was too shy to drop her own hands and be free with him.

He laid her back on the bed and pushed up the chemise. He put his lips to her breasts and kissed them both gently. Then he let go and moved down the bed to her feet. He picked one up and began to separate the toes, kissing each one and sucking it. His hands caressed her ankle and ran up her calf.

She stared at him, her eyes huge. He bent her knees, bringing his hands suddenly closer to her secret places. He ran his hand up under her thigh and let his fingers slip under the lace. He slid his warm hand round her thigh till it was at the front.

The tips of his fingers felt the down of her fleece. He too
his hand away and ran the finger over the outside of he
drawers, between her legs.

She was damp.

'Stand up,' he ordered. 'Here. By me.'

She stood by him where he continued to sit on the bec
He lifted her chemise and kissed her ribs. He eased h
thumbs under the ribbon at her waist and felt round t
where it was tied in a little bow. He undid the bow an
loosened the ribbon. The drawers fell to her ankles in a sig
of lace.

Her fleecy young thatch was bare before him. He put hi
fingers into its little curls and fluffed it gently. Her stomac
fluttered and he leant in to her and kissed its rounde
softness. His hands went round behind her and gripped he
buttocks. He held her against his face and kissed her sto
mach, moving down till he was kissing her fleece direct. He
bottom clenched involuntarily and he resisted the urge t
force her cheeks apart.

Still she trembled like a bird and did not touch him.

He tilted his head sideways and began to bite at her projec
ting mound. At the same time his hands went back up he
body and found her breasts. He felt her nipples and sh
pressed forwards against him, shaky on her legs, almos
fainting with emotion.

He put a hand between her thighs and pushed up till i
touched wet flesh. She fell then, and he caught her and laic
her on the bed.

He moved himself up beside her and laid himself agains
her nakedness, stroking her hair back from her face. His eye
were a deep dark blue, the colour of lust, and his nostrils wer
flared. She looked startled, huge-eyed, like a frightened fawn.

He kissed her throat and came on top of her.

Clumsily she put her arms round him, feeling his weigh
bear her down, feeling his powerful muscled body, feelin
the absolute maleness of him on her. His legs were open and
astride hers which remained tight closed.

His chest crushed her breasts. He lifted himself and kissec
her nipples and then drew himself right up so that he was

itting on his heels astride her. His cock bounced slightly, razing her thighs.

Then he moved and opened her legs by main force, pulling up her knees and pushing them apart. Janine screwed her eyes shut and clenched her fists.

Perspiration beaded Rollo's upper lip. Even her fear urned him on.

He looked between her legs. Her posture forced her thighs vide apart as her legs sagged one to each side. Within the fair curls dark with moisture he could see the pale glimmer of ecret flesh. He sank down and applied his mouth to her closed rosebud of sex.

She mewed.

'I must have you now,' he said, calmly and with steel in his voice.

'Yes,' she whispered.

He could feel her thighs shake with nerves. Her pussy was indescribable, almost unbearable in its sweetness. Its musk was faint and light and the pale pink lobes of flesh were tiny under his tongue.

He lapped her and saw her flush a deeper rosy colour, becoming plumper, more free-standing as her inexperienced flesh prepared instinctively for ingress. He slipped his tongue into her vagina.

Even his tongue could feel the obstruction. She twisted slightly and he heard her pant. He sucked, not too hard. Though he did not know it, he emulated his wife in not wanting to rupture her membrane in this way. He wanted his cock to have the honour of first entering her palace.

He sat up and began to lower himself over her, ready now to penetrate her and complete the act of defloration.

Her hands were on his shoulders. 'Now?' she whispered.

He was beside himself, almost incapable of speech. 'It'll hurt,' he said roughly.

'Hurt me, please. Please!' Her voice was wild.

He pushed her legs wide apart, as far as they would go. His cock was so stiff with lust it needed no hand to guide it. He moved his hips and began to push at her entrance.

Above them tears coursed down Fiona's cheeks. She

wiped them savagely away. She was close to orgasm herself

Janine screamed and went rigid. Rollo stopped, hardly an⟩ of his long prick inside her. Janine forced herself to relax. 'G⟨ on,' she whispered.

Rollo pushed again. She jerked under him and he pushe⟨ on. The tightness was unbelievable. Her fanny gripped an⟨ attempted to repel his cock. He hung still for a moment, no⟨ to help her but to savour fully the moment of violation.

He pushed again and felt her resistance tear. She gave ⟨ sobbing moan and he drove the full length of his cock withi⟩ her. He was gripped by a fantastic tightness, both hard an⟨ dry. His cock bloomed within her, its muscle adjusting to he⟨ narrowness and forcing her riven flesh apart.

'Are you in?' she asked, her voice little more than ⟨ plaintive whimper.

'Yes.' He looked down on her tearstreaked face, and no⟩ that he was free to feel pity without it preventing what he wa⟨ doing, he had some sympathy for her. 'Is it so very bad, m⟩ poor sweet child?'

'It stings but I love it.'

He began to move in her, very slight movements because she was so tight and dry. She held him so tightly that he wa⟨ almost in pain himself. Then, gradually, he began to lubricate them both and movement became easier.

Her eyes were shut and her brows drawn together in a⟨ frown of concentration. Rollo felt his temperature rise and he began to move in earnest. Each stroke was difficult but the sensation was fantastic. He wanted to extend it though he knew for Janine's sake he should keep it short. But for himself, he longed for this unique nexus to last forever.

He felt her soften slightly and his bruised prick eased a little. She grew a little turgid under his inner caress. Her sexual organs were beginning to work properly. He speeded up, trying not to drive too roughly into her but glorying in the force he still needed for each penetration. His climax was approaching and he felt his balls slap against her and his shaft rippled within her flesh.

His orgasm took him, a white-hot explosion in the length of his prick. He hit into her and felt her jerk. His spunk was

eleased and out of control he spent himself in her in a series
f harsh juddering blows.

He rested on his elbows when he was done, his head
anging and his dark blond hair flopping wetly down. She
ay quiescent, his shaft still within her, and he could feel her
trangeness all about him. Very slowly he began to slip out of
er.

His spunk frothed pink from her. She lay docile, the
hemise rucked up above her breasts and her legs splayed
vide apart. He could see what he had destroyed and what he
ad created at one and the same time.

'Janine,' he said.

Her eyelids were veined with delicate blue lines. They
luttered and opened.

'Janine,' he said again.

'Yes.'

'Look at me.'

'Yes.' Her eyes were drowned and mysterious, her face
serene.

'Does it hurt bad?'

She considered. She smiled and it was like the sun
reaking through. 'It hurts good,' she said.

'Welcome to the world.' He began to pull back.

'You're leaving me. Now!' Her voice squeaked in panic.

'I'm going to the bathroom to wash. OK? I don't think we
are finished yet, are we?'

'Oh. Should I wash?'

'You are fine the way you are.'

Alone, Janine drew up her legs, grimacing slightly, and
tried to see herself. She touched the spunk that dribbled from
her fanny curiously and sniffed at what was on her finger.
From above Fiona looked down on the girl's open legs fro-
thing with spunk from her own husband and felt wetness
between her own legs.

Rollo came back, the tension gone from his body though
his eyes had a satyr's glitter to them. 'I want you to play with
me,' he said.

She smiled shyly. 'You'll have to tell me what to do,' she
said.

'Follow your instincts. Explore me. Be as dirty as you like. There's nothing to get embarrassed about. Find out what m' body feels like. Go in what you can get in and go round wha' you can't. I'm quite tough, Janine. You needn't worry abou' hurting me.'

Thus licensed Janine began to rove.

She was hesitant at first, self-conscious, but as Rollo lay peacefully letting her do what she willed and not speaking, she began to move with more confidence. She ran her hands over the smooth planes of his body, feeling his chest and shoulder and cupping his muscles. She was fascinated by his breadth and strength, the veining on him, the bulge of muscle.

She felt his stomach and hips, delighting in the satin skin over iron-hard bone and muscle. She was shy of his groin bu' she explored the column of his thighs with their powerfu' tendons, so different from hers, and his strong knees and calves and feet.

'Now here,' said Rollo, touching his soft cock.

Her hand brushed him like a butterfly's wing.

'You've never touched a naked man before,' he marvelled.

'You are the first,' she replied with strict truth. She lifted his limp penis and lowered it again. It stiffened slightly.

Rollo opened his legs and put his balls into Janine's hands. 'Go easy,' he said.

She played with him as Fiona had taught her whilst up above Fiona watched, her green eyes hard.

His cock grew a little stiffer.

'Kiss me,' he said.

She came up his body, the chemise slipping as she did so.

'No. Down here.'

She looked startled and he laughed and took the chemise up over her head and tossed it to one side. 'Go on,' he said.

She kissed the side of his shaft with lips primly pursed. She repeated this several times.

'Put the damn thing in your mouth,' said Rollo.

She took the very end between her lips.

'Suck,' he snarled, his eyes shut.

She sucked and felt him grow hard and large within her mouth.

226

'Go on. Suck harder.'

She sucked hard. He was swollen in her mouth. She tasted the strange head and sucked with a will.

'OK.' He knotted his hand in her hair and pulled her head off him. Her eyes were large and soft. His were bright and hard.

'He's ready for more,' he said. 'Can you take it?'

'In my mouth?' Her voice rose to a terrified squeal.

'In your cunt.'

'Yes.' She lay back eagerly but Rollo caught at her hair again. 'Look at him now that he's ready, see?'

She looked at his great swollen darkened pole with its bloated head. She saw the pale purple of a vein running beneath the silken skin. She reached out a tentative hand and touched him. He bounced under her touch, alive and strong.

'Cradle my balls,' he said.

She cupped their warm hairy fullness, feeling the two hard nuts within the sac.

'Now grasp my cock with your fist. Ease the skin up and down. That's it. Not too much. Firm but not tight.'

An opaque droplet, a tear, oozed from the eye in the head. Rollo sighed. 'Your tongue,' he said. 'Lick it off.'

She took the droplet on the very tip of her tongue and then tasted it.

'Now I'm going to enter you again.'

Obediently she lay back and Rollo came on top of her. His shaft nuzzled into her tight place but this time the passage was not sealed and she was slimy wet from his previous ingress.

He felt his knob slip firmly in. She squeaked slightly but was otherwise silent. He forgot her, concentrating on the rare tightness and constriction around his burning shaft. He pushed very slowly in, enjoying the increasing pressure as he gradually forced her new-made channel apart. Its wet walls stuck together and tried to resist the stranger but the resistance served only to inflame him and he increased the force he used and penetrated her fully. Her tiny young passage gripped him tightly and then relaxed very slightly as her new womanhood eased around his shaft and made the first tentative stirrings to welcome him.

When he was right in, up to the hilt, he bit her ear lobe. She jumped and he pulled back and drove in again.

This time as he fucked her he kissed her mouth and her breasts and her throat and under her arms till she was moaning beneath him. He continued his deep steady plunges in the slickness of his previous come, bringing himself smoothly to the peak of pleasure.

'I'm going to come,' he said into her hair. His shaft trembled. She lifted her hips and for the first time met his plunge so that their wet flesh thudded together.

'Oh, good girl,' he groaned.

His cock swelled and as he prepared for the glorious moment of release she pushed up, meeting him and triggering his climax. He jerked, driving into her harder than he had intended, and driving again and again till he had emptied himself and spent his lust in her.

Her hands were at the back of his neck, her back arched so she was driving her body up into his. He felt her nails gouge his skin. He rolled over, holding her hard by the waist so she would not slide off him, and settled her astride his diminishing rod. He put his hands behind his head and smiled up at her, the smile of a satisfied lecher.

'You adorable little whore,' he said. 'A virgin whore. Who'd have thought it?'

'Did I do it right, Mr Cambridge?'

'You sure as hell did.'

She looked smug, childishly pleased at her success. Between her legs the golden man was like a god to her.

'Another time,' said Rollo deliberately, 'I'm going to take that delectable little pussy of yours and suck it free of spunk.'

'I'm bleeding,' she confessed.

'You won't be next time.'

Above them Fiona sat up rubbing her eyes and easing her cramped stiff body. She ached with randiness.

Her plan had worked, worked with a vengeance. Remembering what she had seen and knowing what she knew, it was hard to say who had seduced whom.

16

The following morning Fiona was startled to hear on the news that one of the pirates held in captivity had escaped. There were few details yet, no doubt the sufficiency of egg on people's faces was obscuring the free movement of information, but they had a picture of the violent and dangerous man now at large.

Of course it was Will.

Fiona wanted desperately for him to get away. There was no way she could help him and it was obvious to her that he would make for the city where he had friends and a kind of life. There could be no other place safe for him to hide.

She made love in the afternoon with Janine, free at last to explore within the girl as she had wanted to do for so long. She did not admit that she had spied on the girl making love with her husband. That was a piece of knowledge she kept fiercely close to her breast. She made Janine tell her, bit by bit, everything that Rollo had done to her and with her and how she had felt, pain and triumph and glee.

Over and above the undercurrent of jealousy, Fiona felt the power of the puppetmaster. She had manipulated Janine to her will. Now she had manipulated Rollo through Janine, the girl playing her innocent part so completely that she would have fooled Fiona herself, had Fee not known better. And though she had bent the unknowing Rollo to her will, he would bear the burden of guilt and feel that he owed her.

Fee enjoyed hearing Janine talk dirty, hearing her tell her mistress what her mistress's husband had done with her body. Fee touched her and copied, as far as she was able, what Rollo had done to the girl. She and Janine had more, far more that they could do together. There was self-love in the way they exploited each other's bodies. And Janine, who had pretended to be shocked when Rollo had wanted her to take him in her mouth, sucked his wife to climax with a will. And with growing expertise. Awareness of her own fanny made her more responsive to Fiona's. And Fiona, touching lips, breast, vulva and bottom, found a woman exciting and arousing and mysterious to be with.

She sucked Janine to climax. The girl twisted with pent-up desire and yelled aloud when she felt the orgasmic release within her for the first time. Fiona found the flood of wet in her mouth divine. This was nectar. This was ambrosia. With Janine, she tasted the food of the gods.

On Janine's day off Fee answered a call to the door.

'Who is it?' she asked through the grille.

'Let me in, Skelton. They are right behind me.'

She triggered the door release and Will Kid slipped inside and stood panting against the wall.

It was so good to see him that she felt faint. He stood as tall and broad as ever, his wild mane emphasising his slanting, angled cheekbones and his wide-set hazel eyes. But he was different. His eyepatch was missing though Fiona could detect nothing odd about his blind eye save for a tiny opaque blemish in it. He wore prison clothes, dour cheap material, ill-fitting trousers and a grubby shirt.

'How close behind you?' she said.

'Minutes. They'll search here. I can pretend I forced you.'

His voice trailed off. His skin tone was vile, dull, filthy. Fee saw he was exhausted.

'Are they using DNA sniffers?' she asked urgently.

'Yes. I'm sorry it has to end like this for us, Fee.'

She missed the use of her real name. He was done for, she saw, almost at the point of collapse. Her mind meshed smoothly.

'Follow me. Quick.'

'It's no use.'

'Up. Quick.'

She led him to below the loft trap and pressed the device that released the stairs. They lowered silently. He climbed heavily behind her, too tired to argue.

'Here,' she said. 'It's an authentic astronaut's suit. We got t from moonbase one holiday. Get in and I'll seal it. It'll defeat the sniffers.'

She ran back down and got out the multivac, something he never usually touched. It dedusted and ionised the air in he apartment, processing it for allergens and pollutants. And organic traces. Whilst it howled at full blast she activated the carpet enzymes, tiny self-replicating robot chips hat lay invisibly in the floor coverings and ate dirt.

She ran back up the steps and found Will within the suit. She did up the last connections and waved the nozzle of the multivac all around, up the loft steps and into the oft itself and over her own body. Then she descended and sent the steps back up into the loft, closing the trap electronically.

Five minutes had passed.

She ran to the bathroom and turned on the taps, keying the water sensor that would stop the flow well up the rim of the tub. She came back and put the multivac away and turned off the carpet enzymes. She tore off her clothes and heard the front door buzz. She dunked herself in the tub with her underwear still on, grabbed a towel and came back to the door, trying to calm her breathing.

'Who is it?' she queried languidly.

'Police, ma'am. May we come in?'

'Damn you, no.' Fiona achieved a throaty laugh. 'I'm having my bath, officer. Make an appointment.'

'I'm afraid we must insist. There is a criminal loose in this area.'

'The hell there is. How exciting. Do you think he is underneath my towel?'

'We will use an explosive device on your door unless you let us in, ma'am.'

Fiona knew the police had the means and the authority to do this, though she had never heard of it being done to anyone in the Zoo.

She released the door.

She was magnificently angry and allowed her towel to keep slipping, though she kept catching it.

'What is going on? I thought my home was inviolate.'

231

'There is a criminal loose here, ma'am. Our sniffers indicate he has been at your door.'

'How would he get in?'

'That we couldn't say.' There were two of them, lean and
mean-tempered. They carried whip guns. 'Since he broke
out of prison and hacked for a living, maybe he can override
your personal barcode. We have to check it out.'

'This is the missing pirate, isn't it? How thrilling. I must
vidi my friends.'

'Not just now. Wait till we have gone.'

'In that case I shall go back to my bath.' She gave them a
saucy look and flounced off through her bedroom to her
bathroom.

She managed to get off her sodden underwear and dump it
on her clothes, dropping into the hot water. The foamers
tickled her chin and she lay and thought of Will.

She waited.

She heard them move through the apartment and prayed
her plan might work. The suit was genuine and something
manufactured to withstand outer space could defeat a few
sniffers. She considered what might be done to her if she was
caught out helping Will and dismissed the speculation as
pointless from her mind.

There was a tap at the door.

'Come in,' she called frostily. Her entire body was buried
in foam.

The trooper put his head around the door. 'We're sorry to
have disturbed you, ma'am. You can rest assured that you
are alone in the apartment. The criminal has never
penetrated here. There is no internal DNA trace.'

Under the foam Fiona allowed her hand to float from her
cunt to her arse. Will certainly had penetrated here. 'I could
have told you that,' she said to the trooper.

'He stopped at your door. We had to be sure he didn't get
in.'

'It's up to me who gets in,' said Fee ambiguously.

'You are quite safe, anyway,' said the trooper. 'We are
leaving now.'

After a few minutes she levered herself out of the bath and

checked the entire apartment, making sure that they were really gone. Then she phoned Diana and told her of their visit. Whilst she was on the vidi, the police arrived at Diana's and Fee felt she had covered herself sufficiently, her behaviour being normal in the circumstances.

She dried herself and slipped on a housecoat. She knotted up her hair. Then she opened up the loft.

He was half-suffocated when she reached him, for no air could get into the suit and it had no breathing apparatus attached. She helped him out and supported his weight down the steps, no mean feat. He was a heavy man in a bad way. She took him through to the kitchen and sat him at her table.

'What first?' she said. 'Food? Sleep? A bath? New clothes?'

He looked at her. 'Yeah. All that.'

She found high energy food and put it before him with some canned beer from the fridge. She went back to her bathroom and set the bath to empty and self-clean. Then she set it to refill. She took him through and without flirtatiousness she stripped him and helped him in, showing him the temperature control. She took his clothes and incinerated them. She found an old robe of Rollo's and when she went back to the bathroom he was asleep. His face was grey with fatigue. Rollo would be back soon, he was at the gym, and she must have Will hidden before he returned.

She sat on the edge of the bath and woke him up. His eyes blinked and he looked at her.

'OK, do how'd you find me.'

'You were on the Screen. Fee Cambridge, wife of Rollo Cambridge, director of TransFlow.'

'Right.'

'I knew you must live in the Zoo. I checked the listings. That was before I was caught.'

'Were you going to come here?'

'You'll never know.'

She considered him. 'I don't know much about our police service. You'll have to tell me what to do next.'

'I need to sleep. And then eat some more.'

'It'll have to be the attic. My husband will be home soon.

233

We have a maid also, though this is her day off. You've been damned lucky.'

'The devil looks after his own.'

'Will I have to help you out of the tub?'

He started to laugh raggedly. 'You crazy bitch. You have all this and that damned smooth-arsed husband of yours and more money than you could ever spend and you come down to the city to screw a pirate.'

'I did that, didn't I?'

'Was it worth it?'

'Are you asking if you have a good cock?'

'I know the answer to that one,' he said with lazy insolence.

Fiona laughed. 'Get out of the bath, pirate. I'll fix you a bed.'

She made him up a mattress and a covering. Then she heaped food and drink for him. She found him some clothes and put them by the bed also. He was taller than Rollo, though not by much, and his lower dimensions were surprisingly similar. His barrel chest would make Rollo's things look too tight.

'Keep the noise down, huh?' she said, back downstairs. 'I can't guarantee Rollo's behaviour.'

'I need sleep. I'm quiet in my bed when I am alone.'

'There is a light up there. Don't come down. Wait for me to come up.'

'Give me a long time.'

'Hey, look, here's a watch.' She gave him a spare one of her own, an incongruous jewelled thing. 'Shall I leave you the rest of the day and all night? Rollo goes to work early but Janine will be here tomorrow.'

'I know I can't stay.' He checked the watch. 'Come for me in twelve hours. At four in the morning. Will loverboy sleep soundly?'

'He takes a pill. Janine won't be back till nine tomorrow morning but the door is coded for her and she gets in without asking me.'

'Right. Come in the night, then. As you always did.'

She went up the steps with him to make sure he had what

234

he needed, including a bucket. His big naked unaroused body fascinated her. He was sweet-smelling from the bath and he had used her teeth-cleaning device. His loose wet curls clustered on his neck.

He slid into the bed she had prepared for him and she knelt and stroked his brow for a moment.

'Glad to see you aren't beat,' she said lightly. 'I didn't like to think of you in jail.'

'Chain's dead,' he said.

'I'm sorry. He was a raping son of a bitch but he did me no real harm.'

'He was my brother.'

'I'm sorry, Henson Carne.'

He looked startled. 'You know that?'

'Yes. Look, sleep now. We'll sort something out.'

'Fee Cambridge,' he said and gave a crack of laughter. She left him.

The rest of the day passed and Fiona found it hard to remember at times that she had a pirate in the attic. She worried over how to help him. He needed a new persona, that much was obvious. He couldn't stay hidden in her apartment for long.

Then, with a queer pang, she realised all she had to do was lead him over the wire and back to the city. He would need nothing else from her, so why was she worrying about papers and a new identity?

She knew, of course. She wanted him able to move in her world. She wanted him accredited, a legal person, able to live and work.

And screw.

She woke herself at four in the morning using an intra-aural alarm so as not to disturb the sleeping Rollo. She left him drugged into peaceful oblivion whilst she operated the mechanism that released the steps to the loft. She retracted the steps behind her. She didn't want Rollo to come looking if he woke.

She padded softly across the floor to Will.

He was awake, watching her, his eyes glittering in the dim

light. He looked considerably better for his food and rest, filled out somehow, his tight lines dissipated.

She felt the force of his personality as she moved towards him and suddenly became queerly aware that he was not a safe man, not tame, and he would not abide by her rules. Exhaustion had temporarily tamed him when he came tumbling through her door. Now he was fit again.

When she got to him he pulled her roughly down and kissed her, his mouth as fiery as she had remembered, spiced liquid gold.

She slid on to the mattress beside him. 'We have to talk.'

'We have to fuck.'

'Will, this isn't the time.'

'Take what's offered when it's offered. Tomorrow might not happen.' His tongue was in her ear.

'I haven't offered.'

'I have,' said Will. 'Now take it.'

He slid her robe off and kissed her breasts hard, pulling at the nipples so that she was instantly pierced by pleasure and the need for sex rose in her strongly.

There was no time for sophistication or foreplay. He hauled her long pale body down beside his and rolled on top. He entered her hard and fast with his fully erect cock and began to work her, feeling her juices run and bathe his shaft.

Fee gripped his hair and kept her mouth shut.

He fucked hard. His wonderful prick flamed inside her and she felt a possessive pride that she could take such a man and please him. She rose violently to meet his thrusts and their flesh smacked between them.

Their climax was not long delayed. Their pounding escalated in speed and violence until they clung together in an ecstasy of savage thrusts. Fiona's blood was pounding and through a red haze she felt his shaft pulse strongly as he ejected sperm into her. Her own muscles rippled in concert as she sought to drain him and fill herself with the lava of his sexual eruption. Her own climax was upon her and she tossed her head from side to side in an effort to keep her mouth shut. She jerked violently against him, rigid with exploding lust. She felt the enormous heat of their come foaming round his slackening shaft, oozing onto her thighs, crushed by his balls. She squeezed down on his fading erection, breathing hard.

He kissed and sucked her ear. 'Fantastic bitch,' he said. She felt him laugh. The bastard took all the credit, no doubt, for the quality of their fucking. Gradually her dizziness passed.

'Are you going back to the city?' she asked. 'I can take you the way I went, over the Zoo, on the wire.'

'What else is there?' He nuzzled her warm sweaty body and kissed her soft skin.

She took her time to answer. She rolled on to her back, green eyes narrowed to fierce bright slits. Her mind ran smooth and slick the way it did sometimes after good sex, as slick as her wet thighs.

'Will Kid was a pirate.' she said.

'Yeah.'

'They hanged him in 1701.'

'The things you know.'

'But six years earlier he had been granted the King's commission to seek out and destroy pirates.'

'Fancy that.'

'What made you, Henson Carne, choose the name of Will Kid?'

'I didn't know any other.'

'Were you a policeman?'

There was a long silence. 'No,' he said.

Fiona stayed quiet. She had a feeling he wasn't finished.

'You're a clever bitch,' said Will presently. 'My brother was.'

'Chain.'

'Yes.'

'What happened?'

'He found corruption. He was framed to make his evidence of no value. They were going to imprison him for life on fabricated charges to protect themselves. I took him out and we went to the city.'

'You were OK yourself?'

'Not after I sprung Chain.'

237

'What were you?'

'A molecular biochemist.' He started to laugh. As Fee caught on, she started to laugh with him.

'A locksmith,' she gasped.

'You've got it.'

Locks were based on an individual's gene structure which was unique – except for that of identical twins. This was called the genetic fingerprint and it could be read as a barcode using any part of the body, though the finger itself was easily the most convenient. Locks were constructed using the skills of advanced genetic biologists.

No wonder Carne was good at locks. He had made the damn things for a living. Computer hacking was not in essence any different. You had to match patterns to get in if you did not have the genetic code of the owner which gave programmed access, and although the patterns were electromagnetic, not genetic, there was a biological analogy involved because increasingly machines mimicked nature which had had four and half billion years to get it right.

It had taken geneticists half a century to unravel the genome of a simple nematode worm, one millimetre long. Mimicry made sense. They weren't going to come up with anything more complex than nature's own blueprint for life.

'Could you have broken my doorcode?' Fee asked. The word from the manufacturers was that they were inviolate.

'How many people is it coded for?'

'Three.'

'No.' He smiled at her. 'Where I can win is with a door whose control code has a large number of permitted entrants. The barcode gets less and less complex as it incorporates more and more combinations and the chances of you tripping a combination that lies within its parameters get better and better. The prison had old-fashioned locks, far simpler than the design you have on your door. Even so, it took me eight days. I'm a little rusty.'

'You had to guess the barcode, the combination of a specific guard? The odds against that must be terrific.'

'No. Your door, say, has a forty-aspect code. It is coded for three people who probably have nothing in common gene-

238

tically. So at maximum it allows any combination of forty within the programmed one hundred and twenty aspects. Any combination. Not specifically yours or your husband's or your maid's. If someone came along who happened incredibly to fall within that one hundred and twenty aspects, they could get in. The prison was using a ten aspect code and it had about a thousand acceptable aspects. That shortened the odds.'

'Old-fashioned keys would be simpler.'

'You try telling that to the prison authorities. Newer is better to them. And they don't reckon to have a lockmaster in the jail, I guess.'

'Do you ever want to go back to that world? This world, I should say.'

'That's a question.'

'William Kid wanted to.'

'But I am not William Kid, as we have established.'

'Chain is dead. You can't help him now. How about getting on with your own life?'

'Too expensive. I don't deny it can be done but it is a hell of a complicated procedure and I might have to hide for some time.'

'It depends on someone real dying, doesn't it?'

'Yes. You have to have someone with a rough physical fit and you buy their papers before they are filed dead. The papers have to be copied and returned to the widow or whatever with a null code inserted so that when the papers are filed, the computer rejects the information of death.'

'No one realises?'

'They use low quality staff. And a viral null code can take many forms. It isn't easy to recognise even if you are looking for one.'

'How expensive is all this?'

He told her. 'Yes,' she said thoughtfully. 'It could be done but it would take time. I would have to fix the accounting to hide such a large sum of money going out.'

Will shrugged. 'I'll go back to the city.'

'If you had a new persona, could you make out? I mean, could you get a job worth a damn?'

'I reckon.'

She looked at him speculatively. 'You need something dangerous or you'll go bad again.'

'I've always been bad,' said Will. He licked the inside of her mouth. 'I always will be. Like you.'

'I'm losing the taste,' she said grimly. 'I went back to look for you after the news of police raids. I didn't know if you were free or not.'

'Is that so? Didn't you like the city without me to cheer it up? There are plenty of others with nice big prongs to help a little lady like you. A greedy lady.'

'The games were on. I went to the stadium. The damn place caught fire and scared me half to death.'

'You were in that? I heard about that.'

Her green eyes slid over towards him. 'To tell you the truth, I don't want to go back.'

'Not even if I am there?'

'Perhaps that's why I want you somewhere else.'

'Space roughnecks aren't asked too many questions. Mining moonside has a high casualty rate so they don't get picky over who applies. Nor are they fussy about third-degree deep-sea manganese divers nor uranium miners. Good pay, too. Lousy insurance, of course.'

'Diving pay won't hold up,' said Fiona.

'Why not?'

'They have found an enhanced way to extract all the elements from seawater and sell the fresh clean water at the end of it.'

Will stared at her. 'Commercially viable?'

'Yes.'

'Won't that ruin the profitability of TransFlow? I mean, technologically-speaking, it's out of the ark.'

She was pleased at his acumen. 'It could but it won't.'

'Why not?'

'Rollo personally owns the patent on the process.'

Will began to laugh. 'The bastard,' he said. 'The clever no-good bastard. You have it all sewn up, don't you?'

'We hope so. There are always unplanned factors.'

Will slumped back at this glimpse of high-financial

jiggery-pokery. 'Perhaps I'll take you up on your offer,' he said. 'I reckon you can afford me.'

It was six in the morning before she was ready to slip back into bed beside Rollo, clean from her bathroom.

Rollo woke as she got into bed. He reached out a lazy hand and stroked her skin.

'Morning, darling,' said Fiona. 'Sorry I disturbed you. Go back to sleep.'

But Rollo had other ideas. His hands caressed her breasts and he found her lips and kissed her hungrily.

'Do something dirty with me,' he said. 'I'm morning-horny. Or would you rather I was disgusting with you?'

Fiona had checked that Rollo was still asleep once or twice during her long session with Will. She hadn't explained why there should be a peephole above her bed and Will hadn't asked. She could only hope Will had gone back to sleep.

'You be disgusting with me,' she said. This was the first dividend from the episode with Janine. It was nice to know she had not handed her husband over to the girl for nothing, but she could wish his timing had been better. Will didn't leave much of a woman unused and his strength seemed to have returned abruptly.

So Rollo felt disgusting, did he, after the pure little games with Janine? Now there was a satisfactory turn-up for the books.

She slitted her eyes and watched Rollo thinking about what to do with her. This was nice. She appeared to be going from not getting enough action to being almost not able to handle what was on offer. A laugh started in her throat. She had fucked with the criminal hiding in the loft. She had had the sweetest of sweet female intimacies with the delicious newly-awakened nymphet, Janine, who was so adorably enticing that it made her pussy grow juicy just to think about her. And her husband was at last fulfilling his proper conjugal role, and in an interestingly improper way, it seemed.

All she needed was Jamie in the kitchen and big whorehouse Clive in her bathroom and the house would be complete.

'What's making you grin so dirty?' asked Rollo.

'Get on with it,' she said lazily, trying not to laugh.

He moved across the room and came back with something she couldn't see. She was looking at the ceiling, relieved to see its pristine whiteness.

Rollo grabbed her and heaved her violently upside down. She squawked indignantly as he stood her on her head and he gripped her so that her legs hung down, her thighs against her stomach and her bottom right up in the air. Something went round her legs and back and was pulled tight. Rollo still supported her upside down, but her legs were strapped to her body with a leather belt so that her vulnerable sex was poking up in the air, completely exposed.

'Lovely,' muttered Rollo. 'Now it occurs to me, Fee, that you have been going out too much lately and you need a little correcting. You need to know who is the boss here. I aim to teach you. First of all, let's cool down that sexual heat you feel all the time, you randy bitch.'

He began to push something hard and unyielding into her fanny. Fiona squirmed but the strap held her body trapped to itself and Rollo had her in a grip of iron. She yelled as her fanny froze. The bastard was putting ice in her.

'Now you are nice and cool,' said Rollo maliciously, 'I'll take pity on you, you slut, and heat you up some.'

Fiona's insides burned and tingled with the cold. Rollo was unrelenting. Then she screamed, forgetting the possibility of Will hearing her in the attic. Her vulva exploded with pain. Needles of heat, hundreds of them, radiated sharply through her. Rollo struck her again with his tiny multi-thonged whip, right across her quivering pulpy upturned sex, right across her sensitive clitoris. He flicked her again and again so that the thongs licked into her fanny entrance and stung her there.

Fiona roared and yelled as he scourged her, and her flesh, frozen within and burning without, began to feel very peculiar.

All her underparts were fully exposed to her abuser. They glowed and itched so that she was full of an agony of desire as the individual flicks of the whip faded into a glorious generalised stinging heat. As the ice melted cold water bubbled up from her fanny and dripped over the assaulted flesh. Rollo yelled as he beat her.

At this moment, at Rollo's bizarre mercy, exposed, humiliated, degraded, assaulted and ravaged, Fiona knew for certain Will Kid would be watching from above, alerted by the noise. He would see her husband fiercely admonishing the very parts of her that had clasped his cock in frantic desire less than an hour previously. The ironic reversal of roles, Will seeing her and Rollo like this as she had witnessed Janine and Rollo, produced in her a desire for sex that made her want to scream. Almost she wanted Will in the room as Rollo fucked his cock into her boiled frozen cunt. As Rollo fell on her and plunged into her, she wanted the two cocks shoved in simultaneously.

Rollo did not remove the tight leather belt. He let her fall so that he could ram his rigid shaft into her fiery cold hole. The outer heat and the inner sodden cold stimulated his frenzied efforts to new heights of greedy lust. He took his pleasure on Fiona and he took it as hard as he could.

When he was done with her, he withdrew and looked at his handiwork. Her bruised vulva bubbled with his spunk. He laughed and released the strap.

Fiona unrolled and slapped him hard across the face. He roared with laughter and pushed his slimy prick between her luscious breasts, deep into the lovely cleft and rolled it about.

'Stop yelling, woman, and be grateful,' he said insolently. 'One day you'll be a dry old crone and have to live on your memories whilst you watch younger people rutting away. Now is for living.'

This was reminiscent of Will. Fiona eyed the ceiling trying to spot the little dark blip which would indicate a silent watcher.

Rollo opened her legs and began to kiss tenderly what he had abused.

Quite suddenly, she fell asleep.

17

Fiona awoke to find Janine sitting on the bed.

'I'm sorry, Mrs Cambridge,' said the girl. 'I didn't mean to wake you.'

Fee reached up a long arm and caught Janine by the neck. She drew her down and they kissed lovingly with open mouths. 'Come into bed with me a minute, pussycat,' she said sleepily. Janine's sweet softness would be a pleasing antidote to the male rudeness she had enjoyed in the night. Enjoyed very much as well.

Rollo, his sexual sleep over, the prince awake. The pirate in the attic.

'Darling,' she said as Janine slipped naked between the sheets. 'Here, where Rollo lies. Cuddle me some and kiss me. Rollo blew my cunt up last night and I want you to kiss it better.'

Janine rubbed her warm yielding body against Fiona's sleep-dopy one. 'I love you before you've bathed in the morning, Mrs Cambridge,' she confessed. 'I love the smell of the night on you, and the smell of Mr Cambridge where he slept with you.' She began to kiss Fiona between her breasts where a slight trail of sweat always accumulated, sliding her hand down over Fee's belly to her crotch. 'You're all sticky,' she said in surprise. Fiona was always clean. She never left her body meaty after sex.

'That was Rollo. I went right off to sleep before I got to the bathroom to shower. Do you mind?'

Janine closed her lips over one of Fee's nipples and sucked intently whilst her hand moved round Fiona's groin. When her mouth was free, she whispered: 'I love you mucky from him. Can I go down on you.'

'Sure baby,' said Fiona, opening her legs and relaxing. Janine was gentle and soft with her. Her clever knowing ittle mouth tenderly lipped and tongued and very gently sucked all Fee's musky underparts. Her snub nose rubbed Fee's clitoris whilst her rounded tongue gentled the bruised flesh lovingly. Fee let her own hand drift comfortably within the girl's fleece and slid a thumb within her pink wet orifice. Her bladder nagged her faintly and suddenly her eyes opened and she stared up at the ceiling.

She could see the minute black hole.

'You're so sucky,' breathed Janine.

Her orgasm knifed through her, catching her by surprise. Janine was her secret, her creation, almost. Will was her secret, her tiger in the loft. That one of them should spy her with the other both frightened and exhilarated her.

She clasped Janine's bottom between her two hands and sucked the girl to climax, almost hoping Will was watching.

Only then did she rise from her bed to start the new day.

In the bath she pondered the problem of Will's new identity. It was a shame that it should be such an expensive business. It wasn't that she couldn't afford to provide the funding. The problem was to provide so large an amount and then cover her tracks. There was no way she could imagine explaining to Rollo why she should find it necessary to give a criminal a large sum of money in order to lead a new life. She had just spent a considerable time arousing her husband and she didn't mean to lose him as things got really interesting between them again. Rollo on sexual form was unbeatable. She aimed to keep him that way.

Moreover, Rollo was not stupid. He knew she had pulled an insurance scam and he knew how she had done it, more or less, although he knew nothing of Jamie's part in it, in her, for example. He had never closely questioned her as to how she had succeeded in making the police believe her. But if his mind started to run along the lines of where she got her circumstantial detail, accurate enough to fool the police, from, he would not be satisfied with the only safe answer she had come up with so far. She could claim she had used the Screen romantic drama as the basis for her descriptions of the pirates, but anyone intelligent knew that the real thing and the swashbuckling melodramatic adventurers portrayed on the Screen were worlds apart. It simply wasn't a credible explanation. So she had to keep his mind from even beginning to go over her story.

It would be easier to make up a lie about what the money was for than to cover up its transferral. The trouble with automated credit transfer was the record. Everything was detailed in black and white at the end of the day. The cashless society such as she and Rollo inhabited had its disadvantages if you wanted to play at something criminal. She might be a smart-arse computer expert but she did not have the financial wizardry that she now required.

She was being massaged after her bath when a far more satisfactory solution to the problem occurred to her. It contained a delicious hint of danger that brought a sparkle to her cheeks.

Inadvertently she clenched her buttocks sharply.

'I'm sorry,' said Janine. 'Did I hurt you?'

'No,' said Fiona.

'Are you sure?' whispered Janine naughtily. Her fingers slid within Fiona's legs and she giggled.

'Hey, hey,' protested Fee. 'You don't feel sucky again, do you?'

'I could do,' said Janine slyly.

'Could do what?' said Rollo. He must have come out from his work station. He was leaning against the bathroom doorframe, his piercing blue eyes considering the two women he was fucking, the one massaging the other.

'Oh, Mrs Cambridge,' said Janine in pretty confusion. She blushed and dropped her eyes.

'She could do my front now,' said Fiona in a deep voice. She rolled over. She was quite naked. 'Come on, Janine. I have work to do today and I am stiff, for some reason.'

Rollo continued to stand where he was, his arms folded, watching the maid massage his wife's nude body. He had taken both of them sexually over the previous evening and night and he assumed that neither of them knew about his copulation with the other. He rather enjoyed watching Janine handle Fee. He was visited by the idea that he would like to come round the back of Janine as she worked and slip down her breeks and enter her from the rear. Then he could gently pump away at her whilst he watched her hands feel all over his wife's body.

'I'm sore between my thighs, Janine,' said Fiona. 'Do what you can.' She opened her long legs and Janine slipped her hands between them and worked there, grazing Fee's vulva with her knuckles.

'Rollo,' said Fee. 'Why am I so sore? Perhaps I'm getting old, hey?'

Rollo strolled over and looked down at her. He could see the wetly gleaming fissure of her sex right by Janine's hands. Her large breasts fell one to each side of her body and moved slightly as Janine dug into the knotted muscles of her thighs.

'I'm older than you, sweetie,' he drawled. 'Perhaps Janine wouldn't mind massaging me sometime.'

Janine turned scarlet.

'It's up to her,' said Fiona. Her eyes were almost closed but Rollo knew she was watching him. 'It's outwith her maiding duties to me, though. If she takes you on, I think she should be paid more. She might not want to, anyway.'

'I wouldn't mind,' squeaked Janine breathlessly. 'You pay me very generously already, Mrs Cambridge. I would be happy to oblige Mr Cambridge if he thinks I am good enough.'

'Watching you with my wife, I am sure you are good enough,' said Rollo. He bent over Fiona and very deliberately kissed each of her breasts in turn, taking his time and making it an explicitly sexual gesture. As he did so, his hand came round and ran up the inside of Janine's thigh. Janine squeaked and her hands bumped Fiona's clitoris.

Fee purred.

That afternoon she sent Janine out on some trifling errand and then ascended the stairs to the attic.

He was on his back, hands folded behind his head, apparently half-asleep.

She came across the ill-lit space conscious of his eyes.

'You whore,' he said. 'Come here.'

'You were looking?'

'You bet I was looking. Not with my bad eye, either.'

'A voyeur as well as a pirate.'

'You ought to be grateful you are worth looking at. I'll say this for that smooth tight-arse you are married to. He doesn' miss a trick.'

'Don't call him that all the time. Rollo has always exploited all his assets.'

'Come and be exploited some more.'

'I don't now I can keep it up at this rate.'

'I didn't ask how you felt about it. It's how I feel I'm thinking of.'

'Lay your pole bare, pirate. I'll tell you what I've been thinking of whilst I sit astride you.'

It was good to feel him in her, pushing up so hard it was an effort to keep right down on him. She knew her gluttony could not last but Will would have to leave soon and this craziness would be over. Meanwhile she was determined to have the stamina to enjoy it. It was a unique situation, after all.

'Listen,' she said. By way of response he flexed his prick inside her, making her wriggle with pleasure. 'Concentrate,' she protested. But she laughed at what he did to her and ran her fingers through the hairy mat on his chest and laid her hands on his tattooed shoulders.

'I don't want to do this thing about the papers,' she said. 'I don't want to lay out all that money.'

He went still under her. Then he began to move again. 'Congratulations,' he drawled, thrusting gently up. 'It's not many women who would choose a moment like this to tell a guy how little he is worth.'

Fee rode up and down a couple of times. 'A beautiful cock,' she misquoted. 'It's price is far above rubies.'

'You don't think.'

'Hear me out before you judge me, pirate. I have another idea. I have this little company. It's nothing, really. Keep moving, damn you. It's just in place should I ever want to capitalise on the software I created for TransFlow. Come on, can't you think and screw cunt at the same time?'

'Is there any angle you rich bastards don't cover?'

'Sure. The ones we don't think of in time. Don't you knock it. My foresight could prove very useful to you. This apartment is fully extended with Rollo's work station. We couldn't site a new company here even if we wanted to.'

'I'm so sorry,' said Will, doing something that made Fee groan with pleasure.

She wriggled again, savouring his knotty fatness and her muscle-extended fullness. She could get to like living like this, she thought dazedly.

'So I have this little suite of offices in the shopping and business complex. Nothing much. A few rooms with on-screen facilities and storage and basic communications.'

'So?'

'You could hang out there and get out of my loft and let my husband synch with me without me being spied on.'

'I bet you liked knowing I was staring at you whilst he whipped your pretty little fanny.'

She grinned naughtily and squeezed down on him.

'If I DNA record you to use the offices and the company credit, no one will know you don't have documentation. You could lead a normal life, almost. You could spend money.'

'Access your company accounts? You're not being entirely close-fisted over credit, then.'

'I wouldn't let you have an overdrawing facility. You would only be able to spend what I put in.'

'You don't trust me, huh?'

Fee bent over him and kissed his lips, tasting his fiery mouth. Her breasts swung under her, pointed and heavy, the nipples brushing through the hair on his broad chest.

'My dear,' she whispered. 'You are a thief by trade. It's no part of my plan to make you change your spots, leopard-lover. On the contrary.'

'What then?'

Fiona rode up and down on him some more. Somewhere far off her climax was starting to gather. 'The Central Computer,' she said. 'The one that stores all societal data.'

'Yeah?'

'Hack it, sweetie. Change the record.'

He laughed aloud. 'I can't do that.'

'Why not?'

'It'll need time and skill and powerful facilities.'

'You have all three. I'm giving you the time and th facilities with my company equipment. I'll up its power if it i insufficient. You have the skill yourself.'

He lay idly beneath her, thinking, whilst she pulled slowl up and down in long movements on his prick. Her cunt ha the velvet of bloodstock with the kick of a mule. For Fee, th long slow union whilst they planned a major crime added new and pleasant dimension to sex.

'My DNA,' he said softly. 'It's on record. I could mayb use it to access your company doorlock, but never to enter a account. They'll be scanning for it everywhere. They know am cut off from funding. All institutions will have me on blacklist. It's routine.'

'We can't alter your genetic code,' said Fiona. 'Can we?'

'We could polarise it,' said Will suddenly. His muscl went slack in her as he thought furiously and Fee cried ou indignantly. He laughed and hardened up.

'It's a sensational cock, pirate,' she said. 'I have to sav it.'

'It can't be bought.'

'I own enough things already. It's the use of it I need.'

'I was working on polarisation four years ago when I took Chain out and we went to the city. We were using X-rays to generate the code. So far it's not been necessary in the marketplace because unpolarised genetic coding is so compli-cated anyway. Fiddling with the amplitudes wasn't neces-sary. But if I can polarise my own code and create a device to exhibit it that fits over my finger, and we register that polarised code with the banking facility your company uses, then I can make daily use of a unique living code I carry about with me but it won't match that of Henson Carne, escaped criminal. Until the police catch on and start keeping more complete records, of course.' He laughed softly. 'Only one step ahead maybe, but one step can be enough.'

Fee leant over him and bit his ears. She felt creamy smooth inside. He was so big in her. Her orgasm was gathering speed and momentum now.

'Can you make such a device?' she whispered. 'It would have to be practically invisible.'

'I'll need a shopping list. I think the answer is yes.'

The firebolt struck and as their planning climaxed, so did their joined bodies.

Before Janine got back. Will emerged from the loft and bathed and dressed in Rollo's clothes. Rollo was in and working but Fiona rather enjoyed the danger, as she had enjoyed it by having Janine act sexy with her in Rollo's presence in her bathroom that morning. She cut Will's hair and removed his earrings and then she took him out. They rode the walkways quite openly, convinced that the police would not continue to check the Zoo. The simple changes they had made to Will's appearance would fool the optical scanning devices, the video cameras that monitored the Zoo public areas. Faces were at once too vague and too complex to process with digital precision and facial recognition by machine had proved as faulty as its counterpart by human agency.

They went to a restaurant and then shopped for personal clothes and equipment. Fee took him to her offices and showed him round. He would be a prisoner until he had perfected his device. She arranged for food to come in every day in the meantime. Then it was time to go.

'I'll vidi you to see how you get on, huh?' she said.

'Sure.'

'You can make your own future if you are clever enough,' she added slyly.

'And if I'm not?'

'Zoo folk are notoriously ruthless. Sink or swim, Will Kid. You aren't a pirate for nothing.'

'You don't want me straight, do you?'

'I guess I'm kinky about criminals. But be careful with my company. Don't foul the nest.'

'You like wickedness for its own sake.'

'I'm not admitting that.'

'That doesn't make it untrue.'

They kissed lingeringly and she headed for the door. As Will saw her go across the carpet, her high tight arse jutting

251

out from under her clothes, her high heels making her leg look slim and slinky, and the arrogant line of her shoulder where she threw them back to counterbalance her deep heav breasts that hung with captivating pendulous grace on her slin body, he felt lust rise savagely in him once more. This was tame way to let her go, like he was some rich woman's pet o something. He remembered seeing her playing with her maic in bed that morning. He had not mentioned it and he was sti in shock at both her versatility and her appetite. She was woman who would continue to amaze him, he knew.

Will shot across the room and grabbed her. Fiona squealec but that only served to arouse him more. He manhandled he roughly so that she dropped her bag. He forced her agains the desk and pushed her face down so that keyboards scat tered. With his other hand he wrenched up her skirt and tore her knickers off. He freed his cock and shoved hard at her.

Fee wriggled impotently and shouted but her voice wa muffled by the desk and drowned in her own hair. Wil forced his cock at her arse. She felt her tightness yield before his onslaught and he got into her tight hard passage. He gave her no quarter, keeping her forced down over the desk as he rogered her, raping her arse. He saw the skin flush across he buttocks and knew that despite her outrage she could no help responding. She was all woman. She enjoyed a man too much. For that matter, she enjoyed sex so much in any way it came, that unless it was positively life-threatening, she revelled in it.

Will fucked till he was spent. Then he jerked his cock out and put it away. As he released Fee she spun round and tried to slap him. He caught her upraised wrist and crushed her to his chest, kissing her fiercely.

'I'm a thief, remember?' he said when their mouths parted.

'I could kill you,' she snarled.

'Yes,' he said. He believed her.

'What if I told the police?' she half sobbed.

'I'd go back to jail. But it was one hell of a fuck.'

She half laughed now. 'You bastard. You can't go around raping women.'

'I don't,' he said.

'You do it to me.'

'To you yes. That's how we are, Skelton. No one else is like you for me. Or ever could be.'

He let her go. She was still mad at him but he knew she would be back.

That's how it was with them.

Fiona spent a few days after this catching up on sleep and business affairs and clearing the loft of all evidence of occupancy. She met with Diana and led a normal life, except in so far as she made love with her maid as well as her husband at different times. Janine was better and better. Fiona had some more long conversations with the girl. She knew Rollo was now inside her on a regular basis, but since he was giving plenty to his wife as well, she had no complaints. Always she made Janine give a blow-by-blow account of what Rollo did with her and during these auto-voyeuristic episodes she would suck or paddle Janine to climax. Janine adored talking about what Rollo did to her whilst his wife had her tongue where his cock had been.

Then her plans came to their full fruition.

Rollo put his arms around her in bed one night without having taken his pill. His fingers went intimately into her whilst his mouth fed with hers. For a while they lovered each other up in this fashion, then Rollo moved down in the bed and began to burrow into her fanny, one of her legs up over his shoulder.

He had his back to the bedroom door. He was holding Fiona open with his fingers and licking her vulva with long strong licks when Janine stole into the room. He jumped hideously when Janine's hand caught his swinging erection and began to frig him.

He turned like a snake but Janine was faster. Without letting go of his cock, she got between him and Fiona on the bed and put her mouth where his had been, on Fiona's naked aroused cunt. Fiona moaned with pleasure as the girl nibbled and licked where her husband had been.

253

Janine was naked. Rollo held still, his mind racing. His prick softened and hardened again in Janine's grasp. What he was seeing was something he had fantasised about since the episode where he had witnessed Janine massaging Fee. His fantasy had had none of the colour and the excitement of the real thing. He could hardly comprehend it. Fee was writhing and moaning with the girl up between her legs, mouth at her sex. And he was there, watching, Janine's hand holding him.

Suddenly Janine released Fee's fanny and Rollo and Fee met each other's eyes. He looked almost helpless. Fee rose up and she and Janine came either side of him. In concert they began to kiss and caress him, their four hands weaving an erotic web over his body so that he could hardly have told who caressed his throat, his balls, his backside and his hair. There were two hands on his prick and they didn't belong to the same woman.

Rollo fell back on the bed and gave himself up to their voluptuous demands. Either side of him, each sucked a nipple on his gleaming chest with one hand in his groin, stroking, teasing, frotting, cradling and arousing him to undreamt-of heights.

Janine got astride the man, eyes meeting Fee's and dancing wickedly. Fee was grinning. Her hands went in under Janine and she guided the girl's pussy to centre over Rollo's prick, holding his prick as Janine lowered herself to help drive it within her opening rose of sex.

Janine began to ride up and down on her master.

Fee got astride Rollo also, astride his face with her back to Janine in a crazy train of sex. He found her fecund wet luxuriant silken cavern just above his panting mouth. His tongue sneaked out and he began to suck her.

Janine put her hands around her mistress and caught her breasts, caressing them avidly. Rollo saw and was unable to control himself. He spunked up into Janine, yelling with pleasure.

The two women fell off him and crowded together over his groin to lick him clean. Now they let him see that not only did their two tongues tangle over his manhood, but that they kissed each other over and around his cock.

Then they lay back side by side, provocatively, wanting im to inspect them together as they loved to be.

Rollo saw his wife, a long pale shaft of exotic sophistication nd maturity, full breasts elegantly heavy with experience, he large plum-coloured nipples tilting outwards in graceful arnal beauty.

Janine was warm, her almost butter-coloured, creamy kin-tones a contrast to Fiona's magnolia porcelain flesh. anine was dusted with freckles across her young breasts and hey were tipped pale chestnut red. Her wheaten hair ningled with Fiona's raven locks.

She was shorter than Fiona but side by side Rollo could see 'ee's naked bulge of satin-smooth depilated mound, and anine's pale golden silky tangle of curls. Fiona was utterly mooth, but Janine was lightly furred all over with fine, short ed-gold hairs that blurred her image and kept the sweetness f her youth even in her new maturity.

Rollo was enraptured, as Fee had intended him to be. He vatched as they turned their faces together and kissed each ther fully on the lips, a deep succulent kiss of desire and for he other. His cock rose and he possessed his wife.

He rode her slowly, his first flash of lust satisfied. As he went moothly in and out of her, Fee kept her face turned to Janine nd they continued to kiss each other even as he fucked. Then anine broke from Fee and came astride her mouth, facing Rollo over her body. Rollo saw Fee suck Janine's sex, filling her mouth from Janine's pussy with his spunk even as he pre-pared to fill her other end with the same thing.

Janine kissed him, holding him lightly on his hips, leaning owards him over Fee so that her breasts brushed his chest. He slid one hand down between mouth and cunt so that he could feel Janine's pussy and Fee's lips and tongue whilst his cock came to climax within Fee's body and Janine kissed him passionately on the lips.

They released him and smiled at him.

'You've taken me, both of you, you greedy witches,' he said, his voice a little hoarse and his eyes glittering fiercely. 'Now you have only each other to play with. I'm done for tonight.'

Fee looked at Janine and the girl looked slyly back at Fee.

'I don't believe that's true, Mrs Cambridge,' she said.

'No do I,' said Fee huskily. 'Let's prove him wrong darling.'

They began with each other. Whilst he rested they enjoyed each other, lazily kissing and sucking breasts and sampling each other's fine salty spunky body.

They turned top to tail. They began to caress each other's parts and Rollo's eyes darkened as he watched. He could see Fiona's long dark wet crimson slit, a purplish fissure breaking the smoothness of her pale flesh. Janine teased her way expertly through the lovely convolutions of flesh until she was centred on Fee's clitoris, languorously playing with the tiny female shaft.

He could also see Janine's paler, tighter, neater sex. Fee picked it apart with her fingers and began to blow into the narrow passageway, then dipping her tongue in with its wicked pointed tip and tickling the inside of Janine's pussy. When she released it, the newly opened channel closed and clung to itself as if still shy after its violent initiation into sexual activity. Rollo felt proprietorial about Janine's pussy. He had opened it first to the world of loving. He held the patent on her sex.

Fiona could hold her own dark flesh apart using muscles long-skilled in the arts of love for she was self-trained to extract maximum pleasure from her body whilst she gave her man maximum pleasure in coition. Janine would learn but meantime she was naturally tight. She could expand to take Rollo, she could distend about his full mature erection, but he was still a voyager there, an explorer. Where Amundsen had explored the Antarctic, Rollo Cambridge had explored the Cuntarctic. He felt he had the better of the deal, though there was no glory, no renown in his achievement.

Fiona was known territory, much used but delicious to penetrate afresh and strangely different lately. She deserved better than she had had recently, Rollo thought. He had not given her what she needed.

He saw the two cunts he had had that night and felt his cock prickle and his balls begin to swell.

256

He reached forward and inserted fingers from each hand into each woman. He knew he need feel no compunction about interfering between them. He knew they were here to pleasure him for the night and he might do as he pleased. They would be compliant to his will. His cock hardened slightly. Fiona gripped his fingers within herself and laughed. Janine's spongy walls pressed tightly against the invading digits.

Fee nodded to Janine and they both turned to Rollo again. Once more he was stroked and kissed in a maze of teasing delight, dark hair mingled with fair, their tangled limbs weaving between his. They adored him and with their bodies, ravishing his senses with breast and lips and hands and vulva.

Fee fed a nipple into his mouth and Janine came beside her and did likewise so that he could suck the both of them simultaneously. They bent over him and tongued his ears, exploring his whorls of sensitive skin, kissing him as they threaded his hair with their fingers and massaged his scalp. Fee pressed her open mouth upon his and then Janine pressed hers so that he could taste them one after the other. Then they pressed their mouths to each other above him so that he could put his hands into their four breasts as they were crushed nipple to nipple over his face.

Fiona looked down on her golden husband and took his cock in her mouth. She thought she had never loved him so much. Skilfully she licked him to life. Janine climbed astride Rollo and bent forward, putting her face to Fiona's outstretched rear. She ignored the lovely dark wet slit, almost dripping its musky fragrance on to the man they worshipped below, and instead she applied her fingers and then her mouth to Fiona's rear entrance. Fiona felt Janine's lips over her arse, and at the same time Rollo's cock jumped within her mouth as he saw what was happening.

Fee had planned this scene from the start. The wickedness of her scheme was surpassed only by its success.

Janine took spunk from her own fanny and used it to lubricate Fiona's rear. Her tongue darted at the sealed entrance and she tried to penetrate its forbidden mysteries.

257

Just above Rollo's face was her musky bush. He could see every move of her lizard tongue as it tried to bugger Fiona. He came to full erection in Fiona's mouth.

Janine abandoned Fee's rear and moved down the bed. The two heads, one dark, one fair, bent over the erect prick and between them they played at sucking it together and in turn. Rollo was presented with their two upraised bottoms side by side. He was entranced with pleasure. He reached out and stroked their lovely flesh, their long soft rounded female haunches, and felt them quiver in response under his hands.

Janine rolled round and laid Rollo's fat prick along her pink and swollen vulva, so that his muscle nestled in her sexual organ surrounded by her curls. Fiona kept working with her mouth only now she licked from cock to vulva and back again, tasting his gland as it lay snug within Janine's labia. The maid was up on her elbows, watching, and now two sets of hands cradled his balls and tickled him exquisitely.

'I'm going to come,' groaned Rollo. He couldn't hang on and he couldn't bear it to stop.

Fee smiled at Janine and they both turned wicked grinning faces to the man.

'Where would you like to come?' enquired Fee politely in her cool husky voice.

'Come here,' pleaded Janine prettily. She fingered her own sweet pussy.

'Be milked by me,' said Fee and her eyes were heavy-lidded as she smiled.

'Come in my mouth if you like,' said Janine eagerly. Throughout this carnal glut she seemed able to retain an enchanting air of innocence and naivety quite at odds with her knowing and sexually wise behaviour. She was like a wicked nun. Innocence is such a sweet bedfellow to corruption.

'Or my mouth,' said Fee, baring her teeth.

Rollo's throat was dry. He did not normally have trouble taking decisions. This was outside his previous experience.

'I have another orifice, especially tight,' drawled Fiona.

'Don't do that with me,' begged Janine, simulating alarm.

'Unless you really want to.' Her face softened and grew sinfully happy again. 'I'd like to watch you do it to Mrs Cambridge, though.'

Rollo broke into a sweat. 'You bitches,' he said faintly.

They leapt off the bed and with surprising strength hauled him into the bathroom. They showered him and themselves with cold water, yelling and fighting like puppies under the spray of water.

'Now,' said Fiona cheerfully, 'let's have something to eat and the champagne I put on ice earlier. Rollo, we'll let you get away with just one more climax tonight. Don't worry. We can bring you back to where you were. We are just keeping your strength up, darling.'

Rollo's eyes flashed blue fire. 'I never said I was worried,' he said.

Janine went for the food whilst Fiona stripped the bed and put fresh clean sheets on it in place of the tangled musky mess they had made Janine came back with trays laden with lobster claws, salty shrimps, cherries, grapes, durian, nectarine and a magnum of champagne fat as a swollen erection in its bed of ice. Fiona slit the rind of a durian and broke out the luscious civet-smelling cream-coloured pulp. She smeared it on her vulva and laughed.

They sat cross-legged and attacked the food greedily. Fiona could slot shrimps into her fanny and eject them on muscle power alone, into Rollo's open eager mouth. He lay on his back and felt Janine's breast rub his shoulder whilst she fed him grapes and cherries.

Each of the women raised herself on her shoulders and let Rollo fill their cup of sex with champagne and he drank from them like this, one after the other.

They cleared the food away and faced him, two cats with their prey. But Rollo was no mouse.

'Turn over,' he ordered Fiona. She did so. 'Put up your rear,' he said and she obeyed him.

'Janine,' he said.

'Yes, Mr Cambridge.'

'Lick my wife's arse.'

Janine caught her hair back out of the way and lowered her

head. She began to lick tenderly at Fiona's crimped flesh. It moved slightly under her tongue.

Rollo licked his finger and moved Janine off. He began to push his finger into Fiona. Now Janine could see the valve flexing hard as Fiona tried to repel the invader but was unable. Rollo forced his finger in.

Fiona quivered, her buttocks taut and strained. Janine reached up and began to stroke them, to ease their tension.

Fee remembered Will's cock up her arse and almost came. Rollo drove his finger further in and brought his thumb under Fee and began to caress her clitoris with it. He sank his finger within her to the hilt and her sundered flesh convulsed around the invader. Simultaneously he frotted her clitoris with his thumb.

Rollo began to pump his finger in and out, in and out, whilst he rotated the pad of his thumb to masturbate Fee's clitoris. Janine abandoned Fee's buttocks and reached under her to savour the long pointed swinging breasts. She drew one to one side and put the erect nipple in her mouth. She began to suck with long steady sucks.

Fiona heaved and began to perspire. She was moaning with ascending pleasure now. Rollo took her backside faster and faster with his finger.

She jerked violently and cried out and then slowly she sagged down, the rigidity gradually leaving her body.

'Janine,' said Rollo. 'Feel her.'

Janine put her fingers into Fiona's pussy and found it richly wet.

'Now,' said Rollo. 'I am going to fuck the life out of you, Janine, whilst Fee extracts her revenge. You understand?'

'Yes, Mr Cambridge.'

'Lie back and open your legs.'

Janine did this but Fiona raised herself and put a hand over Janine's sex.

'I discovered this,' she said. 'You don't own the rights even if you had first ingress.'

The two of them faced each other over Janine's slack body.

'You women might play together,' said Rollo insultingly,

'and I admit it has pleased me to watch you. I trust there'll be other times.'

'If Janine consents,' said Fiona.

'But I am the man around here. If you want my cock in you, you do as I say.'

'There are other men,' Fiona's chin came up in defiance.

'I'm the man for you.' Rollo's voice was low and diamond hard. 'You know it and I know it. For your damned impudence I'm going to warm my cock in you before I fuck it to death in Janine. Lie down and shut up. You are too juicy to waste in argument. You know you want what I am going to give you.'

Fiona laughed and lay back. She grabbed at Janine before Rollo could move and pulled the girl on top of her, as if she was a mattress to support Janine. Her arms came round the giggling girl and held her steady.

Rollo looked down at the two cunts sandwich-style, one on top of the other. He gave a deep happy sigh and looked down at his own rigid sex. He came forward between the double set of legs and slid his shaft slickly into Fiona's foamy gape. Lusciously she drew him and he felt dizzy as her hot inner velvet lapped him, lapped his prick on every side, squeezing and pressing his member till it felt ripe and rich.

He pumped very slowly for a few moments, just to savour her, both bodies moving as he worked. Very slowly he withdrew his prick, watching its glistening length come from the clasp of Fiona's lips. There was an audible sucking noise as his gland popped out. His eyes raised to Janine's cunt just above, paler and drier. Without using his hands at all he took his prick from one cunt and slid it into another. As he pressed deep into the tightness of Janine's elastic clinging passage, she sighed with pleasure to feel herself distend to absorb his mighty muscle. Her young flesh adored him. Her rounded body wobbled slightly as he began to move slowly in and out of her. She flushed with sexual heat as she came to full arousal.

He was content for a while to move in and out with deep slow regular strokes. Each inward thrust required firm action. She lubricated until she was wetly tight, a slimy tight cushion for his member.

They were interrupted briefly as Fiona wriggled free. She came round behind him and stroked his hairy swinging balls. She looked over the food tray and found a pot of thick mayonnaise a good-sized globule and then as Rollo came back on one of his long dreamy strokes, she greased his rear and allowed her finger to slip within his orifice.

He grunted and plunged into Janine. As he came back, she impaled him on her finger, letting it sink right in. He came off her and went down into Janine. But as he pulled back his rear was again invaded by her greasy finger sinking deep within it.

Rollo's fucking began to change. He began to swoop down into Janine's pussy with powerful urgent strokes, As he thundered into her, she writhed with delight. Fee could feel the base of his shaft as he pulled back from Janine, hot and sticky wet. He was almost there.

Janine cried out and began to shudder violently as she orgasmed. Fee kept time with Rollo's huge plunges, penetrating his arse more gently but still as persistently. She ducked her head down and kissed his balls as they swung.

His back arched and he cried out. He exploded into Janine. His long beautiful shaft rippled its release of pent-up foam. He creamed richly into the girl, spurting all around her as he emptied himself for the final time, emptying himself absolutely into her fresh eager rosebud cunt.

Fiona eased her fingers free and he fell over sideways and lay on the bed. Janine's eyes were huge, love-drugged and slumbrous with satisfaction. Fiona, his dangerous half-tame alley-cat wife, narrowed her glacier-green eyes and smiled with deep pleasure. Her heavy hanging breasts seemed full, her slim powerful body at last satisfied.

Fee laid herself down so that Rollo was between his two women, caught in their sensual web, their warmth pressing him from both sides. His skin savoured the luxury of ripe womanhood as they pressed belly and thigh and breast against him. He was caressed by their fecund generosity, by their adulation of him, by their exploitation of him.

'May I stay, please?' asked Janine.

'Stay,' said Rollo, his voice full of tiredness as he edged closer to sleep.

'And welcome,' said Fiona in her deep rich voice.

For a few minutes Fiona held sleep at bay. She was creamy with satisfaction.

Rollo was a wonderful vigorous inventive lover again, powerful and commanding as she loved him to be.

Janine was adorable. She would tire of them but they would not stop her when she wanted to move on.

If Rollo ever slackened again and she failed to arouse him as was her duty, there was extraordinary pleasure to be bought. She would never quite forget Clive's startling personal equipment and his impressive professional prowess.

She would not tangle with Jamie again, but he was a sweet memory. She must not misjudge people again as she had done with him.

Out there somewhere, wicked all through, dangerous, deviant, fearless and charismatic, was her pirate lover, flesh of her flesh, bone of her bone whether they liked it or not. They were two of a kind, she and Will Kid, and they were not done with each other yet. Not by a long way.

Janine was warm and soft. Rollo was cool and firm. Fee laughed as she tumbled into sleep.

Life was good if you were wicked enough to take what it offered. That was what she had found.

But then, she had always been wicked.